THE FÜHRER'S PROPHECY

Also by Brian Klein

The Counterfiet Candidate

BRIAN KLEIN

THE FÜHRER'S PROPHECY

Cover photo credit: Shutterstock.com

First edition

ISBN: 978-1-3999-3637-8

Cover art by www.patrickknowlesdesign.com

Typeset by RefineCatch Limited, www.refinecatch.com
Printed and bound in Great Britain by Clays Ltd, Elcograf S.p.A.

To Charmaine and Jessica
who remain my inspiration.

Prologue

Auschwitz

November 1943

I t was a blisteringly cold morning. The freezing air, fuelled by a savage easterly wind, spun the unrelenting giant snowflakes into menacing patterns that aptly framed the entrance to the world's most notorious death camp. The Mercedes-Benz 770, only used by the Nazi elite, pulled to a halt outside Auschwitz. Despite the cruel elements, the armed guards either side of the wrought-iron gates looked immaculate in their field grey tunics. They instantly recognised the status of the approaching vehicle, lowered their Karabiner 98k rifles and moved forward to the back passenger door to check the identity of their unexpected, but clearly distinguished, visitor.

As the mysterious VIP slowly wound down the window, their eyes fixed on a familiar face, and they weren't disappointed. The insolent expression glaring back at them belonged to a prominent high-ranking figure in the Nazi regime. He was the man who had conceived and created the extermination camps across Poland and Germany; the infamous architect and driving force behind the Holocaust.

Heinrich Luitpold Himmler held the illustrious title of Reichsführer of the Schutzstaffel but was more commonly known as the head of the notorious Waffen SS, the combat division of the Nazi party. He was the second most powerful man in the Third Reich, but was, without doubt, the most feared.

The two guards reeled back on their heels and immediately performed the familiar Nazi salute while proclaiming a hearty "Heil Hitler". Himmler ignored their enthusiastic greeting, leaned out of the window and adjusted his celebrated pince-nez to focus his piggy hazel eyes on the giant handmade sign that dominated the entry to the camp. An arrogant smirk crept across his pencil-thin lips as he read the notorious words that greeted every individual, "ARBEIT MACHT FREI" – work sets you free. Himmler failed to spot the slight imperfection in the sign; the letter "B" had been inverted deliberately as a covert mark of rebellion by defiant Jewish inmates tasked with creating the sign a few years earlier.

The huge iron gates swung open, and the eight-cylinder engine fired up inside the giant Mercedes, pumping smoke from its exhaust, charring the virgin white snow. The Nazi staff car glided effortlessly into the camp, exuding the same authority and arrogance as its eminent passenger.

Although Block 10 had originally been designed for male inmates, everyone at the camp was aware that in recent months it had been transformed into a massive testing laboratory housing hundreds of female human guinea pigs. Inside the notorious two-storey brick barracks, conditions were atrocious and inhumane. Female prisoners were crammed into triple wooden bunk beds layered with straw bedding, which housed rats, lice and other vermin. The women were routinely subjected to appalling medical experiments performed without anaesthetic, and the complete lack of hygiene ensured the death rate was phenomenally high. Only a handful of inmates lasted longer than a month.

In one of the darkest corners of the block, a young male doctor was struggling to find a usable vein in the almost-lifeless bony arm of his twenty-year-old patient. He swore under his breath as he focused on his fifth attempt to find a landing zone for the hypodermic needle in his right hand. He was determined to make this attempt count when his concentration was broken by the unmistakable voice of the camp commandant, Rudolf Höss. The frustrated SS Major at once knew something was amiss because this was the first time the commandant had deigned to visit his makeshift laboratory.

"Doctor Schumann, you don't seem to be having much luck today, but that might change. You have an esteemed visitor waiting for you in my office. I suggest you get moving."

Two minutes later Doctor Horst Schumann cautiously entered the commandant's office where he encountered Heinrich Himmler lounging in a black leather chair. His short stubby legs were stretched out across the massive oak desk Höss had shipped in from Berlin when he'd first taken over the camp three years earlier. Schumann's gaze was weirdly drawn to the pristine black rubber soles of the Reichführer's jackboots that mysteriously showed no sign of snow in their deep crevices, Himmler nodded to acknowledge the arrival of the doctor and then his eyes flicked down to the manila folder in his right hand, which he brandished in the air with the panache of a seasoned orchestra conductor. He waited a moment before switching his gaze back towards the doctor and then let rip.

"Schumann, I totally condemn your recent behaviour, as does the Führer. Furthermore, it simply won't be tolerated. Maybe you would like to swap places with one of your loathsome Jewish patients? How dare you choose to ignore our weekly requests for updated figures? In the last two months you've ignored countless telexes from my office asking for information on the trials."

The doctor recoiled from the desk – his body physically rocked from the verbal onslaught. His mind raced while he considered the possible consequences of his inaction. He was well aware of the ruthless violence the obnoxious psychopath facing him was capable of dishing out.

"Reichsführer, I do of course owe you and the Führer an apology. As medics we are working in dreadful conditions in Block 10. Many of our patients are so wasted and frail they die before the results of our tests can be processed. Therefore, the figures are much lower than we expected and ..."

Himmler's body snapped into action. He rounded the desk to come eye to eye with Schumann and whipped the doctor's face with the folder before slamming it down on the desk.

"Doctor, as you know, this is the Führer's pet project. He conceived it and therefore it will succeed. I anticipate exceptional figures in your next report."

Himmler didn't wait for a reply. He scuttled past the humiliated doctor and stormed out of the commandant's office. Schumann stood stock-still for almost a minute. His only movement the trembling fear of his body. He slowly reached down and picked up the folder, the disturbing contents of which currently threatened his very existence. The front cover bore the crest of the majestic German military eagle and underneath were typed two words: *Operation Gesamtkunstwerk.*

Chapter 1

Buenos Aires, London, New York, Sydney,
the Caribbean

April 2022

The global Zoom meeting was drawing to a close. It was no different to thousands of others taking place across the world at the same time, except the encrypted passcodes required to gain entry were impenetrable. The participants were based in four continents, with varying time zones, and the call had been scheduled to start at 23:00 GMT. Despite their different nationalities, all the contributors were fluent in a second language – German. The Zoom gallery, displayed on the five computer screens, revealed the images of the participants but didn't list their names. The call lasted just under an hour and the host brought it to an end with a disturbing declaration.

"The ongoing pandemic is a gift. It's already helped us cover our tracks with some of our tests and now the main operation needs to be brought forward. In the name of our grandfather, we mustn't squander the opportunities it brings."

The other four participants nodded in agreement. Just before they logged off, the host resumed speaking.

"One last matter to cover. Eva, this one's for you. I'm emailing through details of the escape plan for an old family friend who is currently languishing in a maximum-security cell. We badly need an operative in the field whom we can trust and, after ten years of incarceration, his loyalty to our cause is undeniable."

In Buenos Aires Eva Castillo closed her laptop and reached for the glass tumbler of Jim Beam that sat on a red leather coaster on the brushed steel desktop. She drained the contents in one swallow and walked across the tumbled marble floor towards the fifteen-foot-high curved glass windows, a signature feature of her waterfront penthouse apartment in Puerto Madero Harbour on the east side of the city. It formed part of a luxury high-rise development comprising some of the most expensive real estate in Buenos Aires.

Eva glanced down at the spectacular pedestrian suspension bridge spanning the harbour and the picturesque dockside restaurants that attracted tourists and locals alike. The area was renowned for its upscale steak and seafood bistros, and she smiled to herself as she spotted the usual queue snaking around the front of El Mirasol, her favourite eatery. She knew a simple text to the maître d' always guaranteed her a table overlooking the water, regardless of the waiting times being handed out to hopeful customers who stood in line. She was born to entitlement and privilege which, to date, had smoothed her path through life.

Eva loved playing the card that, right from birth, she was destined for a life in politics because her parents had named her after the First Lady of Argentina, Eva Perón. In reality, her Christian name was a tribute to her paternal grandmother,

Eva Braun; the wife of the most notorious dictator of the twentieth century. She'd inherited the natural beauty of her grandmother, with her crystal blue eyes and curly strawberry blonde hair combining to stunning effect. At twenty-nine, she was the youngest senator in the National Congress and deputy leader of the extreme right-wing party Sovereignty. In the recent midterm elections, they had caused a political earthquake by winning twenty-three per cent of the national vote, reflecting the popularity of the growing fascist movement inside Argentina.

Although the sound was switched off on her cell phone, Eva felt the faint buzz created by the arrival of a fresh email and retrieved the super-encrypted iPhone from her jean pocket. The incoming message displayed no subject, just an attachment that she immediately double-clicked. The top half of the screen showed the colour headshot of a man she'd never met but whom she felt she knew intimately. She could see the Word document contained ten pages of copy but, for now, she was content simply to stare at the distinctive features of prison inmate 477815, otherwise known as the Black Scorpion.

Chapter 2

Valledupar, Colombia

The maximum-security wing in Valledupar Penitentiary was not for the faint-hearted. It was the first prison to be built inside Colombia using US funding and was designed to secure inmates who were seen as a potential threat to both the Colombian and US governments. Its clientele was a heady mix of drug lords, serial killers, rapists and political extremists and, more than two decades after its opening in April 2000, it had deservedly earned the reputation of being the worst hellhole in South America.

The prison stank of vomit, faeces and urine because prisoners only had access to running water for three hours a day. Most of the time they deposited their liquid and solid excrement in plastic shopping bags and dumped them in the communal areas scattered around the sixteen-hectare site. Most of the fourteen hundred prisoners were lifers, confined to tiny barren ten-foot-square cells for twenty-three hours a day, surviving on a diet of stale bread, rice and peas. Visitation rights were down to the goodwill of the warden, of which very little was ever shown.

Matias Paz, also known as the Black Scorpion, was one of the inmates. He was approaching the tenth year of his life sentence, having been found guilty of the multiple murders that terrorised Buenos Aires in January 2012. At the time, Paz fronted a corrupt security company that took orders directly from the CEO of a major US-based pharmaceutical corporation, who was exposed as the secret son of Adolf Hitler. Paz had found himself at the centre of a worldwide firestorm as he became the ugly face of a show trial that dominated the front pages across the globe for almost two months. Throughout the entire process, he didn't utter a single word.

Now in his sixties, Paz was a former mercenary and lifelong fascist. He still didn't carry an ounce of spare fat on his muscular frame, and before his incarceration he'd dyed his platinum-grey hair jet black to disguise his age. For many years he had kept two glossy black-skinned emperor scorpions in a large terrarium in his office, earning him his nickname.

He was just over halfway through his morning workout, simply dressed in white vest and underpants, when he heard footsteps approaching his cell. This was highly unusual as the guard who patrolled his level and dropped off his food twice a day, always at the same time, wasn't due for another seven hours. Paz cursed under his breath – the disruption to his routine and the consequent break in concentration meant he lost count of the number of press-ups he'd completed, so he'd have to start again. A few seconds later the metal hatch in the middle of the cell door slid open and the guard's face filled the void. Curiouser and curiouser, thought Paz – an event like this hadn't happened in the previous ten years of his incarceration.

"Get some clothes on, Paz – you have a visitor. I'll be back in five minutes."

The Black Scorpion was stunned. He'd not had a single visit since the day he'd entered the disgusting institution. He scrambled out a reply.

"Who ... is it?"

"It's your nephew, Theodor, and it's your lucky day. The warden has sanctioned the visit."

The hatch slid back into place and Paz made a grab for his brown dungarees, neatly folded on the mattress of his bunk. The imminent visit was indeed unusual, particularly as he didn't have a nephew.

* * *

The compact rectangular visiting room was stark. The white paint that had been applied to the plastered brick walls twenty years before had long since discoloured and now resembled a weak cappuccino. In the centre stood a small square pine table with a chair on either side – one of which had its legs cemented directly into the grey concrete floor. Two iron manacles secured to that end of the table were tightly clamped around Paz's wrists and, to complete the restraints, a four-inch-wide black leather safety belt secured his chest to the back of the chair. He felt like a trussed chicken and the message was clear: the warden may have granted him a visit, but he was obviously taking no chances with his high-profile inmate.

The digital clock on the far wall read 11:27, so Paz figured he only had three minutes to wait before meeting his mysterious nephew. He wasn't wrong. At precisely 11:30 the door facing him opened to reveal a guard he'd never seen before, accompanying a tall, painfully skinny early twenty-something, dressed head to toe in denim. The young man's overall appearance was unassuming and somewhat bedraggled; he was unshaven with a mop of hippy-length black curly hair. Paz figured his visitor was a struggling college student in desperate need of a decent meal. His angular features were dominated by high, pronounced cheekbones and his dark brown eyes, partially hidden behind a pair of cheap wire spectacles, looked slightly haunted as they focused on Paz. There was an ominous silence while he drew up the other chair to face his "uncle". Neither of them seemed sure how the initial greeting should play out but then the young man broke into life – as if he had just received an action cue and launched into his rehearsed script.

"Hello, Uncle. How are you doing?"

Before Paz could reply, the burly guard who'd escorted Theodor into the room interrupted them.

"You have exactly fifteen minutes for the visit, but if I see something I don't like, it'll be over. Do you understand?"

He didn't wait for a reply. Instead, he strolled over to the corner of the room, just far enough, Paz decided, to be out of earshot, and began playing a game of solitaire on his cell phone.

Paz was ready to begin his interrogation of the young visitor who was pretending to be his nephew. "Firstly, we both know Theodor isn't your real name. Who sent you and what do they want from me?"

The young man lent forward so his face was no more than six inches away from Paz. "Señor Paz, I'm an actor, a struggling actor who makes a grubby living as a waiter in a nightclub in the city. Last week I saw an online advert for a Zoom casting audition and … guess what? This was the part."

He smiled for the first time as he witnessed a look of total bewilderment on Paz's face. "The fee was huge and the woman who interviewed me said all I had to do was alter my appearance, take on the role of Theodor and deliver the following message to you in person, word for word."

"Who gave you the part? And don't bullshit me," Paz hissed, his reply dripping with threat.

"The woman never put up a live image of herself – there was just a caption on the screen saying 'casting director', so I've no idea who she was. But she made one thing very plain, I am not allowed to answer any questions."

Paz nodded his understanding and furtively glanced at the guard who was deep into his card game. "Go on, Mr Actor, let's hear what you've got to say."

Theodor shut his eyes for a couple of seconds, his forehead creasing up – almost as if he were rebooting his brain. Then he resumed eye contact with Paz and began to recite his lines. "Next Tuesday, exactly one week from today, at 13:09, nine minutes into your daily one-hour exercise break, you'll walk across the open courtyard to the middle of the western wall, turn and face it and maintain that position, regardless of anything that might go on around you. You'll be safe from harm as long as you don't move. By 13:15 you'll be out of the penitentiary and on your way to meet an old admirer."

The young man deliberately scraped his chair when he stood to catch the attention of the guard who glanced up from his phone, irritated his game had been disturbed.

"Guard, I'm ready to leave."

Paz's eyes never left the actor as he made his way across the room and out the door shadowed by the disgruntled guard. He sat passively in his chair, desperately trying to work out whom the young man was working for and what the hell was going to happen next week. For now, all he could do was wait.

Chapter 3

Valledupar, Colombia

T he week had dragged so slowly, Paz felt as though seven months rather than days had passed since his bizarre encounter with his phoney nephew. He'd tried hard to rationalise the scenario and find some answers. His shrewd brain played through all the possible angles, yet he was always left with two questions: who wanted him out and why now? He'd been rotting for years in this vile hovel, which had the audacity to call itself a correctional institution, and suddenly, out of nowhere, an outside force was set to free him. None of it made sense.

At 12:55, after the prison officer had opened his cell door, any lingering doubts Paz had that the whole set-up might be a sham vanished. The uniformed guard, who'd never uttered a word of small talk in the preceding ten years, reached into his pocket and retrieved two tiny yellow polymer foam earplugs. He held them in the open palm of his hand and gestured for Paz to take them.

"I've been instructed to give you these."

Paz stuffed them firmly inside his ears while the guard

turned, and they set off down the dark narrow corridor, beginning the long walk to the communal exercise courtyard. Paz could feel pure adrenaline surging through his veins. More questions flooded his thoughts: how had his rescuers persuaded the warden to allow last week's visit and how had they got to the guard – who'd always seemed incorruptible?

The recreation yard was jam-packed, with over three hundred prisoners taking their daily one-hour escape from their dismal cells. The convicts were monitored on the ground by thirty armed guards, ably supported by four elite officers perched on fifty-foot-high brick-built turrets positioned at the corners of the exercise area. All four were armed with an M249 light machine gun, capable of spitting out 5.56 mm rounds at a rate of two hundred per minute and, between them, the machine gun nests had clear sight lines of every inch of ground inside the yard, leaving no hiding place for the inmates should trouble break out.

Paz entered through the only access – a massive fifteen-foot-high, twelve-inch-thick iron door that formed part of the south wall. He at once found himself shoulder to shoulder with dozens of prisoners all arriving for their break at the same time. Although Paz could sense the busy chatter, the earplugs were doing their job muffling the noise to a distant, unintelligible hum. He glanced down at his cheap digital watch displaying the time 13:06. Three minutes to go.

He casually strolled towards the centre of the yard, deliberately avoiding eye contact with inmates and guards, all the while desperately trying to stay calm and focused. Paz sensed a rapid increase in his heartbeat and felt a slight sweat break on his forehead. He cursed the ten years of incarceration that had dimmed the natural operational skills he'd taken into the field so successfully on countless occasions. Yet again he furtively checked the time – 13:08. Just one minute to go but nothing was amiss. Nevertheless, he made his way across to the western wall and, at exactly 13:09, turned to face it.

Forty-five minutes earlier, unsuspecting tourists in the popular coastal resort of the walled city of Cartagena, witnessed two black dots flying in above the massive expanse of the Caribbean Sea, heading directly east over the old Spanish town, heading inland. The Sikorsky UH-60 Black Hawks were armed to the teeth. Both choppers were loaded with sixteen air-to-ground Hellfire missiles, usually employed to take out armoured tanks, and two M134 Miniguns were mounted on the bottom of the stub wings. These Gatling gun-style rotating barrel weapons could dispense a payload of six thousand rounds a minute.

The two Hawks circled around before coming in low and fast, attacking the penitentiary from the west. Although the four turret guards had heard and watched them approach thirty seconds earlier, they had no real sense of the violent attack heading their way. That all changed instantly as four Hellfire missiles slammed into the top half of each of the turrets, obliterating the solid brick structures and incinerating the guards. The deafening shriek produced by the four-bladed rotors hit an eye-watering 160 decibels and muted the screams of terror from below. Mayhem broke out as hundreds of inmates desperately raced towards the main entrance trying to escape the assault. Dozens were ruthlessly cut down by thousands of tracer rounds that carved a path across the concrete yard, taking out prisoners and guards indiscriminately.

Paz stayed jammed against the western wall but turned to get a close-up of the murderous attack. It was sheer carnage –

bloody body parts flying high into the air and corpses dancing on the ground as bodies were riddled with an endless hailstorm of incoming rounds. Paz's mind flicked back forty-five years to the Angolan Civil War, specifically to the tiny village of Cabo in the deep south of the country, where he and his band of mercenaries had created killing fields of their own, working for the National Liberation Front.

His mind snapped back to the present when he spotted a figure dressed head to toe in black commando fatigues winching down at breakneck speed from the open door of a Hawk maintaining a hover position directly above him. The second chopper was still wreaking mayhem with its Miniguns relentlessly pursuing any remaining signs of life in the courtyard, which had, in a matter of minutes, become an open burial ground. The winchman, his features hidden by a black balaclava, was now suspended three feet off the ground directly in front of Paz, who was relishing the enormity of the attack. He instinctively moved away from the wall towards his rescuer. An unmistakable American accent yelled instructions as a leather strap was flung towards him.

"Get this over your arms and back. We are going up."

Paz couldn't quite make out the exact words because of the earplugs but grabbed the strap as though it were a lifeline and, within moments, the two men were physically bonded together. Eighty feet above them the winch operator, leaning out of the Hawk's open door, triggered their ascent. In the chaos of the firefight three prison guards had miraculously made it to the safe zone of the western wall, the only untargeted area in the courtyard. One of them fired his Fara 83 automatic rifle directly at Paz and the winchman, while the other two took aim at the small rear rotor of the second Hawk, which continued to spit out punishing rounds from its Miniguns. He felt a sudden impact as two bullets ripped into the back of the winchman's skull, whose body immediately went limp. Soaring above the bedlam below, Paz realised he was now harnessed to a corpse.

The ferocious exchange of fire between the guards and the Minigun operator in the Hawk led to catastrophe for both sides. Now that Paz was no longer there, the Western wall had ceased to be a no-fire zone and the guards were mown down by dozens of strafing rounds and, moments later, the second Hawk stuttered in mid-air as a spray of bullets smashed into one of its rear rotor blades, upsetting the balance of the chopper. Tiny titanium fragments from the shattered blade flew into the air and the nose of the Hawk lurched forward. The gunship emitted a grinding mechanical scream as it began its descent, spiralling downwards at great speed.

The chopper smashed into what was left of the south turret and the entire courtyard shuddered from the impact, which created a giant fireball rising hundreds of feet in the air. Paz was within touching distance of the open door of the remaining Hawk when he felt the heat of the blast around him. He gasped for breath as burning hot petrol-fuelled black smoke filled his lungs. Seconds later he lost consciousness, unaware of a powerful pair of arms seizing his shoulders and bundling him and his dead companion inside the body of the helicopter. As soon as he was on board, the pilot began a steep climb and the Hawk made its exit, heading directly north for the coastline.

When Paz finally came around, he was aware of a silicone oxygen mask on his face and, at the same time, realised he was laying prone on the metal floor of the Hawk, in the narrow aisle between eight black leather seats. A male crew member was kneeling in front of him and, as soon as he saw Paz stir, shouted a greeting, fighting to cut through the deafening noise created by the rotors. Paz struggled to hear until he remembered the earplugs, which he took out and threw to the floor. His eardrums were instantly assaulted by the cacophony of sound that boomed around the tiny cabin. The man moved closer and tried again, pointing to the oxygen mask.

"Mr Paz, we just wanted to clean out your lungs from the blast. Try removing it now."

Paz gratefully obliged, slipping off the mask and taking a large gulp of fresh air that helped clear the fog from his mind.

"How long was I out?"

The man glanced down at his watch. "Maybe fifty minutes."

Paz nodded. He sat up gingerly, leaned forward and looked to his right through one of the large square side windows. The Hawk was flying fast and low, speeding over the stunning turquoise waters of the Caribbean.

"Where are we heading?"

"Take a look over there, Mr Paz."

The man pointed north, where a large white dot could clearly be seen in the distance. Paz narrowed his eyes until he could make out an enormous boat ahead of him.

"That's your new home. A sweet upgrade from your previous lodgings." The crew member laughed at his own joke.

Paz ignored him and maintained his gaze on the superyacht below. Every second that passed brought the seven-tier luxury boat into clearer focus and, three minutes later, the Hawk was ready to begin its descent manoeuvre onto one of the two helipads marked out on raised platforms at either end of the top deck. The landing was smooth and surprisingly easy. As soon as the three rubber tyres made contact, one of the crew slid open the door and Paz was ushered to the opening. He clambered out and stooped under the still whirring fifty-three-foot rotors and set eyes on a slim olive-skinned male running towards him. The man, in his thirties, was tall, slim and elegantly dressed in a light blue designer linen suit. He smiled warmly and offered his hand, which Paz happily accepted.

"Welcome aboard *The Blonde Lady*, Mr Paz. Allow me to introduce myself. My name is Anwar Al Kathib. Please follow me. Your saviour is extremely keen to meet you."

Chapter 4

The Blonde Lady, Caribbean Sea

The superyacht was truly spectacular. The 110-metre streamlined aluminium hull was the length of an American football pitch. It was powered by an innovative diesel-electric propulsion system that produced an impressive top speed of thirty plus knots. Its multilayered decks housed ten sumptuous staterooms, two swimming pools, a surround sound cinema, and a forty-square-foot wooden-beamed loggia. Attached to the stern was a three-man mini submarine capable of diving to fifteen hundred feet. The endless luxury was heavily protected by armour plating and bulletproof glass, as well as a ballistic missile defence system. What appeared at first glance to be an opulent gin palace of epic proportions was, in fact, an incredibly sophisticated, heavily protected vessel manned by a highly skilled crew of sixty.

The two men had only walked a short distance from the helipad when they heard the Hawk rev up and, a few seconds later, felt a savage downdraught as the chopper took off. Paz and the Arab stood and watched as the state-of-the-art Sikorsky gunship headed north towards the horizon. Paz briefly wondered where it was destined but his random thought was interrupted by Al Kathib, who turned away from the departing Hawk and gestured towards an oval glass lift protruding from the side of the deck.

"Let's go, Mr Paz."

After a short descent, the single door smoothly peeled open on the third level to reveal a magnificent oak-beamed double-height gallery partially wrapped in light gunmetal grey tinted glass. Paz savoured the luxury of the decor as he followed Al Kathib across the polished maple floor. The subtle cream and brown fusion of colours, creating the overall colour scheme, was broken up by giant artworks, many of which appeared to be floating in mid-air. This effect was created by a combination of free-hanging paintings dangling from semi-invisible wires and mounted sculptures on transparent Perspex plinths. In his previous existence Paz had always appreciated the trappings of wealth and power but right now, dressed in a pair of filthy, blood-strewn dungarees, he felt like a tramp who didn't belong.

They headed for the seating area at the far end of the vast loggia, where Paz could make out the back of a fair-haired man, sitting on a chocolate brown calfskin couch. He was leaning forward, seemingly preoccupied with a large glass container positioned on a circular ivory and glass coffee table. The man sensed the presence of his guests and stood, turning to greet them. He was tall and lithe, his face dominated by a bushy light brown beard that made him appear older than he was. Paz instinctively felt he was looking at someone from his past but, frustratingly, he just couldn't nail it. There was something about the nose and cheekbones that seemed slightly odd, and then he realised the face he was looking at had undergone significant reconstructive surgery. However, one feature remained unaltered – the man's piercing sky-blue eyes which, at that moment, were firmly fixed on the Black Scorpion.

"Mr Paz, I can tell from the look on your face that the thousands of dollars I've spent trying to disguise my features hasn't worked."

It wasn't until the man spoke that everything suddenly fell into place. Paz knew that voice so well. But it wasn't from any previous face-to-face meetings – in fact, the two men had never set eyes on each other before in the flesh. The man who had masterminded his escape from the hellhole in Valledupar, the man with the unmistakable voice, was a dead man: former presidential candidate, John Franklin, who, ten years earlier, had been publicly disgraced when he was exposed as the grandson of the world's most reviled dictator, Adolf Hitler. A man who supposedly had taken his own life.

Paz uttered the first thought that came to mind. "I knew your father well."

"You worked for my father for thirty years. You were never friends."

The bluntness of Franklin's reply was slightly softened by his gesturing towards the couch, indicating he wanted Paz to sit next to him. Al Kathib took his own cue and walked across to the armchair opposite. As he sat, Paz caught sight of the contents of the large glass terrarium on the coffee table which housed two glossy black-skinned emperor scorpions. He leaned forward and studied them in closer detail, instantly captivated.

Franklin noted Paz's reaction but was done with the niceties and keen to begin his pitch. "Consider them a gift. I'll have them installed in your stateroom. But now we have much to discuss."

Paz eased back on the couch and turned to face the man

who, after his exposure by the world's media, had been dubbed 'the Counterfeit Candidate'. "I'm ready to listen, Mr Franklin. A man who brings in two Black Hawks to rescue a single prisoner has my undivided attention, especially as I am the beneficiary of the raid."

Franklin beamed at the third man in the room. "I'm afraid I can't take the credit for the choppers. They were down to the talents of Anwar here, who used his personal friendship with senior figures in the Taliban to acquire them."

Al Kathib smiled as Franklin continued.

"Did you know that old fool of a president screwed up the withdrawal of US troops from Afghanistan so badly, he left behind thirty-three Sikorsky Black Hawks worth ten million dollars each? They now belong to the Taliban."

The Syrian paused for a moment and then became animated. "The irony is, the jihadists have no one in their ranks with any idea how to fly those machines, so for months they lay in the desert deteriorating. Add to that the cold reality of the Taliban's foreign accounts being frozen by the West and the timing of my cash offer of one million dollars for two Hawks was, under the circumstances, extremely generous and welcome."

Paz couldn't help but be impressed by the silky smooth-talking Syrian. He was evidently a man not to be underestimated.

"We hired a group of mercenaries – former US marine pilots and engineers to crew the Hawks, and the rest you know."

Paz turned to face Franklin, who was relishing hearing the detail behind the ingenious purchase of the Sikorsky killing machines. "So, Mr Franklin, why am I here? What do you want of me?"

"First of all, before we get to that, I want you to relax and enjoy your freedom. Get out of that revolting garb, scrub yourself clean and start to refresh your mind. As my guest, I want you to take full advantage of the facilities on offer. You'll find a range of designer clothes in your stateroom far more fitting for a man of your status. And, in case you were about to ask, this superyacht was originally commissioned by a Russian oligarch who crossed the wrong people in the Kremlin and never lived to enjoy it. To the relief of the shipbuilders, I stepped in and took over the contract. It's registered out of Hamilton, Bermuda, to a holding company based in Liechtenstein and its ownership is so deeply buried it can never be traced back to me. So, for a dead man, it provides the perfect hideaway. I can move around freely without any hassle, never having to worry about border or passport checks."

Paz was suitably impressed and stood to leave, sensing the meeting was over. At the same time, Franklin leaned to his right and from the end of the couch picked up two large files that he held in the air.

"Before you leave, take these. Over the next day or so, I want you to study their contents in detail. I've had the relevant sections translated into Spanish for you. Digest the material well and, the next time we meet, you'll have a good understanding of why I require your services."

He switched one of the files to his free hand and waved it in the air.

"This one is irreplaceable. It's almost eighty years old and the contents were the brainchild of my grandfather. It's quite magnificent."

Paz took the files and before withdrawing fired off a parting shot. "You realise the authorities will come looking for me."

Franklin frowned as if let down by the comment. "Paz, you do me an injustice. The carnage we created at Valledupar was a deliberate strategy to create a smokescreen for your escape. We systematically wiped out all the guards and convicts in the exercise yard, as well as the exterior CCTV cameras. The authorities are left with the painstaking process of piecing together hundreds of body parts to try and work out exactly who died in the attack. We believe they'll conclude it was the work of a Colombian drug lord looking to kill incarcerated rivals. Then, of course, we had the fortunate unplanned bonus of the fireball that cremated dozens of bodies. That will further hamper the identification process. It will be weeks, or possibly months, before they realise you're missing. If they ever do."

Paz stared in silence at his new captor for a few seconds and then glanced down at the two files in his hand, wondering what sort of evil was contained inside them. He was desperate to leave the meeting and escape to the sanctuary of his stateroom, but Franklin hadn't quite finished.

"Paz, I'm not sure of your sexual preferences, but just let your steward know and he'll arrange some suitable company."

Paz didn't react but wondered how much Franklin knew of his secret weakness for young blonde rent boys. A flaw he certainly wasn't going to admit to, despite the tempting offer.

An immaculately turned-out steward escorted Paz to his new prison: a beautifully appointed stateroom decked out with a queen-size circular bed – that on its own was bigger than his old cell, and a massive green marble jacuzzi. He stripped off his filthy dungarees and foul underwear and ran the taps as he contemplated his first bath in over ten years. Paz figured it would take at least ten minutes to fill the jacuzzi so, with time to kill, he flopped onto the bed and reached for the aged manila file. The first thing he noted was, despite the Spanish documents inside, the eighty-year-old folder had a German title printed on the front: *Operation Gesamtkunstwerk*. He flicked it open, began reading and quickly forgot about his bath.

For Paz, after a ten-year hiatus, the fun was about to start.

Chapter 5

Buenos Aires, Argentina

T he banner headline of the *Clarín*, Argentina's best-selling daily paper, contained a single word: *¡Masacre!*. A high-angle photo taken from a press drone, displaying the carnage inside the exercise yard at Valledupar following the helicopter attack at the maximum-security prison, dominated the rest of the page.

Nicolas Vargas of the Buenos Aires Police Department finished studying the lead article for a second time and dropped the newspaper onto his desk. The story made for a bizarre read. The female journalist who'd written it was suggesting that a crazed Colombian drug lord who, she suggested, might be Carlos Vásquez, had used two stolen helicopter gunships to wipe out some of his rivals being held at the notorious Valledupar Penitentiary.

At just over fifty, Vargas was at the very peak of his powers and was regarded by his peers as the brightest chief inspector on the city force. He was a tall man with film-star good looks enhanced by a natural charisma that matched his physical attributes. His attractive features hid a painful personal secret, as thirteen years earlier his life had been brutally derailed by the untimely death of his wife, Sophia. Her loss, and the loss of the future they'd planned together, had left him devastated. She was irreplaceable, so since then his sole focus had been his work.

The vivid description of the aerial assault at Valledupar intrigued him. An estimated two hundred prisoners and thirty-four guards had been slain in the military-style attack – although it was expected to be weeks before a confirmed list of the dead was made public. Vargas couldn't wait that long; there was one question he needed answering right away. He had to know if one of the slain convicts was a man he had personally sent there. A monster called Matias Paz. Vargas had led the arrest team responsible for Paz's capture back in January 2012 and had later given evidence against him at the show trial a few months later. If the mass murderer had been killed in the attack, good riddance. But Vargas needed to be sure.

When he'd first heard about the incident the day before, he'd contacted a colleague in the Colombian Police Force, based in Cartagena, to ask for everything he could find out about prisoner 477815, Matias Paz. The wait for a reply was killing him. Vargas was hoping to receive confirmation that Paz was one of the victims but when the news came through it didn't play out like that.

His cell phone rang and he instantly recognised the Colombian area code displayed on the screen. Vargas took the call knowing it would be from Police Captain Arturo Jiménez. The deep baritone voice of the Colombian boomed down the earpiece. He wasn't a man who wasted time on small talk.

"Chief inspector, I think you'll be pleased to hear the findings of my research. Your friend Matias Paz is no longer in his cell, so we can reasonably assume he was killed in the attack."

Vargas let out a huge sigh of relief. "They've identified his body?"

"I didn't say that. It will take weeks to identify all the corpses, especially those virtually incinerated in the inferno. They'll be identified through dental records eventually. But if he's no longer in the prison building, we have to assume he's dead." The police captain seemed keen to end the call. "So, there you have it, chief inspector."

Vargas could see the logic and had only one remaining question.

"Captain Jiménez, have you seen Paz's prison records? Was there anything strange or suspicious I should know about?"

"Nothing at all – he appears to have been a model prisoner. I've emailed them through to you so you can see for yourself. Now, I have to go."

Vargas ended the call and placed his iPhone next to the newspaper on the desk. Paz was dead, along with hundreds of other evil men, none of whom would be mourned by anyone other than their immediate families. He felt a huge sense of relief, but until official identification came through there would continue to be a tiny element of doubt. He took a sip of cold coffee from a white polystyrene cup while he flipped open his laptop and clicked on his inbox. He had twelve new emails but was only interested in one, which he quickly opened and double-clicked on its attachment. It contained the ten-year prison record of inmate 477815.

It was a short document, and Jiménez was right – the information it contained was routine and low-key. Paz's behaviour had been exemplary. Maybe, despite his life sentence, the Black Scorpion had secretly hoped that somewhere down the line his good conduct might catch the eye of the parole board, however unlikely that was. He was about to close the file when something slightly off caught his attention. Under the heading "Communication" there were two sub-columns: "Visits" and "Correspondence". The second, which related to any incoming or outgoing letters, showed the figure zero. The first showed the number one.

Vargas wasn't at all surprised by Paz's lack of communication with the outside world but was curious about the lone visitor. He assumed it must be a lawyer who had perhaps visited the Black Scorpion shortly after he had begun his sentence, but when he saw the date of the visit, he felt a searing pain deep in the pit of his stomach. Why on earth would Paz have had his only prison visit exactly one week before the attack? Moments later, when Vargas saw the name of the visitor – Theodor Paz, he knew the answer.

Chapter 6

Los Angeles, United States

Troy Hembury wasn't quite sure what to make of the WhatsApp message that had popped up on his cell phone, even after reading it for the third time. The police lieutenant was waiting in line at a McDonald's drive-through in his Hybrid Lexus having made a quick pit stop on his way home.

I need your help, Troy. We must visit Valledupar Prison. I think the Black Scorpion is out. There's a red eye from LA that gets you into Cartagena at 7. I'll meet you off the plane and we can drive the rest of the way. Will explain when we meet. Nic

Hembury clicked on the phone icon to contact Vargas, but the call diverted to voicemail. He figured the chief inspector was probably already mid-air, so didn't bother to leave a message. His thoughts flashed back ten years to when he and Vargas worked side by side on an extraordinary high-profile case that unravelled across North and South America, starting with a safe-deposit robbery in Buenos Aires and concluding with the exposure of John Franklin, the fraudulent US presidential candidate.

A key figure at the heart of the investigation was a psychopathic killer, Matias Paz, aka the Black Scorpion, who had personally tortured and murdered multiple victims and almost succeeded in taking out Vargas. The fallout from the case had affected Hembury's life in many ways, the most significant being that he'd scrapped an early retirement and now, here he was, fast approaching his sixty-first birthday and still holding down the challenging role.

Despite his age, the African American lieutenant was in great condition. Remarkably, his black hair showed no sign of grey and his waistband size hadn't changed since he was thirty, being the fitness addict he was. But, at that precise moment, he felt every one of the sixty odd years of his biological age. Ironically, he'd been planning to contact Vargas to discuss another critical matter but realised now that difficult conversation would have to wait, having been hijacked by these latest events. He paused for a moment, contemplating the potential implications of Paz's escape. There was only one possible reply he could send.

See you there. Sounds like old times! T

Hembury ditched the burger and headed straight to his West Hollywood apartment. Two hours later, armed with just an overnight bag, he grabbed a taxi to LAX. As the yellow cab pulled up outside the terminal, his phone pinged.

I really hope not! Nic

Chapter 7

Cartagena, Colombia

The nine-hour night flight was uneventful. Hembury spent most of the time online, catching up with news coverage of the sensational prison attack before grabbing a couple of hours' sleep. Forty minutes after the American Airlines plane touched down, the two detectives were travelling in a hire car on the main road heading east to Valledupar with Vargas at the wheel. It didn't take long for the Argentine to bring Hembury up to speed, and Troy quickly picked up on the significance of Theodor – Paz had been the CEO of a covert security company named Theodor Consultants, and whoever had come to visit him seven days before the attack had used that name as a trigger sign.

"Apart from the name, what do we know about the visitor?"

"Not a lot, Troy. All we know is he was an impostor – Paz has no brothers or sisters. The man posing as his nephew applied for the visit through a now defunct email address and, of course, his ID was fake. The Colombian police have some decent photos from the meet, but I suspect he was heavily disguised, so I'm not holding my breath. One thing really bugs me, though. Why, when it falls within his discretion to refuse visits, did the warden let this one happen?"

Hembury nodded and glanced across at Vargas. "Great minds, Nic. Why, indeed?"

For the next few minutes they sat in silence, surveying the passing scenery. Then Hembury sought to lift the sombre mood.

"Nic, do you remember the last time we were together in a rental, heading out to El Calafate?"

Vargas broke into a smile and glanced across at his passenger.

"How could I ever forget our meeting with the delightful Eva Braun. It's burned into every little cell in my brain, and don't forget I've the scars to prove it."

The two friends laughed and for the rest of the two-hundred-mile journey forgot about Paz and caught up on each other's lives. The pair had last met ten months earlier in Washington for their annual face-to-face briefing with the deputy director of the FBI. The detectives were part of a small clique of high-ranking government officials, including the president, who were aware of some complex loose ends connected to the Franklin scandal that were still live and constantly monitored under a cloak of secrecy.

It was just after three when the Hertz rental approached the main entrance of what was left of the maximum-security penitentiary. An enormous section of the front elevation had been blown away leaving a smouldering pile of concrete rubble, reminiscent of a Middle Eastern war zone. Vargas brought the car to a halt about twenty yards from what remained of the front gates. He and Hembury stepped out and walked to the front of the black Ford Taurus to take a closer look at the sheer devastation. They were stunned by the appalling sight that faced them. The visual impact of the decimated prison was heightened by the disgusting stench of charred human flesh that hung in the air, forming a pungent cocktail with the smell of burnt diesel.

As the two men continued their approach by foot, they became aware of activity taking place inside what was left of the former exercise yard. Dozens of military soldiers were carefully laying out lines of thick black plastic body bags containing the charred remains of the guards and prisoners. The grotesque tableau also featured the crumpled, twisted and burned-out wreckage of the Black Hawk that had crashed into the south wall of the yard, causing total carnage.

Hembury watched a female soldier pull up the heavy-duty zipper on a body bag just a few feet from them. He turned to Vargas and pointed at the plastic mobile graves.

"Jesus, Nic. I'm praying Paz – or what's left of him, is inside one of those because if this operation was solely to extricate him, God knows who we're dealing with."

Vargas was looking down at his iPhone, reading a text. "Let's try and find out. The warden's waiting for us in his office in the admin block. He's sent a prison officer down to find us."

* * *

Victor Quintana felt uneasy about his upcoming meeting with the Argentine chief inspector and his American colleague. He'd held the position of warden for almost twenty years – the latter fourteen of which had been at the helm of hell on earth, otherwise known as Valledupar Prison. Quintana was an imposing hulk of a man whose six-foot-five frame, and twenty-one-stone bulk combined to create an intimidating presence.

His pockmarked dumpy face housed two small brown eyes and a thin slit for a mouth that gave the unfortunate appearance of a permanent smirk. The few strands of greasy brown hair left on top of his head were combed forward in a feeble attempt to disguise the creeping baldness. As the prison officer opened the door to his office and escorted the two detectives into the room, Quintana felt his armpit sweat seep through his white cotton shirt and settle on the lining of his navy-blue linen jacket.

After a brief handshake Vargas and Hembury dropped into two low black chairs strategically positioned in front of a high black metal desk behind which the obese warden appeared enormous. Vargas kicked off with a conciliatory tone.

"Warden, thank you for seeing us at such short notice. I can't even begin to imagine what chaos you're dealing with. Where do you start?"

The warden felt a sense of relief at the supportive comment and replied in his native tongue. "Thank you, chief inspector. I confess I share your concerns. This sort of event is unprecedented and nothing in the prison manual prepares you for it."

"Warden, Captain Jiménez told me you were able to converse in English, which would be helpful for my colleague, Lieutenant Hembury."

Quintana's sweaty forehead creased to a frown while his tiny eyeballs darted around like a crazy pair of pinballs. "Yes, of course. I apologise if my English isn't perfect. But I will do whatever I can do to be of help. I must admit, I am confused as to why you are both here. Are you involved in drug administration? Is that what the assault was about?"

Hembury joined in for the first time. "No, warden. We're

here because we believe the attack may have been a cover for the escape of one of your inmates. Matias Paz, to be specific. We've heard from several eyewitnesses along the coastline that two Hawks flew inland but only one headed out to sea about an hour after the assault. We believe Paz may have been on board."

Quintana lurched forward, genuinely startled by the suggestion that one of his prisoners had somehow escaped under cover of the attack – especially if the man involved was Paz. He felt nauseous and fought back the impulse to vomit.

"With respect, lieutenant, this sounds more like a James Bond plot than reality." His half-hearted laugh died a slow death before Vargas spoke.

"Warden, why did you allow Paz his first ever private visit just seven days before the attack took place when in the last five years you haven't permitted any of the lifers a single visit between them?"

The warden now realised he was under suspicion but tried to stay calm and keep his wits about him. "Chief inspector, unlike most of the scum in here, Paz was a model prisoner. He didn't give us a single moment of trouble in ten years. All he did every day was work out in his cell for hours at a time – the man was a machine, and if all the lifers behaved like he did, my job would be easy. Unfortunately, they don't." He paused for a moment to see if either detective was buying his story, but by their grim faces he guessed they weren't, so he ploughed on. "When his nephew applied for the visit, I could see no harm in allowing it to happen, which is why I sanctioned it. Right now, I still can't see any connection between that and what took place two days ago."

Vargas went in for the kill. "Paz doesn't have a nephew. The visitor was an impostor, who no doubt informed Paz of the escape plan." That bombshell was swiftly followed up by an even bigger one. "Warden, I believe you know this information already and that you were paid a great deal of money to allow the visit to take place. As part of my investigation's remit, I have the power to gain access to your bank accounts. I'm betting they'll show—"

Quintana didn't allow Vargas to complete the accusation. "Chief inspector, you can do whatever you like. I have nothing to hide, nothing at all."

Both detectives spotted the momentary telltale flicker of the man's eyes.

Although the warden was lying, he was unconcerned at the thought of them digging into his affairs as his twenty-thousand-dollar bribe wasn't sitting in a bank account – he was wearing it on his wrist. His bravado returned and he stood, towering over his guests.

"I'm happy to make my accounts available to you without the need for a warrant. Now, I suggest you leave my office and take your fantasy ideas with you as I have serious work to get on with."

Having delivered his final statement, the warden rounded the desk and flew past them at a speed that belied his size. Moments later he exited his office.

Vargas watched him go and glanced back towards Hembury.

"What the hell did you make of that?"

"Nic, that colossus was lying through his yellow teeth. Here's a question for you – how the hell does a prison warden earning thirty thousand a year afford a gold Rolex Submariner?"

Chapter 8

El Calafate, Argentina

14 May 1948

I t was an industrial-scale rant, even by his standards.

"I am sick to the very pit of my stomach. I am repulsed by this event. Thinking about it makes my flesh crawl ... It's the ultimate mark of failure and betrayal."

The Führer was incandescent with rage. Adolf Hitler's piercing blue eyes burned with fury as he let rip at Martin Bormann. The two notorious Nazis the world believed had died in Berlin were very much alive and mortified as they listened to the world news on a Zenith Console Radio Phonograph, which was in imminent danger of being destroyed by the Führer's flailing arms.

For almost three years Hitler, Bormann and Eva Braun had been living in secrecy in the obscure town of El Calafate, situated near the edge of the Southern Patagonian Ice Field in the Argentine province of Santa Cruz. Bormann had masterminded the trio's escape from Berlin twenty-four hours before the Red Army reached Hitler's infamous bunker, and the three of them now lived under fake identities in an enormous farmhouse known as El Blondi, along with four guards, a maid, a housekeeper and a cook. They'd taken the surname Franklin, with Hitler and Bormann posing as brothers Gerald and Ronald, and Eva Braun playing the role of Gerald's wife, Emilia Franklin.

The cultured voice on the radio that had sparked Hitler's anger belonged to David Ben-Gurion, the executive head of the World Zionist Organization, who was declaring the establishment of a Jewish homeland to be known as the State of Israel. An Argentine commentator was talking over the Hebrew speech in Latin American Spanish, which Bormann was doing his best to translate.

"Führer, as we feared, Jews, whatever their nationality, now have a permanent homeland. With the unqualified backing of the United States – prompted by its despicable Jewish lobby, this new country of Israel will become a beacon for Jews across the world."

The two men were inside Hitler's vast pine-panelled study listening to the broadcast. Bormann was sitting in a brown leather armchair close to the radio, while the Führer paced the room spouting profanities every time his fellow Nazi threw him another nugget of information.

"Martin, the creation of this new country represents an enduring threat to everything we believe in. For so many years we were successful in culling this subhuman race and now the Western powers – in their madness, have given it the chance to procreate and prosper in a state of legitimacy."

As the broadcast came to an end, Hitler, who had been animated throughout the transmission, appeared to run out of energy, as if a mystery force had somehow disconnected his batteries. He slowly walked across the room to his imposing desk and slumped into the chair behind it, shaking his head in denial of the new reality.

Bormann, the ultimate arch-manipulator, had known this day was coming for months and had prepared a surprise to lift his beloved Führer's spirits.

"There might be a long-term solution to this new problem, Führer. I have arranged for a special house guest to arrive at El Blondi in the morning – a respected scientist who shares your passion for *Operation Gesamtkunstwerk*."

Hitler looked up at Bormann, who was now standing in front of the desk, and for the first time that day the hint of a smile appeared on his face.

The following morning, at precisely ten thirty, Bormann escorted the visitor into the main reception room of the farmhouse, where the Führer was reclining on a small black couch listening to one of his treasured opera recordings. Wagner's *Die Meistersinger von Nürnberg* was the four-and-a-half-hour operatic odyssey Hitler had chosen to be performed in Berlin in March 1933 to mark the founding of the Third Reich. Bormann knew the significance of the aria and was relieved to hear it, confirming as it did Hitler's upbeat mood that morning.

"Führer, may I introduce you to Doctor Horst Schumann, who also served during the campaign as an SS major."

Schumann found himself totally awestruck, both because he'd believed the Führer was dead and because he was coming face to face with him for the first time. He wasn't sure whether to use the Heil Hitler salute but decided to play safe. The Führer nodded his appreciation at the greeting and gestured for Schumann to sit on a matching couch opposite him. Bormann moved across to the phonograph and lifted the needle from the seventy-eight. He took a seat in a single armchair between the two men and continued the introduction.

"Schumann worked as one of the principal doctors at our celebrated Auschwitz camp, where he carried out a number of experiments under direct instruction from Mengele. He was a pioneer of *Operation Gesamtkunstwerk* and now, as we plan for the future, I believe his research can be put to good use in our pharmaceutical company."

The doctor looked bewildered, so Bormann elaborated.

"Dr Schumann, two years ago we created a major pharma company in Buenos Aires and it's already the third largest in South America. As you can imagine, we have invested significant funds and have recruited leading research biologists who are sympathisers to our cause. They work out of a secret laboratory in Neuquén. I want you to spend a few months there passing on your knowledge."

Before Schumann could reply, Hitler spoke for the first time. His question was blunt and laced with suspicion.

"Major, where have you been hiding out since the war ended?"

"Führer, I left the camp in December forty-four and went to work on the front line as a military doctor. In early April I was captured by the Americans but had taken the precaution of accessing forged papers with a fake identity showing no connection to Auschwitz. They accepted my story that I was just a regular doctor and released me after a few weeks. I travelled to Gladbeck in the North Rhine region where I had an old medical friend who was happy to put me up. I've been there ever since, practising as a sports doctor in plain sight."

Hitler seemed suitably impressed and glanced at Bormann,

signalling his approval. The Führer's henchman rose and walked across to the doctor, placing a hand on his shoulder.

"So once again you will have the honour of working directly for the Führer. You'll stay here tonight as our guest and tomorrow I'll arrange your transport to Neuquén to begin your vital work."

Schumann was canny enough to play the game in such exalted company and, besides, the prospect of spending a few months in Argentina appealed to him. "Führer, this opportunity is a huge honour and I'll do everything I can to take the project forward."

The obsequious doctor saluted and, just before he turned to leave, Hitler leaned forward on the couch indicating he had one final question. His voice dropped to a menacing whisper.

"Tell me, doctor, how many Jewish bitches did you personally sterilise?"

Chapter 9

The Blonde Lady, Caribbean Sea

Paz had been busy. In the forty-eight hours since his game-changing meeting with Franklin he'd meticulously studied the documentation in the two files and had also put the burner phone his steward had provided to good use. In theory he was now a free man but appreciated his unexpected liberty came at a cost. For the second time in his life his very existence depended on the patronage of the infamous Franklin family. He'd worked for Richard Franklin, John's father, for more than thirty years and shed no tears when he learned of his suicide. Franklin Senior had been an arrogant, violent sociopath who believed he was untouchable and was the only man Paz had ever truly feared. Although he'd only met John two days before, he sensed the former presidential candidate was cut from the same cloth.

The contents of the files were fascinating. They read like an enthralling history lesson that began in 1942 as the Third Reich swept across Europe rounding up millions of Jews into death camps and ended in the present day with a compelling, ingenious plan code-named *Operation Gesamtkunstwerk*. It would either work brilliantly or fail disastrously, and the more Paz contemplated it the less certain he became as to which outcome was most likely.

Once he felt he had gleaned everything he could from the documents, he wrote out a list of former associates and contacts from his past life who he thought might still be loyal or at least owe him. He dived into the murky depths of his memory and retrieved one cell number for a source he knew would have contacts for everyone else – and he was right. The select few were stunned to hear from him, but once the initial shock passed, they quickly fell into line.

Buenos Aires had always been his hunting ground and, as well as providing loyal foot soldiers, it was also the home of a secret bank account containing over three million dollars and a lock-up warehouse with over half a million in cash stashed behind a dummy wall. Maybe he'd have a chance to spend some of it after all.

As he waited for the steward to come and collect him for his follow-up meeting with Franklin, he studied his reflection in the full-length mirror on the back of the bathroom door. His restored jet-black hair, courtesy of a bottle, was perfectly slicked back and his muscular frame was coated with a black linen Prada suit. His sockless feet wore a pair of Christian Louboutin boat shoes that completed the look. The Black Scorpion was back.

He was collected from his stateroom at midday and a few minutes later was back inside the vast loggia, together with Franklin and Al Kathib. As if by design, the three men took up the same positions they'd held at the previous meeting. It was as though they'd never left. The only obvious difference, apart from Paz's new apparel, was the strong scent of Giorgio

Armani emanating from him, replacing the stench of stale urine that had taken him hours to scrub off.

Franklin poured them all a glass of red wine from a stunning Venetian glass decanter and handed them around. "Paz, I know you favour fine red wines, so I'm sure you'll find this one to your liking. It's a Château Cheval Blanc 1947 St-Émilion. Quite rare."

Paz enjoyed the distinctive liquorice and berry fragrance of the French Merlot before taking a couple of sips and nodding his appreciation to his host. Franklin took the cue.

"So, I assume you've gone through the documents and are now well versed in the operation we are planning. You'll have a key role to play, alongside Anwar, to bring it to fruition. As I'm sure you've worked out, we have a great deal to do if we are going to hit the proposed date."

Paz took a massive gulp of wine before replying, not sure how his response would go down. "I think it's incredibly ambitious, Señor Franklin, but, then again, the entire plan is verging on the brink of fantasy."

Franklin flashed his teeth in a sign of unguarded anger. "Paz, you're in no position to cast doubt on an operation that has been years in the making. I expect total, unquestioning loyalty, just as my father did."

Having been well and truly slapped down, Paz realised this wasn't the time to push his luck. "Of course, Señor Franklin. I understand our working arrangement and I'm ready to go through the details with you both right now. Looking at some of the prep that needs to be put in place, I assume I'll be heading back to Buenos Aires."

"Indeed so. But first I have a little job for you back in

Colombia – an assignment that'll both hone your skills and prove to me the Black Scorpion hasn't lost his sting."

Paz was intrigued. His mouth broke into a fake smile at Franklin's weak pun.

"I want you to pay a visit to your young nephew, Theodor. You see, I hate loose ends."

"Where will I find him?"

"He lives in a tiny studio in Bogotá. We'll arrange your travel and source a suitable weapon."

Paz's thoughts flashed back to his last bout of killings, ten years earlier. "Don't worry about that. I'll source my own."

Chapter 10

Bogotá, Colombia

Mateo Silva had never seen a nail gun before. Yet here he was being interrogated by a maniac who was holding the work tool a few inches from his face. He was a prisoner in his own home, strapped like a helpless mummy to a plastic chair by six leather restraints.

A few hours earlier the young unemployed actor had been living it up at one of Bogotá's most exclusive nightclubs, blowing a large chunk of the sizeable cash fee he'd just received. The psychopath holding the repurposed weapon was the same man Mateo had visited in Valledupar Prison the week before, when he'd given a one-off performance as the man's nephew.

Paz was relishing every moment of the encounter. For the first time in a decade, he felt truly alive and relevant. He pressed the plastic muzzle firmly against the terrified actor's forehead and held it there for what seemed like an eternity but was in reality no longer than ten seconds.

"Mateo, you look so different without your wig, glasses and make-up – I hardly recognise my own nephew. Now, we need to have a little talk. Let me begin by asking you a question. Do you know what this is?" He gestured to the black and orange heavy-duty plastic nail gun in his right hand.

Silva was shaking with fear and tried in vain to articulate an answer but, in the end, just about managed to shake his head.

"It's a top-of-the-range VonHaus cordless nail gun armed with a unique action trigger that delivers precise placement and depth control. This little baby can fire up to sixty nails a minute."

Paz reeled back as the young actor's body shuddered, letting fly an uncontrollable torrent of vomit. The Black Scorpion was enjoying the moment and was keen to prolong the suffering.

"Now, Mateo, tell me, how much were you paid for playing my nephew? Whatever it was, I guess at this moment you're thinking it wasn't enough."

Silva choked out a reply through a mouthful of vomit. "Ten … thousand … dollars."

"So now we know the value of your life."

Paz felt a surge of adrenaline pump through his body as he registered the terror in Silva's eyes now that the actor realised he had just been given a death sentence.

"I followed you tonight as you left this shithole and ended up downtown at Piso 30 where you no doubt blew most of your fee. Now, here's another question for you – have you told anybody about your starring role as my nephew?"

"No one – nobody knows about it."

Paz moved closer with the weapon, content the man was telling the truth in a desperate bid to save his life. "Mateo, that's excellent. Now, I have some good news for you. I calculate that after the first two nails penetrate your brain, you won't feel a thing when the rest follow. And I'm thinking it will take at least fifty to create a nice symmetrical halo around your head."

Paz's gruesome calculations were slightly off. During the next few seconds Silva was sure he sensed at least five insertions before everything went black.

As the Black Scorpion let fly with his lethal weapon, his mood was euphoric, and it never occurred to him that the final answer the actor had given was a lie.

Chapter 11

Cartagena, Colombia

After their confrontation with the warden at Valledupar Penitentiary, Vargas and Hembury remained in Colombia for a couple of days to see what they could dig up now that they were convinced the attack was a smokescreen to facilitate Paz's escape. They based themselves at the Hyatt Regency on the oceanfront in Cartagena where they hunkered down with their laptops, learning as much as they could about the prison attack. The two nagging questions that urgently needed answering were, who was behind the breakout and why?

The only time the detectives emerged from their rooms was to gorge on the sumptuous breakfast buffet that fuelled them for the day. Vargas was ploughing his way through an enormous plate of scrambled eggs, bacon, and hash browns with a toasted bagel on the side, while Hembury opted for the healthier choice of pink grapefruit accompanied by a bowl of muesli topped with fresh berries.

"Nic, we need to focus on our only two leads, however thin they are. We must find the fantasy nephew Theodor – a name like that would have tipped Paz off that it was something to do with his past life, and then there's the Black Hawk. Where did it fly to after the attack? Where did it deliver Paz?"

Before he could reply, Vargas's cell phone pinged, signalling an incoming text.

Are you still in Colombia? There's been a development that will be of interest. Jiménez

Vargas showed Hembury the message then called the Colombian police captain, who picked up after the first ring.

"Chief inspector, thanks for calling. There's been a gruesome killing of a young male actor in Bogotá. I believe he may well be the mystery man who visited Señor Paz a week before the prison attack."

Vargas glanced across at Hembury who was staring at his friend, desperate to know what was being said.

Jiménez continued to fill the chief inspector in on the grisly details of Mateo Silva's murder, and at the end of the call Vargas agreed to jump on the next flight to Bogotá to meet at the crime scene. Hembury dived straight in.

"Tell me."

"It seems we've found the first of our two leads, although by the sound of things Paz got their first."

A few hours later, following a ninety-minute internal flight and a taxi ride, the pair entered a tiny squalid studio apartment located in a narrow backstreet in the colourful district of Ciudad Bolívar in the south of the city. The grim six-hundred-square-foot apartment was populated by a team of hazmat-suited forensic officers fighting for space alongside a team of detectives. Jiménez escorted Vargas and Hembury through the human maze to the open-plan kitchen where a horrendous sight awaited them. The young actor's body was slumped in a plastic chair that gave the impression it was floating in a pool of congealed blood, courtesy of the damage caused by the fifty or so two-inch nails hammered into the top of his forehead creating a gruesome crown of thorns effect.

The corpse's face was swollen, distorted and blood-soaked, making identification pretty much impossible. Vargas turned away from the disgusting scene and addressed Jiménez.

"What on earth makes you think this is Theodor?"

The Colombian police captain gestured for the detectives to follow him, and they made their way down a narrow staircase onto the street where they entered a small shop located below the studio. Three more police officers were inside along with a smartly dressed middle-aged man sitting in the corner. He was clearly distressed – his tearful red eyes staring straight ahead into space. He didn't notice the three men approach until Jiménez spoke.

"Señor Silva, these are the detectives I told you about. Please can you tell them exactly what you've already told me."

The man snapped out of his trance and stood to greet them. Despite being understandably distraught, his voice was strong and unwavering.

"My name is Arturo. Mateo was my baby brother. What they did to him," he paused, fresh tears in his eyes, "is inhuman. I know this must somehow be connected to the last job he took on – visiting that murderer in Valledupar."

Vargas placed his arm on the man's shoulder in a genuine gesture of sympathy. "Arturo, my name is Vargas. I'm a chief inspector working out of the Buenos Aires Police Department. I'm so sorry for your loss but right now if we are going to find the person who did this to your brother, I need to ask you a few questions."

Arturo nodded his consent.

"How do you know about the visit to Valledupar?"

"Mateo was a young, ambitious actor desperate for a break but, in truth, he spent months at a time working in bars and nightclubs, scraping a living, constantly failing auditions. Then, a couple of weeks ago, he secured a Zoom interview for a major role. He was so excited he could hardly sleep. He asked me to help him because he didn't have a laptop, so he came over to my apartment in the old town and I stood to the side of him, well out of view, and watched his entire audition."

Vargas could hardly contain himself. "You witnessed the entire thing – which means you can help identify the people who recruited him. Can you tell me exactly what took place?"

"I can do far better than that, chief inspector – I can show you. I recorded the entire Zoom call."

Chapter 12

Bogotá, Colombia

Arturo Silva and the three police chiefs left the dilapidated newsagents and drove to the old town where they set up camp in Silva's spacious apartment in Plazoleta del Rosario, a small square in the historical La Candelaria neighbourhood. They based themselves in the expansive lounge, which featured floor-to-ceiling windows with views directly over the pretty square. After handing out cold bottles of water, Silva made a quick trip to his office to retrieve his MacBook, which he carefully placed in the centre of a long coffee table, angling the screen towards the policemen.

"I am a lawyer and senior partner in one of the city's leading property law companies based in the old town. As the oldest of five siblings and the head of the family, I take my responsibilities very seriously. Mateo was the youngest and neediest of all of them. There's a big age gap between us but he was my baby brother, I've always tried to be there for him ... and now he's gone and ..."

Tear welled up in Arturo's eyes as he visualised the painful image of Mateo's brutal killing and he paused before slowly sitting down. No one spoke until the broken lawyer composed himself and continued with his tale.

"A couple of weeks ago he called me, buzzing with excitement. He couldn't wait to tell me about an online Zoom audition he had coming up with a production company casting for a new movie to be shot across South America. The problem was he didn't own a laptop and so, of course, I suggested he use mine."

He nodded towards the black Mac on the table.

"We both agreed the backdrop for the audition would look far better here, so he came over about midday to prepare for the two o'clock Zoom. Mateo had replied to an online ad and the audition was set up following an exchange of emails with the production company. They insisted on several conditions ahead of the call – one of which was that it couldn't be recorded. However, Mateo was insistent he needed a record of the audition to analyse his performance. As you'll see in a moment, we cleared the centre of this room, closed the blinds and I stood over there in the corner so I couldn't be seen. The call lasted about forty minutes and when it was over I pleaded with Mateo not to pursue the bizarre role – the whole thing smelled to high heaven. Clearly I failed."

Vargas gestured towards the laptop. "Señor Silva, that information has been incredibly helpful. Now, please can you play the recording."

For the following forty minutes, the Zoom audition ran on the laptop and Vargas played the role of translator for Hembury's benefit. The screen was split in half, with the left-hand side showing Mateo, while the other box showed no people, just a black-and-white caption that read "VIVA SA FILMS – CASTING". In total, there were three participants on the Zoom, but only Mateo was visible. Just the voices could be heard of the other two – a young woman, who did most of the talking, and a male who interjected occasionally.

The female voice was blunt and to the point. The role on offer was a one-off performance to take place at Valledupar Prison, where Mateo, in disguise, would play the part of Theodor Paz. He would be emailed his lines the night before the visit, and in return for his performance he'd receive a fee of ten thousand dollars – half on agreement and the other half after the job was carried out. The woman stressed the need for total confidentiality. It was obvious the audition angle was a total sham.

When the picture froze at the end of the recording, Arturo stood up and closed the laptop. "I told Mateo not to pursue it but there was no talking to him. He was excited and intrigued by the proposal – and then the size of the fee was the clincher. The rest you know."

Vargas nodded, reached across the low table, and picked up the laptop. "We'll need to take this away for our IT guys to work on. I suspect VIVA SA and its email address will prove to be dead ends, but the Zoom call might give us something. Señor Silva, I believe the person who tortured your brother was the same person he visited at Valledupar. We'll do everything we can to bring him in."

With the viewing over, the meeting came to an end. Vargas and Hembury said their goodbyes, split from Jiménez and booked themselves into a Hilton close to El Dorado International Airport. They found a quiet corner section in one of the ground-floor bars and the chief inspector placed an international call to FBI headquarters in Washington. It wasn't long before he had fully briefed Mike Berrettini, the deputy director, who asked for the Zoom call to be emailed over, along with any other information concerning VIVA SA. They concluded the conversation and agreed to speak again in a few hours once the FBI tech specialists had been given a chance to pore over the recording.

"Troy, the bad news is it's impossible to work out where a Zoom call is placed from, even though the laptop that issues the invite has its own unique address. So, the two voices we heard could have been located anywhere in the world when they spoke with Mateo. But you never know, those guys in Washington might come up with something."

Hembury downed the remains of his beer before replying.

"Look, it's clear we're dealing with a serious player who has the know-how and military might to break Paz out of a maximum-security penitentiary. Now we need to know where they're keeping him and what comes next."

Vargas smiled at his close friend. "What comes next for me is a long, hot shower followed by a giant rib-eye."

"I'm up for that. I'll see you in reception at seven."

* * *

The Factory Steak & Lobster was only a short cab ride from the hotel, and the two men were enjoying a beer and waiting for their surf and turf to arrive when Hembury decided to change the subject and the mood.

"Nic, before all this blew up, I'd been meaning to call you, but kept putting it off."

Vargas picked up on the change of tone. "What is it, Troy? What's happened?"

Hembury took a large gulp of beer, put his glass down and

glanced up at his friend. "A few months ago I started to suffer from bad headaches that I initially assumed were migraines. They persisted during one bad week and coincided with bouts of violent sickness. I felt strangely tired, drowsy, almost as if I'd been drugged. Anyway, I went for a check-up with a private doctor, had all the tests, and then came the results – a double whammy."

Vargas had started to tear up but tried his best to fight it as Hembury continued.

"Seems I have a massive tumour just here." He raised his right hand and tapped the left side of his forehead. "Grade three, not good. Inoperable. He's put me on steroids, but the prognosis isn't great."

Vargas's stomach churned as his mind flooded with the excrutiating memory of the exact moment his late wife Sophia broke the awful news to him of her own inoperable tumour.

"How long, Troy?"

"That's the goofy thing about it. He can't say. Could be six months, could be five years – maybe a bit longer. It all depends how the tumour reacts to the steroids. Right now, I've been headache free for the last three weeks and I feel great."

"Troy, you're the fittest guy I know. You'll get through this somehow and the drugs will keep it under control."

Both men stood and embraced in a bear hug before Hembury broke away and they resumed their positions across the table.

"Nic, your support means a lot. In fact, it means pretty much everything right now – you're the only person I've told."

At that moment the server arrived with two fresh beers and the mood changed again. They seamlessly moved to the topic of basketball and Hembury's collection of tropical fish, named after his all-time favourite players from the LA Clippers. Then

Vargas's cell phone rang with a withheld incoming number. Vargas had no doubt who the mystery caller was.

"Mike, what news? Have the guys come up with anything?"

"Nic, I assume Troy is nearby. I hope you're both sitting down."

Their booth in the restaurant was easily far enough away from any other diners for Vargas to feel comfortable hitting the speaker icon. He straightened in his chair, reacting to the tense tone of the FBI deputy director.

"Mike, Troy's right here and we can both hear you."

"Okay, guys, here's what we've got. As expected, the Zoom address and email details gave us zilch, so the guys ran our latest voice recognition software on the two mystery participants, and we hit pay dirt. The male voice drew a blank, but we struck gold with the female. The young lady who auditioned Mateo Silva is someone we all know well, even though we've never actually met her. We've been monitoring her movements for the last ten years, ever since the Franklin fiasco. The voice on the Zoom belongs to Eva Castillo, Adolf Hitler's secret granddaughter."

The FBI deputy director wasn't finished. "This all ties in with a much bigger picture that's rapidly emerging and one that we urgently need to discuss in person. What we know is the Franklin clan are on the move and everything right now points towards Argentina, with Eva playing the role of ringleader. Nic, get back to your home turf as soon as possible and I'll fly out tonight on the red-eye with a couple of senior operatives. Let's meet tomorrow in Buenos Aires. I'll take a room at the Marriott and see you both there at 1 p.m."

Just as Vargas pocketed his iPhone, the server arrived with their main courses.

"Things are unravelling and right now I've no idea what we're facing," said Vargas. "I suggest we make the most of this feast – it could be the last decent meal we have for a while."

Chapter 13

The Blonde Lady, Caribbean Sea

Following his excursion to Bogotá, Paz was now back in the sanctuary of his stateroom on board *The Blonde Lady* studying his two black scorpions that were busy devouring their live lunch of assorted insects and mammals – a delicious concoction of spiders, centipedes and lizards, complemented by a tiny drugged grey mouse. He was furious when a steward entered his cabin before his beloved pets had started work on the rodent, and his mood further darkened when he was summoned to the third deck loggia for an unscheduled meeting with Franklin.

As usual, his new boss was accompanied by his Syrian sidekick, Al Kathib, and Paz, exuding an air of sullen insolence, quietly took his regular position on the large couch. Franklin ignored the clear sign of defiance and laid straight into the Black Scorpion.

"When I asked you to tidy up an annoying loose end, I wasn't expecting theatrics. You left a bloody giant calling card that will alert many of our potential enemies to what should have been the death of an insignificant young actor but is now front-page news. You must learn to harness your sadistic nature if we are to continue this journey together. Maybe I made a miscalculation breaking you out, but I won't accept any more mistakes like this. Do you understand?"

The Black Scorpion reluctantly accepted the humiliating reprimand because he knew the alternative was far worse. Franklin was deranged and so was his plan but right now he had no choice but to play along. "Old habits die hard, Señor Franklin, but of course you are right. I promise I won't make any more mistakes and you have my unequivocal loyalty."

Franklin's irate mood softened when he heard the apology. "My father used to talk about you, Paz, especially around the time of the safe-deposit robbery when he really needed your services. He always said you were unstable and right on the edge, but he respected your unbridled loyalty. I remember him telling me that when the chips were down, you would do whatever he asked, no matter the consequences. That's why I knew we needed you back on board."

Franklin rose to his feet, grabbing his tumbler of bourbon and raising it high in the air, indicating to Al Kathib to do the same with his glass of white wine.

"A toast to the return of the Black Scorpion!"

Paz did his best to produce a genuine-looking smile of appreciation, but his brain was already hatching a plan to take down the madman standing in front of him and currently controlling his life.

* * *

The FBI deputy director's corner suite was on the top floor of the spectacular Marriott Park Tower Hotel, where Vargas and Hembury found him sitting on the large red-brick terrace reading through some briefing papers. One of his foot soldiers, who simply identified himself as Agent Roberts, escorted them through the suite, directly to his boss.

Berrettini was not an imposing man in the physical sense of the word, but his appearance belied the razor-sharp intellect that had taken him to the peak of his profession. He carried far too much weight – his five-foot-eight frame tipped fourteen stone, and his olive-skinned face, courtesy of his Italian heritage, was partially hidden by a neatly groomed black beard peppered with small grey pebbles. His strongest features by far were his striking pearly-blue eyes that shone through the rimless frames of his glasses and radiated an air of confidence and alertness. He was casually dressed in a pair of denims, complemented by an open-necked white cotton shirt. No one would ever have guessed his occupation, which made him the perfect man for the job. Berrettini was genuinely pleased to see the two detectives, and after a warm greeting, they all grabbed a coffee and settled back to begin the meeting.

"Firstly, guys, great job on the Paz breakout. The scale of that operation is a clear warning of what we're facing – two Black Hawks, for Christ's sake and you won't believe where they came from. Get this, they were courtesy of the Taliban."

Hembury was shocked by the latest twist imparted by the FBI man. "How the hell do they fit into all this?"

"No idea, but the downed chopper recovered by the Colombian police matches one of the Hawks we left behind when we got the hell out of Kabul."

Vargas was equally bewildered as he took on board the implications of Berrettini's revelation. "Mike, are you telling us that the descendants of the leader of the Third Reich are in league with the Taliban?"

The post-mortem investigation that followed the fallout of the Franklin political scandal ten years earlier had unearthed some highly sensitive information that at the time the president and the FBI deemed should be withheld from the public domain. This material revealed that John Franklin, Hitler's secret grandson, who the world believed had taken his own life, had four younger siblings: three half-brothers and a half-sister, who lived under false identities across four continents. John's father Richard Franklin had murdered his wife shortly after the birth of their son and he then went on to do the same with four of his mistresses. Each of them had borne him a child and was then disposed of, never to be heard from again. The babies were passed into the care of an inter-country adoption agency in Buenos Aires, which placed them with families across four continents. Richard Franklin ensured each set of adoptive parents were loyal Nazis who knew the identity of the infant's father and were honoured to be tasked with bringing up one of Adolf Hitler's grandchildren.

It was rapidly becoming apparent to Vargas and Hembury that recent events were somehow intertwined with at least one of Franklin's secret children.

Berrettini took a swig of coffee and shared the classified information so far discovered by the FBI.

"Okay, so here's what we know. Since February 2012 we've been monitoring the movements of the four kids as they've grown into adulthood. To the best of our knowledge, they've absolutely no idea of our surveillance – or indeed that anyone knows of their very existence. There's never been any evidence to suggest they ever communicate or even know about each other, until a few days ago. We always suspected they may use secret email addresses and burner phones, but nothing has ever come to light ..."

Hembury cut in. "Until now?"

"Yes, about a week ago they finally broke cover. Three of them, the half-brothers in London, New York and Sydney, all booked a long weekend break for the same dates to the same location – a remote lakeside hotel in a small city called Bariloche in the Río Negro province of Argentina, at the foothills of the Andes. We believe this could be the first time they've ever met in person."

Hembury jumped in again, curious to know about the eldest and only female of the four siblings. "What about Eva Castillo?"

"She's also booked leave for the same weekend, but not yet shown her hand as to where she might be heading. Remember, she is a high-profile politician in Argentina and plays her cards close to her chest. The reality is that, compared to her three half-brothers who live in other continents, Bariloche is just down the road from her base in Buenos Aires, only a two-hour internal flight away. I've no doubt she'll be there – in fact, I'm convinced she's behind this whole event. I think she's summoned her three siblings for a face-to-face meeting on her turf. They've all booked their own suites, but David Williamson, who's flying in from London, has also taken a meeting room in the Moreno Wing of the hotel, which takes up an entire floor and has a private lift for access. In addition, he's booked four other suites under his name, one of which I'm sure will be taken by Eva. As for the other three – who knows who they're for?"

Berrettini paused to finish his coffee before winding up.

"So, it looks like a party of seven, and we need to find out precisely what's on their agenda."

No one spoke for the next few seconds, then Vargas broke the silence. "Mike, we've two days before they arrive. Let's get down there with some of our intelligence guys and wire the hell out of that meeting room."

"I'm ahead of you, Nic. We have a private jet on standby to take the three of us to Candelaria Airport, about an hour's drive from the hotel. We also have a tech team heading down there, and by the time they're finished we'll have a remote viewing gallery set up in one of the hotel rooms that would make Spielberg sick with envy. I'll need you to schmooze the hotel manager because we'll want access to their internal CCTV and utter secrecy regarding our presence there. We've checked him out and he seems a straight shooter. You can give him the classic spiel about national security and how he'll be helping the country and all that crap."

Vargas and Hembury glanced at each other knowingly. During the previous ten years both men had often speculated on whether Hitler's grandchildren would prove to be a live threat in their lifetime. Now they had the answer, and they only had to wait another forty-eight hours to discover the exact nature of that threat.

Chapter 14

Bariloche, Argentina

E arly the following morning Vargas spearheaded the small, elite task force that arrived at the exclusive resort. He was confronted by the German general manager, Heinz Schneider, whose initial reaction was to call his in-house security team to escort the chief inspector off the premises. Schneider was a bright, ambitious man, who wanted to protect the reputation of his exclusive hotel at all costs. However, his hostile mood quickly softened after he read a personally signed letter from Vicente Lozano, the Argentine foreign secretary, granting Vargas special powers on behalf of the national government in a matter of international security.

At first Vargas was slightly perturbed by the awkward coincidence of the hotel being run by a Spanish-speaking German. Meanwhile, Schneider had suspicions of his own.

"Chief inspector, if this is about a drugs operation of some kind, I can assure you none of our clientele would be involved in such a matter. Very wealthy, often high-profile guests come here seeking relaxation and privacy, so I insist on a guarantee you and your men will be discreet, or our reputation could be severely damaged."

Vargas needed the hotel manager to be compliant so was happy to reassure him. "Look, we're both on the same side. It's vital to the success of our operation that nobody ever knows we were here, especially the guests we'll be monitoring. We have no interest in challenging or arresting any of them – you have my word on that. We simply need to observe, eavesdrop on their meetings and allow them to go on their way, none the wiser. We know they'll be based in the Moreno Wing because they've booked seven suites as well as the Lakeside Meeting Room. Mr Schneider, we require immediate access to it so we can install surveillance equipment, and we also need a secure base close by."

The general manager's demeanour brightened – he sensed Vargas was a man he could trust, and his German instinct for precision and organisation kicked into action. "Give me a few minutes to sort out the exact arrangements. I think I know the perfect place for you to situate your team. It's less than twenty metres from the meeting room."

* * *

"These look as if they've been lifted straight out of a CBS control room!"

Hembury was swivelling around in a black leather office chair, facing a large bank of television monitors. In total there were three rows of two twelve-inch screens forming a small surveillance tower. Vargas and the deputy director were standing next to him in the Moreno Lake Suite, which had been transformed into a mobile television gallery by a small team of bureau engineers.

Berrettini stepped forward to the control desk positioned on top of a large table – the same one that was supporting the monitors. A young technician was sitting off to the side, focusing some of the cameras. It was clear this wasn't the deputy director's first surveillance rodeo.

"Gentlemen, we have six cameras in total. Four are fixed and the other two are remotely operated by James here, who can pan and zoom the lenses as required. All their output is recorded directly on to these babies." He pointed to a stack of thin black SanDisk five-terabyte G-drives. "I wanted to go for ten cameras, but our boys struggled to find enough safe hides, so in the end we played it safe. In addition to the video coverage, we have four directional Sennheiser mics hidden around the room, and I think that means we're well covered for all eventualities. In a few minutes I'll send in a couple of our operatives to hold a phoney meeting, which will give us a useful rehearsal prior to the main event tomorrow."

The two detectives couldn't help but be impressed by the deputy director's slick presentation. Hembury stood and joined him.

"So, what happens after the run-through?"

Berrettini's oval face gave way to a large grin. "After that, the three of us get to sample the five-star cuisine in the lakeside restaurant."

* * *

The next day, the first of the seven guests arrived just after eleven in the morning. Daniel Anderson was the third eldest of the five Franklin siblings and had travelled the furthest, enduring a twenty-three-hour trip from his home in Sydney. Daniel was a software developer – a rising star in the booming world of computer coding, who ran his own boutique video game publishing house.

In the following three hours the rest of the party arrived. The clandestine group included two of Anderson's half-brothers: Simon White, an investment banker for Morgan Stanley who was based in New York, and David Williamson, the youngest member of the family who lived in London where he worked as a corporate lawyer specialising in mergers and acquisitions. Eva Castillo had the shortest journey to make but was the last to arrive, having taken the two-hour internal flight from Buenos Aires. On the face of it, the Franklin siblings formed a respectable and formidable quartet consisting of a high-profile politician, a leading computer games developer, a banker and a lawyer.

In the Royal Suite, only one floor below, John Franklin was settling in. He, Al Kathib and Paz had arrived courtesy of Franklin's Global 7500 jet, which had made an incredible non-stop seven-hour flight from Aruba. He relished owning one of the only private planes in the world that could possibly take on such a marathon journey.

Thirty minutes after checking in he summoned the two men to his suite to run through his plan for the meeting with his four siblings scheduled for five o'clock that afternoon, with a private dinner to follow. He had no plans to meet them beforehand; the family reunion would happen when he was ready and on his terms.

He had just taken a shower and was sitting in a white towelling robe, briefing his two subordinates, when he was interrupted mid flow by the arrival of room service – a waiter armed with coffee and a selection of pastries on a silver trolley. The uniformed blond-haired young man was still in his teens and his supple, athletic body immediately caught the attention of Paz who couldn't take his eyes off the boy's buttocks. He ensured his knee brushed against the unsuspecting waiter's calf as he leaned down in front of him to place a fine china cup of steaming black coffee on a side table next to his armchair.

The young man served Al Kathib next, and by the time he reached Franklin he could sense Paz's persistent leering at his rear. He was now a bag of nerves and, as Franklin shot out an arm to take the cup from his shaking hand, the pot slipped from his grasp and scalding coffee gushed over his exposed right shin and foot. Franklin cried out in pain, jumping to his feet like a startled cat, hopping around in agony. His foot was stained bright red and part of the skin around his ankle had started to blister.

"Get out of here, you imbecile."

The horrified waiter turned and darted out of the suite, pursued by a further mouthful of abuse from Franklin. Paz held his position, praying his boss hadn't realised his role in the sorry episode, while Al Kathib ran to the bathroom and grabbed a hand towel that he quickly soaked in cold water and wrapped around the wound. Franklin lay writhing on the floor, still yelling with pain.

Ten minutes later, the hotel doctor arrived and covered the burned skin with a moist bandage, while simultaneously feeding his patient strong painkillers. However, even after the treatment Franklin's fury failed to subside, and as he rested on his giant Emperor-size bed with his leg supported on a cushion, he shouted a message through the open door to Paz and Al Kathib, who were still in the suite.

"There's no way I'm making a grand entrance hobbling into a meeting room like a senile old man. They'll have to come to me. Call Eva and tell her the meeting will take place here in my suite. Now, both of you, get out of my sight."

Chapter 15

Bariloche, Argentina

Vargas, Hembury and Berrettini, accompanied by a lone technician, sat patiently in the Moreno Lake Suite waiting for the action to play out on the screens in front of them when Schneider burst into the room waving a large brown envelope in his left hand. The hotel manager was panicked - his normal calm, efficient German persona had vanished. He dropped the envelope onto the table and gestured frantically towards the bank of monitors.

"The meeting is off... I mean it's moved... It's not going to happen in that room."

Berrettini cut straight in. "Herr Schneider, just calm down and tell us what the hell has happened."

"Ten minutes ago, Señorita Castillo called reception to say the party is no longer required in the meeting room. She requested four chairs plus a whiteboard and all the refreshments that had been pre-ordered to be delivered to the Royal Suite instead – one floor down from us. She wants everything in place by four forty-five. She informed us that later in the evening seven people will be dining in the suite and requested our à la carte menu be sent along."

While Schneider blurted out the disastrous news, Vargas focused on the envelope that he knew contained several black-and-white A4 prints. He slid them out, carefully placing them in a tight line across the table.

The hotel manager switched his attention towards Vargas. "Chief inspector, those are the best still images we could grab from our CCTV cameras at the check-in desk. They're photos of the seven guests you requested."

Hembury and Berrettini moved closer to Vargas and the three men began the identification process. The FBI deputy director flicked open his laptop to cross-reference the low-quality, slightly blurred black-and-white images against the clean colour headshots he had on file. It took only seconds to confirm the identities of the four Franklin siblings, who'd all signed in using their real names. That just left the three remaining guests, whose suites had been booked under the name of Williamson.

The first of these images displayed a swarthy, unshaven face that drew an instant blank from the three policemen. The second headshot was virtually useless – the bearded man had a baseball cap slanted across his face, obscuring most of his features, and his head was tilted towards the floor as though he were deliberately avoiding the CCTV camera lens. Vargas leaned down and picked up the final photograph, holding it high in the air directly in front of them. No one spoke for a few seconds as they studied the unmistakable features of the man staring back at them – a face none of them had seen for almost ten years. It belonged to the man they all knew as the Black Scorpion. Vargas was the first to react.

"Christ! It's Paz. What the hell is he doing here?"

Hembury was equally astonished to see the face of their old adversary. "Presumably Eva's brought him down here for the big family get-together. The question is why?"

Berrettini's ice-cool brain smoothly shifted into gear. "Gentlemen, we have two immediate priorities to resolve. Firstly, we need to get a handle on what the meeting is about and, secondly, we need to ID the two unknowns. Why on earth have the Franklin kids flown halfway across the world to meet up for the first time with these three men in attendance?"

Vargas was still holding the headshot printout of the Black Scorpion. "Mike, there's also the question of Paz. We could take him into custody, but I don't see the point as he's evidently only a small part of a bigger operation. I agree we need to focus on the meeting, find out what's on their agenda and who the two other men are."

Berrettini glanced down at his watch. "Okay, I'll email their images to the tech boys in Washington and that leaves just under an hour for the three of us to figure out a way into the Royal Suite."

Chapter 16

Bariloche, Argentina

B errettini had been wrong when he'd speculated this was the first in-person meeting of the Franklin siblings. It was, in fact, the second. The first had taken place on the oldest brother's superyacht five years earlier. Ahead of it, John Franklin had spent several months planning the secret meeting, which went wholly undetected by FBI observers. It took place over a long weekend in August 2016 when the other Franklin kids had appeared to be travelling to different parts of the world for their respective summer vacations. However, courtesy of four fake passports and some ingenious sleight of hand at international airports, the five grandchildren of Adolf Hitler met for the first time just off the north coast of Crete in the Aegean Sea.

It was a remarkable meeting on many levels. Firstly, up until that fateful weekend only a handful of people knew the former presidential candidate was alive and that his suicide had been a sham. John Franklin was anything but dead and he was ready to break cover to meet with his four siblings. The four younger Franklin children were each aware of their unique heritage –

their specially chosen adoptive parents were Nazi sympathisers who were honoured to have a direct descendant of the Führer in their personal care. However, up to that point they'd had no knowledge of each other's existence or that their infamous older brother, John, was still alive.

It was a momentous, emotional, chaotic rollercoaster ride for them all, with John playing the role of ringmaster and Eva quickly emerging as his second in command. Two of the younger brothers, Daniel and Simon, were captivated by the charm and stature of the man whose features had dominated the world's media once his identity had been exposed. David, the youngest of the group, was a newly qualified law graduate living in London and, although he tried to conceal his emotions, it was apparent to everyone his interest and enthusiasm in being part of this bizarre cloak-and-dagger clan was lukewarm to say the least.

In the five years since that initial encounter the new "family" had kept in touch via burner phones, encrypted email and zoom. Even though John had no awareness of the FBI surveillance, he insisted they all behave as if they were under scrutiny and no risks were ever taken ... until now. Which is why, at short notice, he had summoned them to the lakeside hideaway in Bariloche.

John greeted them all warmly as they entered his suite, although no explanation was given as to why they were forced to approach him standing as he stood rigidly on the spot behind an armchair with his arms resting on the back to support his body weight. After their initial greetings his four siblings took their seats opposite him, Paz and Al Kathib, who was busy writing on a whiteboard.

Hitler's five grandchildren were meeting in the flesh for only the second time in their lives and the game-changing session was about to begin.

* * *

One floor up, another meeting was coming to an end.

"Just make sure the trolleys are left sideways on at both ends of the suite – and don't screw up."

Berrettini delivered his orders to the two FBI operatives who were now dressed as room service waiters and armed with tea, coffee and sandwiches. The improvised brushed stainless-steel trolleys were topped with a black oval melamine top, under which was strapped a one-inch black Lavalier microphone, secured in position courtesy of some gaffer tape. As the two virgin waiters moved towards the door, Hembury gave them a final note.

"Try and grab a good look at our mystery man with the beard. We urgently need a lead on who he is. Good luck."

Three minutes later, Eva Castillo opened the huge ornate wooden door to the Royal Suite and ushered in the waiters who carefully manoeuvred their surveillance vehicles into the room. Al Kathib was still standing next to the large whiteboard that now displayed a map of the Middle East and some handwritten notes. It was obvious the Arab had been holding court prior to the interruption. He glared at the pseudo-waiters, impatient to carry on where he'd left off. Special Agent Grant Brookes parked his trolley in front of a huge marble fireplace, while his colleague, Jack Leonard, rested his a few feet away from the door, next to a long coffee table.

"Please don't hesitate to call reception should you require anything more."

Brookes made the brief announcement and then crossed the room in silence, making his way towards the door where Leonard was waiting, having already opened it.

They were nearly out when Eva Castillo's raspy, arrogant voice reached them, "Before you go, set everything up on the coffee table and take the trolleys away. There's no room for them."

The two FBI agents glanced at each other, knowing any queries might arouse suspicion, and did as they were instructed.

* * *

Berrettini was pacing the room, trying to figure a way to salvage something positive from the total carnage of the operation. Hembury and Vargas watched as he conducted the debrief of his two agents.

"Okay, Brookes, let's summarise what we've got."

The young agent loosened his black tie and undid the top button of his white shirt before nodding towards his boss

"The Arab seemed to be running the show, but he went schtum as soon as we entered. Our mystery man with the beard was sitting next to him, close to Paz, and the four Franklin children were in an arc facing them."

Vargas couldn't resist butting in. "What more can you tell us about the bearded man?"

"Not a lot. I'd say he's in his early fifties, blonde, blue-eyed, with a heavy beard. Hard to judge his height because he was sitting down, but I'd guess he's well over six foot."

Berrettini took back control of the interview. "Tell us everything you can about the whiteboard?"

"Most of it was covered by a hand-drawn map of the Middle

East. I could easily make out Egypt, Israel, Syria and Jordan and there were seven blue dots randomly placed around the edges of the Israeli border. At the top right-hand corner of the board was an underlined date – May 4 and below the map was the word "Prophecy" written next to a long German word. I tried my best to memorise it, but I've no idea what it means."

Jack Leonard, the younger of the two agents, cut in. "Sir, I studied languages at college and majored in French and German. The word was *'gesamtkunstwerk'*."

The FBI deputy director barked back at his agent, "What the hell does that mean?"

"It's actually more of a phrase than a single word. I think the closest English translation would be 'Total Work of Art'. I'm pretty sure it's somehow associated with Wagner – he might even have invented it."

Berrettini shot a puzzled glance towards Hembury and Vargas, desperately looking for inspiration, but the blank expressions on their faces suggested that neither of them had a clue as to what this new information meant or the potential threat they were now facing.

That same level of ignorance was shared by the young room service waiter who'd accidentally spilt boiling coffee over a guest's ankle in the Royal Suite. An action that forced a last-minute change of venue for a surreptitious meeting that couldn't now be monitored. He had no idea his clumsiness may have inadvertently led to tragic consequences for thousands of innocent people.

Chapter 17

Bariloche, Argentina

"Chaos often brings opportunities in its slipstream."

John Franklin may have been forced to sit but he remained animated and consumed with excitement as he brought his siblings up to speed.

"The success of the Covid vaccines means we probably only have a few more months of cover from the pandemic before the world begins to function normally again. That's why I'm bringing forward the timing of the operation, and what could be a more apt date to aim for than May 4? For Jews across the world, it marks the celebration of the creation of the state of Israel, a milestone they believe offers permanent protection from future persecution. But, in years to come, May 4 will instead be remembered as the date when the Jewish race began its inexorable path towards extinction. Eighty years ago, our grandfather came up with the genesis of an inspired idea that he named *Operation Gesamtkunstwerk*. Now, it's our destiny to bring it to fruition."

Franklin paused for dramatic effect before delivering a chilling statement.

"The mass sterilisation of Jewish women of childbearing age was a brilliant vision being tested by Josef Mengele in the summer of 1943 at Auschwitz. In those early days the methodology was primitive but nonetheless ground-breaking. Doctors working in the camp injected a caustic substance into the cervix of female patients that blocked the fallopian tubes and caused permanent infertility. The tragic turn of events in the war meant those early tests were dropped in their infancy but, post-war, the creation of Franklin Pharmaceuticals in South America enabled our grandfather to continue with the precious work.

"He invested millions of dollars into research, pursuing the development of an undetectable waterborne drug that needed to be tasteless and odourless, yet powerful enough to create infertility when consumed by females. Fresh water in developing countries often contains undetectable killer diseases – typhoid, cholera and malaria, and so is the perfect hiding place for a manufactured drug. Despite losing ownership of the pharma operation ten years ago, I've maintained a secret facility in Patagonia where a small team of brilliant chemical biologists have finally achieved what many of their predecessors believed impossible – the creation of a wonder drug that can be added directly to a fresh water supply and when imbibed will effectively sterilise women of childbearing age. The fast-acting chemical agent furs up the fallopian tubes and causes a blockage that, we believe, is irreversible. It'll be a knife in the very heart of Israel from which it will never recover.

"In the last eighteen months we've carried out undercover field testing with the drug in the remote town of El Bolsón, in the Río Negro province of North Patagonia. Covid provided us with the perfect smokescreen as during that time very few people visited their physician or hospitals for medical check-ups, so if women weren't conceiving, they didn't get to see a doctor about it. The town has a population of just under twenty thousand and would normally expect to see around one-hundred-and-forty births per year. In the last twelve months that figure dropped to nine, which I think you'll agree is a pretty remarkable result."

Franklin's mouth formed a twisted self-satisfied grin as he looked across at his siblings for acclamation. Three of the four smiled back. Al Kathib was still standing next to the whiteboard and took the reins, just as they'd rehearsed. The Syrian's cut-glass British accent had been honed during a four-year stay at Oxford where he'd studied modern history and politics.

"Israel is fundamentally an arid country where rain falls only in the winter and then, mainly, in the north of the country. This means they're forced to look elsewhere for their drinking supply, and their two main sources are the Sea of Galilee – the lowest freshwater lake in the world, up on their north-eastern border – and a number of seawater desalination plants dotted along their Mediterranean coastline. We've identified seven principal plants and pipelines that supply freshwater to over ninety per cent of the population, and it is those we intend to corrupt with the drug. As John said, we're working towards D-Day being May 4 which means we have a huge amount of work ahead of us. You all have essential roles to play and now is the time to start drilling into the details."

* * *

At almost two in the morning Hembury and Vargas were still awake, working on their laptops in the monitoring room, piecing together the few crumbs of information they'd managed to acquire and desperately trying to make sense of it all. Berrettini had moved to an adjoining room a few hours earlier but returned just as the two detectives were about to call it a night.

"Guys, I've set up a Zoom with Mossad's director, Doron Bekher, who's a good friend of the agency. I've worked closely with him in the past on various terrorist threats and he has an amazing resource at his disposal. They're six hours ahead of us and we're on in thirty minutes. I've also sent him images of our Middle Eastern friend along with baseball cap man in case they can ID them."

The FBI deputy director glanced down at his watch. "We've got half an hour to get our ducks in a row ready for the call."

Hembury looked at the random notes on his laptop screen. "Nic and I have been working through everything we know to date. We've put together a summary but I'm afraid it's paper-thin."

Berrettini pulled up a chair and leaned forward. "Okay, let's hear it."

"So, one fact we do know for sure is that Matias Paz was busted out of Valledupar by Eva Castillo, courtesy of the Taliban, who provided the high-class transport. We assume our mystery Middle Eastern friend played a role in securing the Hawks for the prison attack and is working with, or for, the Franklin family, along with baseball cap man. Then we have the information your guys obtained from the whiteboard. We think May 4 could relate to the date Israel celebrates Independence this year, but we can't be sure. And then there are the mystery blue dots on the map – what the hell do they represent? It seems like Israel is the potential target for an attack, possibly on their Independence Day. Finally, we have the word 'prophecy' along with the historic German word *gesamtkunstwerk*, which translates as 'Total Work of Art' or 'Ideal Work of Art'. We think Leonard was correct when he credited Wagner with creating this historic phrase, or at least adopting it as his own. And, of course, Hitler idolised the legendary composer, but what does it mean in this context?"

"Troy, a lot of unanswered questions but enough detail, I think, to justify reaching out to Mossad. We'll use my laptop for the call as it's—"

Vargas cut in. "Mike, I assume the first thing we'll need to do is explain to the director the confidentiality around the existence of Franklin's grandchildren, before we update him on recent events."

Berrettini's rotund poker face broke into a large smile. "Nic, get real. We're talking about the director of Mossad. Of course, he'll already know of their existence. Anything that poses a potential future threat to the state of Israel will be on his agenda and, in this instance, we're talking about Adolf Hitler's progeny. What he won't be expecting to hear – or be prepared for, is the notion of an unholy alliance between the Taliban and the direct descendants of the leader of the Third Reich."

Chapter 18

Buenos Aires, Argentina

October 1954

The man known to millions of Jews as the "Angel of Death" was a significant figure in the development of the sterilisation drug in the post-war years. Although Josef Mengele was based in Buenos Aires, he spent a great deal of time working in an anonymous research facility in Neuquén, financed by the Franklin Pharmaceutical Corporation, that had been established in Argentina eight years earlier by Hitler and Bormann.

His crude methods at Auschwitz paved the way for the creation of *Operation Gesamtkunstwerk*. Mengele shared the Führer's obsession with sourcing a method that could deliver the final solution to the Jewish problem and believed mass sterilisation would be the ultimate weapon in delivering that goal.

After the war, Mengele fled Nazi Germany and travelled to Argentina, assisted by a network of former SS colleagues. He changed his identity and began a new life in Buenos Aires as

Wolfgang Gerhard, running a small mechanical equipment shop in the suburbs.

Although he'd been on the run and was forced to travel light, rather than clothes and personal possessions, his three pieces of luggage were stuffed full of original documents and research papers stolen from the records department at Auschwitz. They contained in-depth information on the two areas of human experimentation that dominated his period at the Polish death camp. Between 1943 and 1945 he personally supervised a series of abominable tests on Jewish twins. He was desperate to enhance the ability of racially desirable German females to improve their reproduction rate because he believed that would strengthen the genetic superiority of the Aryan race. He also headed up the small medical team run by Horst Schumann that carried out primitive sterilisation tests on Jewish female inmates of childbearing age. The latter was the area of research Hitler demanded he focus all his attention on once he settled in South America and went back on the Nazi payroll.

Mengele stretched across the bed to reach for his gold Oyster Perpetual Rolex that sat on his side table, a souvenir from his time at Auschwitz. Every time he strapped it on his wrist his mind momentarily flashed back to the haunted face of the inmate he'd stolen it from. The man had owned a large chain of jewellery stores in Berlin that were confiscated by the SS before he and his family were shipped to Poland. He'd been at the camp less than two hours, having made the horrendous three-hundred-mile train journey with thousands of other Jewish prisoners jammed into wooden cattle trucks with no light and very little air.

He was being herded along the platform with a large group of men, heading towards the shower block where a horrendous death, courtesy of Zyklon B awaited him, when Mengele spotted the gold timepiece on his wrist. He had the man pulled aside and offered him a deal on the spot: he promised the jeweller his family would enjoy special privileges if he traded the watch. After the brief transaction he sent him on his way to the gas chamber.

Mengele hadn't slept well since receiving an intimidating call from Bormann two days earlier summoning him to a meeting at El Blondi, Hitler's farmhouse hideaway in South Patagonia, to report on progress with the sterilisation programme. He suspected it could be a difficult encounter with the Führer as, the truth was, there hadn't been any progress, so he'd have to be inventive.

Right now, he needed the money tap to keep flowing as he was planning to marry his late brother's widow, Martha, who shared an apartment with him in Buenos Aires and he required funds for the wedding. When he'd evaded capture and escaped from Germany, his first wife, Irene, had disowned him as a war criminal and begun divorce proceedings. Now, under the guise of Wolfgang Gerhard, he was to wed for the second time.

Bormann had organised a small private plane to transport Mengele directly south on the seventeen-hundred-mile journey; valuable time he could use to concoct a believable report – although he knew how sharp Bormann was, which meant he had to be careful with his story. It was just after midday when he arrived at El Blondi. The house was drenched in sunshine – ironic, Mengele thought, as he was expecting a frosty reception. He was met at the front entrance by Eva Braun. She greeted him like a long-lost friend, which was disconcerting as they'd never really been close. She escorted him through the entrance hall to the wood-panelled study where Bormann and Hitler were waiting to interrogate him on the latest test results. The Führer was perched behind his imposing desk and the former party secretary of the Nazi regime was standing alongside. Together they formed a menacing united front. No handshakes were exchanged but Hitler gestured towards the empty chair in front of his desk and Mengele responded, sitting down opposite him.

"Josef, it's good to see a familiar face. I spend so much time hidden away here, I sometimes forget what it's like to share the company of trusted old friends. Martin has been disparaging about the lack of recent progress at the laboratory, but I told him you would have good news to impart and I'm sure that's the case, isn't it?"

Hitler's voice was laden with menace, a smouldering volcano close to eruption, and Mengele knew he'd have to tread carefully to avoid a manic outburst that could lead to disastrous consequences. His survival instinct kicked into gear as did his default defence mechanism of obsequiousness.

"Führer, it is such a delight to see you looking so well and, yes, I'm pleased to report our research programme is making steady progress—"

"Specifics, Mengele. We need specifics."

Bormann's brutal interruption dented Mengele's already fragile confidence. The truth was he knew the science required to create and manufacture the drug Hitler had in mind simply didn't exist, and the team of chemical biologists working under his guidance were nowhere near creating a potent sterilisation drug that could be mass produced and successfully hidden in food or liquids. It was one thing sterilising individual female patients in Auschwitz but quite another producing a drug that could be hidden in plain sight and eaten or drunk without the victim's knowledge.

"Führer, it's still early days but we have begun experimenting with both tablet and liquid forms of the drug. Right now, it produces a pungent smell and leaves a bitter aftertaste in water. It's partially hidden in milk but of course it must be totally undetectable. Nevertheless, the early signs are still encouraging. Eventually we hope to create a formula that's tasteless and odourless but, more importantly, we need to find a satisfactory way of testing the efficacy of the drug to see how well it corrupts the fallopian tubes. The problem is, unlike Auschwitz, we don't have access to human guinea pigs."

The Führer slowly rose from his padded leather chair and leaned across the desk to face the Angel of Death. Even by Hitler's standards, the next words he spoke were so chilling they shook Mengele to the very core of his soul.

"Josef, we have unlimited funds for this operation. Set up your own version of the camp near the lab in Neuquén. There are plenty of young single peasant women living in obscure towns in that part of the country. Buy them, kidnap them – do whatever it takes. It's vital we discover if the drug you're developing really works. Martin will source a location for the camp and sort out the payments. Josef, your role is crystal clear. You need to put the foundations in place for the future implementation of *Operation Gesamtkunstwerk*."

Chapter 19

Bariloche, Argentina

D oron Bekher, the director of Mossad, had been in place for five years and was only answerable to the prime minister. However, most Israelis believed he held the most important post in the country because it was his responsibility to keep the people safe. At thirty-eight he was the youngest man ever to hold the position and was one of the most respected and feared intelligence chiefs in the world.

Bekher was a former paratrooper who moved directly from the military across to Mossad, where he was employed as a case officer running agents in foreign countries, before working his way up to the top job. His dark, striking features included an angular nose, deep-set hazel eyes and a crown of black hair, slightly frosted at the sides. He hosted the encrypted Zoom call from his Tel Aviv office and warmly greeted Berrettini, who introduced him to Hembury and Vargas.

"It's great to meet you both. The president has told me of the roles you guys played in the Franklin episode and, from what I've just been reading, it looks like here we go again.

"I'm about to bring one of our agents from our Kidon unit

online to join the call. She's currently based in Israel but has worked extensively across South America in our embassies in Buenos Aires and Montevideo. She could prove invaluable and speaks fluent Spanish – a bonus I think will prove extremely useful. Her name is Leah Katz."

Over eight thousand miles away in the hotel suite in Bariloche, the FBI deputy director was the only one of the three detectives to fully appreciate the significance of Bekher's comment: Kidon was the special unit inside Mossad responsible for carrying out the assassination of foreign nationals who posed a threat to Israel's national security. Basically, a highly trained killer was about to join the call.

A third screen burst into life as the Mossad director granted his agent access to join the Zoom. The first thing about Leah Katz that struck all three men was her eye colour – emerald green, an extremely rare feature shared by less than two per cent of the world's population. Her oval face was dominated by high, wide cheekbones and her coal-black hair was precision cut into a short bob. She wasn't beautiful in the conventional sense, and there was an unnerving hardness in her eyes that seemed threatening, but she had a face that once seen, you would never forget. Her opening words made it plain she wasn't one for small talk – she was all about the business in hand.

"We have a match with one of the CCTV images you sent through. His name is Anwar Al Kathib, a high-ranking Syrian gunrunner and dealmaker who is a well-known collaborator with our enemies. He's been on our blacklist for the last three years."

"Blacklist?" Vargas clarified.

"Our kill list, chief inspector. Through a number of his

'business deals' he has been indirectly responsible for the deaths of dozens of our citizens. He has homes all over the world, but we believe his main base is in London. Mayfair, to be precise. Although we've got close to him, this is the first new image we've seen for almost fifteen months." Her next comment was clearly directed at her boss. "I think we should take him out immediately, as we currently have eyes on him."

Berrettini jumped in straight away. "Leah, just slow down. The first thing we need to do is update you both on what we know so far."

The FBI deputy director briefed them on Paz's breakout and the information gleaned from the whiteboard, ending with the reference to May 4, gesamtkunstwerk and its meaning.

Bekher processed the new information for a few seconds before replying. "Mike, we don't have enough information yet to properly nail these guys unless you fancy popping a grenade into their suite right now, which I'm sure Leah would approve of but, I assume, isn't a realistic option. So, for now, we need you to monitor them all as closely as possible while we try and work out just what sort of attack they're planning."

Katz jumped in. "Sir, with Al Kathib in the mix we could be looking at a nuclear or biological threat. The man is consumed with hatred when it comes to Israel and will do anything if the price is right."

The Mossad director quickly weighed up the options before showing his hand. "Leah, you need to get on this as soon as possible. We'll sort out a jet to get you over there and, Mike, you and I should start working up a plan."

Berrettini couldn't help but be impressed by the dynamic response from his Mossad counterpart, although he wasn't surprised. "Okay, Doron, what's the first thing on your agenda?"

Bekher leaned towards his laptop screen and his face gave way to a hint of a smile. "The first job I have to do is not easy. I need to warn the prime minister of Israel that his country is in imminent danger of a major terrorist attack masterminded by the Führer's grandchildren."

Chapter 20

Bariloche, Argentina

Operating on just a few hours' sleep, Berrettini, Hembury and Vargas were back at their desks at seven in the morning putting together a surveillance plan for Al Kathib, Paz and baseball cap man. Berrettini was running the operation, but Vargas had access to police foot soldiers on the ground as it was all happening on his turf. The FBI man stopped punching the keys of his laptop and took a huge slurp of coffee.

"We know that four taxis are booked for Candelaria Airport at nine this morning and that three of the Franklin kids have international flights scheduled to take them back to their respective countries, while Eva's hopping on an internal flight to Buenos Aires. But Al Kathib and Paz have nothing booked in their real names, and then, of course, we have no idea what name baseball cap man might be travelling under. We have three plain-clothed officers at the airport waiting to see what flights they check in to and the plan is for our guys to jump on the same plane or planes. Once we know where they're heading, we'll alert Interpol to have agents waiting at their respective destinations to continue the surveillance as double insurance against losing them. We also have four additional officers confirmed on the Franklin children's flights, just to ensure they go straight home."

Vargas nodded his approval as he dipped his chocolate croissant into his lukewarm coffee. "Mike, it sounds like we're well covered for now. And with the three of us booked on the Buenos Aires flight departing an hour after Eva's, we should be back by three thirty. Leah isn't due in until eleven this evening and won't make the hotel before midnight. She's suggested a seven thirty breakfast meet, so I guess the woman has no intention of letting jet lag hold her up. Seems she just wants to get straight down to business."

Hembury smiled at his fellow detectives. "I suspect Leah is going to keep us all on our toes. Nic, I hope you're up to it."

The banter was suddenly cut short by the unmistakable whirring of an approaching helicopter that was heading towards the resort at great speed from the south. The three detectives ran across the room to a large picture window overlooking the landscaped grounds abutting Lake Moreno. A silver-grey unmarked twin-engine Hermès EC135 was hovering above the lawn by the side of the water, preparing to land. As it began its descent, three figures appeared below them, striding towards it. The man leading the way was hanging on to a red baseball cap to keep it safely on his head. Two minutes later, Franklin, Al Kathib and Paz were safely strapped into the soft leather seats of the world's most luxurious helicopter. The million-dollar machine smoothly took off without missing a beat and thirty seconds later it was nothing more than a silver dot in the distance.

Hembury was the first to turn away and react. "Jesus Christ, once again we're behind the eight ball. Unless they're just taking a quick ride to San Carlos Airport, we've lost them already."

Berrettini was still peering out the window, watching a gaggle of geese fly over the lake, presumably returning to the water having been disturbed earlier by the downdraft and noise of the chopper. "Troy, I strongly suspect they're heading for a private airstrip where, no doubt, an unmarked jet is waiting to transport them to their next destination. It's a total disaster – and not a great way to start our relationship with one of Mossad's leading assets."

* * *

Berrettini's hunch was correct. Less than two hours later the three fugitives were on board Franklin's private plane heading towards the Caribbean and the sanctuary of *The Blonde Lady*. Franklin was checking through his latest emails while Al Kathib and Paz were catching up on some sleep. Franklin reread one of the recent messages three times before waking the other two men.

"We have a slight problem that could delay the timing of our operation and, of course, that is totally unacceptable. Our lead biochemist, who is running the operation out of our main laboratory in Patagonia, has asked for an immediate meeting to explain his concerns. I've arranged for him to be waiting for us on the yacht when we arrive. Meanwhile, I suggest we all use the time to familiarise ourselves with the drug Quentiline, because right now the lack of it appears to be a major issue and, Paz, we might well need your help to appropriate some as quickly as possible."

Although Al Kathib was listening, he was also scanning

a WhatsApp message that had just popped up in his inbox. "John, it seems as if we may also have a problem down in El Bolsón, with a doctor who is making waves."

Franklin eased back in his chair and took a sip of bourbon while he collected his thoughts. "Paz, on second thoughts, leave the drug research to us. I would get as much rest as you can over the next few hours. It seems you might have two fires to put out."

Chapter 21

Buenos Aires, Argentina

The lavish buffet breakfast at the Marriott catered to all tastes and judging by the varied selection of food piled up on Leah Katz's plate, she clearly approved of what was on offer. The three male detectives were making do with a selection of toast and jam washed down with black filter coffee, while they watched her devour a concoction of scrambled eggs, sausages, hash browns, mushrooms, tomatoes and black beans.

The vast dining room was heaving with random groupings of transient businesspeople, enjoying their meals ahead of a full day of meetings, and no one paid any attention to the FBI deputy director and his three dining companions.

Hembury made the big mistake of kicking off the conversation with some small talk. "Leah, how was your flight and how are you feeling?"

"I'm fine, Troy. Where did our three suspects travel to once they left Bariloche?"

Berrettini caught the uncomfortable expression on Hembury's face and cut in to pass on the latest intelligence to the Mossad agent. She plainly wasn't impressed.

"Shit, you boys really were caught with your pants down." She allowed the put-down to take hold and then moved on. "Do you think they were tipped off?"

Berrettini responded with a quizzical, non-committal look, so she moved on with her verbal mugging.

"Mike, I've read the notes you emailed through on the flight, so I know as much as you. Nic, are we working out of your office downtown or what?" Her machine-gun delivery didn't show any sign of easing up and she continued without giving Vargas the space to answer. "I've thought a lot about the true interpretation of *gesamtkunstwerk*. I think 'Total Work of Art' is a classic phrase stolen from the past, but Al Kathib and the Franklin family have given it a sick update that somehow relates to creating a huge hit on the Jewish people through an orchestrated attack on Israel."

Vargas nodded in agreement and looked to take her theory forward. "Leah, five of the seven blue dots that Mike's agents identified on the map of Israel were spread along the west coastline, while one was located in the south and one was in the north of the country. They could indicate multiple points of attack – maybe multiple bombs."

For the first time since she'd joined them at the table, the Mossad agent stayed quiet as she contemplated the implications of Vargas's theory.

* * *

Franklin had pretty much downed a whole bottle of bourbon during the long flight back to *The Blonde Lady* and his mood was dark. Fifteen minutes after landing, he dispatched a steward to collect Samuel Rivero, his head biochemist, who had been waiting patiently in one of the staterooms two decks below. Rivero had been heading up the test facility in Neuquén, in the north of Patagonia, for the last four years and had spearheaded the final push to create the formula for CDF830, the chemical name for a waterborne drug that could cause infertility in females.

Prior to running Franklin's team of biochemists and genetic engineers, his specialist research had focused on the thermodynamic analysis of the four biological macromolecules that make up a human cell's dry mass. He was the leader in his specialist field and had been headhunted for the lead biochemist position by an esteemed recruitment agency – one that had no idea of the reality behind the role they were filling, for what they believed was a respectable company, which it appeared to be. Franklin had used an established research lab that he owned through one of his numerous holding companies as a cover to attract top talent. Once inside the net, the lure of quadrupling his salary plus a seven-figure bonus if successful in developing the new drug were powerful enough drivers to bring the senior biochemist on side.

It was only his third face to face with Franklin, whom he knew as Jim Anderson – a wealthy American businessman who had an unhealthy obsession with creating a super drug that could affect female fertility. The previous two meetings had taken place at the Neuquén research facility in the first few months following his appointment, and since then they had communicated mainly by email, along with the odd phone call. As he entered the enormous loggia, he focused on keeping his nerves in place and made his way over to the designated seating area where his employer was waiting, flanked by Paz and Al Kathib. Franklin gestured for him to take the empty seat opposite and didn't bother to introduce the two observers.

"Doctor Rivero, any delay to the manufacturing schedule we have in place is totally unacceptable, so if there is a major problem, you need to solve it. Failure at this point is simply not an option and you'll be held personally responsible if our timetable is not adhered to. Do I make myself clear?"

The biochemist was well used to Franklin's candid style but hadn't been prepared for the thinly veiled threat. "As I explained in my email, the amount of CDF830 we need to produce over the next few weeks is hampered by the short supply of one of its many components. Quentiline, which as you know in its native form is an antimalarial drug, accounts for just over five per cent of the formula but, nevertheless, it is still a vital ingredient. In recent years, it's been banned by most countries as a carcinogen and old stocks are low on the ground and almost impossible to source."

"There has to be a way, Rivero. Someone must still be sitting on some."

"There is a large chemical manufacturer in Córdoba who I believe still has a substantial supply that it hasn't got round to destroying, but if we were to place an order, it would obviously be refused and throw suspicion our way."

Franklin had heard enough. He downed a fresh glass of bourbon in one giant swallow and nodded towards a small notebook and pen that were resting on the ivory and glass coffee table between them. "Write down the exact quantity you require as well as full details of the facility in Córdoba. You'll have what you need in the next seventy-two hours. After that, Rivero, I expect to hear no more excuses, or the five million bonus you received two years ago will need to be returned ... with interest."

Rivero knew the meeting was over and, after scribbling down some notes, took what felt like a walk of shame across the vast open space, heading towards the door, cursing the day he first met the uncouth American maniac.

Franklin's mood had slightly brightened, and he gave himself a large refill before turning towards Paz. "Sort out a team and hit that chemical factory as soon as possible. Steal at least ten other drugs as a diversion."

Paz rose to his feet and picked up the note the biochemist had left behind. "Leave it with me. I have some old friends in Córdoba who owe the Black Scorpion a debt that I'm about to call in."

* * *

In the end they agreed it was safer to set up a makeshift office in Berrettini's suite at the Marriott rather than in Vargas's station, and extra phones were installed along with a crime board, work desks and technical equipment. The open-plan lounge was a hive of activity with Vargas, Hembury and Katz at the hub of it, while the FBI deputy director worked from a makeshift desk in the bedroom. The crime board was positioned against one of the floral wallpapered walls, dressed by the chief inspector with an assortment of photographs and documents related to the case. Vargas was carefully studying a picture in the centre of the board – an aerial colour image of what remained of the exercise yard at Valledupar Prison.

"We need to follow the evidence. The Hawk that took Paz headed north out to sea and then disappeared. Where did it land to drop him off and where is it now? We know that by the time it passed the coastline it had anything up to eight hundred miles of fuel left in its tank, assuming it didn't stop to refuel. There's no intelligence to suggest it landed at a recognised airport, so the chances are it came down on a remote island somewhere in the Caribbean. We need to find it."

Vargas looked at Katz. "Leah, then there's our Syrian friend. Can Mossad check on all his known previous addresses just in case he's returned to one of them? I'll do the same with Paz – he may well have returned to Argentina to one of his old hunting grounds."

"I've spoken with Doron and he's already on it. Our agents on the ground are monitoring any known locations or contacts of Al Kathib but, let's be honest, he could be anywhere by now." Katz paused before issuing her reprimand. "I just hope you guys don't come to regret not taking him out when you had the chance."

Chapter 22

Córdoba, Argentina

The modest three-acre site that housed the Pagina GA Chemical plant was in the heart of the Santa Isabel district, a vast industrial area carved out of the south-west of Córdoba, Argentina's second largest city. The footprint of the plant was dwarfed by the massive Renault car factory that pretty much surrounded it on three sides – the largest manufacturing complex in the area. However, the chemical manufacturing facility more than made up for its lack of size with its state-of-the-art interior that had been installed two years earlier when it was completely refurbished. With more than fifty robots, twenty automated guided transportation vehicles, digital workstations and 3D printers, the plant was at the very forefront of technology.

The three-storey structure was divided into five main sections: milling, granulation, coating, tablet pressing and storage. Tens of millions of pills and liquids were securely stored on the ground floor, inside a specially designed air-cooled unit where they were kept in giant reinforced plastic pallets.

It was just after midnight and the two occupants of the silver-grey Mercedes-Benz Sprinter van had been monitoring the comings and goings at the plant for the previous twelve hours. They'd found a partially hidden vantage point in a public car park situated about one-hundred-and-fifty feet from the entrance to the building. Héctor Rojas and Bruno Chávez were both in their late sixties– former mercenaries and career criminals who had come out of retirement to do one last job for their former boss, the Black Scorpion. Their loyalty to him was instinctive and the lure of a fifty-thousand-dollar fee per man meant these old-school hardmen were prepared to do whatever the job demanded.

They both heard the distinctive sound of the six-litre V8 Cadillac Escalade approach seconds before they spotted it turn into the car park and pull up alongside their van. The men waited for Paz to emerge from the driver's seat before leaping out to greet him with a couple of bear hugs and cheek kisses. Rojas was euphoric at seeing his former boss for the first time in ten years.

"We thought you'd been killed by the chopper attack at Valledupar. Then we suddenly hear from you. How the hell did you get out?"

"There'll be plenty of time for that story when we're on our way to Neuquén with the goods."

Paz glanced away from them towards the gated perimeter of the chemical plant, where he spotted two armed guards standing by the security entrance.

"Right now, bring me up to speed as to what we're facing down there. What's our route in?"

Chávez walked towards the back of the Mercedes van and

came to a stop by the rear doors. "Boss, everything you need to know is inside here."

A few seconds later the three gangsters were standing in semi-darkness inside the Sprinter peering at a figure who was lying sideways on the heavy-duty rubber floor. His body was trussed up like a turkey and his mouth was covered with a huge chunk of black duct tape. His body was static, and the only obvious sign of life came from the furtive movement of his dark brown eyes, which emanated pure terror. The rest of his face was bloody and swollen, the deep cuts and heavy bruises a testament to the beating he'd endured during a prolonged interrogation a few hours earlier, courtesy of Rojas and Chávez.

The Black Scorpion licked his parched lips, relishing the session he was about to initiate with the terrified prisoner. He indicated to Chávez to remove the man's mouth tape and he dutifully obliged, yanking it off with such force, tiny fragments of bloodied skin flew into the air. With Rojas's help, the man was pulled upright onto his knees so he could face his new inquisitor. Paz's voice dropped to a threatening whisper.

"I have a few questions for you that I need answered truthfully. Please don't try and lie to me as the consequences will not be pleasant. Do you understand?"

The man, who was petrified, nodded his head, subjugating to Paz.

"Very good, tell me your name and your position at the plant."

"My name is René... Houseman... I'm a duty manager at the chemical plant."

"How many armed guards are there on the night shift?"

"Two at the gate ... and ... two inside."

Paz put the slight pause down to fear rather than deceit. A

rare mistake for such an experienced interrogator but then, the Black Scorpion was still a little rusty.

"Why so many guards?"

Houseman sensed the ongoing dialogue was somehow keeping him safe, so decided to expand his answers. However, he couldn't help wondering what the endgame was. "We've had many attempted break-ins during the last two years – mainly organised crime gangs looking to steal drugs to sell on. Plus, of course, there are plenty of desperate druggies who'll risk their lives trying to get a hit."

"Do you have stocks of Quentiline in storage?"

Houseman was genuinely bemused by the question – why would anyone go to these lengths to steal a banned antimalarial drug? "I think so … but I can't be sure. We have over five thousand different drugs in the storeroom unit and—"

Paz cut in. "Señor Houseman, for your own sake, let's assume you do. Where exactly would I find it?"

"The storeroom unit is located at the end of the main corridor on the ground floor, at the very rear of the building. All the drugs are meticulously labelled and catalogued. The pallets are stored in alphabetical sequence, so it would be somewhere towards the right-hand side of the unit."

Paz moved a bit closer, almost as though he were trying to befriend the bewildered duty manager. "How does the internal security work?"

"Everything in the building works on a biometric access control system. All the doors on the ground floor have fingerprint entry units. It's the only way to get in."

The hint of an ominous smile appeared on the Black Scorpion's face as he cut short the interrogation, turned around and indicated to his henchman they should all exit the van.

Once outside, Paz walked over to the Escalade, opened the passenger door, and reached for a large brown leather bag. He unzipped it and pulled out a large stainless-steel Japanese chef's knife. The ultra-sharp edge of the blade glinted in the moonlight as he carefully balanced the weight of the weapon in the palm of his hand.

"Go inside the van and untie his hands."

Rojas and Chávez exchanged a knowing look and disappeared inside the back of the Mercedes. A minute later Paz joined them and moved slowly across to Houseman, still on his knees and flanked by Paz's men who were holding him rigidly in position.

The Black Scorpion leaned forward and at the same time lifted his right hand, ensuring the duty manager caught a perfect view of the elegant chef's knife. "Now, Señor Houseman, would you be kind enough to tell me which two fingers you use to access the entry system?"

Chapter 23

Córdoba, Argentina

Chávez was monitoring the guardhouse through the telescopic lens of a ThOR thermal imaging night scope mounted on top of his Remington M24 stainless-steel sniper rifle. The image intensification component inside the scope was made of phosphorus and its luminescence capability produced a vivid green image that was invisible to the naked eye.

Rojas and Paz were standing a few feet away, partially cloaked from view by the Mercedes van that was parked sideways on, looking down the hill towards the entrance of the chemical plant.

"Boss, the night guards who work the grounds normally come together for a cigarette break every two hours or so. The one who patrols the perimeter fence walks out to the front entrance where he meets up with the guard who's based inside the entrance hut. They normally stand behind the red automatic arm barrier for a smoke and a five-minute chat." Rojas glanced down at his watch. "The last break they took was about ninety minutes ago."

Paz glided silently across the car park to join Chávez. He rested his left hand gently on his shoulder to not disturb his concentration. In days gone by the hitman had served alongside him for six months as a mercenary in Angola, where he'd proved himself to be an elite sniper, taking out hundreds of enemy soldiers single-handedly.

"Bruno, next time they meet up for a smoke, take them out. Two head shots."

Paz left the marksman in place and joined Rojas, who was carefully checking all seventeen rounds in his Beretta M9 semi-automatic pistol were present and correct. He figured one magazine gave him more than enough bullets to take care of the two unsuspecting guards they would encounter inside the plant. Paz let him finish the check before issuing his next orders.

"As soon as Bruno takes out the guards, remove the fingers from our friend inside the van. They'll only work while they're still warm, so we'll have to move fast."

Nothing happened for almost thirty minutes and then the attack began. The guards had only just lit their cigarettes when two rounds, fired within two seconds of each other, took off the tops of their heads. The 6.5-millimetre hollow point boat tail bullets were renowned for their accuracy and designed for rapid expansion on impact, which meant they literally blew the guards' brains apart.

Rojas took his cue and ripped open the back doors of the Sprinter van. He found the duty manager curled up in a tight ball in the far corner, shaking with terror as he contemplated his inevitable fate. A few minutes earlier he'd lost control of his bodily functions and the stench of liquid excrement inside the van forced the hitman to stop in his tracks and retch.

For reasons unknown, Rojas decided to show an element of compassion towards the wreck in front of him and paused by the doors to casually fit a silencer to the muzzle of his Beretta before firing a single shot into Houseman's forehead. He justified his generosity as a good way of testing the efficiency of the weapon he'd sourced only two days earlier.

As the body slumped to one side, he pulled the Japanese knife from his inside jacket pocket and carefully sliced through the knuckle bones of the dead man's middle and index fingers of his right hand. The chef's knife was more than up to the task of carving through human bone and cartilage, so it wasn't long before Rojas was cradling the two fingers in several layers of white kitchen roll that immediately soaked blood red.

Less than two minutes later the three-man assault team, all wearing black woollen balaclavas, arrived at the front barrier to the plant in the Escalade. Chávez jumped out of the passenger side and raced into the entrance hut to release the electronic barrier. The SUV glided into the grounds and Paz parked the black Cadillac a few feet away from the grey solid-steel electronic entrance door. There was a silver unit to the right of it that housed an entry phone button with a small black glass panel below it.

Paz carefully unwrapped the two bloody digits and pressed the pads firmly against the glass. He held his breath for what seemed like an eternity before he heard the whirring sound of the door mechanism kick into action. He cautiously pushed the door open, and the three men entered the dimly lit reception area, where there was no sign of activity. It was much wider than it appeared from the outside, with a metal winding staircase to one side and two large corridors – one veering off to the left and one running straight down the centre.

Paz walked across to the oblong reception desk, which had a large black leather chair positioned directly behind it. To the side was a deep shelf with six black-and-white monitors displaying live CCTV footage of the front of the chemical plant, where they had just entered. Something was wrong. Where were the two internal guards? Why wasn't at least one of them monitoring the security output?

As he peered down the centre corridor, Paz could just make out a set of double doors at the far end, which he assumed led to the storeroom. He nodded to Rojas and Chávez to follow, and they began moving along the passage. They hadn't taken more than a few steps when they heard a door shutting upstairs and footsteps heading their way, accompanied by chatter and laughter. Paz and his men simultaneously drew their weapons, retreated to the desk and dived behind it for cover. They waited as the footsteps grew louder.

The two security guards had broken every rule and code of behaviour in the book. They'd left their positions unmanned at the same time when they'd sneaked off to watch the edited highlights of an international soccer match between Argentina and Colombia on a television in a room upstairs that was designated as a communal break area for staff to make use of during the day.

As they made their way to the bottom of the stairs and back into the reception area, they were greeted by a relentless hail of bullets, courtesy of three semi-automatic Berettas. Their bodies were ripped apart by the sheer scale of rounds. Both men were clinically dead after being struck by initial head shots, but by the time they'd tumbled to the floor they had been hammered by over twenty bullets each. The whole shooting match was over in less than thirty seconds.

The Black Scorpion put his gun away and Rojas and Chávez followed his lead. For the second time in as many minutes they made their way down the central corridor towards the storeroom. The three men felt more relaxed and focused their attention on locating the stocks of Quentiline. Once again, the duty manager's bloody fingers did the trick, triggering the dual lock mechanism that protected the reinforced steel double doors.

As they made their way inside the vast air-conditioned unit, they had no idea that a third guard – the one the Duty Manager, Houseman had neglected to mention – had heard the massacre, hit the panic button that connected to the local police station and was hiding inside the giant storeroom behind a huge pile of pallets with his SIG Sauer P938 pistol locked and loaded.

Chapter 24

Córdoba, Argentina

The sheer scale of the drug storeroom took Paz by surprise. The two upper floors had been removed, resulting in an internal height of over thirteen metres which, combined with a floor footprint of ninety square metres, created a massive open-plan area. It was crammed full of thousands of pallets, many piled high in the air. For a moment, the Black Scorpion's mind flashed back to the memorable final scene from *Raiders of the Lost Ark* and the enormous government warehouse where the Ark was secretly stored.

The two-metre-square drug pallets were clearly labelled. Paz noticed large stacks of Adapalene and Alprazolam positioned to the left of the double doors and remembered Houseman explaining the alphabetical storage system. His eyes flicked to the other side of the storeroom, where they briefly settled on piles of Pantoprazole and Perindopril. He scanned right before landing on the prize. There were only two pallets of Quentiline on display and the diminutive pile looked a bit sad compared to the huge stacks of other drug stocks surrounding it.

Paz didn't give a damn as he'd hit the jackpot. One pallet contained almost double the quantity requested by Franklin's head biochemist, so it was a big win for the Black Scorpion. For the first time since breaking out of Valledupar he felt he was back to the peak of his powers. Adrenaline pumped through his veins as he snarled out orders to his men.

"Héctor, Bruno, let's get on with this. It'll take both of you to carry the Quentiline pallet out to the car and we need to come back for other random drugs. Then we're out of this weird giant pharmacy."

Chávez and Rojas moved swiftly across the unit and bent down to grab the corners of the top two-metre-squared plastic pallet, containing two hundred bottles of Quentiline. Focused on the job, they were both taken by surprise as Sergio Aguilar, the third night guard, appeared from nowhere, having silently emerged from his hiding place. He stood in the middle of the storeroom, slightly crouched, with his gun drawn and aimed in their direction. His eyes darted between them and Paz. He had no doubt his fellow guards were dead and knew he was facing a gang of highly trained killers, but he also knew help was on its way.

"The police will be here any moment, so I suggest you all sit on the floor with your hands folded in your laps and we'll wait for them to arrive."

Paz cursed under his breath as his mind flashed back to his recent interrogation of the plant manager and the slight pause the man had taken before revealing the number of armed guards inside the chemical plant. It was always the small details that caught you out and he knew in the past his razor-sharp brain wouldn't have missed the obvious clue. Nevertheless, he remained calm and tried to take back control, playing the only card he had left.

"How much money will it take – maybe a hundred thousand dollars?"

Aguilar was about to give a dismissive reply when Chávez dived to the floor, desperately seeking cover from a pile of nearby pallets. He hit the ground hard yet still managed to pull out his Beretta in the same movement. His index finger twitched as it searched for the double-action trigger, but before it could wrap itself around the lever three rounds came his way. The first two whistled past his head but the third lodged deep into his brain, just above his right ear. A dark wet patch quickly seeped through the black woollen balaclava as he lay prone on the white-tiled floor.

Four more shots rang out and Aguilar reeled backwards, his chest struck by a volley of rounds that blew him off his feet. The Black Scorpion kept his gun waist-high as he walked across to the still-breathing stricken guard and finished him off with a head shot. In the distance, he could just make out the sound of approaching sirens. He turned to Rojas, who was kneeling over the body of his dead partner.

"Let's grab the Quentiline and get the hell out of this shitshow."

The third-row seats in the rear of the Escalade were already lowered, and after hurling the drug pallet on top of them, the black Cadillac sped away, disappearing up the main entrance to the industrial estate a good thirty seconds before the first police car arrived on the scene.

They headed north-east for the next forty minutes, towards the city centre, looking for cover, and finally came to a stop in a large car park at the side of a Holiday Inn. Paz jumped out of the passenger seat and stormed away from the car as if it were to blame for the giant screw-up that had just taken place. He gulped in some cold fresh air and his mind quickly began to clear. He knew what he had to do next. He hadn't forgotten the chilling threat from Franklin for the way he'd dealt with the young actor in Bogotá, so he wasn't about to confess to another botched job. He reached for his cell phone and scrolled through his contacts, taking one more deep breath before placing the call. Franklin answered after the initial ring, which took Paz by surprise. Evidently his boss had been waiting to hear from him.

"How did it go, Paz? Did you get it?"

Paz smiled to himself at the blunt greeting from a man he loathed.

"It was like taking candy from a baby. We got away with almost double the amount requested and we're on our way to the airport. We'll take the jet to the facility in Neuquén, and I'll personally hand over the package to Rivero."

Franklin purred like a baby kitten who'd just been given a saucer of cold milk.

"Really good work, Paz. I knew I could trust you. That's why I got you out of that hellhole in Colombia. Call me as soon as the delivery has been made. We have another urgent matter to deal with."

Paz placed his cell back into his jacket pocket and stared at the half-moon illuminating the charcoal sky alongside thousands of glistening stars. He knew he'd really messed up this time. As well as leaving Bruno's body behind and not covering the true motive of the robbery by taking other drug pallets, there was the small matter of the Mercedes van containing the duty manager's mutilated body and the Japanese chef's knife. All loose ends he'd planned to clear up before everything went haywire. He couldn't help but shudder as he wondered how Franklin would react when he discovered the truth.

Chapter 25

Cape Town, South Africa

May 1958

"I t's clear we share a common cause we are both passionate about – the annihilation of the Jewish race and the destruction of the state of Israel."

Hitler and Bormann listened intently to the words of Gamal Abdel Nasser, the enigmatic president of Egypt, who, eighteen months earlier had provoked the infamous Suez Crisis. He had threatened to destabilise world geopolitics by unilaterally nationalising the Suez Canal, which connected Europe to Asia and was a vital sea trading route for France, the United Kingdom and the recently formed state of Israel. That controversial action led to a bloody invasion of his country spearheaded by the Israelis with the backing of UK and French troops. Over three thousand Egyptian soldiers were killed during hostilities before external pressure from American President Dwight D. Eisenhower forced the British, French and Israelis into a humiliating climbdown, bringing the conflict to a close. Nevertheless, Nasser received a bloody nose from the Jewish state and was desperate for revenge against his new upstart neighbours.

The extraordinary, highly secretive face-to-face meeting between the Egyptian president and the Führer took place in the spacious lounge area of the luxurious presidential suite at the eminent Mount Nelson Hotel in the heart of Cape Town. The encounter was hugely significant because it was the first time since he'd fled Germany that Hitler was brave enough to break cover and leave his Patagonian sanctuary. He was fascinated by the emergence of Nasser as a new political force on the world stage, especially as they shared the same viewpoint when it came to the Jews, so he had badgered a reluctant Bormann into setting up a meeting.

On the other side, the Egyptian president had been tempted into making the arduous flight to South Africa by the transfer of five million dollars into his personal bank account, with the promise of more to follow. The payment was contingent on him meeting a South American admirer who ran a large pharmaceutical corporation that was keen to throw its financial weight behind the Egyptian military. Bormann suggested Cape Town as a suitable venue as it represented the halfway point between Buenos Aires and Cairo, meaning both men travelled a similar distance to take part in the covert summit.

When they met, Nasser was astonished to discover the real identity of Gerald Franklin, especially as, at first glance, the frail sixty-nine-year-old figure standing before him with the aid of an ebony wooden cane, looked nothing like the notorious German dictator he'd believed was long dead. But, as he examined his face more closely, he managed to see past the reconstructive surgery and receding grey hairline to the menacing steely-blue eyes that belonged to the man known to the world as the Führer.

Bormann, as usual, had planned everything to the last detail – including securing the services of a South American translator who spoke fluent Arabic. Once the introductions were out of the way, the dictators spent over two hours discussing current events in the Middle East and the disturbing emergence of the Jewish state. They sat facing each other on matching Chesterfield sofas, while the translator sat to one side on a dining room chair. Bormann observed that Hitler appeared far more animated and engaged in the meeting than at any time since the end of the war. He was energised by the freedom to discuss his innate hatred of the Jews with a like-minded senior politician.

"I first identified the Jewish problem as a young man living in Munich after the end of the First World War. It became apparent to me how our brave soldiers were betrayed by the powerful Jewish lobby of bankers and politicians inside Germany who sold out to the Western powers to feather their own nests. They were – and remain, a corrosive cancer embedded in society that needs to be cut out. Had my deceitful generals not betrayed me at a crucial point in 1945, we would have been victorious, and every Jew in Europe would now be dead."

Nasser seemed fascinated by the Führer's slant on the past, especially as he was hearing it first-hand from the man who'd been at the very epicentre of the greatest war of all time and whose hatred of the Jews matched his own. He was a diligent student of modern history and was in awe of Hitler's achievements when it came to his diabolical treatment of the Jews.

"Führer, I've read about the death camps you built in your commendable pursuit of the final solution. It is a great inspiration to me and tragic that events prevented you from completing the task. Regardless, I believe you took out over six million, which is still a remarkable achievement. My problem is, many of the remaining Jews fled Europe and set up home on my doorstep, in this new Israeli state."

"What about inside Egypt – how many vermin do you have?"

"Before I came to power there were about sixty thousand, but after the war I began a programme of expulsion and today less than a quarter of that number remain inside the country. My ambition, though, is to bring the figure down to zero. In many ways, I followed the blueprint you created inside Germany after you became chancellor – I issued decrees abolishing civil liberties for the Jews and stripped them of their Egyptian citizenship. In addition, I granted special powers to our secret police, enabling them to close their businesses and arrest them at will. Since the recent war over Suez, the people's hatred for the Jews has greatly intensified and I plan to weaponize that discontent across the Middle East by creating a consensus with my fellow Arab nations to build an army powerful enough to eventually wipe out the Israeli state."

Hitler glanced across at Bormann before responding, as if looking for validation before he next spoke. His former party secretary caught his eye and gave a slight nod.

"Martin has access to several dark bank accounts in Europe and will set up a mechanism to transfer significant funds to your government on the sole condition one hundred per cent of the money is spent on strengthening the military. Every dollar must go on equipment and armaments in preparation for a future war with Israel."

Nasser leaned forward in his chair and dropped his voice to a whisper. "What is significant?"

"We're thinking two hundred and fifty million dollars in the first twelve months and then we'll assess how wisely you spend the money. If I'm satisfied, we'll continue annually with the funding."

The Egyptian president tried to maintain a deadpan expression, but his mind had already switched to another place – he was working out what percentage he could safely skim off the top without anyone ever knowing. It would provide him with a nice insurance policy should his position be threatened in the future.

"Führer, that level of financial support will allow us to build an air force capable of taking on the Israelis, who currently have air supremacy. Plus, we'll invest in the new tanks and military vehicles required for a successful land invasion."

Hitler felt empowered to go further, to tell his new ally about his long-term plan to cull the Israelis with *Operation Gesamtkunstwerk*. Even Nasser, who clearly was no fan of the Jewish race, was shocked by the pure malevolence of a plot that would leave millions of Israeli women barren.

A random childhood memory struck a chord, prompting him to laugh aloud. "When I was a little boy, I remember my grandmother reading me a bedtime story about Moses and the ten plagues he inflicted on the Egyptian people. The final and most powerful was the slaying of the firstborn of every female in the country. Somehow, this feels like a wonderful real-life payback for the historical myth the Jews have peddled for generations." He paused before asking, "Realistically, how far away are your scientists from creating this miracle drug?"

"Many years – perhaps decades, but they'll get there in the

end and *Operation Gesamtkunstwerk* will eventually happen. My son, Richard, will one day take over the reins of the Franklin Pharmaceutical Corporation, so continuity in the research is assured."

"How old is Richard?"

The Führer was on a roll now and couldn't resist adding an extra layer of icing to the cake. "He's only twelve, but eventually, when he becomes CEO, he'll move to America, where in time he'll marry and have a son of his own, who'll be groomed from birth to become the most powerful leader on earth. That means my grandson will one day be president of the United States."

Nasser wasn't sure if he was staring into the eyes of an ageing, deluded lunatic or a fanatical genius who knew exactly what he was doing; only time would tell. But by the sound of it, neither of them would live long enough to find out the answer.

Chapter 26

Neuquén, Argentina

F ranklin's Global 7500 jet devoured the six hundred miles between Córdoba and Neuquén in under two hours and touched down at Presidente Perón International Airport at seven in the morning. Paz and Rojas insisted on personally carrying the precious cargo off the plane and loading it into the back of a dark blue BMW X5 that was parked on the tarmac ten metres from the left side of the plane.

The drive to the covert laboratory was just under an hour, and as the car pulled up outside the grey two-storey nondescript building, Paz spotted Doctor Rivero pacing up and down outside the front entrance. Thirty minutes later, having carefully checked and tested the contents of one of the bottles from the plastic pallet, the biochemist joined Paz in the works canteen where the two men enjoyed a celebratory coffee together.

"Mr Anderson called me to say everything went smoothly. Frankly, I'm also impressed by the speed of your work. We have far more Quentiline than we need but that's not a bad thing. You're very good at your job."

Paz took a large swig of black coffee and stared straight into Rivero's eyes, hitting him with a piercing gaze that instantly unnerved the biochemist. "Don't ever patronise or underestimate me, doctor, or you'll regret it."

Rivero suddenly felt nauseous and sensed large blotches of redness breaking out on his face.

Paz eased out of his chair and turned to leave. "This magical drug of yours better work or I'll be back for another visit and, trust me, you really don't want that to happen."

Paz made his way back to reception where Rojas was waiting for him. "Boss, have you not checked your messages? Franklin's been trying to reach you."

The Black Scorpion retrieved his cell phone, displaying three missed calls, and cursed as he recalled muting his iPhone back at the chemical plant. He immediately returned the call and Franklin picked up.

"I told you to call me as soon as you reached the lab."

Paz accepted the put-down. He was more concerned that Franklin may have heard about the chaotic mess he'd left behind in Córdoba.

"I need you back here as soon as possible. I'm taking a trip to Afghanistan with Al Kathib, and I want you to come with. Are your two men still with you?"

Paz glanced across at Rojas who was staring intently at his Galaxy smartphone, deep into a game of *Angry Birds*. "Yes, they are still with me. What do you need?"

"There's a doctor in El Bolsón who needs to disappear, along with his recent medical records. It mustn't look like murder, so it's essential his body is never found. I just need him to vanish. I'll upload full details on our secure site for you to pass on to your boys. Are they up to it?"

Paz gritted his teeth. "Don't worry, Señor Franklin, they'll take care of the problem."

"Good. Now, get your ass to the airport. My jet is fuelled and ready to bring you back."

* * *

Vargas could hardly contain his excitement. For the last twenty minutes he'd been pacing up and down the hotel corridor on a phone call with a senior detective based in Córdoba. Hembury, Katz and the FBI deputy all stopped what they were doing as the chief inspector burst back into Berrettini's suite.

"Late last night there was a break-in at a chemical plant in Córdoba. Three armed men took out five guards and a duty manager – who also had two of his fingers sliced off." He answered his audience's bewildered stares with a wave of his hand, "The biometric security system required his prints."

Hembury was just as puzzled as his two colleagues as to why Vargas was on such a high. "What did they take, Nic?"

"One pallet containing a banned antimalarial drug called Quentiline – but that's not the interesting part, at least not compared to the rest of the crime report. One of the criminals shot dead in a gunfight with a guard has been identified as Bruno Chávez, a former colleague of Matias Paz. They were mercenaries together back in the day and, more recently, he worked for Paz in Buenos Aires at Theodor Consultants. The detective I spoke with told me Chávez has been retired for many years and he was genuinely shocked to see his corpse at the crime scene. But there's more ..."

Vargas felt a bit like Houdini, about to produce another rabbit out of a hat.

"They found a van in a nearby car park. It contained the body of the duty manager along with one other object – a Japanese chef's knife, which was obviously used to carve off the poor guy's fingers. We got two clear sets of prints from it – and guess what?"

Berrettini smiled as he deduced what was coming. "I think we might be ahead of you, Nic."

Vargas savoured the moment nonetheless. "Yep, one of them belonged to the Black Scorpion."

Chapter 27

El Bolsón, Argentina

The quiet, unassuming town of El Bolsón in the province of Río Negro in the north-west of Patagonia, nestles on the fertile banks of the Quemquemtreu River. Its tiny population of just over nineteen thousand survives mainly by living off the fruits of the land. Although it is one of the oldest settlements in Argentina, its single claim to fame occurred back in 1901 when the infamous bank robbers, Robert LeRoy Parker and Harry Alonzo Longabaugh, better known as Butch Cassidy and the Sundance Kid, took refuge there in a small, remote log cabin while on the run from US marshals.

In the hundred and twenty years following that newsworthy event, nothing much happened in El Bolsón, which made it the ideal testing ground for CDF830, the secret drug created by the team of biochemists and chemical engineers based in John Franklin's research facility in Neuquén; a drug with a heritage that could be traced back to 1943 and the primitive sterilisation tests instigated by the Angel of Death, Josef Mengele, at Auschwitz.

El Bolsón, was a sleepy town with an alpine feel and pretty, wide streets, perfectly framed by the magnificent Andes Mountain range which created a breath-taking backdrop. The town had been personally selected for the test by Eva Castillo, John Franklin's younger half-sister, after she made a visit there in her capacity as a senator in the National Congress. As part of her high-profile visit, she toured the newly developed reservoir complex and filtration plant that served the entire population of El Bolsón with fresh drinking water. The senator hailed this state-of-the-art facility as a wonderful innovation.

Although the outside of the plant was reasonably well protected, she noted a conspicuous lack of security inside the main structure, where a clarification and filtration process removed sediment and particles from the reservoir water. Chlorine dioxide was then added as a powerful disinfectant to further enhance the water's purification. Castillo figured a lone intruder, with the aid of a generous bribe, could easily gain entry to the plant, and once inside could add unlimited amounts of the colourless, odourless, and tasteless liquid drug, CDF830, into the final filtration process.

The potency of the drug meant a small amount entering the water system would, when imbibed, be enough to cause irreparable damage to the unsuspecting female population of El Bolsón and render them infertile. Six months after her visit in October 2020, Castillo recruited a young, unemployed drug user in downtown Buenos Aires, who was more than happy to carry out the required task in return for a small brown package containing five kilos of uncut cocaine. The live human test, sanctioned by John Franklin, was underway.

* * *

Doctor Tomás Eduardo had earned his first-class honours degree from Buenos Aires School of Medicine in 2005. After finishing his obstetrics and gynaecology residency in Ricardo Gutiérrez Children's Hospital, he completed a two-year fellowship specialising in following up preterm babies in a small clinic based in Buenos Aires. In 2008 he married another young doctor whom he'd first met at medical school when they were both teenage students. A few months after their wedding, they moved to her hometown of El Bolsón, where they opened a small surgery on Avenida San Martín in the town centre where Julieta worked as a general practitioner and Tomás was the town's sole obstetrician and gynaecologist.

It was late afternoon and he had just treated his last patient of the day and was back sitting behind his desk studying a collection of hysterosalpingography tests taken on four of his patients during the last couple of days. The young doctor was staring at a bewildering conundrum that just made no sense. The HSG images were produced by a unique form of X-ray known as fluoroscopy – a procedure undertaken when it was necessary to examine the uterus and fallopian tubes. He shook his head in disbelief at the anomalies in the new images, which were pretty much identical to six others he'd seen two weeks earlier.

In all ten cases the fallopian tubes had significantly narrowed and there was a thin, sinister dark patch running through the middle of them. The X-ray images resembled the common disease atherosclerosis, where arteries gradually fur up over time and eventually block; a condition that tends to be more prevalent in older people. In this instance, all his patients were aged between twenty-five and forty and were actively trying for a baby. The doctor had never come across anything like it before, and in the past few days had scrutinised his large collection of medical journals, desperately looking for an answer, but nothing showed up that could provide a plausible explanation.

Eduardo had sent the first set of images, along with an assessment report, to the government's chief medical officer at the Ministry of Health, requesting a mass programme of HSG tests be carried out in the town as soon as possible among women of childbearing age. A seemingly reasonable request, but it had so far gone unanswered.

Unbeknown to Eduardo, the contents of his email had been seen by someone outside the department, a female Senator, who had passed the details of the explosive report to her half-brother, John Franklin. He'd responded immediately by ordering a semi-retired hitman to take a trip to El Bolsón.

* * *

Héctor Rojas hired a fresh rental and set off to tackle the six-hour, three-hundred-mile drive heading south-west on the legendary RN40 State Highway, the longest route in South America. The former mercenary felt energised by the events of the previous twenty-four hours and was relishing every moment of his unexpected reunion with the Black Scorpion. Resting on the empty passenger seat alongside him was a one-page email containing the name and address of his target, along with a colour headshot of the doctor.

The drive was uneventful and traffic-free until Rojas reached the outskirts of Los Repollos, a small hamlet twelve miles north of El Bolsón. His silver Chevrolet Prisma slowed to a halt as it joined a one-mile tailback caused by lane closures at the location of a road widening scheme.

As his rental crawled past a concrete mixer truck, he became mesmerised by the giant drum mounted on the back trailer slowly churning as it poured freshly made concrete down a curved extension chute into a massive hole on an unmade section of road. An idea formed in his mind as he reflected on his favourite book, *Killer – Autobiography of a Mafia Hit Man.* It was the life story of a contract killer known simply as Joey, who had worked his way up the ranks of a New York-based Mafia family. Over the years, road building projects had provided mobster families with custom-made anonymous cemeteries to conceal their victims' bodies. A faint smile appeared on Rojas's face as he visualised the slain body of the eminent doctor forming part of the renowned state highway.

An hour later he parked the rental directly across the street from the surgery, placed the headshot of the doctor on the dashboard and began his surveillance, prepared to wait for as long as it took.

Chapter 28

El Bolsón, Argentina

Eduardo and his wife rented a comfortable two-bedroom apartment above their workplace, although access was from a separate front door situated at street level, about ten yards from the surgery entrance. That's where Julieta was, upstairs preparing dinner in the kitchen when Tomás finally closed the file containing the mysterious X-rays and called it a day. He was deeply concerned by the growing number of patients suffering from an unknown condition he had no explanation for and therefore was unable to treat. Tomás resolved to call the CMO in the morning to force an emergency meeting in Buenos Aires where he could meet up with the best medical minds in the country to try and determine what the hell was going on.

He suddenly remembered that Julieta had mentioned they were having a tenderloin steak dinner and his mood lightened. He glanced at his watch and saw it was nearly seven, which meant he just had time to nip to the corner mini market to pick up a bottle of their favourite red wine. As he exited the tinted-glass surgery door and turned right towards the shop, he had no sense of the man across the street furtively stepping out of the driver's door, crossing the road, and falling into step about ten yards behind him.

A few minutes later Tomás strolled out of the shop clutching a bottle of Malbec in one hand and a small bunch of pink roses in the other. He was only five yards from home when a figure moved out of the shadow of a doorway and grabbed him from behind. The assailant's left arm wrapped itself around the doctor's upper chest like a giant anaconda and the barrel of a handgun wedged itself firmly against the bottom of his spine. The rapid injection of fear Tomás experienced was further intensified when he heard Rojas's sinister voice for the first time as the hitman whispered in his right ear.

"Doctor, just walk across the street to the silver Chevrolet and everything will be fine. Any attempt to deviate from my instructions and I'll blow a giant hole through your back."

Julieta was standing by the kitchen window, peeling baby potatoes on the drainer of the stainless-steel sink, when she saw her husband being bundled into the passenger seat of a silver car by a stranger holding a gun in his right hand. For a moment she did a double take – she couldn't quite believe what she was witnessing, but then she leapt forward and almost pulled the sash window out of its runners as she pushed it upwards and screamed her husband's name. She saw the anguish on Tomás's face as he turned and stared up at her. Moments later, Rojas hit the throttle and the rental shot off like a bullet.

The hitman kept his right hand on the wheel while his left rested on his knee, cradling the Beretta that was aimed at his passenger. Neither man spoke for about ten minutes as the car headed north, back the way it had come a few hours earlier. Finally, Tomás broke the insufferable silence.

"Is this about drugs? Is it a kidnapping?"

"Relax, doctor, I'm not after any of your magic pills. Just stay quiet. We don't have much further to go and then, I promise you, I'll explain what's happening."

* * *

Although Julieta was in a deep state of shock, she had the presence of mind to dial the personal number of the town's only senior police officer. Chief Inspector Juan Ojeda picked up on the heady mixture of terror and panic in Julieta's voice and his thirty-years' experience on the force kicked into action. The first thing he did was attempt to calm down the near hysterical doctor.

"Julieta, I promise we will find Tomás and quickly. Just lock your doors and wait for me and my men to arrive and, whatever you do, don't let anyone else in. I'll be there in a few minutes."

An unmarked police vehicle screeched to a halt outside the surgery. Ojeda, accompanied by a uniformed officer, entered the flat while a third man stood guard on the street in case the kidnapper returned looking for another target. Ojeda sat down opposite the woman he knew to be a wonderful doctor in the community – a woman who was normally so calm and self-assured. She was a bag of nerves now, her ghostlike face drained of any colour and her hands trembling with fear as she nursed a mug of black coffee on her lap.

"Julieta, tell me again exactly what happened? Have you any idea who might be behind this? What did the man look like and what make of car was he driving? What direction did they head off in?"

It only took her a few seconds to answer the questions. The whole episode had happened so quickly, she couldn't really provide the detective with any useful answers, and as that became more apparent, Julieta's distress rose. Ojeda stood up and walked to the window to look across the street at the empty space where the silver car had been parked just a few minutes earlier. He tried his best to process the titbits of information Julieta had imparted and then wondered what the hell was happening in his quiet little town.

* * *

It was pitch-black and the only illumination came from the rectangular LED headlights of the Chevrolet Prisma as it made its way along a narrow gravel side road and came to a sudden stop a few hundred yards away from the state highway. Rojas turned off the engine and switched the gun to his right hand while his left reached for the driver's door handle.

"Okay, doctor, it's time to take a walk."

They got out of the car and Rojas steered Eduardo around to the boot before issuing his next command. "Open it and take out the shovel."

The doctor froze with sheer terror, unable to raise his arms, which suddenly felt as though they were laden with ten-ton weights. However, a moment later, when he felt the stark coldness of the Beretta steel barrel jam hard up against the back of his head, he somehow summoned the mental and physical strength to follow the order. He flicked open the boot to reveal a wooden-handled steel shovel, a toolkit and two green twenty-litre jerrycans. Rojas backed away, allowing Eduardo the room to grab the work tool, then pulled out an iPhone from his jacket with his left hand and switched on the torch.

"Okay, let's go. We need to get moving."

"Can you at least tell me ... what this is all about?"

"Doctor, you'll find out soon enough. Now, start moving."

The two men walked along a gravel track until they reached the side of the highway, which was bordered by a large ring of three-foot-high, red-and-white barriers marking out the perimeter of the construction site. Situated between each one was a red flashing lamp, strategically positioned to warn motorists of the potential hazard. Rojas kicked a barrier aside and gestured for Eduardo to walk through the newly made opening and onto ground that was uneven underfoot. The doctor slowly moved ahead until he came to an abrupt stop by an enormous hole that had been carved out of the ground by the giant diggers that were now parked up for the night. Eduardo couldn't quite work out how deep it was but sensed he was staring at his own grave; a petrifying reality that made his entire body shudder. He kept hoping that at any moment a random event would suddenly free him from this horrific nightmare, but it was blatantly obvious his captor had brought him there to die.

"Doctor, it seems you have been making too much noise and you've become a problem for my boss."

Tomás desperately tried one final plea for clemency. "There's been a huge mistake – I'm just a doctor, for God's sake ... At least tell me what I'm supposed to have done!"

Rojas raised the Beretta and took aim. "Doctor, I really don't know but it's of little interest to me."

The former mercenary fired his two trademark shots: one to the head and one to the heart. Eduardo's limp body fell to the ground and ended up in a twisted heap, half in and half out of the hole. Just as Rojas had planned, the freshly laid concrete was still fluid and workable, so it only took a few minutes' effort with the shovel for the body to be completely covered by a grey blanket that would harden overnight.

Rojas made his way back to the car and placed the shovel inside the boot, alongside the two jerrycans. He switched off the torch and sent a short text to the Black Scorpion.

The medical problem has gone away and will never return. Still need to tie up some loose ends.

He pocketed the phone and slid back into the car where he gunned the engine to life. The night was still young, and he had plenty of work to do.

Chapter 29

El Bolsón, Argentina

Detective Ojeda stood on the pavement in front of the surgery entrance briefing the plain clothes officer who was sitting in his unmarked car with the window down.

"Acosta, park up across the street about fifty yards down so you can keep an eye on the surgery, just in case our mystery friend in his silver car makes a surprise reappearance."

The veteran detective wasn't quite sure what was unfolding but his instincts told him there might yet be more to come. He had already released the officer from the apartment, and so decided to re-join Julieta and keep her company while he waited for news on her husband's whereabouts. She was relieved to see him return, desperate for any news.

"Chief inspector, do you think this might be a kidnapping for drugs?"

"It's possible, of course, but I'd expect to have heard something by now if that were the case. Did anybody threaten Tomás at all or did anything unusual happen in the last few days?"

The doctor shook her head and tears welled up in her eyes. "Please, just find him and bring him home."

The silver Chevrolet cruised to a halt directly outside the medical practice. Up ahead and across the street, the young police officer who'd been on lookout for over an hour ducked low inside his car and watched in his rearview mirror as Rojas emerged from the rental and made his way to the clinic's glass door. He grabbed the radio from the dashboard.

"Sir, I think our man is back. He's parked up in a silver Chevy and right now is trying to work the lock on the surgery door."

Julieta heard the message on the detective's radio and jumped out of her chair like a bat out of hell. Ojeda nodded at her to stay calm and clicked on his handset.

"Keep monitoring for now. I'm calling for backup."

It took Rojas less than twenty seconds to break the lock, but instead of entering the building he returned to his car where he opened the boot and retrieved the two jerrycans. Acosta immediately keyed the radio.

"Sir, he's just taken two fuel cans out of the car boot and is walking through the entrance."

"Christ. I'm on my way down. Wait for me outside the door."

Less than a minute later Ojeda and his officer cautiously entered the front door of the surgery and crept into the hallway that was bathed in darkness. They flattened their bodies hard against the wall as they inched forward towards the surgery door bearing the name "Doctor Tomás Eduardo" on a silver plaque. It was slightly ajar, allowing a hint of torchlight glow to spread into the hallway. Inside, they could hear the unmistakable sound of footsteps shuffling around and a sloshing noise that sounded like fuel leaving a can as it was randomly spewed across the floor.

Rojas was fully focused on spraying gasoline around the consulting room and didn't hear the door slowly creak open. He had his back to it, emptying the dregs of the first can onto the doctor's desk when he was stopped in his tracks by a shout from the chief inspector.

"Throw the can to the floor and slowly turn around with your hands high in the air!"

The former mercenary froze to consider his options. Concealed in the palm of his left hand was a brushed steel Zippo that he'd been about to use on an oily rag to create an improvised fire starter. Thinking quickly, he dropped the can from his other hand and, at the same time, flipped back the top of the Zippo with his thumb and flicked the flint wheel back to create a flame. In one fluid movement he threw it to the floor where it ignited the gasoline, creating a line of flame that raced around the room.

Ojeda was momentarily taken off guard by the sheer speed of the move and hesitated slightly as Rojas fell to his left and withdrew his Beretta, letting off three rapid shots. Two missed their mark but the third impacted human flesh. In the hiatus and partial darkness, no one had noticed Julieta enter the room. The .22 calibre round penetrated her chest, striking the sixth rib before lodging in the tissue of her left lung. She collapsed to the ground, her hands instinctively clutching the small fountain of blood that spurted from the open wound.

Ojeda gathered himself and fired his Glock 17 back, and in the mayhem of crossfire a single bullet caught Rojas to the right of his neck, shattering his collarbone into tiny fragments. His gun slipped from his grasp as he writhed around in agony, and moments later Acosta had him pinned to the ground before applying a set of heavy-duty handcuffs, immobilising the hitman. Ojeda reeled around and dropped to the floor to attend to Julieta who had lost consciousness and was lying in a heap, blood pumping from her chest and leaking from her mouth. He hauled her still body away from the smoke and flames.

Ten minutes later, two green and yellow Ford Venari ambulances sped away from the medical practice, heading for the general hospital two miles away. One of the patients on board was fighting for their life.

The chief inspector stayed behind to help extinguish the fire and secure the crime scene, after which he decided to check out the arsonist's car parked outside. He tried the handle and found it unlocked. He immediately spotted the photo of Doctor Tomás Eduardo on the dashboard, along with a printed email lying on the passenger seat. He leaned across to pick up the single white sheet that had the address of the medical practice and a chilling message printed in type.

Make sure the doctor permanently disappears and destroy all his records.

Ojeda read the message twice before leaving the car and walking back inside the medical centre, which was now a hive of activity with firefighters, officers, and photographers scouring the crime scene, searching for evidence. The fire had been brought under control quickly, so hopefully most of the records remained intact, but any confidence he'd previously fostered of finding the doctor alive had now faded. Nothing made any sense. Why on earth would someone dispatch a hitman to El Bolsón to take out a respected doctor and burn down his surgery?

One thing was for sure: whatever it took, the chief inspector was determined to discover the answer.

* * *

Paz was a worried man sitting in the rear section of Franklin's private jet on the way to the International Airport in Kandahar. He'd been waiting for his boss to summon him when a news alert pinged on his phone – an arsonist had been shot and arrested in the small town of El Bolsón in the Río Negro province. He cursed under his breath. The mistakes were piling up and it was only a matter of time before his employer found out about them. He wondered about cutting off the head of the snake, but that still left Eva and the other siblings as potential enemies who would, without doubt, look for retribution. And then there was Al Kathib. There was something unnerving about the Syrian that Paz couldn't quite put his finger on, but he instinctively knew he wasn't a man to be crossed.

His train of thought was broken by the sudden appearance of a male flight attendant who beckoned him forward for a meeting with the man who had recently become his new jailer.

The front of the plane contained a luxurious seating area with four cream leather and chrome armchairs neatly positioned, forming a small circle. Franklin and Al Kathib were occupying two of them and Paz took his place in one of the empty seats. His American boss was, as usual, accompanied by a large tumbler of bourbon from which he took a giant swallow.

"What news from El Bolsón?"

"The doctor is no longer a threat and won't be found. All his records have been destroyed in a fire." Paz lied with ease – he had no choice but to roll the dice.

Franklin nodded his approval. "That's good work, Paz. Give your men a healthy bonus. Now, we need to brief you on our upcoming meeting with two senior members of the Taliban."

* * *

Berrettini had shuffled the cards: he and Hembury stayed in the hotel suite in Buenos Aires, working the case on the internet, while Vargas and Katz flew north-west to Córdoba to check out the chemical plant Paz and his team had hit twenty-four hours earlier.

Once they arrived, the Chief Inspector and Mossad agent found themselves standing in the massive drug storeroom in Pagina GA, accompanied by the general manager and the local detective covering the break-in. Vargas led the charge and directed his initial questions towards the perplexed plant manager.

"Señor Blanco, what can you tell us about the drugs that were stolen?"

The manager was a wreck. His close friend, Houseman, had been mutilated and killed along with five guards. His short, squat figure appeared to wobble as he struggled to overcome his nerves.

"As far as we can tell, all they got away with was one pallet of Quentiline."

Vargas and Katz both pulled expressions demonstrating their ignorance of the name.

"Look, I'm no pharmacist but I do know something about it. It's an old antimalarial drug that was banned a few years ago because of suspected carcinogenic side effects. We only have a few pallets left and they're all due to be destroyed in the next few weeks, along with other banned drugs. I can't see why anyone would kill to get their hands on it – it doesn't make any sense."

Katz glanced across at Vargas, practically reading his mind. "Don't worry, Señor Blanco, nothing much about this case does."

Chapter 30

Kandahar, Afghanistan

T he Global 7500 touched down at Ahmad Shah Baba Airport in Kandahar a few minutes before midday. Waiting on the tarmac, about fifty yards away, was a black armour-plated Mercedes G-Wagon that drove the three VIPs north-west towards the city where it headed for the palace formerly owned by the governor.

Despite eight months of neglect, the imposing structure still made for an impressive sight as the Mercedes swept through the ornate iron gates and parked up in the enormous courtyard. A single flagpole flew the unmistakable white Taliban flag decorated with black Islamic writing that translated as: "I bear witness that none deserves worship except God and I bear witness that Muhammad is the messenger of God".

The three men were escorted from the car by two heavily armed guards who led them across the courtyard into a huge labyrinth of corridors and doorways, eventually depositing them in an L-shaped room that was once the governor's office. The opulent decor and china-blue walls were daubed with black hand-painted slogans and signage written in Pashto. The second incarnation of the Taliban had taken possession of the governor's palace eight months earlier, on August 15, along with Kabul and the rest of Kandahar, the two nerve centres of the country.

The Taliban 2.0 were willing to recognise and work with almost every country in the world, including the United States with whom they had fought a bloody twenty-year war in Afghanistan. There was just one exception to their new-found policy of openness and friendship when dealing with their foreign affairs: the State of Israel, which they refused to recognise or have any relationship with. That inbuilt hatred of the existence of a permanent Jewish state located in the Middle East had been a major factor in John Franklin's planning when searching for an ally for *Operation Gesamtkunstwerk*.

Waiting to greet Paz, Al Kathib and Franklin were two of the Taliban's high command, who sat next to each other on low chairs parked in the middle of the governor's former office. Facing them were three upturned wooden crates – clearly the designated seating area for their guests. Al Kathib took care of the introductions, revelling in the role of greeter and translator; enjoying the fact he was the only one of the five men present who could fully understand every word being said. Paz, in contrast, felt the unease of an outsider as it became clear this wasn't the first time Franklin and Al Kathib had met with the two senior Taliban figures.

Abdul-Azim Habibullah was a major player in the re-formed Islamic Emirate, holding the post of Minister of Foreign Affairs. Twenty years earlier, he'd served as Minister of Information in the first incarnation of the Taliban government and was regarded by his enemies as one of the shrewdest and most experienced figures in the regime, second in importance only to the supreme leader. He was in his early fifties, although his bespectacled face, fuzzy grey beard, gaunt features, and heavy-lidded hazel eyes made him look a great deal older. He was a stick of a man, standing almost six foot tall but weighing only ten stone, with his black cotton tunic and woollen baggy pants hanging loosely off his bony frame.

Habibullah's physical features couldn't have been more of a contrast to the bear of a man who awkwardly squatted on the chair next to him – Firooz Mohammedzai, a senior military commander in the Taliban grand army. For the previous twenty years he'd been one of the most effective soldiers in the resistance and was heavily linked to the infamous massacres at Shi'a villages in 2001, as well as the summary execution of hundreds of Afghan soldiers who were found hanging off temporary scaffolds at random roundabouts throughout the city of Kandahar. During the long war, he'd proven to be a constant thorn in the side of the US military who had put a one-million-dollar bounty on his head. The problem was, there wasn't a single person brave or stupid enough to cash it in.

His towering, six-foot-six-inch frame, combined with a fifty-inch girth, created a Goliath of a man whose intimidating, stone-cold dark brown eyes completed the appearance of a human killing machine. He was dressed entirely in black robes, along with a traditional Peshawari turban that struggled to cover the top of his enormous head. Paz tried to avoid his piercing gaze as, for once, the Black Scorpion knew he'd more than met his match. Resting on the floor next to the commander was an M4 carbine fully automatic rifle, recently appropriated from a US arms stockpile that had been left behind in the mayhem of the panicked withdrawal. For the newly revived Islamic regime, the days of the Russian AK-47 being the Taliban's go-to weapon were consigned to the history books.

Al Kathib kept the conversation flowing. To Paz's surprise, the foreign minister spoke reasonable English while the giant gorilla next to him needed every word translated. The Syrian explained how a large shipment containing CDF830 would be flown into Kandahar no later than 29 April, some six days before it was required for the operation.

Habibullah took up the reins of the meeting, skilfully running through the details of the planned attack on the Israeli state. "My friends, once we have the full quantity of the drug in our possession, it will be packaged into refrigerated pallets and placed into transport containers attached to two Volvo trucks. They'll convey them on the two-and-a-half-thousand-mile journey from here to the first location in Eilat. The drugs will be hidden inside hundreds of halal processed-meat packages, all branded with the Kandahar Meat Company logo. This is one of the most respected brands in the Middle East. No one will challenge the cargo."

Al Kathib and Franklin were enthralled with the sheer level of detail the foreign minister was dishing out. Suddenly everything seemed real and within touching distance. Franklin was keen to hear more.

"Tell me about the planned route and the border crossings involved."

"The lorries will travel west from Kandahar and enter Iran at the Islam Qala border in the western province of Herat. From there, they'll make their way to Haji Omeran in the Erbil Governorate where they'll cross into Iraq. Then they'll head for the Al Karamah border crossing – the only road route available to enter Jordan. Finally, they'll pass through the soft border with Israel at the Wadi Araba Crossing, straight into Eilat. Once inside Israel, the trucks will make their way north along the Mediterranean coastline, hitting the designated desalination plants along the route. Finally, they'll travel north-east to the giant pump station in Galilee, their final destination."

Al Kathib clapped his hands together in a gesture of spontaneous delight. Habibullah returned the smile and turned to the Taliban soldier on his right-hand side, reverting to Pashto.

"Gentlemen, my colleague Commander Firooz Mohammedzai will take you through the security of the entire operation, but first we need to eat and drink to cement this holy alliance."

The foreign minister glanced towards the open door the three men had earlier entered by and, as if by magic, two male servants appeared in the doorway, each carrying large copper trays on which were placed two gold and black Arabic teapots and five unglazed clay tagines containing the treasured national dish, kabuli: a slow cooked stew of seasoned lamb, rice, raisins, carrots and nuts. The five men toasted each other with small china cups of black tea and set about tackling the feast.

A few minutes later, the commander used a large piece of warm naan to mop up the last piece of stew on his plate, then raised his claw like hand to his mouth and devoured the bread in one mouthful. He was the first to finish his meal and showed no interest in waiting for his fellow diners to complete theirs. When he spoke, his booming voice appeared to come from the very depths of his size fourteen boots.

"Each lorry will have two men on board who'll share the driving. But they aren't regular drivers. I have personally selected them from our Badri 313 Battalion, an elite unit of the Islamic Emirate Army."

Al Kathib had resumed his translation duties and couldn't resist adding his own insight for the benefit of Franklin and Paz. "Think of the US Navy Seals and then imagine a group of men twice as tough and with no conscience. They are capable of undertaking unspeakable acts."

Mohammedzai had no idea Al Kathib was embellishing his words and ploughed on.

"My men will be fully briefed and primed to carry out the specific duties requested of them for this complex operation. They know the importance of the mission and are prepared to die for it."

The commander switched his gaze to Paz before continuing with a direct question to Al Kathib. "Is this the man you told us about who'll be travelling with us? Will you be with him?"

The Syrian nodded before replying, "Don't worry, commander. I'll be there along with Paz … and I hope we won't be alone." He glanced back at the foreign minister. "I believe you have some sleepers inside Israel who can help us with the operation?"

Habibullah stopped eating but ignored Al Kathib, turning to the commander instead. "Yes, we have loyalists in the country who we'll activate to enhance your numbers. But the success of this mission revolves around stealth and secrecy – the smaller the band of brothers the better."

The colossus nodded his understanding and rose from his chair, shouting, "Baahir … Baahir."

A few moments later a Taliban soldier entered the room dragging the nearly dead body of a semi-naked man across the polished floor, creating a disgusting trail of blood and skin.

The beaten and tortured prisoner was semi-conscious, and the sight of his mutilated torso was not for the faint-hearted.

"Baahir, bring him over here."

The commander reached for his M4 carbine and raised it high in the air with his right hand. Then he lurched forward with surprising speed and grabbed the hair of the prisoner with his left hand and wrenched his head upwards.

"This piece of shit worked as a translator for British paratroopers stationed in Kabul and was responsible for the deaths of hundreds of our brothers." He gestured to Paz to take the rifle. "If I am to place the lives of my best men at your disposal, I want to know what kind of man you are."

Al Kathib smiled perversely as he translated the death order with relish.

Paz ignored the Syrian and turned towards his American boss. "Señor Franklin, I'm not a show pony who performs at the whim of a deranged fat slob of a soldier."

Franklin edged forward and glared at the Black Scorpion. "I think you've momentarily forgotten your place in our little hierarchy. Do it ... and do it now."

Paz took a moment to gather his thoughts before slowly standing and snatching the rifle from the commander's hand. The Black Scorpion decided it was time to show the Taliban giant exactly who he was dealing with, and in the following ten seconds he peppered the broken body of the prisoner with over twenty rounds, rendering the four onlookers speechless.

Chapter 31

Córdoba, Argentina

Vargas and Katz were sitting in the bar of the Gran Rex, a small boutique hotel located in downtown Córdoba, a couple of miles away from the chemical plant. They had exhausted the limits of the tiny menu and were feasting on a bowl of roasted peanuts and a plate of mixed hams, accompanied by two cold beers. Vargas had been on his laptop searching for more information on the banned drug that appeared to be the motive for the elaborate robbery masterminded by the Black Scorpion.

"Leah, what on earth would Paz and the Franklin clan want with a banned antimalarial drug? Somehow, it has to relate to the plot against Israel and *Operation Gesamtkunstwerk* – whatever that is."

"I've already emailed Doron regarding the Quentiline. He's recruiting a biochemist in Tel Aviv to run a full report on it. Obviously it has other properties that aren't immediately apparent and that gave it a value worth killing for."

Vargas shifted on his bar stool and downed the dregs of his

Peroni. "Leah, whatever the threat is to Israel, like you, I have a personal stake in the outcome."

The Mossad agent shot a quizzical look across the small bar table and leaned forward.

"Like most people in my country, I was born a Catholic – although I've never really cared about the whole religion thing. When I was thirty, I married a girl – the love of my life. Her name was Sophia ... she was a kindergarten teacher, and she was Jewish." Vargas stopped mid-flow, choking up as fragments of distant memories flooded his brain. His stomach cramped as though a giant knot had suddenly formed deep inside it, creating a sharp stab of pain. "She died of a brain tumour when she was just thirty-three. Ever since, I've kept a close relationship with her family. I visit them at least once a month – normally we share a typical Friday night Sabbath dinner. In the early days, having Sophia's family around me helped with the grief ... the pain. These days it's become more of a duty, but I've grown incredibly close to them."

Katz waited for an appropriate moment to reply, her voice softer when she spoke, "Nic, I'm so sorry. What a nightmare. I had no idea."

"There's no reason you should. It was a long time ago, but as you can see, the pain never really goes ... it just lurks beneath the surface. The thing is, Sophia has a younger sister, Nadia, and I'm incredibly fond of her. Three years ago, she married an Israeli lawyer who works for a firm of solicitors in the capital. I went to their wedding in Jerusalem, which was truly amazing, and about eighteen months ago they moved to Netanya. If Nadia is facing an imminent Nazi threat, I need to warn her."

The Mossad agent was taken aback by Vargas sharing such an open wound with her. She didn't know how to respond, and before she could the slightly awkward silence was relieved by the sound of Vargas's phone and an incoming call from Hembury who was still in Buenos Aires. The chief inspector hit the speaker icon and placed the phone on the table so Katz could hear what was said. The unrestrained excitement in Hembury's voice was palpable.

"Nic, they say lightning doesn't strike twice but there's always an exception to the rule – at least as far as our friend Matias Paz is concerned. I've just spoken with a detective based in the south in an out-of-the-way town called El Bolsón. He's filled me in on the details of a peculiar kidnap and arson attempt that's just taken place at a GP surgery there. I'll go through the details in a minute, but here's the golden nugget. The thug who was sent to kill the doctor and burn down his practice is currently in the local hospital with a shattered collarbone but alive and conscious. His name is Héctor Rojas. He worked at Theodor Consultants for nearly twenty years – yet another of Paz's closest allies. I thought it might be nice if you and Leah picked up some flowers and paid him a surprise visit."

* * *

It was a fifteen-hour non-stop flight back to the Caribbean, but the eight-thousand-mile journey was well within the range of Franklin's private jet. He spent the first thirty minutes locked on the phone, most of the time just listening. Al Kathib sat opposite him, intrigued by this unusual situation. Towards the end of the conversation, Franklin arrogantly waved an arm in the air, gesturing for the Syrian to disappear. Al Kathib obeyed the order, even though he was aching to know what was going down and the identity of the person on the other end of the line.

A few minutes later, Franklin brought the call to an abrupt end and summoned Paz for a briefing while Al Kathib remained alone at the back of the jet, fuming at being excluded. As soon as the Black Scorpion caught sight of the malevolent scowl on Franklin's face, he instinctively knew he was in for a rough ride, but even he wasn't prepared for the hurricane coming his way.

Hitler's grandson brandished a Smith & Wesson in his right hand, which he aimed at Paz's forehead. The white-hot rage in his voice was unmistakable as he began his onslaught. "Do you know that if I fire a single bullet directly into your futile brain, even if the round fails to lodge in a piece of bone and exits the back of your head, penetrating the fuselage, the aircraft's automatic pressurisation system will instantly kick in and within ten seconds the jet will be stable but most of your brain will be splattered on my carpet?"

Franklin paused a moment, allowing the threat of imminent death to hang in the air. Paz was in little doubt he was seconds away from oblivion, but Hitler's grandson hadn't finished his verbal tirade.

"You might as well have left your name and address at the chemical plant – your prints were all over the knife you left behind in the back of the van. You also failed to inform me that one of your associates was killed and that the entire raid was a total farce."

Paz was genuinely shocked by the sheer amount of detail Franklin had, but there was far worse to come.

"And then there's the fiasco in El Bolsón. Your geriatric

hitman screwed up the job and right now is in hospital waiting to be interviewed by the police."

Franklin enjoyed reading the blank look of bewilderment on Paz's face and continued to twist the knife.

"So, it's down to me to clean up your dirty mess. I've already sanctioned an immediate hit on Rojas before he gets a chance to talk."

Paz sensed he was about to be given another chance when Franklin lowered his pistol.

"How do you know all this? You seem to know more than me and that's—"

"Never make the mistake of underestimating me, Paz." Franklin paused for a beat, as his mind shifted to other issues. "I have much more to impart, some of which will be of particular interest to you. It appears that Vargas – the man who put you in Valledupar ten years ago, is running a small close-knit team which includes his old colleague Lieutenant Hembury, the FBI's deputy director and a female Mossad agent. They seem to know a great deal about our plans but, fortunately, nothing that can hurt us. Information is king, you see?"

Paz struggled to process the barrage of information coming his way but had to admire the display of pure cunning he was witnessing. The abrupt silence was an obvious sign the meeting was over, so he rose to his feet. As he turned to leave, Franklin, the ultimate control freak, couldn't resist firing off a parting shot.

"Paz, in case you're wondering, I have someone deep on the inside working for me, which means I'll always stay one step ahead."

* * *

Vargas and Katz had no way of knowing they were literally following in the footsteps of Héctor Rojas, the hitman they were planning to visit in the general hospital in El Bolsón, by driving south-west on the RN40 State Highway from Córdoba. As their Toyota rental crawled through the traffic works just outside Los Repollos, with Katz at the wheel, for a few seconds they were less than fifty yards away from Doctor Eduardo's unmarked concrete grave.

Thirty minutes later, the Corolla pulled up outside the surgery, where they'd arranged to meet Chief Inspector Ojeda. A thin strip of yellow tape draped across the entrance marked out the crime scene that was patrolled by a single uniformed officer. Vargas flashed his ID to the policeman, who'd been expecting them, and the pair were escorted into Eduardo's consulting room where Ojeda was waiting. Vargas made the introductions and then the local detective brought them up to speed with the investigation. Katz was full of questions, mostly about Rojas.

"So, you're convinced Rojas killed the doctor and then returned to burn down his surgery? What about his wife – did he try to kill her too?"

"No, I'm convinced that was an accident. He was firing at me and one of my men and she got caught in the crossfire by mistake. But there's absolutely no doubt about his motive."

Ojeda handed over the email he'd found in Rojas's car. The Mossad agent quickly read it before passing it over to Vargas, who made a copy with his iPhone.

Katz turned to Vargas to gauge his reaction before saying, "I agree the order is conclusive, so that begs two questions – who ordered the doctor's execution and why?"

Vargas placed the email containing the one-line death

order back on the desk. "The connection with Paz can't be a coincidence, so we have to assume he issued the order to his former henchman. But God knows why."

He scanned the fire-damaged room, his eyes settling on a large grey metal filing cabinet with four deep drawers. "Maybe the answer lies somewhere inside his patient files. We'll need to take them with us when we head back to Buenos Aires, but right now I'd like to have a chat with Héctor Rojas."

Ojeda shook his head. "I checked in with one of the doctors at the hospital a couple of hours ago. Although his wound wasn't life-threatening, he's packed full of painkillers and is drifting in and out of sleep."

Katz was already on her way towards the door. "Let's get over there and wake the bastard up."

Chapter 32

El Bolsón, Argentina

C hief Inspector Ojeda led the way across the tiny car park and through the entrance of the hospital, with Vargas and Katz following closely behind. The unimposing single-storey structure coated in rough white plaster and crowned with a wooden vaulted roof with a matching arched doorway appeared at first sight to look more like a church than a hospital. Directly inside the main entrance was a small A & E reception area and running off it to the left was a single narrow corridor with ten rooms for inpatients.

Rojas had deliberately been placed in a room at the very end of the corridor, so no one had any reason to pass it. As they approached, Ojeda slowed down and pointed to the last door on the right.

"He's in that one but, as I said, I've no idea if he'll be conscious."

Katz stopped and looked around the corridor. "Where's the doctor's wife, Julieta?"

"She's gone. They moved her earlier today to a far better equipped hospital in Bariloche, about seventy miles away. She's in a coma and needs a level of medical care they simply can't provide here."

Ojeda pushed open the blue door and the three of them entered the sparse, dimly lit room containing nothing more than a side table on casters positioned alongside an ancient black metal bed, currently occupied by the unconscious hitman. Rojas was propped upright against the bedhead and the right side of his neck and shoulder were heavily bandaged where his collarbone had been blown apart, courtesy of Ojeda, less than twenty-four hours earlier. A plastic intravenous line running the painkiller Meperidine had been inserted into one of the larger veins of his right arm.

Katz brushed past the two detectives, leaned down towards the bed and shoved the hitman's upper body with such force the drip line ripped from his motionless body and his torso almost rolled onto the floor. Despite her best efforts, Rojas remained unconscious, and all Katz could do was utter an Israeli curse under her breath. Ojeda watched on in silence and then attempted to prop Rojas back into a central position before moving away from the bed.

"They've pumped him so full of painkillers, it's hardly surprising he's completely out of it."

The Mossad agent wasn't having any of it. She frowned and shook her head. "This is total nonsense. We've no time to waste. We need to interrogate this bastard as soon as possible. Tell his doctor to cease all painkillers overnight. Let him suffer. By the morning the pain will be unbearable and he'll beg to tell us everything he knows in exchange for some drugs."

Ojeda was startled by the cold-blooded ruthlessness of the Israeli agent but Vargas was firmly onside.

"Leah's right – we have no time to play games. We need some answers."

Katz turned towards the door and Vargas followed suit but wasn't quite finished with issuing instructions.

"We need an armed officer placed outside the room. The man who recruited Rojas is more than capable of sending a second hitman to take him out if he thinks he might talk. We'll meet you here at eight in the morning to begin the interrogation."

* * *

The Cypress Hotel, located close to the surgery, was the only one in El Bolsón with decent Wi-Fi, making it the obvious choice for their one-night stay. Both were famished, so immediately after checking in they met up in the cosy ground-floor steak restaurant where they demolished a couple of sirloins, accompanied by a local Pinot Noir – the most expensive bottle on the menu, even though it was less than twenty dollars. They spent most of the time talking through every aspect of the case, although Katz seemed particularly interested in learning every detail she could about the man known as the Black Scorpion.

"Nic, the break-in at the chemical plant to steal a banned antimalarial drug and the murder of a small-town doctor are two random events directly linked to Paz, who we know has been working for the Franklins since they broke him out of Valledupar. There must be a connection – but what the hell is it?"

"Right now, we can't see it, but trust me, Leah, we're really close. We might get a break when we see Rojas in the morning. That was a good call to turn off his drug supply, although I'm not sure Ojeda was overly impressed."

For the first time since they'd met, Katz momentarily let her guard down and burst into spontaneous laughter. "Well, I doubt if he or the good people of El Bolsón have ever had a Mossad agent pay them a visit before. Was I too direct?"

It was Vargas's turn to smile. "Maybe a touch, but you said what needed to be said. Hopefully we'll reap the benefits in the morning."

For the next few seconds neither of them spoke. Vargas drained his glass and Katz checked through the latest messages on her phone. The chief inspector finally broke the silence with a blunt gear change.

"Leah, how did you end up becoming a Kidon operative?" It was a roundabout way of asking how she'd ended up becoming an assassin for the world's toughest secret service.

Katz held his gaze and then took a deep breath before replying. "Do you want the full story or the cut-down version?"

"I'd love to hear as much as you want to tell me."

Her remarkable green eyes momentarily flicked away from his, as if she were about to reveal a guilty secret.

"I guess it all started with my father. Although he never admitted it, the truth is he always wanted a son. After he got over the initial disappointment of my birth, I was brought up as a tomboy. As a kid I was more into toy guns than dolls – more a Ken than a Barbie. I was born in Holland, and my parents lived and worked in Amsterdam, but when I was five, they emigrated to Israel. My dad was a successful engineer and my mum worked as a lawyer. We settled in Tel Aviv where it was commonplace to see soldiers roaming the streets and I was totally captivated by the sight of them. I fell in love with the Israeli Army uniform and my dad bought me a full set of fatigues for my seventh birthday. After that, I was hooked."

She paused for a moment as if sensing she'd said too much, but Vargas was fascinated and wanted to hear more. He gestured towards their empty glasses.

"Shall we get a refill?"

She nodded and picked up where she'd left off. "I couldn't wait for my eighteenth birthday to arrive – when I'd be conscripted into the Israel Defence Forces for a minimum of two years. Most of the girls looked for admin roles to pass the time before they could get back to civilian life, but I was different. Within three months of initial training, I joined the Caracal Battalion, a light infantry force that patrols the Egyptian and Jordanian borders looking for potential terrorists trying to gain entry illegally. I was so proud of the day I received my first rifle, a Tavor TAR-21 fully automatic assault rifle chambering 5.56 calibre rounds. It was a thing of absolute beauty – a treasured possession that meant everything to me."

She paused as a waiter returned to refresh their glasses and Vargas took the opportunity to steer the conversation.

"Did you see any action on the border? Is that when you were recruited by Mossad?"

"No. I spent eighteen months desperate for any excuse to test my Tavor but absolutely nothing happened and, as my conscription came to an end, my parents insisted I return to full-time education. Two days after my twentieth birthday I enrolled as a student at Haifa University to study history and modern politics, and for two years I went through the motions but then—"

"But then what?"

"Then a game changer. I was carrying out some research in the vast reading room inside the library when a lecturer I'd seen around the campus pulled up a chair. I didn't know him, but he started chatting, and before he'd even said anything meaningful, I realised exactly who he was and why he was talking to me. His name was Asher Cohen – a recruiter and handler for Mossad."

"And when did you move into Kidon?"

"You mean when did I become an assassin?" For a moment it felt as if she was teasing Vargas.

"It was just a natural progression. I was good with guns and fearless, so they fast-tracked me into Kidon. You've got to remember, most of the time I'm working undercover as an agent in a foreign country. Killing plays a very small part in what I do. I'm basically a spy and my principal role is to help keep the country safe from potential foreign threats."

"Like we're doing right now?"

Katz's mouth gave way to a knowing smile. "Exactly like what we're doing now."

"Is that why you asked me so many questions about Paz?"

She savoured almost half a glass of Pinot Noir before answering. "Yep, Nic. I suspect that before this is over, I'm going to have to take out the Black Scorpion and, if you want to know the truth, I can hardly wait."

Chapter 33

El Calafate, Argentina

September 1967

Richard Franklin's twenty-first birthday present from his father came as a complete surprise. Adolf Hitler's son and heir was secretly hoping for a new car – specifically a Series 2 red Alfa Romeo, which had only come out the year before, or a limited-edition Cartier Tank watch with a midnight-blue Lapis Lazuli dial. What he was presented with instead was a twenty-five-year-old worn manila folder containing a set of original documents from the records department at Auschwitz. The discoloured cover bore the distinctive black image of the German military eagle above the words *Operation Gesamtkunstwerk*.

Hitler's son was sitting in his father's study, alongside Bormann, when his father proudly handed over the ancient folder with the same level of enthusiasm Richard might have expected had they been the set of keys to a new car.

The Führer was seventy-eight and suffering ill health, and all three men in the room knew it wouldn't be long before his liver and bowel cancer caught up with him, leaving Richard as his sole heir.

"Richard, the time has come for you to learn more about the huge responsibility that rests on your shoulders because I won't be around forever. Read carefully through the contents of this folder as tomorrow Martin and I are taking you on a trip to visit a research facility in Neuquén that belongs to Franklin Pharmaceuticals, a facility which technically doesn't exist."

Richard tried his best to hide his disappointment, made easier by a heightened level of intrigue to discover what secrets lay inside the folder. He said his goodbyes and retreated to his bedroom where he spent the following hours transfixed by its contents.

The following morning the trio were up early to board a small private plane for the five-hour flight to Neuquén. Just before midday the Lear Jet 23 touched down in a small private airfield on the outskirts of the industrial area, where a black Mercedes-Benz 600 Pullman Limousine was waiting to meet them. Thirty minutes later they were being shown around the interior of the research facility by Josef Mengele, who was as obsequious as ever. He moved slowly to accommodate the snail's pace of the Führer who, he calculated by the grey pallor of his skin only had a few months left to live at best. Personally, he would be counting the days. He decided to focus on the future, and that meant gaining the trust of Richard who no doubt would soon be calling the shots. Mengele figured the young man would have no basic knowledge of the complexities involved in creating and manufacturing a new drug and he turned the dial up to full volume on the bullshit meter.

"Richard, the biotech industry has come a long way in the

last few years. With the advance of technology comes the opportunity for state-of-the-art research and development facilities such as this one to thrive as we pursue the goal of creating a drug that can ably fulfil your father's dreams. Our biochemists are making breakthroughs all the time and we are gradually coming closer to finding the correct formula. Under my careful stewardship, it will only be a matter of time before we get there."

Bormann was quick to pour cold water on Mengele's bragging. He despised the old man who he believed to be a fraud. "Mengele, for all the millions of dollars the Führer has poured into this enterprise, there appears to be a remarkable lack of progress. As far as I understand it, up to now none of the female captives who have been tested with the drug over the last twelve months have successfully been sterilised. So, where the hell is the progress?"

Mengele bit his tongue, fully aware of the huge influence Bormann wielded over Hitler. He secretly hoped that in time Richard would prove to be his own man and not remain in the pocket of the former Nazi party secretary.

"I assure you, Martin, we are making amazing progress, but patience was never one of your virtues. Remind me, which ones do you have?"

Richard stifled a laugh at Mengele's sharp riposte. He was genuinely impressed by Mengele's demeanour and in-depth knowledge on a subject he'd only learned about for the first time the previous day. He was fascinated – intrigued even, by the history surrounding Auschwitz and was determined to hear first-hand details from the man the Jewish inmates named the "Angel of Death".

"Doctor Mengele, I'm keen to learn a great deal more about

this whole operation, so I'd like to spend substantial time here during the next few months. Would that be all right with you?"

Before Mengele could reply, Hitler, breathing heavily, spoke. "That's an excellent idea. Richard, I suggest you forget about returning with Martin and me in the morning and move into a hotel nearby. I'll tell Eva to arrange for some of your clothes and essentials to be flown up here. Why don't you stay for at least a month and then you can return to El Calafate and give me a full report of your findings."

Richard nodded his head in agreement. Once again, his control freak of a father was shaping his destiny, although, on this occasion, he was happy to comply because he was excited to learn as much as he could about the development of the sterilisation drug. The Führer was clearly exhausted but at the same time seemed delighted by the way events had panned out. He thanked Mengele for his time and led Bormann and Richard towards the reception area of the facility.

"Let's get back to the hotel. I need a rest and then we'll enjoy a meal together." Hitler glanced across at Bormann. "Martin, I hope you remembered to send the hotel chef my full list of requirements."

"Yes, Führer. He's preparing a fresh dish of Leberknödel with a side portion of mashed potatoes."

* * *

In the evening they sat in a small private dining room where a revitalised Hitler did very little talking at first – his entire focus was spent demolishing the contents of a white bowl of hot broth containing two liver dumplings, cooked just to his liking. It didn't take him long to polish it off and then he set about tackling a plate of mashed potatoes coated with a sprinkling of peas and carrots.

Bormann had planned to use the dinner as a convenient backdrop for digging his knife deeper into the middle of Mengele's back but observed how good Hitler's mood was and decided to save his scripted rant for another occasion. Instead, he resolved to play the sycophant card.

"Führer, it gives me so much pleasure to see Richard following in your footsteps. It must make you feel proud to know your legacy is in such safe hands."

Richard thought it strange Bormann was addressing his father about him as if he weren't in the room, but he was genuinely thrilled to have apparently pleased his demanding father.

Hitler spoke for the first time since finishing his meal. "Martin, it validates everything you and I have worked for during the last thirty-five years." The Führer then turned his focus to his son. "Richard, be wary of Mengele. I'm not sure he's totally trustworthy and I suspect the research and testing is not going as well as he suggests. I believe this process could take many years to perfect, so you must promise me you'll never give up until you have the drug safely in your hands, as well as the means of delivering it on a mass scale. I won't be alive when it happens, and it's even possible it may fall to your own son to fulfil my prophecy, but you must swear an oath to me it will remain a priority in your life long after I've gone."

Richard leaned forward and took hold of his father's right hand, which was vibrating against the top of the table. "Father, I swear on the sanctity of the Third Reich that I, and indeed my son, will pursue your vision and one day we'll bring it to fruition."

Richard looked directly into his father's eyes and made a vow there and then. He promised himself that when his future son reached the age of twenty-one, he'd have a similar talk with him to ensure the legacy would be passed on. As things worked out, on 15 November 1991, he did exactly that.

Chapter 34

The Blonde Lady, The Caribbean

F ranklin, Al Kathib and Paz were on board *The Blonde Lady*, relaxing in the hazy sunshine on the main deck by the side of the fifteen-metre pool, which had its tinted glass sunroof fully retracted. Nearby, a white-uniformed chef was checking the food inside a giant red-brick pizza oven, and for once Franklin was holding court on a subject other than the immediate plans facing them. He loved to boast and reminisce about his unique heritage, and while the Syrian appeared to lap it up, Paz struggled to conceal his boredom because he'd heard it all before from John's father, his previous boss.

"My grandfather was not just a genius; he was an innovator who began to tackle the Jewish problem head-on soon after he came to power in 1933. He'd already characterised the effect of the Jewish presence inside Germany as a 'race-tuberculosis of the peoples' to be eradicated at all costs. Then in January1939 he made a remarkable speech at the Reichstag that contained a key section that subsequently became known as 'The Führer's Prophecy'. I know that part by heart. My father taught it to me when I was a small boy and it's truly inspirational."

Paz grimaced; he knew he was about to hear a word-for-word recitation whether he liked it or not. Franklin was enjoying his memories far too much to notice the disinterested expression on the Black Scorpion's face.

"'If the international Jewish financiers in and outside Europe should succeed in plunging the nations once more into a world war, then the result will not be the Bolshevising of the earth, and thus the victory of Jewry, but the annihilation of the Jewish race in Europe!'"

Al Kathib was genuinely enthralled by Franklin's personal recollections of the most reviled dictator in history. The man who almost succeeded in taking out the entire Jewish race in one pass was regarded as a demigod by the Sunni Muslim.

"John, you have your grandfather's blood and passion coursing through your veins. Together, in his name and in the name of our beloved Prophet Muhammad, we will strike a huge blow against the Jewish race."

Paz couldn't believe the sick love affair he was witnessing, but equally knew he was a hired gun who owed his freedom to these two men, so, for now, he had no intention of rocking the boat. In fact, he sensed a large dose of sycophancy wouldn't go amiss following his recent screw-ups.

"Señor Franklin, I too am in awe of your heritage and am honoured to play a small part in the forthcoming operation."

Franklin soaked up the flattery without spotting the insincerity of the delivery.

"Paz don't underrate your role in all this. You'll be standing alongside the Taliban warriors as our plan plays out almost eighty years after my grandfather first had the idea tested in a shitty cell block of Jewish lab rats in a Polish concentration camp."

Franklin picked up his ever-present tumbler of bourbon and proposed a toast. Al Kathib and Paz raised their respective glasses in unison.

"Here's to *Gesamtkunstwerk*, an ingenious attack the Israelis won't even know has hit them until months later, and by the time they discover what's happened it'll be too late to do anything about it. And the best bit? When they try to work out who the perpetrator is, the Taliban's fingerprints will be all over it."

* * *

The hooded figure parked the rental in an unmarked country lane almost a mile away from the hospital, ensuring there was no chance of it being recorded on CCTV. Franklin's assassin avoided the main road and created an impromptu route through the woods that led to the west side of the small car park. A quick glance at a digital watch confirmed it was almost three thirty in the morning, the optimum time for an unscheduled visit when planning a murder.

Bypassing the front entrance and walking to the rear of the building, the killer stealthily searched for a way into the hospital. Two green industrial waste bins were parked on a raised slab of concrete about six feet away from a white metal door that had a toughened glass panel in the upper section featuring the words "Delivery Entrance" embossed in red. The three-lever mortice deadlock was in place, but it proved a minor obstacle for the professional, who made short work of it with the aid of a stainless-steel lock pick.

Once inside, the assassin moved silently along the narrow, green-tiled passage until reaching the small open-plan A & E reception area. The front desk was unmanned and the only sound to be heard came from inside the staffroom, where two night nurses were on a break. A swift surveillance revealed a gloomy corridor running off to the right, accommodating inpatients in ten single rooms.

The killer hugged the wall that formed a ninety-degree corner with the corridor and silently inched forward, gaining a partial view of the hallway. There was sufficient light to distinguish the outline of a figure sitting on a chair propped up against the back wall. The uniformed protection officer had been asleep for over an hour, but his Bersa Thunder 9 pistol was still firmly gripped in right hand, resting on his left knee.

The intruder retreated into the passage and fished out a Beretta 70 from a deep inside pocket. The aluminium frame already had a Spectre suppressor fitted, so the single-action semi-automatic pistol was good to go. Dropping to the floor with athletic ease, the lithe murderer slithered back to the corner, where a clear shot at the officer was now possible. The sound of a gentle thud echoed around the corridor as a single.22 calibre round penetrated the centre of the guard's forehead, creating a small hole. The officer's body slumped to the side but remained in the chair. However, his right hand relaxed its grip on the gun and the weapon clattered onto the tiled floor.

The killer spun on instinct to face the staffroom, expecting the nurses to react to the unexplained sound, but nothing happened. They were still engrossed in their conversation.

After checking the uniformed officer's body to confirm the kill, the assassin turned to face the end door on the right-hand wall and calmly pushed down on the chrome handle. No movement registered in the bed when the door opened. The assassin moved silently across to the bed and stared down at their helpless victim.

Suddenly all hell broke loose as Rojas's eyes flashed open. At the same time his left arm flew into the air, striking the right arm of his assailant and knocking it skywards. For a moment, the tables dramatically turned, as Rojas reacted to the intruder's presence in a desperate, instinctive attempt to save his life.

But the assassin was just too quick. The gun barrel and suppressor came crashing down from a great height onto what was left of Rojas's smashed collarbone. The impact was so violent, he let out a howling scream as his brain flooded with a searing burst of pain. Mercifully the agony only lasted a nanosecond and disappeared courtesy of a bullet that entered his left ear and blew the side of his head clean off.

Mission accomplished; the assassin fired off a two-word text.

Problem nullified.

Somewhere in the middle of the Caribbean, John Franklin heard his phone register an incoming message. He rolled across the bed, grabbed his cell and read the good news. A menacing, self-satisfied smile broke out on his face. All was well and, at that precise moment, he felt invincible.

Chapter 35

El Bolsón, Argentina

Vargas and Katz were in the hotel dining room just after seven the next morning, picking at a traditional Argentine breakfast of toast and medialunas, accompanied by fresh orange juice and steaming hot coffee. They looked slightly the worse for wear courtesy of the two bottles of local Pinot Noir they'd consumed the previous night, but their quiet mood abruptly changed when Vargas took a call from Ojeda, who was already at the hospital.

Twenty minutes later they were in the A & E reception along with a heavy police presence. There was no sign of any visitors or patients as an active crime scene meant the hospital had been closed to the public. Ojeda waved them through and led them along the corridor, stopping by the body of the slain officer.

"A clean, precise headshot that we figure was fired from roughly twenty-five feet away – from the other end of the corridor. Evidently a professional assassin who didn't give my officer a chance."

Katz turned and stared back down towards the reception.

"It's strange, though, because the guard would have had a clean sight line of any intruder coming his direction."

Vargas nodded his agreement. "Yes, but I guess the assassin had the element of surprise on their side." He pointed to the door on the right. "Let's take a look at our friend in there."

Ojeda led the way inside the room where Rojas's head wound was being photographed by a forensic pathologist who moved away from the bed to allow access for the three visitors.

Ojeda placed his hand on the doctor's shoulder. "Henrique, give us five minutes on our own and then we'll leave you to it."

What was left of the hitman's head was not a pretty sight.

Vargas grimaced as he leaned over the bed to take a closer look. "Another headshot and, judging by the damage, this one was fired at close range."

Katz had clearly seen more than her fair share of mutilated victims and didn't seem fazed by the bloody carnage laid out on the hospital bed in front of her.

"Nic, this operation has Paz's calling card all over it. Do you think he was here?"

"No, he's a psychopathic killer – this is the work of a trained assassin. I don't think there's any doubt he gave the kill order, but he didn't pull the trigger himself." Vargas was despondent. "This is a real setback for us. We needed to find out why Rojas killed the doctor but instead we've had another door slammed in our faces … another lead closed down." Vargas walked to the door where he stopped and turned to face the Mossad agent. "Leah, there's nothing for us here. Let's get back to Buenos Aires and regroup with Hembury and Berrettini. I've a horrible feeling we're running out of time."

* * *

The huge screen inside the cinema room of *The Blonde Lady* was divided into five sections to accommodate a Zoom meeting between John Franklin and his four siblings. Franklin was positioned on a black leather couch directly facing the screen, while Paz and Al Kathib parked themselves on separate sofas, deliberately out of shot.

After a brief greeting, John zoned in on Simon, the investment banker based in New York. "We're getting close to initiating *Operation Gesamtkunstwerk* now, so let's make sure our ducks are nicely lined up. Simon, have you actioned the closure payment with our Afghan friends?"

Simon's body language was like an over-excited child as his words tumbled out. "Absolutely! Yesterday, I personally authorised a thirty-million-dollar transfer from your bank in Geneva using dummy accounts I'd already put in place. The funds went via twelve different routes before hitting the Taliban's account in Beijing. I received a WhatsApp message this morning from the foreign minister confirming the money had hit, so we are good to go."

"Excellent work, Simon."

Franklin switched his attention to David, the legal eagle and youngest member of the family, who was based in London. "David, are you happy with the paperwork the Arabs have prepared for transporting the goods from Kandahar to Israel, especially the permits for the three critical border crossings?"

The London lawyer was far less euphoric and reassuring than his half-brother in New York, and a slight undercurrent of contempt was evident in his reply. "John, as you'd expect, the documentation is written in Pashto, so even though I've had it translated, I can't vouch for its validity. For all I know, the paperwork could be sound, or it might all be complete dog shit."

Franklin wasn't impressed by the insolent reply from the baby in the group and made his feelings clear. "David, you need to watch your tone, remember exactly who you are and show some respect for your heritage. Let's hope everything is in good order or I'll hold you personally responsible if the convoy gets delayed because of second-rate documentation. Do I make myself clear?"

Before David could reply, Eva interrupted with a change of subject, trying to lighten the mood.

"John, I see Paz took care of the meddling doctor before he was able to create too much of a problem, and I've taken care of the initial report he sent through to the Ministry of Health. It's well and truly buried."

Franklin couldn't resist using Eva's information to throw a quick put-down in Paz's direction. "Actually, Eva, Paz's soldiers screwed up on that particular assignment, but, fortunately for him, I was around to clear up the shitstorm he left behind in El Bolsón."

Paz's body physically flinched at the barbed comment hurled his way. He glanced across at Al Kathib who didn't even bother trying to suppress the hint of a smile that broke out across his thin lips.

Franklin signed off the Zoom with an impassioned call to arms. "We're all part of the same family. We share the same blood – the blood of the Führer. We stand on the verge of fulfilling a lifelong vision he first hatched at Auschwitz but never brought to fruition because he was betrayed by his own generals. He dreamed of achieving the final solution and now we have the means to deliver it. In years to come, the events of

May 4 2022 will be regarded by millions around the world as the greatest day in contemporary history."

* * *

Vargas and Katz were back in the familiar surroundings of the junior suite at the Marriott in Buenos Aires, where they were briefing Hembury and Berrettini on their visits to Córdoba and El Bolsón. The FBI man struggled to make sense of the brutal murders that had taken place.

"It seems to me, the killing of this doctor is inherently linked in some way to *Operation Gesamtkunstwerk*. The speed at which they moved to take out Rojas tells us they know we're on to them and were terrified we might've learned something vital from his interrogation. Fortunately, they failed to destroy Eduardo's files, so they've become a priority lead our team will go through, looking for clues as to what motivated his kidnapping and death. Nic, what's the status of his wife?"

"Not good, Mike. Sounds like she's in a coma for the long haul. It's doubtful she'll ever come round."

"Okay, so let's take stock. The stolen antimalarial drug must have other applications and we have just over a week to figure out what they are and how they relate to an attack against Israel." Berrettini turned to Hembury, deferring to the oldest person in the suite in pursuit of some wisdom. "What do you think, Troy?"

Hembury's lips formed a rueful smile. "I think we need a lucky break and, in my experience, the harder you work, the luckier you get."

Vargas patted his old friend on the shoulder. "Troy's right. Maybe it's time we started creating our own luck. I think a one-to-one with Eva Castillo is long overdue. We know the senator's up to her neck in this, even if she isn't the one pulling the strings. I'm going to pay her a surprise visit and see if I can spook her into making a mistake."

Hembury nodded his approval but added a cautionary note. "Go shake that tree, Nic, but be careful. Be on your guard for unpredictable behaviour. Remember, the bottom line is you're dealing with Adolf Hitler's granddaughter."

Chapter 36

Buenos Aires, Argentina

E va's day was steadily going downhill and, unbeknown to her, it was about to get a lot worse. She'd had a huge row with the head of her political party about a foreign policy matter, followed by a live car-crash interview for TN – the rolling news channel, with a left-wing reporter who'd accused her of being a fascist. Not only that but, in the last five minutes, she'd received a call from the porter at her apartment block, informing her the building had suffered a major power outage.

However, none of those events compared to the seismic reaction she experienced when her secretary entered her office to inform her she had an unscheduled visitor. "Senator, there's a Chief Inspector Vargas in reception requesting an urgent meeting with you regarding a security matter. I explained you had no time today but he's insistent he sees you right now. He won't take no for an answer."

Eva felt her entire body go limp as it slipped into meltdown. She found it impossible to catch her breath and could feel her heart pounding wildly inside her chest, as though it were trying to escape. The name Vargas triggered uncomfortable teenage flashbacks involving her adoptive parents educating her on who she really was and where her birth family originated from.

Nicolas Vargas was the man who'd humiliated and bullied her birth father, Richard, into killing himself with Hitler's infamous Walther PPK. He was also responsible for exposing the identity of her older half-brother, John, forcing him into faking his own suicide. One moment in time John was about to become the forty-fifth president of the United States and then, thanks to Vargas's intervention, he was forced to go into hiding as an exile from the world. Now, ten years later, just as they were within touching distance of pulling off a sensational blow against the Jewish nation, the man she'd been brought up to revile had surfaced once again. What did he know and what did he want with her?

She was desperate to call John for advice but equally was aware she had to somehow regain her composure and face Vargas down herself. After all, she knew her heritage.

As soon as she regained control of her breathing, Eva instructed her secretary to bring Vargas up to her third-floor office. The man who confidently strode through the door a few moments later looked exactly like the photos she'd seen, which was slightly unnerving as they were at least ten years old. Most people would have described Vargas as a handsome, charismatic man, but to Eva he was the devil incarnate with the sex appeal of a hideous gargoyle. *Sin vergüenza de mierda* – a shameless piece of shit.

Even the tone of his voice freaked her out when he introduced himself. "Senator Castillo, thank you for seeing me at such short notice. I really appreciate it."

Eva nodded and shot a glance at the wall-mounted clock. "It's a pleasure, chief inspector, but I can only give you ten minutes as I have back-to-back meetings stacked up with government ministers."

This time it was Vargas's turn to experience a flashback, which he chose to use to try and disorientate her. "That's ten minutes more than your father granted me the first time we spoke. It was on the phone, and as soon as I introduced myself, he cut me off."

Eva was bemused. To the best of her knowledge Vargas had never met her adoptive father. Where was this heading? "When did you call my father and why?"

Vargas took a short breath and readied to launch an initial hand grenade. "I called him around ten years ago to ask what he knew about the contents of a stolen safe-deposit box and why he'd sanctioned a trained killer, Matias Paz, to carry out a number of interrogations and murders."

Eva's crystal blue eyes couldn't hide the wave of shock and terror that overwhelmed her brain as the impact of Vargas's revelation struck home: the man facing her knew her true identity. Now the question was – how much more did he know? Rather than employ a strategy of denial, she decided to remain silent and try to regain her wits.

Vargas saw her utter bewilderment and looked to make a surgical strike. "Senator, the people of Buenos Aires believe you were named after their beloved Evita but we both know the reality. You were named after your paternal grandmother, Eva Braun."

Vargas paused for a reaction and was granted one as a series of worry lines magically appeared on the senator's forehead. Still she refused to speak, so he ploughed on.

"We know about your brothers and your secret get-togethers. In fact, I was in the hotel in Bariloche when you and your family and my old friend Matias Paz, recently met up. The Black Scorpion – you know, the man you personally helped escape from Valledupar?"

Eva's brain felt as though it were in a terminal spin as Vargas continued to deliver killer blows.

Having hit her with a catalogue of revelations, Vargas felt now was the right time to try a calculated bluff. "We know all about your planned attack on Israel and *Operation Gesamtkunstwerk*. Let's talk about why it will never work, and if you cooperate with me on preventing it, we can probably sort out a deal."

Vargas was now on a fishing trip, but suspected Castillo had no way of knowing that because his other claims had been bang on the money.

Finally, Eva found her voice. "Chief inspector, go screw yourself. I have nothing to say to you. If you or your colleagues dare go public with any of these false accusations, I will sue you personally, as well as the entire Buenos Aires Police Department. Now, get the hell out of my office."

Vargas realised he'd hit a dead end, so didn't bother to try another angle. He turned abruptly and walked across the office to the door but paused in the doorway to fire a final salvo that he hoped would hit home.

"Richard Franklin was an evil sociopath who did the world a favour by killing himself. Eva, you really are your father's daughter."

Chapter 37

Buenos Aires, Argentina

va's face was drained of colour and matched the porcelain tiles on the floor of the cubicle inside the female washroom, where she took some respite, desperately trying to regain her composure. She was perched on the pedestal with her cell clutched in her right hand, waiting for the phone to ring. Two minutes earlier she'd sent a short text to her older half-brother.

I've just had a visit from a ghost.

Franklin's curiosity got the better of him and he listened in silence as Eva gave him a word-for-word account of her confrontation with Vargas. He insisted she rerun the conversation three times and was calm enough to dissect and then identify the key moment of their conversation.

"Vargas knows nothing about our specific plans for Israel – he was bluffing. Most of what he came up with was nothing more than a history lesson. He and his associates gain absolutely nothing by outing your identity or those of our siblings. In fact, in their own interests they've deliberately kept everything a secret from the public since our father's death.

I told you before, we have somebody on the inside keeping me up to speed. Vargas and his colleagues are desperate to learn the intricacies of our plan but really have no idea what it is."

His utter self-confidence helped lower Eva's anxiety levels and she started to think rationally about the situation.

"John, what should I do next?"

"Inform the others that Vargas is scratching around for anything he can find out about our operation and tell them to keep their mouths shut. As for you, Eva, you just need to hold your nerve."

* * *

"How did it go with the wicked witch?"

Hembury and Berrettini were desperate for a positive debrief from Vargas following his meeting with Castillo. They hoped he'd gleaned something that might help them understand the nature of the imminent attack on Israel. The chief inspector leaned on his desk in the makeshift office the FBI deputy director had created inside his hotel suite.

"I definitely rattled her cage big time and she's running scared, but she refused to offer anything up. In the end, she told me to get the hell out of her office."

Hembury pushed his colleague for any possible strand of news. "What about Israel – did she say anything?"

"Honestly, Troy, not a word. All I can tell you is that by the look in her eyes, I hit the spot when I brought it up, but she just wouldn't give."

Berrettini sensed the drastic drop in morale both detectives were experiencing. "Guys, what we've proved is we're definitely on the right track, and Nic, now you've spooked Eva, there's every chance the Franklin clan will start making mistakes."

* * *

It had been almost twenty-four hours since Eva's fierce clash with Vargas and the wounds were still fresh. However, the chief inspector wasn't her only problem. She had another one far closer to home in the shape of Rocío Agüero, her personal research assistant who'd joined her staff eighteen months earlier.

Rocío was young, beautiful, extremely bright, and highly ambitious; an intoxicating combination of qualities that made her a formidable force of nature. She was named after the Virgin Mary, María del Rocío, although there was nothing virginal about her. She had the looks of a supermodel with her leggy, size-eight frame and her heart-shaped face, perfectly framed by a cascade of long curly black hair that complemented her glistening cornflower-blue eyes. She was without a doubt the full package. To complete her repertoire, she was also a martial arts champion, specialising in Kendo.

Rocío had an inbuilt awareness of her own beauty and knew exactly how to use it to maximum effect. But her stunning appearance only told half the story. Her superior intellect – an IQ of 159, placed her in the top one per cent on intelligence quotient scales, and in 2020 she graduated from Buenos Aires University with a first-class degree in history. Rocío's heroine was Eva Perón and, like her idol, she was driven by political ambition, so it was no surprise to any of her friends when her first job after completing her studies was a junior research assistant role inside the Argentine National Congress. It was while working there she first met Eva Castillo. But that was no accident. She was besotted with the senator and, like millions of voters who passionately supported her, had no idea of her real identity.

Rocío was one of three graduates offered coveted six-month contracts working inside the neoclassical Congressional Palace, located on Avenida de Mayo and home to the two houses of the legislature: the Senate and the Chamber of Deputies. She was based inside the enormous library where, along with a small, closely knit team, she was on call to senators who required information or extracts from the millions of books, articles and historic legal documents that were stored inside. When she wasn't chasing down material to photocopy and compile at extremely short notice, she was kept busy cataloguing new papers that arrived every hour of the day.

However, Rocío wasn't content to stay within the confines of the government library; her aspirations lay elsewhere. She'd identified the youngest senator in the National Congress, and deputy leader of the right-wing party Sovereignty, as a potential role model and, if she were going to follow in her footsteps, she needed to get close, and that meant taking a few risks.

When an urgent request appeared on the library computer hub from Castillo's office, asking for detailed information on the newly built reservoir and filtration facility near El Bolsón in northern Patagonia, Rocío printed out a hard copy and deleted the email from the system before any of her colleagues noticed it. She worked through the night, compiling everything she could possibly lay her hands on that might prove relevant, however obscure. By the time she'd finished, she'd created a stunning Word document containing dozens of photos, illustrations and articles presenting a comprehensive insight into the reservoir complex that provided clean, fresh water for the population in the Río Negro province.

When she was finally happy with the document layout, Rocío printed off the file and created a physical folder using a deep ocean-blue plastic cover with a small white circular label in the centre that simply read: "El Bolsón – reservoir and filtration plant. FAO Senator Eva Castillo". The eye-catching file and its contents were articulately and intelligently laid out, producing an exemplary presentation; in many ways the research folder was a perfect reflection of Rocío herself, and now she needed to hand deliver it to the woman she'd earmarked as her future employer.

The senator's third-floor office was located on the east side of the Congressional Palace, an area out of bounds to Rocío's laminated identification lanyard. However, the fact her ID failed to open some of the security doors en route from the ground-floor library was easily overcome by a combination of charm and smooth-talking, and at precisely eight thirty in the morning she found herself standing outside Castillo's office door, the blue file gripped firmly in her right hand. She paused for a few moments to stare at the brass nameplate in front of her and took a mighty breath before opening the door, preparing to make the pitch of her life.

Inside, she was greeted by Ana Paredes, Castillo's personal secretary, who glanced up from her desk with a slight hint of surprise on her face as she didn't recognise the young intern but was immediately struck by her beauty and presence. Rocío ramped up the charm to full volume as she explained she had completed an urgent research document for the senator and wished to hand it over in person. Three times she was asked politely to leave it and go and each time Rocío held her ground, emphasising her need to talk through some of the finer points of the presentation with the senator in person. Finally, Paredes ran out of patience and was reaching for the phone to call for assistance from in-house security when the door swung open and Eva Castillo appeared. She immediately sensed tension in the air and the obvious stand-off between her secretary and the young lady whom she thought was one of the most stunning women she'd ever seen outside the cover of *Vogue*.

Rocío was quickest out of the blocks. "Senator, my name is Rocío Agüero. I am a research assistant in the house library. It's such a privilege to meet you in person. I'm a huge supporter of your work, particularly the campaigning you do for our people in the northern regions who are suffering at the hands of immigrants from Paraguay and Bolivia – who our government are allowing to pour into the country."

Eva was taken back by the unexpected, passionate outburst from the young beauty in support of her politically controversial right-wing policies.

Rocío seized the moment and held up the blue file in her right hand. "Senator, I have prepared a detailed document for you on the El Bolsón water project and, if you'll allow me the time, I can take you through it in person."

Parades had heard enough. She cut in abruptly, "Senator, you have a Zoom with the deputy leader of the House in five minutes."

Castillo ignored her secretary and turned towards Rocío, who was still holding the file. "Rocío, how do you like your coffee?"

Agüero had done her homework on the senator and knew she

survived on a diet of black coffee and Red Bull, supplemented by fish and eggs. "Americano, no sugar."

Castillo gestured towards the inner door leading to her private office, and as she moved towards it, called over her shoulder to her secretary, "Ana, two Americanos and cancel the Zoom."

Chapter 38

Buenos Aires, Argentina

D uring the following eighteen months, Rocío thrived in her role as Castillo's personal aid and the two women became almost inseparable. Her natural beauty and sharp intellect often wrong-footed political opponents, which delighted the senator, and with only a seven-year age difference, she treated her assistant, in many ways, like a younger sister. Rocío helped prepare detailed speeches and presentation documents for the House and hardly put a foot wrong. The only time the two young women ever had an issue was when Eva blanked out her diary for certain Zoom calls and meetings, the nature of which were kept secret from Rocío. Eva would simply taunt her by saying they were beyond her pay grade – a comment Rocío found patronising but also intriguing.

However, as the months passed, another problem emerged that developed into a constant, sensitive issue between them. Rocío was a social climber as well as a political one, and the Buenos Aires newspapers and celebrity magazines embraced her in their glamorous world. Her model looks and status as a political influencer working for one of the most powerful senators in the country made her perfect tabloid fodder. She was forever being photographed in the company of rock stars, famous actors and wealthy socialites and she revelled in the attention. At first, Eva found it quite amusing, but as the pressures associated with the imminent approach of *Operation Gesamtkunstwerk* began to increase, she became irritated by the constant exposure and decided to confront Rocío over her nocturnal behaviour. The two of them were being chauffeur driven across the city to a meeting with a local business leader when Eva, never one for small talk, cut straight to the chase.

"Rocío, you need to put a brake on your social life, at least for the next few weeks. The problem being every article about you inevitably references me as your boss and right now I could do with keeping a lower profile."

Castillo was astonished by the waspish retort that came her way.

"Eva, I work my butt off for you, so just keep your nose out of my private life. What I get up to when I'm away from work is my business. You have your ambitions and I have mine."

Rocío had seriously crossed the line but didn't care. She knew she held strong insurance for her insolent behaviour and remained unfazed as the senator predictably let rip.

"You stupid, ungrateful slut. I gave you a break from that dead-end job in the library and this is how you dare speak to me? You think you're irreplaceable? I've got news for you, you're not. Don't bother coming in tomorrow. As of right now, you no longer work for me. When the car stops, you can piss off to one of your sleazy bars and hang out with your cronies."

Rocío held her nerve and pulled out her ace card. "That's not how it's going to play out, Eva. I think I'll stay in the job for as long as it suits my purposes, unless you want me to start talking to some of my journalist friends about your involvement in the Valledupar Prison massacre. I'm sure they'd love to ask why you hired a young actor to visit an infamous lifer just a week before it kicked off – an actor who was then found mutilated in his apartment a few days later. They'll hold the front page for that story. Oh, and by the way, what did that chief inspector want yesterday?"

Castillo was stunned into silence by Rocío's brazen blackmail threat, and for the remaining few minutes of the journey neither spoke. Their meeting with the business leader lasted barely fifteen minutes before the senator made her apologies and left on her own. Eva jumped into a yellow cab and headed for her apartment in Puerto Madero. She was shaking with rage at being held to ransom by her impertinent assistant who knew far too much for her own good. She was reluctant to contact John again so soon, but this matter was urgent, and she felt she had no choice. She fired off a text to the one person she knew could make her problem go away.

I have an urgent issue with my personal assistant that requires the special skills of the Black Scorpion asap.

As soon as Eva sent the text, she regretted the flagrant show of panic, and when the reply came through a few seconds later she regretted it even more.

Eva, you're a big girl. Clean up your own mess.

Castillo cursed as she read the devastating reply but knew Franklin was right.

Once she was back in the sanctity of her own home, she poured herself a large Jim Beam and began work on a removal plan for Rocío Agüero. Her assistant held information that could lead to her arrest and public disgrace, as well as potentially screwing up the entire operation she'd been working on for months with Franklin and her other siblings. There had to be a quick, simple way of eliminating Rocío; she was far too dangerous to have around.

Strangely, the answer came to her later that evening through the unlikely vehicle of Netflix. It was past midnight and Eva was in bed, scrolling through the menu looking for a new thriller that might be absorbing enough to distract her from the problem at hand. As the cursor sped across the box set offerings, a moment of clarity sparked an idea. She was staring at an image of Kevin Spacey posing to camera in his role as President Francis Underwood in the award-winning series *House of Cards*. She'd viewed all the episodes at least twice and recalled how he'd removed the troublesome journalist Zoe Barnes, who'd posed a threat to his presidential aspirations, with a simple shove in the back. She clicked on the boxset and began searching for the opening episode of the second season and a particular scene set in the fictional Cathedral Heights metro station in Washington.

Chapter 39

Buenos Aires, Argentina

E va knew she had to work quickly. She left her dockside flat in the east of the city an hour earlier than usual, although she still made her regular fifteen-minute cab journey to the Palace of the Argentine National Congress. Once she arrived, she strolled directly past the neoclassical facade and headed for the entrance to the nearest metro station, less than a hundred yards away. The underground system in Buenos Aires, known as *Subte*, was the oldest in Latin America, having opened in 1913, and Congreso Station, on the blue Line A, was one of the first to be opened in the city.

Eva made her way down the concrete steps, commuters weaving past her, shoulder to shoulder, in the opposite direction. She used cash to purchase a ticket, enabling her to pass through the barrier with no digital trace, and headed straight for the platforms. Eva knew Rocío made the brief daily commute from her apartment located near the 9 de Julio Station, five stops to the east.

She walked along the narrow white-and-red platform, glancing at the massive, tiled frescoes adorning the wall, illustrating Argentine farmers working in the crop fields. A line of floor-to-ceiling posts, painted red and positioned a couple of feet away from the electrified line, ran the length of the platform and provided the potential for a natural hiding place. Once she'd seen what she needed, Eva retraced her steps and emerged on Avenida Rivadavia, where she hailed a cab and headed for the city centre. There was more work to be done – she needed to secure a few crucial props and that meant a quick shopping trip to the Galerías Pacífico mall.

It took her less than fifteen minutes to track down the random items on her list: a khaki cotton-twill trench coat, a pair of black thick-framed glasses, a navy-blue headscarf, and a synthetic short blonde wig with a fringe. Armed with one large carrier bag, she opted to walk the two miles back to the National Congress building, which gave her some valuable thinking time.

Once she entered the palace, Eva walked straight past the bank of lifts in the central hallway and headed for the back of the ground floor where she spotted a single unisex toilet positioned a few yards from the rear entrance. She'd never seen it before but, then again, she'd never entered or left work from the rear of the building. Walking towards the lifts, she smiled inwardly as she noted that today would be the first time she'd ever taken a human life and, strangely, she felt good about it.

The rest of the day flew by in a frantic blur, which wasn't unusual as countless meetings, phone calls and Zoom conferences ran into each other and, with no time to break for lunch, sustenance came via a cold egg salad courtesy of a delivery bike. Eva had three short sessions with Rocío and went out of her way to be warm and friendly, acting as if nothing had happened the previous evening and hoping her vain assistant would assume her thinly veiled threats had done the trick. At five o'clock she was ready to begin her calculated play, which began by calling Rocío into her office for an unscheduled meeting.

"I'm going to head off early and carry on at home." Eva swept her right hand over her forehead in a flamboyant gesture. "I can feel a migraine coming on and, as you know, tomorrow morning I have that mother of a speech to give to those bastards at the Association of Latin American Commerce that I still need to work on. Can you do me a huge favour and go through the current draft one more time and email over a new copy with your extra notes included?"

Having undeniably secured her job with her performance the previous day, Rocío was happy, for now, to revert to playing the role of enthusiastic puppy desperate to please its owner. "No problem. It'll take me the best part of an hour and some, so I'll get it over to you by six thirty at the latest."

"Perfect. I'll see you in the presentation hall tomorrow at nine. Have a good night."

With that, Eva stood up from her desk, grabbed the shopping bag and almost raced out of the office. Five minutes later, she was standing inside the small toilet she'd recced earlier in the day, altering her appearance using a handful of props. She carefully placed the headscarf on top of the wig, deliberately allowing a small amount of blonde hair to remain uncovered, as if by mistake. She used a wet wipe to completely remove her make-up, and once she put on the heavy-framed glasses the transformation was complete.

Eva took a few moments to study her reflection in the small wall mirror, relishing the reality that the face staring back at her belonged to a virgin killer. Her thoughts were interrupted by the piercing sound of her smart watch alarm signalling five thirty. By her own schedule, it was time to make her way to the east platform at Congreso Station, where she would position herself behind the first red pillar facing the entrance stairway and wait for as long as it took, for her victim to arrive.

* * *

Rocío made a final check of the tracked Word document containing the senator's speech before saving it as an attachment and firing it off with an email to her boss. She was pleased with her notes and had gone the extra mile as a way of reingratiating herself with Castillo following their dust-up the day before.

She glanced down at her watch – it was six thirty-five. It had taken a bit longer than she'd planned but the pay-off would be worth it in the morning if the speech was a stormer. There was still time to get back to her apartment, grab a quick shower and just about make an eight thirty dinner date at Don Julio's, the hottest steak restaurant in the city, with an equally hot companion. She gathered up her things and dashed out of the office, her thoughts now sharply focused on the night ahead.

Rush hour was at its peak and Rocío literally fought her way down the station steps, forming part of a bulging wave of commuters, all heading in the same direction. As she reached the congested platform, she registered the sheer number of bodies standing between her and the open doors of a train that had just pulled in. Rocío knew she had no chance of making it but was determined to catch the next one, and so began to weave her slim frame through some improbable gaps between people that didn't really exist. Somehow, she made it to the platform edge just as the double doors to the carriages slid to a close, jamming the passengers inside like sardines. For a moment, her body was pinned hard against the yellow aluminium frame of the train exterior by the weight of the human surge behind her. The pressure eased after a few seconds and, as the train pulled away from the platform, Rocío caught her breath and took a small step back from the edge, pleased she was now in pole position.

Eva kept a careful eye on her from the cover of the wrought-iron pillar less than six feet away. She turned up the collar of the khaki trench coat and checked the digital display on the overhead read-out that showed the next train was due in one minute. It was time to act. She threaded her way through the throng of bodies with the finesse of a lioness silently eyeing up unsuspecting prey, and as the sound of the approaching train rang through the tunnel, she eased into position directly behind Rocío, whose mind was faraway, contemplating her outfit for her date.

The threatening noise of the incoming train was almost deafening as Eva made her move. She leaned forward and pressed the weight of her right elbow into the middle of her assistant's spine and then casually pushed down. Rocío felt the impact immediately and stumbled forward towards the open rails below her, but in a desperate, instinctive attempt to save her life, her highly tuned martial arts reflexes kicked in and she swivelled around in a tiny circle, allowing her arms to lunge forward, randomly searching for something to catch hold of to maintain her balance. The outstretched fingers of her right hand grabbed Eva's collar in a vice-like grip. For a nanosecond the women caught sight of each other as Castillo pushed forward again, this time even harder, underestimating the strength of her young assistant.

The train came barrelling towards the platform, just as their bodies tumbled over the edge together, entangled in an ugly fight to the death they were both destined to lose. As the pair smashed down onto the electrified rails, they locked eyes once again before everything went black and they disappeared under the front of the train. Piercing screams from horrified onlookers echoed around the platform as witnesses watched on in stunned disbelief. A few minutes later, when the traumatised driver reversed his train back up the track, there was nothing about the hideous bloody mess splattered across the rails that resembled a human body.

Chapter 40

Buenos Aires, Argentina

The Buenos Aires transport police worked through the night, desperately trying to get a lead on identifying the remains of the two women who'd tragically fallen under the metro train at Congreso Station. Eyewitnesses spoke of a violent struggle between them in the immediate moments before they fell onto the track.

There were two angles of CCTV available, both of which covered the incident, but only on wide-angle lenses that didn't help when it came to identification. The investigators zoomed in on the footage but the best they could ascertain was that a dark-haired young female – the woman closest to the edge of the platform, appeared to turn and attack the blonde-haired woman standing right behind her, and then, within a couple of seconds, they both fell forwards onto the track. The only other clues to their identities were the remnants of a blonde wig and a platinum ring inlaid with three small diamonds. Their remains had been scraped off the rails and taken away for forensic examination and DNA tests, but all that would take time.

The first breakthrough for the investigators came at about nine twenty, nearly three hours after the incident occurred. One of the witnesses, Martina Duarte, a young language student, was convinced she'd recognised the dark-haired woman from social media postings and magazine articles. She couldn't name her but was pretty sure she was a minor celebrity. One of the officers sourced a link to relevant online publications and Duarte diligently searched for a matching reference. It didn't take long. A full-length photograph of Rocío wrapped around the torso of a popular daytime soap actor as the pair emerged from the legendary Jet Lounge nightclub hit the jackpot. Duarte swore the face on the computer screen belonged to the young woman she'd seen earlier that evening at the station.

Events moved fast after that initial identification. It was quickly established that Rocío's phone was switched off, no doubt crushed during the incident, and a work colleague confirmed she commuted every day via Congreso Station. No one had seen or heard from her since she'd left the National Congress building earlier in the evening, supposedly on her way home. Furthermore, it soon came to light that Rocío worked as a personal research assistant to Senator Castillo, the high-profile right-wing senator. Therefore, the tragic death of the young woman was undoubtedly going to make front-page headlines. The breakthrough that followed was a game changer for the investigation.

One of the officers, Sebastián Kempes, was the first to put two and two together when he discovered Castillo's cell was also off the grid. There was no answer from her home landline either and the porter in her apartment block confirmed he hadn't seen her arrive back that evening. Kempes tracked down the senator's secretary, Ana Parades, who confirmed two vital pieces of information: firstly, Castillo had left the office at about five, supposedly to go home and work on a speech, and, secondly, she wore a platinum ring inlaid with three diamonds on the index finger of her left hand. Although the investigators had to wait for forensic confirmation, as they moved into the early hours of the morning and with no sign of either of the women, they were convinced they had the correct identities of the two victims.

No one found out who leaked the story or seemed to care if it was true or not, but at eight in the morning, millions of breakfast television viewers and radio listeners across the country woke up to the news that Senator Eva Castillo and her personal assistant Rocío Agüero had died in bizarre circumstances following a fight on the platform at Congreso Station. Their headshots were televised next to each other by news broadcasters across the country, and before midday their images were plastered on the front pages of every national print publication.

* * *

Franklin was in his stateroom mulling over the implications of the shocking death of his half-sister, which had completely taken him by surprise. However, his ruthless, robotic brain was unaffected by emotion – it had no space for anything other than his own well-being and the success of the forthcoming operation in Israel. Undoubtedly, Eva's issue with her personal assistant had been far more serious than he'd imagined, and he briefly regretted not intervening to sort the problem when he saw the frenzied media coverage created by her death, which he despised. Franklin consoled himself with the thought that this was obviously a personal drama, which would hopefully disappear once the initial hysteria had calmed.

He typed out a holding text to his half-brothers and hit send:

Eva died in a tragic accident. Nothing to do with our work. Just hold your nerve and all will be well. If you are approached by any police officials, especially Vargas, do not engage. Call me immediately and I'll take care of it. We are nearly there.

Eva was the only one of his younger siblings he held an ounce of respect for, although he wondered if her premature death might turn out to be a blessing in disguise. Ultimately, she was a potential loose end who'd pretty much served her purpose, and he made a mental note that once *Operation Gesamtkunstwerk* was successfully enacted, it would be prudent to take care of his half-brothers. For now, he needed to keep them onside. After which, they were fair game.

* * *

Hembury was sitting at his desk working on his laptop. He was ploughing through countless media accounts of the sensational double tragedy that had captivated the nation.

"Christ, Nic, what the hell did you say to her?"

Vargas was pouring out coffee for Katz and Berrettini and the three of them broke into a sudden bout of laughter.

"Thanks for that, Troy. But, seriously, how weird is this entire story? I smell Franklin and Paz's fingerprints all over it. Maybe I spooked Eva to the point where she was going to break cover and tell us what the Israeli play is?"

Berrettini shook his head and sipped his coffee.

"I don't think so, Nic. Our team have seen the CCTV footage and it looks like a frantic catfight between Eva and her assistant with no one else involved. Listen, I really hate coincidences – they very rarely happen in our game, but, for once, I think we're looking at an unfortunate event that has nothing to do with our case."

But Vargas was like a dog with a bone and wouldn't let go. "I can't accept that, Mike. Eva's death must be connected to Franklin somehow." He shook his head slowly. "Though I suppose whatever the answer, it's yet another potential route shut down."

"I know Nic, but it's not all bad news. I've had my team chasing up a new lead that might just blow this whole case wide open."

Chapter 41

Roseau, Dominica

T he volcanic Caribbean Island of Dominica, with its tiny population of seventy-five thousand, lies between the former French colonies of Guadeloupe to the north and Martinique to the south and is known for its natural hot springs and tropical rainforest. It's also home to the imperial amazon parrot and the world's second largest hot spring, known as Boiling Lake.

Apart from those few highlights, it's regarded as one of the remotest and quietest of the Caribbean islands where not a lot happens apart from an excessive amount of drinking of the local bush rums. Dominicans have been processing sugar cane for centuries, creating a ground zero version of rum known to the locals as "Caribbean Moonshine". Most of the island's social life revolves around the western port of Roseau, which is also the capital and home to a small collection of bars and cafés. The Restless Python was one of the newer and more popular beachfront establishments to spring up, and locals and tourists alike packed in most nights to sample the famed python pie, with its mystery ingredients, accompanied by a selection of rum-based cocktails.

It was approaching midnight and Pete Renton and Neil Piotrowsky were sat at the same wreck of a wooden table they'd occupied for thirteen nights in succession. They were fully absorbed in a game of dominoes, borrowed from the bar owner Joseph with whom they'd bonded after numerous rum sessions that usually lasted till the early hours. No one knew Joseph's true age, but Pete and Neil speculated he could be anywhere between forty and seventy.

The two men were former US military turned mercenaries, who in previous lives had proudly served in the Virginia National Guard 2nd Battalion, 224th Aviation Regiment. In recent years they'd grown disillusioned by the constant defence cuts and postings in Afghanistan and Iraq, which had made little sense to them. They were now highly paid freelancers working for private military contractors who dispatched them to war zones around the globe at short notice, but unlike their spell in the military they could always say no if they didn't fancy the smell of the mission.

In their late thirties, they were both pretty much at their physical and mental peak, prepared to take on most challenges that came their way. The pair were human fighting machines, equally at home with hand-to-hand combat or flying attack helicopters. Right now, they were in between missions and enjoying spending their hard-earned bucks on a paradise island where nobody knew or cared who they were. They were casually decked out in nondescript T-shirts, cut-down denims, and cheap trainers, happily playing the role of a couple of regular American tourists.

Neil was holding a solid bone domino tile in his right hand, carefully weighing up his options, when the noise of a smashed bottle coming from the bar area broke his focus and that of his companion. Their good friend Joseph was standing behind the bar, facing up to four young locals, all wearing matching black T-shirts and jeans, as though it were a uniform.

They were taunting him, and it was apparent that one of them, who was built like an all-American footballer and was probably the leader of the group, had just smashed a perfectly good bottle of rum on the bar top, drenching it with dark brown alcohol and tiny glass fragments. Neil was too far away to hear what was being said but it was obvious their friend was being threatened. He was frantically nodding in agreement to whatever was being asked of him. The leader of the gang grabbed hold of Joseph's shirt and lifted the frightened man off his feet, dragging him over the bar until his face was only inches away from his persecutor. Neil had seen enough and leapt out of his chair, but Pete gripped his arm and shook his head.

"Neil, not now. Just chill until those boys leave and then we'll find out what's going down."

Neil nodded and slowly sat back at the table, just about holding his temper as he watched the four men laugh while Joseph yelled in pain when the tiny shards of glass pierced one of his elbows. Everyone in the bar, other than Neil and Pete, was looking at the floor, ignoring the browbeating playing out in front of them.

A few moments later, after the four young men had strolled out of the bar, laughing all the way to the exit, the mercenaries sprung out of their chairs and ran across to Joseph, who was attempting to clean up the bar top with the aid of an old blue tea towel. He was ignoring his injuries, but his entire body was shaking with fear from the episode. Both men made their way to his side of the bar and Neil put his arm around his shoulder.

"Joseph, let me take a look at your elbow and Pete will clear this mess up."

The relieved barman dropped the soggy cloth and walked across to the small stool normally used by staff for short rest breaks. Neil went with him and on the way stopped to rip off a stack of paper towels from a small pack he'd spotted on one of the shelves underneath the bar. The bloody wounds were only superficial and Neil ran the towels under a cold tap before wrapping them around Joseph's elbow.

"What the hell did those jokers want?"

Joseph eased his back against the wall and smiled at his friend. "Money, of course. They're part of an established gang who work the bars and cafés in Roseau, demanding protection money. If I don't pay up, they'll smash the shit out of the place, which will force me to close, so either way I'm screwed. We've been open three months and I knew it was only a matter of time before they hit me."

"How much do they want?"

"Two hundred dollars a week, but that's just for starters because we're a new business. Most of my friends along the beach pay five hundred. The two biggest bars pay seven fifty."

Neil thought for a moment before asking his next question. "When are they due back?"

Joseph was slightly puzzled but happy to reply. "Same time tomorrow, when they'll expect to collect their first payment."

Chapter 42

Roseau, Dominica

The following evening, at about eleven o'clock, Pete and Neil returned to the Restless Python and shocked Joseph when they ordered a couple of Diet Cokes on the rocks.

"Boys, at least let me lace it with some of my moonshine."

Pete laughed but shook his head. "Not right now, Joseph, but we promise normal service will resume just after midnight."

The mercenaries nursed their soft drinks while keeping an eye on the time. When it reached eleven forty-five, they casually stood up and wandered out of the bar without attracting a ripple of attention. The Restless Python was the last property on that stretch of beach, and as soon as they were outside, they walked across the rough black sand to the side wall of the nearest café – about ten yards away. Then they tucked themselves into the shadows and waited.

Just after midnight they heard chatter, and as it grew louder it became clear the young gangsters were heading their way. Neil and Pete held their positions until the very last moment and stealthily emerged from the semi-darkness, creating a human shield between Joseph's bar and the four men. The gang had no option but to come to an abrupt stop, slightly bemused as to how the two strangers had appeared from nowhere and wondering what they wanted. Their designated leader quickly regained his composure and puffed out his massive fifty-inch chest as an act of intimidation. His left hand withdrew a giant carving knife from the brown leather sheath hanging off his belt.

"What do you old white men want – maybe a good cutting?"

His backing boy band laughed on cue. Neil, however, was unimpressed and seemed almost bored as he replied.

"Big boy, put your bread knife away and run back home to your mother. We work for Joseph and have some money for you."

Neil reached into one of the front pockets of his denim shorts and retrieved a single five cent coin, which he threw onto the sand with as much contempt as he could muster.

"Pick it up, then piss off and don't come back."

The leader's face broke into a twisted snarl. He took a half-step back to join the line of his three amigos who simultaneously produced different sized knives that they arrogantly flashed in the air. But Renton and Piotrowsky held their ground, their hands resting by their sides, waiting for one of the knifemen to initiate an attack.

The leader's bravado returned – basic maths reassuring him that four knives to zero gave him and his boys an unassailable advantage. He'd no idea he was about to take on two human lethal weapons and, in reality, the odds were heavily stacked against him.

He let out a war cry and the four youths leapt forward in unison, brandishing their blades. Renton reacted a millisecond ahead of his colleague. He spun on the spot and catapulted himself into the air like a guided missile. His right foot was at least six feet off the ground when it connected with the leader's left temple, just above his ear. The stomach-churning cracking sound that coincided with the moment of impact failed to drown out the piercing scream of the stunned man that echoed out across the sea. His body folded like a cheap pack of cards and his crumpled figure slumped onto the black sand.

A moment later Piotrowsky landed a murderous kick to the groin of another assailant, who fell to the ground as though someone had opened a trapdoor under his feet. The mercenary used his forward momentum to barrel into the body of the third knifeman with such force that the youth flew backwards under the sheer weight of the physical assault. He released his grip on his knife and, as his right arm frantically searched for it in the dark, a forceful left elbow smashed into his windpipe so hard his Adam's apple disappeared, as did his life.

Renton was now in a crouched pose facing up to the last man, who was trying to process the shocking turn of events he'd just witnessed. He launched his knife towards the lapping waves of the Caribbean and scampered away with the speed of an Olympic sprinter. The former soldiers were leaning down to check on the body count and collect the weapons when they heard the familiar sound of safety catches being released from a pair of automatic rifles. A single voice boomed out from the looming darkness behind them, issuing a command.

"Raise your hands high in the air and slowly turn around."

They glanced at each other for a moment before doing as they were instructed. Facing them in the gloom were two island policemen, immaculately dressed in white shirts and dark blue cotton trousers with matching caps. Both officers held Remington assault rifles that were currently aimed at their heads. The policemen had witnessed the brutal demolition of the local gangsters and were wary of the two men standing in front of them. Unbeknown to the mercenaries, Joseph had taken matters into his own hands and earlier that night had informed the police about the extortion he was being threatened with by the local gang.

"Now, lie face down in the sand and place your hands behind your backs."

* * *

Berrettini had been pacing around the suite for over forty minutes, thoroughly involved in a long-distance call. When it finally came to an end, he was desperate to break the news to his colleagues, who could feel the excitement vibrating off him.

"That call was from a colleague at Interpol who looks after the Caribbean region. One of our agents contacted him yesterday when they saw a report concerning two American tourists who were arrested in Dominica for killing three local villains with their bare hands. Once they sent through fingerprints and headshots, it didn't take us long to identify them as Pete Renton and Neil Piotrowsky, a pair of former US Army vets who work these days as top-of-the-range mercenaries."

Vargas was running on a short fuse, as were Hembury and Katz. "Mike, where is all this heading?"

"Patience, Nic. I promise you I'm getting there. When I checked out their army records, I noticed they flew attack helicopters in Afghanistan for over three years during the war. That got me thinking about what the hell those guys were doing on a Caribbean Island in the middle of nowhere, so I asked my contact to check out the hangars at Canefield Airport, which is just outside the capital where the soldiers were arrested. Guess what they found?" Berrettini didn't give any of them a chance to answer his question. "A gleaming Sikorsky UH-60 Black Hawk, last seen transporting the Black Scorpion out of Valledupar Prison."

Chapter 43

Roseau, Dominica

Berrettini laid on an FBI company jet to fly Vargas and Hembury from Buenos Aires to the island haven of Dominica, where the two American mercenaries were being held in the state prison in Roseau. The Gulfstream V took just over seven hours to cover the three-and-a-half-thousand-mile journey. The elegant landing at Canefield Airport provided spectacular viewing for the two men as the single runway butted hard up against the Caribbean Sea on the island's west coast and waiting to greet them on the tarmac was the police commissioner, Lincoln Valerie, a veteran officer who was delighted to be involved in an international crime investigation, even though he'd no idea why Interpol had instructed him to fully cooperate with the two visiting detectives. He was an honest, proud man who had served in the police force for over forty years, joining as a junior officer in 1978 when he was eighteen, the same year the island gained its independence from the United Kingdom.

He welcomed Vargas and Hembury with a beaming smile and a firm handshake. "Gentlemen, I assume the first thing you'd like to do is check out the Black Hawk." He pointed east of the runway. "It's just over there in one of the private hangars."

* * *

The iconic helicopter was named after the Native American Sauk warrior, Black Hawk, and the Sikorsky UH-60 looked as imperious as its namesake, positioned in the centre of the grey steel hangar, one of three huge storage units located at the far end of the airport complex. When the giant automatic doors slid open on their tracks, the four matt-black titanium rotors glistened as they were illuminated by the bright sunshine that flooded inside, transforming the interior of the hangar from a dull darkness into full daylight. The Hawk's impressive footprint was sixty-five feet long and eight feet wide, with a height of just over sixteen feet. The massive rotors had a span of over fifty-three feet. The police commissioner held back as Vargas and Hembury positioned themselves in front of the squat nose and took in the view of the magnificent fighting machine.

Vargas had never seen a Hawk in the flesh, other than the burned-out remains of the downed one in the courtyard at Valledupar. "It's a beast but at the same time it's a thing of real beauty. Do we think it could have made it all the way from Colombia to here in one journey?"

Hembury was walking towards the side door of the Hawk, which was open. "Yes. It has a range of almost fourteen hundred miles and Valledupar to Dominica is just under nine, so I don't see why not. What we badly need to find out is whether Paz came all the way here or if he was dropped off on the way."

Hembury clambered inside with Vargas following close

218

behind. The first thing they spotted was a coil of wire rope and a winch lying on the floor in the middle of the fuselage.

Hembury pulled on a pair of clear latex gloves that he lifted from his jacket pocket before holding up a small section of the rope. "What's the betting the Black Scorpion's prints are all over this? He probably held on for dear life as they winched him up. I'll ask Mike to send out a couple of his team to crawl over this baby and lift whatever clues they can find."

Valerie was leaning against the door of the Sikorsky, straining to hear what was being said inside. "Gentlemen, if you're done here, I'll drive you into Roseau where you can begin your interrogation of our two prisoners."

Vargas turned and made his way to the door, where he stepped down to join the commissioner. "We're good to go, but before we do – what can you tell us about when the chopper arrived and how it ended up in this hangar."

Valerie had been secretly hoping they would ask those exact questions as it gave him an opportunity to impress the detectives with the investigative work his men had carried out in the previous twenty-four hours.

"It seems the Black Hawk landed here sometime between eleven and midnight a fortnight ago. Because it was so late, the airport was officially closed, but it turns out one of our air traffic controllers was paid a great deal of money to open the airport surveillance radar to supervise its safe landing. Two of my men spoke with him last night and he admitted receiving five thousand dollars in a bank transfer in return for less than an hour's work. He was aware there were a couple of privately owned hangars currently empty, so he opened this one to house the Sikorsky. You're more than welcome to interview him yourselves, although he swears everything was done by email, including the initial approach, and he has no idea who he was working for. At the time he couldn't see any harm in allowing the helicopter to land."

"Great work, commissioner. We don't need to see him but I'm sure our colleagues at the FBI will want full details of the email chain and bank transfer to see if they can unpick anything. Now, let's go and pay a visit to the two human killing machines you currently have locked up."

Chapter 44

Roseau, Dominica

I t took just under ten minutes for Valerie to drive Vargas and Hembury from the airport to the outskirts of Roseau, where the only prison on the island was located. The Mitsubishi Outlander pulled up in the small car park outside the dilapidated two-storey building that looked as though it should be condemned. The tiny jail only had room for one hundred inmates but currently there were over double that number jammed inside, living in appalling squalor. As they followed the commissioner through the wire mesh doors that led inside the ramshackle structure, both detectives were hit by a vile stink emanating from the main cell block up ahead. Vargas almost gagged as he struggled to cope with the disgusting odour and Valerie noticed his discomfort.

"Chief inspector, I apologise for the lack of sanitation inside this establishment, but our meagre budgets don't allow us to provide anything more than very basic accommodation for our island's criminals. I won't offer you a guided tour – I don't think your stomach would survive it. Instead, I've asked the warden to set you up in the visiting room where the prisoners will be brought across to meet you. Thankfully, it's in another section of the prison where the smell isn't quite so apparent."

The inmate visiting room was basically a bare grey concrete box, no bigger than a hundred-and-twenty-foot square. Its only furniture was a single table with two chairs on either side and a large jug of water with four glasses on top of it. The warden had obviously prepared for their visit, but the white plastic chairs would have benefited from a good wipe down. Unfortunately, the commissioner was wrong about the acrid aroma that still poisoned the air, and to make things worse Vargas spotted a small procession of massive black beetles scurrying along the skirting before disappearing through a mouse hole. Standing in one of the corners of the room were two uniformed, armed guards who stared on impassively with their AK-47s locked and loaded.

"The prisoners are on their way down, so I'll leave you to it. I hope you get what you need from them."

With those parting words the commissioner disappeared, leaving the detectives alone with the guards. Moments later, the far door opened, revealing Renton and Piotrowsky. They were herded inside by two other guards who led them, hobbling, towards their chairs before turning and leaving. Both mercenaries were restrained by heavy-duty handcuffs as well as medieval-style manacles around their ankles. It was clear from their pissed off expressions, neither of them appreciated their new environment. Vargas figured they would do just about anything to get out of the stinking pigsty, or at least he hoped that would be the case.

"I'm Chief Inspector Vargas from the Buenos Aires Police Force and this is Lieutenant Hembury from the LA Police

Department. We'd like to find a way to help you get out of this cesspit."

Renton's poker face switched to a quizzical stare. "You guys are a long way from home. What's your beef with a couple of army vets?"

Hembury glanced at Vargas before beginning. "Fellas, we haven't got a great deal of time, so here's how this is going to work. You're going to tell us who hired you to fly the Black Hawk into Valledupar Penitentiary and the exact location you delivered Matias Paz to after you broke him out during the massacre. A great many people died in that bloody raid, plus we have the three gangsters you took out here, so if we walk out of this room empty-handed, I promise you'll both spend the rest of your miserable lives inside this disgusting institution." Hembury turned towards Vargas before continuing. "Now, my colleague here, the chief inspector, is fighting back the urge to vomit any time soon, and once that happens he's gone, so I suggest you start talking quickly or—"

Renton cut in, interrupting the police lieutenant. "And what's the upside if we play along and help you out?"

"We'll let you scumbags walk out of here and vanish to some godforsaken corner of the world."

Piotrowsky spoke for the first time. "How come you've got the power to make all this disappear? How do we know we can trust you?"

"Here's the thing, we have much bigger fish to fry than you two clowns, so don't waste our time. Start talking or we'll throw away the key."

The two soldiers exchanged a swift knowing glance and Renton began. "A few weeks ago, we were finishing up an assignment in Yemen for a private contractor when we were

223

approached by a stranger at our hotel bar. He seemed to know a great deal about us but specifically wanted to check out how comfortable we were handling Hawks, which for us is a bit of a no-brainer. Our daily rate is ten thousand dollars, but he offered ten times that. At first, we thought he was a joker, but that changed when he came up to my room and produced a suitcase with two hundred and fifty thousand dollars inside, which he offered up as a deposit—"

Hembury butted in. "What was his name?"

"When a stranger offers you that sort of money, you don't ask their name unless they volunteer it. He was an Arab who spoke the Queen's English – I'd guess he was educated in the UK."

Vargas reached for his phone and flicked through his photo album until he found a headshot of Al Kathib. He placed the phone on the table with the screen facing up. "Is this the man?"

Piotrowsky nodded. "Yep, that's the arrogant bastard. Anyway, we signed up for the job and the rest you pretty much know. Pete and I were part of two teams of pilots that collected the Hawks from a small, disused airstrip just outside of Montería, which was controlled by some local drug lords. We flew north-west out to sea and then headed inland to Valledupar for the rescue mission."

Hembury took up the questioning. "Did you know the identity of the man you were rescuing?"

"No, our operating orders were on a need-to-know basis. We were told he'd be waiting by the western wall of the courtyard."

"Okay, here's the million-dollar question that is going to decide your fate – where did you drop him?"

For a moment, neither of the mercenaries answered and then Renton spoke.

"It was weird. We were given exact coordinates that took us about fifty miles off the northern Colombian coastline, bang in the middle of the Caribbean."

"A boat?"

"Yes, a monster private yacht with its own helipad."

Vargas could hardly contain himself. "What was its name?"

"I told you, we never ask for names. But I can supply you with the precise coordinates we were given. You'll be able to check out the name of the boat for yourselves."

Vargas and Hembury exchanged a knowing look, acknowledging they'd finally got the breakthrough they needed. Vargas retrieved a biro from his inside jacket pocket along with a small notebook.

"Okay, hit me with the numbers."

Renton broke into laughter.

"If you can get us out of this stinkhole today, I can save your tech team a great deal of time and effort."

"How so?"

"Neil was doing all the flying when we dropped that goon off and I was doing a bit of sightseeing. As we headed away, I caught the name of the mega yacht from the side of the bow."

Vargas and Hembury held their breath and nodded their agreement to the deal on the table. Renton milked the moment for all it was worth.

"It was called ... *The Blonde Lady*."

Chapter 45

Roseau, Dominica

Vargas and Hembury spent the first hour of their return flight on the Gulfstream preparing their notes before joining an encrypted conference call with Katz and Berrettini to deliver a debrief on their findings from their whistle-stop visit to the island of Dominica. The deputy FBI chief led most of the questioning.

"So once again Al Kathib appears in the background pulling the strings. I wonder if he owns *The Blonde Lady?* Or does it belong to baseball cap man?"

Vargas was quick to offer his opinion. "Somehow my gut tells me it's the latter, but nothing about this case so far has played out the way we expected. How easy is it to pin down the location of the yacht?"

"I've already been speaking to my counterpart at MI6 and I'm sure they'll help us with this. There are dozens of commercial apps out there that provide boat-tracking services, but the facility at GCHQ in Cheltenham in the UK is another level. By the time you land we'll know exactly where *The Blonde Lady* is hiding out and everything about its on-board facilities and ownership. Thanks to your mercenary friends we're already aware it's equipped with a helipad, so we'll prepare for an aerial visit."

Hembury glanced down at the notes on his laptop. "Mike, what about the deal we cut with the army boys?"

"I'm all over it, Troy. Interpol have sent two senior officers to the island to process their release, along with a small forensic team who'll sweep the Hawk for evidence. Now, you guys get some shut eye and we'll see you in a few hours. Leah and I will start preparing everything we need for our surprise visit to the superyacht."

Once they'd finished the call, Vargas grabbed a couple of Buds from a small glass fridge – one of the many perks that came with flying on an FBI private jet. He flipped back the ring pull and downed a huge gulp of ice-cold beer, which provided a welcome shot of adrenaline. Refreshed and invigorated, he felt ready to address the elephant in the room; raising the question that had been on his mind ever since Renton had supplied them with the name of the boat.

"Troy, do you think the use of the word 'blonde' is a total coincidence or a nod to the past? Is it a subtle connection to El Blondi? Could John Franklin possibly be alive?"

Vargas was attempting to join the dots with Hitler's secret hideaway in El Calafate in Southern Patagonia. The sprawling estate he'd settled in after the war, which Vargas and Hembury had uncovered during their investigation of the Franklin family ten years earlier, had been named El Blondi in honour of the Führer's beloved pet Alsatian.

"Nic, I've had the same thought, of course, but the implications are huge. Let's just keep an open mind until we find out more about the boat, and maybe keep this little nugget between ourselves for now."

Hembury took a swig of beer and at the same time the ring finger on his other hand pushed the black recline button on the arm of his leather seat, converting it into a horizontal position. "Let's get some rest, Nic. There's plenty to dream about."

* * *

The Hostage Rescue Team, the elite tactical unit of the FBI, was originally formed to respond to crisis situations across America, but in recent years its special agents had taken part in numerous foreign escapades whenever the national interests of the United States came under threat, whether from terrorists or violent criminals.

For amphibious operations, where they were required to board an enemy ship, their counterterrorist team usually flew in an olive-green tactically enhanced Bell 412 helicopter. The FBI agents inside the chopper were armed to the teeth with an assortment of assault rifles, sub-machine guns and grenade launchers and were ready to deploy on a new mission within four hours of being alerted.

Berrettini, Vargas, Hembury and Katz formed a tight group as they stood on the side of the main runway at the military airport in El Palomar watching a small team of elite agents prepare the Bell 412 for take-off. The FBI deputy director was clearly not messing about when it came to boarding the mysterious yacht known as *The Blonde Lady*.

"Our friends at MI6 have provided us with the exact location of the yacht and are tracking it as we speak. Currently, it's about fifty miles off the coast of Uruguay, south-east of Montevideo, in the South Atlantic – a long way from where it met up with the Black Hawk in the Caribbean. Its ownership is buried in a holding company registered in Liechtenstein, and even the Brits at GCHQ are struggling to ascertain who it really belongs to. We know from its original plans that it's fitted with an antiballistic weapons system, but for all we know, since it was first commissioned, it may have added some offensive weaponry as well."

Berrettini paused to point towards the agents who were loading up the Bell 412. "If we receive a hostile reception when we try to land, these guys are the best in the world in rappelling onto a moving vessel. You guys will be joined on the chopper by three of their best men. Nic, you'll take charge, alongside their senior agent, Tom Leonard – I'll introduce you to him before take-off."

Berrettini left the group and headed towards the helicopter to seek out Leonard. Hembury was the only one of the three who'd heard of the infamous HRT agents and was truly in awe of their reputation. He turned to face Vargas and Katz with a large grin on his face.

"We're in the best hands travelling with these guys. There's a great story about the HRT that really sums up their ethos. They were set up in the seventies by a former FBI director, William H. Webster, who's a bit of a legend himself. A few months after the special unit was formed, he paid a visit to their base and inspected the military equipment inside one of the helicopters. He noticed there were no handcuffs and inquired about it. One of the senior agents replied, 'We normally put two rounds through their foreheads. The dead don't need handcuffs.'"

Katz nodded her head as a gesture of respect to the anecdote. "My sort of men. Maybe some of them are Israelis."

Chapter 46

The Blonde Lady, South Atlantic Ocean

I t took ninety minutes before the pilot flying the Bell 412 first spotted *The Blonde Lady*, which was sailing at a gentle fifteen knots about two miles west of the chopper. Tom Leonard, the senior HRT agent, unbuckled his belt and moved upfront to sit alongside the pilot. Everyone on board had radio comms and listened carefully as he barked out his orders.

"In a couple of minutes, we'll be directly above the yacht. We'll come in low from the south-west and hover about one hundred feet above the landing pad. Nic, we'll tune you in to their radio so you can speak directly with the captain. If we receive a hostile reception, I'll take control of the landing operation. Is that clear?"

Nic gave a thumbs up from his seat. "Crystal. Just give me the nod when you want me to jump on."

The Bell 412 dived down towards its target, tracking directly above the helipad on the yacht, maintaining a height of one hundred feet. Leonard gave the signal to Vargas, who depressed the button on his radio.

"This is a message for the captain of *The Blonde Lady*. We have agents on board from three national governments and intend to board your yacht safely and without incident. Decrease your speed and deploy your sea anchor as soon as possible. Please confirm you understand these instructions."

Apart from the static there was a prolonged silence of about thirty seconds that caused concern among the three HRT agents who started to prepare for the worst. Then the void was broken by a friendly Italian voice speaking in English.

"This is Captain Francesco Ricci on board *The Blonde Lady*. I'm very happy to cooperate with your instructions but how do I know you aren't a band of pirates?"

Vargas was slightly perplexed by the not unreasonable query and thought for a moment before replying. "Okay, give me your email and we'll send through ID."

A few minutes later Ricci's phone was bombarded by emails embedded with PDF attachments containing IDs of elite police forces from across the world. As he issued instructions for the yacht to slow to a stop, the bemused captain wondered what the hell he was caught up in.

The pilot of the Bell 412 made the landing appear effortless. As soon as he cut the rotors, Leonard led the team out through the side door and onto the deck of the superyacht. The first thing that struck Vargas was just how quiet everything was on the seven-tier monster. For a boat that size, there was no sign of crew or passengers; no sign of movement at all. They had their weapons drawn and Leonard stealthily led the way down one level, towards the pilot house, in search of some life.

Just as they reached the triple glass door entrance, a lone figure, immaculately dressed in whites broken up by four yellow stripes on his epaulettes, emerged from the deserted bridge. The bewildered captain raised his arms in terror as he registered six assault weapons aimed in his direction. He tried his best to keep calm but could feel his entire body shaking. Vargas lowered his weapon and, moments later, everyone else followed suit. He could smell the fear Ricci was experiencing and sensed it was the right moment to dial down the terror.

"Captain Ricci, I'm Chief Inspector Vargas from the Buenos Aires Police Department. Please excuse the invasion of your boat but we're here on a matter of great importance."

The Italian regained his composure as well as his confidence. "Grazie, Signor. I can assure you there's no danger for your people on this vessel. Please can you put your weapons away and explain to me what this is about?"

Leonard, accompanied by the two other HRT agents, left to check out the rest of the yacht, while Vargas, Hembury and Katz followed Ricci into one of the lounge areas, sited one deck below the pilot house. By the time they'd settled into four luxurious armchairs, enough small talk had taken place to reassure the captain he was no longer in any kind of personal danger. Vargas did his utmost to establish a rapport with the Italian and led the questioning.

"Captain, is the owner somewhere on board? It's important we meet with them."

Ricci took a few deep breaths before hitting them with his tale, which no one saw coming. "My story is strange and yet it's all true. I hope you believe me because I do not lie."

The captain paused and Vargas realised he wanted some kind of affirmation and obliged. "I believe you are an honest man. Please continue."

"Thank you, Signor. Fifteen hours ago, I was contacted by a freelance agency I regularly work for with an unusual request. They needed me to crew up a superyacht with immediate effect for a one-month duration. I was in Rio, having just finished another job, and the boat wasn't far away, which is no doubt why they chose me. As a freelance I often work at short notice, but I have never been offered a job like this one. At first, I said no, but then, as my countryman Don Corleone famously said in *The Godfather*, they made me an offer I couldn't refuse. Then there was the problem of a crew. A boat this size requires a crew of at least fifty, and it became clear after a couple of hours they could only find thirteen at such short notice. I thought that was the end of it, but apparently the owner made it clear there would be no guests on board and a skeleton crew was acceptable. The money was exceptional, so everyone said yes. We were brought in by helicopter and most of the old crew and any guests had already left by the time we arrived."

Vargas shook his head in disbelief. Once again, they were behind the eight ball. "Captain, what are your instructions?"

"Very straightforward. We're to cruise around the east coast of South America until we receive new orders. Everything about this job is strange but—"

Vargas's headset crackled into life as Leonard came on. "Nic, this boat is like an opulent *Marie Celeste*. There's a handful of crew in the engine room but other than them it's deserted. Worse still, it looks as though anything of any interest has been cleaned out."

"Okay, Tom. Keep searching for any clues and we'll join you shortly."

Ricci spoke, having heard the radio chat. "When we first landed on the yacht, I witnessed the remnants of the old crew frantically throwing items overboard – lots of black bin bags stuffed full of papers and other assorted items. It was total chaos."

Vargas had heard enough. "Captain, thank you for your honesty. Please return to the bridge and we'll speak again later."

Ricci didn't need asking twice. He stood up and scurried away.

Katz waited for the captain to exit before speaking. "Nic, this smells like an inside job. Without doubt, whoever owns this floating palace was tipped off we were on our way."

"Yes, it's not the first time they've been one step ahead of us. Remember the assassination of Rojas – just hours before we were due to interrogate him?"

Hembury nodded in agreement but tried to lift the mood. "Look, they had so little time to clear this boat, let's take a good look around and see what we can find."

For the next three hours, the three of them tore the boat apart, piece by piece, looking for anything that might offer a clue as to who owned *The Blonde Lady*, but the cupboard was bare. Finally, Vargas and Hembury ended up in what was clearly the owner's bedroom. A vast, lavish space occupying almost a third of one of the decks with sensational one-hundred-and-eighty-degree views. The colour scheme was cream and turquoise and the decor oozed decadence, courtesy of an interior designer who'd been gifted an unlimited budget. It was stunningly fitted out, with a massive circular bed positioned in the centre of the open-plan area, alongside a six-person jacuzzi that adjoined an enormous walk-in shower.

All the toiletries had been cleaned out and a pungent odour of cleaning fluids hung in the air. The two detectives sat on the edge of the bed and glanced around at the splendour surrounding them. Vargas was shattered and his mood was darkening by the minute. His tired eyes continued to search the stateroom and settled for a moment on a hand-carved ivory bookcase positioned in front of one of the few walls that wasn't solid glass.

"Looks like the owner wasn't too bothered about leaving some of their books behind."

Hembury half-heartedly glanced across at the bookcase and was about to look away when he spotted something odd, something that couldn't possibly be right, something that triggered a violent memory from many years ago. He looked again and did a double take before jumping off the bed, heading towards the bookcase, his eyes zooming in on a specific book.

He grabbed the red leather first edition and held it for a moment in his right hand before tossing it across the room to Vargas who caught it but was struggling to work out its significance. That was until he read the title, embossed in old gold letters. Hembury couldn't contain his excitement a moment longer.

"Christ, Nic, this is the very book Richard Franklin showed me in his study in San Francisco ten years ago, minutes before he blew his own brains out. It was his prized possession – a precious family heirloom. Hugh Trevor-Roper's definitive biography of his father and John's grandfather, *The Last days of Hitler*. There can only be one reason why it's here."

Vargas gripped it firmly in his left hand. "Troy, this has to mean that John Franklin's alive after all. Can you believe it! This book nails the identity of baseball cap man. The clever bastard faked his own death and is obviously the secret force driving this entire operation, with Al Kathib and Paz in tow."

Hembury was as astonished as Vargas. "Mike will not believe this. The FBI swallowed the suicide bullshit hook, line and sinker. But the question is, where is Franklin right now and can we track him down in time?"

235

Chapter 47

Carmel, California, United States

6 February 2012

J ohn Franklin knew his life was over, so there was nothing left for him to do but formally end it. Incredibly, just twenty-four hours earlier he'd been within touching distance of the White House; the beneficiary of a virtual coronation from the Republican Party who'd anointed him their presidential candidate.

With just nine months before the election, he'd enjoyed a massive poll lead over the incumbent Democratic president, but now that ambition lay in tatters. Hours earlier, his identity had been exposed and the world's media had crucified him. He'd fled his office in San Francisco in search of sanctuary at his father's hideaway sea ranch where, in less than two hours, he'd consumed a bottle and a half of bourbon followed by a barbiturate chaser. A deadly combination he'd hoped would numb his mind and aid his suicide.

Carmel Beach was one of the most iconic spots on California's central coastline, renowned for its surf, and as Franklin walked deep out to sea, battling the fierce incoming waves of the Pacific, he went under for the second time. A few seconds later he surfaced, gulping for air, his lips stinging with seawater. He was determined not to turn back but was stopped in his tracks by the familiar voice of his father echoing inside his head.

"John, swear an oath to me on your twenty-first birthday, just as I did on mine to my father. Promise me, you'll do everything in your power to fulfil the Führer's Prophecy."

Over twenty years before John had made a solemn pledge to continue the relentless pursuit of a perfect sterilisation drug that could strike at the very heart of Israel, the Jewish state his grandfather had vowed to destroy. The dream of one day implementing *Operation Gesamtkunstwerk* was an obsession that had galvanised his grandfather and father and now, at this precise moment, it inspired John to reject death and cling to life. The alcohol-induced fog inside his brain began to clear and he commenced the long swim back to shore.

Franklin burst through the front door of his father's house and began manically ripping off his sodden clothes, leaving a haphazard trail along the maple wood hallway on his way to the ground-floor shower room. Once inside, he allowed the hot water stream to drench him, hoping somehow the scorching water would wash off the events of the previous few hours. It felt like a safe place – an escape from the madness closing in on him, and he remained there for almost an hour. Eventually he got out, towelled off, grabbed one of his father's dressing robes and brewed a pot of coffee. Mug in hand, he returned to the main living area, where he spread himself out on one of the huge cream fabric couches facing out to sea.

He reached for his cell and the screen notified him of over seventy missed calls. He scanned through the list, and one name jumped out at him, beckoning him to return the call. Joe Warner was vice president of Franklin Pharmaceuticals, based in their San Francisco head office, and was one of John's closest allies and personal friends. They had many things in common – including their secret lineage, as both men were direct descendants of prominent Nazis. John trumped him in that respect – his grandfather being the leader of the Third Reich, but Joe's paternal grandfather, Otto Brandt, was no slouch when it came to mass genocide. As a lawyer and SS officer he'd headed up Hitler's controversial euthanasia programme and was responsible for the deaths of over two hundred thousand Germans with incurable diseases, mental illness, or physical handicaps. Brandt claimed to be a "mercy killer" who'd systematically exterminated those vulnerable groups on the direct orders of the Führer to help purify the Aryan race.

Joe picked up the moment he spotted Franklin's ID. "John, where the hell are you? Are you okay?"

Franklin had just downed a second mug of black coffee in an attempt to sober up as fast as possible, and was chain-smoking his way through a pack of Marlboro Red.

"Joe, I just tried to take my own life, but I couldn't see it through."

"Christ. Where are you?"

"I'm at my dad's sea ranch in Carmel. Do you remember you came to one of his summer parties here a few years back?"

Warner was already in the hallway of his house, searching for his car keys. "Sure, I remember. I'll be there in two hours. Don't do anything until I get to you."

"Joe, I need to disappear. You've got to help me."

"Don't worry, I'm on it. I've already got an idea."

* * *

By the time Warner arrived at the sea ranch, Franklin had dressed in a fresh set of clothes taken from the guest bedroom where he often stayed for long weekends with his family. Sheer relief was plastered on his face when he greeted his old friend; he was no longer fighting against the odds alone. For a while they reflected on the events of the previous few hours, both agreeing there was no way back to public life for Franklin. Then Joe listened intently as John recited the details of his botched suicide attempt and immediately spotted an opportunity.

"Before we leave here, we'll gather up your wet clothes and leave a few clues that indicate you drank heavily, took some barbiturates and then went down to the beach on a suicide mission. Your face is so recognisable we need to get you out of sight, and I have a plan to make that happen. We'll hole up here for the next few hours and then I've arranged for my brother to bring my boat down from Pier 39 to the coastline a couple of miles north of here, for about two in the morning. We'll swim out to it – we can't risk using the marina in case someone sees us. Once you're safely on board, it's going to head straight for Costa Rica where I have a house on Nosara Beach with direct sea access. No one will see you arrive, and it's at least a mile away from the nearest residence, so it's the perfect place to hide out while you plan for the future."

"How long's the journey?"

"It'll be a leisurely seven days in safe hands. No one can possibly find you at sea."

Franklin was getting calmer by the second. Now he could see a realistic escape route from his nightmare, but there were still many problems to solve. Just a few days earlier he'd announced to the American people in a TV broadcast that following his father's death, he was handing over the ownership of the Franklin Pharmaceutical Corporation to the US government; a decision that had direct implications for *Operation Gesamtkunstwerk.*

"Joe, now that I'm disappearing, you'll be one of the key board members supervising the legal handover of the company to the government. All that's fine, but it's vital you carve out our R & D facility in Neuquén. I'll provide funds to run it from one of my Swiss accounts, but I need you to ensure it simply vanishes from our balance sheet before the corporation is handed over."

Warner had no idea what type of research took place at the facility and had no intention of asking. He would simply make it disappear.

"John, that's no problem. We own hundreds of research facilities all over the world. Nobody is going to miss a tiny one in Patagonia. I'll prepare predated paperwork that shows we shut it down months ago. Now, I suggest you get some sleep in preparation for our post-midnight swim. I'll check out the fridge and fix us both some food. You need to start thinking about the future and where you want to base yourself after things calm down in a few months."

Franklin was already one step ahead of his friend as far as that matter was concerned. For the past fifteen minutes he'd been searching Google on his iPad, looking at some of the biggest and most luxurious superyachts in the world. A hint of an arrogant smile returned to his face for the first time in a while.

"Don't worry, Joe. An idea is already beginning to form."

Chapter 48

London, England

David Williamson was sitting behind his desk in the London office of the highly respected law firm Grayson and Thompson, feeling increasingly troubled and slightly paranoid because of the recent turn of events. His half-sister, Eva, had died in the strangest of circumstances, and then his oldest half-brother, John, had fired off a text warning him and his two other brothers not to speak with any police officials if they were contacted. He was aware he was starting to panic but that didn't prevent him setting up an emergency Zoom call with his two siblings, Daniel in Sydney, and Simon in New York.

David immediately sensed a frosty temperature in the ether. It emanated from the other two, who'd always been much closer to each other than they were to him. After the blunt coldness of their greetings, he decided to dive straight in with a catalogue of questions.

"Am I the only one who thinks this entire episode is turning into a total fiasco? Are we really meant to believe Eva's brutal death was some weird accident that had nothing to do with the operation John is planning? Surely the psychopath they broke out of prison is somehow involved in all this. Then there's Vargas, the cop who brought down our father and discredited John. How much does he—?"

Simon White, the New York investment banker, had heard enough and cut in. "Let's face it, David, you've never really felt the same about this as the rest of us, have you? I'm devastated by Eva's death, but she'd be the first to point out that *Operation Gesamtkunstwerk* is bigger than any individual. It fulfils the legacy of our grandfather—"

Daniel Anderson, who was Zooming in from his apartment in Sydney, interrupted his half-brother mid-flow. "A legacy we should all be proud of. At this moment, we need to trust John's judgement. If Vargas surfaces, Paz will take care of him. David, above all else, remember your bloodline and respect it."

Before David could reply, Simon jumped back in. "Can we trust you to hold your nerve at this crucial time? Because if we can't ..."

Williamson only paused for a moment before replying. "Of course, you're my brothers – my family, and, yes, for a moment after Eva's death I had a wobble but, as ever, you've reassured me. I'm totally on board."

As the call came to an end, David wondered if he'd got away with that last piece of bullshit. Unfortunately for him, his half-brothers knew he was lying through his teeth.

* * *

Following an early morning visit to a bijou French bakery located close to the hotel, Hembury, Katz and Vargas struggled their way through the door of the Marriott suite, laden with white paper bags full of warm, fresh baguettes, croissants, pains au chocolat and pastries, along with four take-out cups of cappuccino. Their impromptu breakfast was well-received by Berrettini, who was keen to hear about their escapade on *The Blonde Lady* and discuss their next moves. When they'd grabbed a handful of food and taken their places behind their respective desks, he opened the meeting.

"It's hard to believe that for ten years John Franklin managed to avoid detection and suckered us all. Bureau analysts concluded a long time ago he'd died by suicide off the coast at Carmel and, now we know, it was all a brilliant smokescreen. I hate to give the man any credit but the idea of hiding in plain sight on a superyacht is very smart. In the early years after his disappearance, he knew he would be one of the most hunted men in the world, so basing himself at sea meant he was never in danger of being discovered crossing land borders where papers and passports would be checked. On a boat that size, he could travel the world safely without fear of being found."

Hembury downed the rest of his cappuccino and placed the cup on his desk. "Mike, the pieces are rapidly falling into place. Franklin is clearly the ringmaster behind the whole operation, with Al Kathib, Paz and the siblings working alongside. The meeting they had at Bariloche – the one we got locked out of, was obviously set up by Franklin to green-light some kind of Israeli attack. He knows we're on to him, and the fact he was forced into evacuating his main base at such speed means we have him on the run and, hopefully, that will leave him open to making mistakes."

Mike turned to another matter of concern. "There's no doubt Franklin has someone on the inside who's tipping him off. Our immediate priority must be to find the leak and shut it down. Leah, I know you report back directly to Doron in Tel Aviv, but who else has access to your reports?"

Katz wasn't prepared to entertain a leak inside Mossad and her reply was laced with sarcasm. "Mike, I think you need to get your own house in order before looking at ours. Start by looking a bit closer to home – everyone knows the bureau has more leaks than a sieve."

Hembury attempted peace making. "Guys, calm it down. No one is accusing anybody of anything and besides—"

Vargas, registering the significance of a message he'd just received, cut across his friend. "Let's park that one for now. I've just read an email from my assistant at the station. A few minutes ago, David Williamson called wanting to speak with me. Sounds like one of the Franklin clan is finally breaking cover. He's left his number, requesting I call him back straight away."

Everyone in the room held their breath as Vargas made the call to London. He hit the speaker icon and placed the phone on a desk positioned between the four of them. Hitler's grandson picked up after only two rings. It was a dreadful line, with the sound bouncing in and out.

After a brief courtesy greeting, Williamson came straight to the point. "Chief inspector, I need to meet with you as soon as possible. Just you and me – I don't want anyone else present."

"What do you wish to discuss, Mr Williamson?"

There was a prolonged spell of silence and for a moment Vargas feared the line had been cut, but then Williamson spoke again.

"I need to talk to you about my brother, John Franklin, and his insane plans. My sister Eva was murdered, and I believe my life is under threat. I want police protection until that madman has been stopped ... Can I trust you?"

"Mr Williamson, I know you're based in London. How quickly can we meet up?"

"Chief inspector, right now I'm on a plane heading for Buenos Aires. My flight lands at eight this evening. Where shall I come to – where's safe?"

Vargas glanced around at his associates who all looked equally stunned by the rapid turn of events.

"Okay, once you land, grab a taxi to the Marriott Park Tower. I'll text you a room number where we can meet. After that, I'll sort out a safe house somewhere on the outskirts of the city."

"Thank you, chief inspector." Everyone heard the sheer relief in Williamson's sign-off. "Please respect that I've asked to meet alone."

Vargas checked the line was dead and then picked up his cell. "Christ, the Führer would be spinning in his grave if he knew one of his grandsons was about to betray the family."

Katz's face broke into a grin. "Nic, to the best of my knowledge he was never buried, but I take your point."

Berrettini reached for the landline on his desk. "Nic, I'll book you a suite. Do you want one of my men hidden in the bedroom, just in case this is some kind of trap?"

"No, Mike, thanks but I don't think he poses any kind of threat. I'm good to handle this one on my own."

* * *

After abandoning the yacht, Franklin had installed himself in his own safe house – a former monastery on the outskirts of Neuquén, just a few miles away from the secret lab facility, where at that very moment the sterilisation drugs were being packaged, ready for the flight to Kandahar. He was deep in conversation with Al Kathib and Paz, running through timelines and schedules, when he received a call from Simon White in New York. He initially ignored it as an inconvenience, but after the fifth missed call in five minutes he picked up. His half-brother was in full-on panic mode.

"John, I don't think we can rely on David anymore. I'm seriously worried he might do something stupid. He's a loose cannon. Daniel and I think he poses a serious threat to the security of the operation. Also, there's—"

Franklin had heard enough and ended the conversation with a chilling response. "Simon, you and Daniel can relax. I'm already aware of his intended treachery and have put plans in place to address the situation."

* * *

David Williamson exited Terminal A at Ezeiza International Airport in Buenos Aires and jumped into a cab, heading for the city. He powered up his phone and read the text from Vargas:

Room 934. See you soon. Stay safe.

He shot off his reply:

Just left the airport. On my way to hotel.

Williamson pocketed his phone and relaxed back in his seat, playing out the upcoming meeting in his mind. The traffic was surprisingly light and twenty-five minutes later the cab pulled up outside the spectacular exterior of the Park Tower. As he strode across the vast reception heading towards the bank of lifts, his nerves began to take hold and for the first time since leaving London, some self-doubt crept in. However hard he tried, he couldn't shake off the terrifying image of John Franklin's face, twisted in hatred and anger, when he learned of David's betrayal. Then his mind flashed to the recent memory of Eva's savage murder, and he reassured himself he had no alternative but to pursue this course of action. He had to move fast or, no doubt, he would join his half-sister in an early demise.

He was so firmly focused on what he needed to do next, he paid little attention to the two people who entered the lift alongside him. One of them was a smartly dressed middle-aged woman who leaned forward to press the fourth-floor button. The other, wearing a black hoody, hit the button for the eighth floor and retreated to the rear of the lift. Finally, David followed suit and illuminated the button for the ninth. No one spoke and the only sound filling the void was some dreadful piped music – a poor soundalike of an Ed Sheeran classic.

The fourth floor came and went, allowing the woman to exit and leaving the two remaining passengers in the lift. As the moving light flicked through the ascending numbers, the hooded figure moved forward, slightly brushing past David as the eighth floor approached. In a blink of an eye, they made a deadly move, spinning around at eye-watering speed, revealing a cut-throat razor in their right hand, that expertly sliced through David's neck, puncturing both his carotid arteries. An arc of blood spray painted the interior of the lift and David's body crumpled backwards, hitting the floor hard. Within five seconds the silent killing was over, and as the doors to the eighth floor slid open, Franklin's assassin exited and disappeared along the corridor, heading for the fire escape.

Chapter 49

Buenos Aires, Argentina

V argas checked his watch for a third time, assuming Williamson would be arriving any moment. Then his heart sank into his boots when he heard a piercing scream coming from the corridor outside his suite. The hysterical noise continued as he flew out of his room and raced towards its source. As Vargas rounded the corner, he ran into four overwrought teenage girls standing with their backs pressed against the wall facing a bank of three lifts. The doors to one of them were manically opening and shutting like a set of steel jaws that were biting on an abandoned roll-on suitcase that had been flipped onto its side.

As the lift opened, Vargas rushed forward and held down the button to keep the doors open, unwittingly taking in the full impact of the dreadful scene in front of him.

Williamson's body was slumped in the far right-hand corner, drenched in a pool of blood, the result of a precise slit that ran from one side of his throat to the other. The wound was so recent, fresh blood was still frothing around his neck where the point of the knife had struck. Williamson's eyes were wide open, staring upwards towards the exact spot his assassin must have stood when making the kill. Vargas figured it must have happened within the previous two minutes.

The horror-struck girls were still shrieking in the corridor when he moved fully inside, kicking the suitcase out of the way, and closed the doors. He took the lift up to Berrettini's floor and called the FBI man on his cell. The two men quickly secured the crime scene ahead of calling for help.

Fifteen minutes later they were joined in Berrettini's suite by Katz. All four of them were shell-shocked but the Mossad agent seemed particularly on edge. Hembury had swiftly left his own room as soon as he heard about the killing, but Katz had made a phone call first.

"I've just reported in to Doron who completely balled me out. He realises our team has been infiltrated by an insider and has summoned me to Tel Aviv for a grilling."

Berrettini raised a quizzical eyebrow but there was no mistaking the red-hot anger driving his reply. "Leah, is that your way of saying he thinks we're screwing up and doesn't trust us to handle this case anymore?"

"Look, Mike, Doron knows, as does our prime minister, that Israel is facing an imminent attack and right now we still can't tell them what the hell it is, or where it's coming from."

Vargas looked to lower the temperature in the room. "Leah, I promise you, we get it. Every time we think we're about to make a breakthrough, something goes wrong – it's frustrating. I'd like to accompany you on that trip and take part in the debrief if that's okay. It might be helpful to have two heads rather than one."

"I don't know, Nic. You're not a Mossad agent, but Doron

might go for it because your background knowledge on Franklin is far deeper than mine. Let me call him back."

* * *

Franklin read the WhatsApp message confirming the hit and immediately deleted it. The sender's name was listed under "Cleaner", a simple code for his assassin that appealed to his sick sense of humour. He quickly brought Paz and Al Kathib up to speed on the latest liquidation and turned his attention to the imminent departure of the drugs to Kandahar.

"The flight is booked for tomorrow afternoon. Both of you will be on it, so before you go, I've organised a meeting later today at the lab where we'll run through the finer details of the schedule."

Paz wasn't really paying any attention to his boss – his mind was still absorbing the implications of Williamson's murder. "Señor Franklin, like you, I really hate loose ends. They somehow always come back and bite when you least expect it."

Franklin was irritated by the interruption. "Paz, where are you going with this?"

"I think your assassin did a brilliant job with the Englishman but, if I were you, I'd be concerned about your other two siblings. Neither of them are professionals and therefore their behaviour is unpredictable. They're the last significant connections to you and this whole operation."

Al Kathib was quick off the mark to second the idea. "John, I think Paz might be right on this one."

Franklin eased back in his chair and pondered the issue before glancing across at the Syrian. "I think the Black Scorpion has raised a valid concern."

Chapter 50

Tel Aviv, Israel

The National Intelligence Service of Israel, better known as Mossad, employs seven thousand full-time workers and runs an annual budget upwards of two billion dollars, making it one of the world's largest espionage agencies. Its headquarters are located in central Tel Aviv but due to its enormous size various departments are based across the city, cloaked in secrecy. The meeting between its director, Doron Bekher, Vargas and Katz took place inside the Matcal Tower, a seventeen-floor high-rise at Camp Rabin military base in the HaKirya quarter of the city. Bekher constantly bounced around different facilities – knowing a moving target is far harder to take down.

The three of them sat in a small, fortified room in the basement of the tower, one of two "clean" meeting areas on the base that were swept for bugs every six hours. The windowless, airless box was used for meetings of an hour or less and was only available to the director and a handful of senior Mossad employees.

Bekher listened intently as Katz took him through a detailed analysis of the events of the previous few days, ignoring Vargas who was happy, for now, to play the role of spectator. He had tremendous respect for the Mossad Director, who was universally regarded as one of the top spy chiefs in the world and was fascinated to hear his take on the current situation. However, Bekher was keen to grill him first.

"Nic, you know more about Franklin than any of us. What's he like and what's your take on the operation named *Gesamtkunstwerk?*"

"The man is obsessed with his legacy and consumed with the same hatred for the Jewish race his grandfather preached to the German people. The word '*gesamtkunstwerk*' literally translates to a 'Total Work of Art' and is associated with Wagner and his obsession with composing an aesthetically perfect piece of music. Franklin has clearly appropriated the phrase for whatever carnage he's planning."

Bekher was fascinated. "So, what is his plan?"

"Look, we still don't know for sure, although I suspect he's looking to attack your country with some kind of biological weapon. As yet, I've no idea how he plans to deploy the attack but every day we're getting closer."

"Nic, based on what I've heard today from Leah, Franklin has someone working for him on the inside who keeps him one step ahead. That leak must be plugged immediately ... Any ideas?" The Mossad director locked eyes with Vargas. He allowed his question to hang in the air as if it were an accusation.

"Not right now but, trust me, I'm working on it."

* * *

Later that afternoon, Vargas took a forty-minute taxi ride along Route 2, the coastal highway that ran north from Tel Aviv to Netanya where his sister-in-law Nadia had made her home. He'd surprised her a few hours earlier when he'd called to say he was in Israel for a short trip and wanted to meet up. Her apartment was on the third floor of the newly constructed Lagoon complex on South Beach, boasting glorious views of the Med.

Vargas arrived just before six and was greeted at the door by Nadia and her husband, Meir, who'd left his law firm early to join in with the unexpected family get-together. Although it wasn't a Friday night, Nadia had decided to lay on a traditional Sabbath meal in honour of her brother-in-law's surprise visit. After polishing off a bottle of Moët, courtesy of Vargas, they sat down to eat on the spacious tiled balcony where Nic set about attacking a huge plate of chopped liver that he knew was only the precursor to three massive courses, meaning he ought to pace himself. He took a circular matzo from a brown wicker basket in the centre of the table and used it as an improvised spoon to scoop up a large mouthful of the chicken pâté. As he devoured it, he appreciated, for the first time in weeks, that his mind wasn't consumed by his work crisis.

"So, Nadia, how's life on the Israeli Riviera?"

She laughed and glanced lovingly at her husband, who, like Nic, was also demolishing the starter.

"Nic, I really love it here. The sun, the sea—"

Vargas couldn't resist the temptation. "The sex!"

Nadia laughed again. "Yes, and that. Seriously, though, the lifestyle is wonderful and, although I miss Mum and Dad loads, the truth is I've never been happier."

"Nadia, I'm so glad for you. I'm sure Sophia would have loved coming here to see you and Meir."

Nadia nodded. She was delighted to see that, thirteen years on from her sister's tragic death, Vargas could finally say her name without tangible pain being etched across his face. It gave her the confidence to raise a topic she knew had previously been taboo.

"Nic, what about you? It's high time you had a lady in your life, and I know it's what Sophia would have wanted. It's been a long time now – there must be someone?"

Vargas was unprepared for that curveball and for a moment was taken aback. Meir jumped in to fill the tense silence, with a gentle reprimand for his wife.

"Nadia, Nic still might not be ready to talk about such things—"

Vargas raised his hands in protest. "No, Meir, it's fine, it really is. The truth is, I'm about twenty years out of practice, so even if I wanted a relationship, I'm not sure I'd remember how to go about it."

Nadia put her hand on top of his. "Nic, it'll just happen naturally if you allow it to. Is there no one around who interests you?"

Vargas felt the warm outpouring of love and genuine concern exuding from Nadia as a physical force and was greatly moved by it.

"Actually, there is someone I've recently met through work who fascinates me, although I'm sure I'm not even on her radar. And guess what?" He turned towards Meir before completing the sentence. "She's Israeli."

Meir smiled and shook his head. "Nic, my friend, Israeli women are strikingly beautiful and super intelligent but can be a handful when it comes to a permanent relationship. Look at me, I opted out of the dating scene over here a long time ago and found Nadia in Argentina."

Vargas laughed and then neatly switched the subject to football and the upcoming World Cup in Qatar, which he knew would prompt Meir into a passionate debate. Two hours later, having eaten and drunk far too much, Vargas said his goodbyes before getting into a cab to ferry him back to his hotel in Tel Aviv. He hugged Nadia and Meir farewell and, as he turned to leave, couldn't resist a parting question.

"Guys, when are you going to make me a very proud uncle?"

Meir wrapped his arm tightly around Nadia's shoulder and replied with a mischievous grin on his face. "Believe me, we're trying all the time, so hopefully any time soon."

As Vargas settled in the back of the cab, he had no way of knowing that Franklin's abominable plan threatened the future plans of his beloved sister-in-law.

Chapter 51

Neuquén, Argentina

With a population of just over three hundred and fifty thousand, Neuquén was the largest city in Patagonia. Its economy was booming, unusually combining a thriving agricultural base with a vibrant petrochemical industry, and it provided the perfect hiding place for Franklin's covert biochemical laboratory.

Paz, Al Kathib and Samuel Rivero, the head biochemist and operational chief of the lab, were huddled together in a small group inside the dispatch area of the facility surrounded by dozens of wooden pallets housing 50 ml clear glass bottles containing the sterilisation drug CDF830. In the distance they could hear the sound of angry footsteps belonging to John Franklin, who'd just completed a fractious meeting with the plant's logistics manager. As he joined the three other men, he made a beeline for the biochemist, whom he blasted with a verbal assault.

"Rivero, I've just fired that useless piece of shit, Figueroa. He tried to tell me you're half a day behind schedule processing and purifying the final batch. You know we need precise amounts bottled up and ready to go if we're to hit all seven of our targets. Your workers will have to continue their shifts, non-stop through the night, to make up for lost time. Come what may, that plane to Kandahar takes off tomorrow afternoon fully loaded. Do I make myself clear?"

Rivero knew he was dealing with a maniacal control freak who wasn't about to take no for an answer, so there was little point in fighting him, even if he didn't believe he could hit the delivery schedule.

"Yes, sir. One way or another everything will be checked, packaged and on board your plane ready for tomorrow's four o'clock flight."

Franklin didn't even bother to acknowledge the answer from his subservient biochemist; he'd already focused his attention on Paz and Al Kathib.

"You'll both be aboard the flight to Kandahar and once you reach Afghanistan, you'll meet up with our Taliban friends, Habibullah and Mohammedzai. They'll supervise the transportation of the merchandise as well as the repackaging of it into halal meat containers, which will be loaded onto their transport trucks. They've received their final payment and are ready and waiting to carry out their role in the operation."

Al Kathib licked his lips in anticipation of the trip that lay ahead. "It's perfect, John. Everything is going according to plan, and the beauty is those Taliban fanatics have absolutely no idea we're playing them. When the Israelis eventually discover what has taken place inside their country, the shit will hit the fan and their retribution will be ferocious. Their regime will seek a bloody revenge and the fury of the Israeli military will be focused on the Taliban's turbaned heads. They'll kick the crap out of Kandahar and take out anyone associated with the leadership."

Franklin put his arm around the Black Scorpion's shoulders. "What's up, Paz? You seem unusually quiet."

"Señor Franklin, I share the excitement of our Syrian friend, but I still have concerns about Vargas and his associates. They are no doubt trying to track us down as we speak. My past encounters with him have taught me he's a formidable adversary."

"Paz, relax. I've told you before, I've a secure source deep inside his camp, so I can assure you he has no notion as to how we're about to strike at the very heart of Israel."

"And what if your pathetic siblings reach out to him? They know far too much about our plans." Paz had his own motive to continue pushing for the removal of the remaining two half-brothers – with them out of the picture he'd have free rein to finish off John Franklin.

His boss eyeballed his watch and Paz recognised the hint of a familiar sinister smile beginning to form on his lips. "Paz, very soon they'll no longer be relevant."

* * *

The time difference between New York and Sydney is fourteen hours, with the capital of New South Wales being ahead and the physical distance between the two world-renowned cities is ten thousand miles. But even if they had been based in the same continent, half-brothers Simon White and Daniel Anderson would still have had no idea they'd been earmarked to die at precisely the same time and vanish from the face of the earth without the hint of a trail. Their murders were set for eight in the morning and ten at night, respectively.

Simon was a young, hard-working, ambitious investment banker employed by one of the Big Four institutions – Morgan Stanley, working out of their headquarters on Broadway in Midtown Manhattan. Since graduating from Harvard with a prestigious MBA, his career path had been meteoric, and at twenty-seven he was the youngest banker in New York to run his own international wealth management team. His basic annual salary of three hundred thousand dollars was regularly topped up by performance-related bonuses that easily quadrupled his income, so on the surface he appeared to the executive board of Morgan Stanley to be the perfect example of a hungry young man who would boost their funds while building his own career. That impression couldn't have been further from the truth, however, as his personal wealth far exceeded that of any of his deluded bosses.

On the morning of his twenty-first birthday Simon's personal account received a life-changing injection of fifty million dollars courtesy of Goehner and Roths, one of the oldest private Swiss banks, based in Zurich. Fortunately for him, they had no qualms or conscience when it came to hiding the clandestine funds of senior infamous Nazis or distributing part of those funds to their offspring as required. Despite having zero morals when it came to selecting their clientele, as a bank they were incredibly rigorous in charging a twenty-five per cent commission rate on any transactions they were instructed to make from those illicit accounts they had successfully kept secret from the eyes of the world for over seventy-five years.

The money had been left to Simon by his biological father, Richard, who had bequeathed the same amount to all four of his "secret" children, to be paid when they reached the age of twenty-one. The two-hundred-million-dollar pay-out hardly made a dent in the enormous Nazi pot of money Richard had stashed away in Switzerland before he died. Money that originally had been stolen from German Jews by Martin Bormann and Adolf Hitler during the war years.

Having the comfort of a private financial cushion allowed Simon to take outrageous trading risks – many of which his competitors simply wouldn't contemplate, and which enhanced his reputation as the most fearless investment banker in Manhattan. But Simon's hidden personal wealth wasn't the only skeleton in his closet, or his biggest. The secrecy that cloaked his birthright, inspired a burning inner strength and determination to succeed, and the consummate pride he felt as Hitler's grandson meant he was totally committed to the imminent attack on Israel. Despite the recent murder of his younger sibling, David, he had no inkling his mentor and older half-brother, John, had lost faith in him.

Simon was a young man driven by an obsessive work ethic, and part of his punishing routine entailed a regular early morning visit to the Mercedes Club, a luxury gym on West 54th Street, less than a ten-minute drive from his office. As usual, that morning he polished off an intense circuit workout under the guidance of his demanding female personal trainer and, after a swift shower, bounced into the underground car park ready to face another day of pressurised trading.

Simon nonchalantly aimed his key fob towards his petrol-blue Porsche Taycan Turbo S, which was dwarfed by the two giant SUVs it was wedged between – a blacked-out Escalade and a silver-grey Chevrolet Suburban. The fully electric supercar silently unlocked its doors, as commanded, and Simon eased into the driver's seat. Before flicking the drive lever, he took a moment to style his damp hair in the rear-view mirror. An anonymous male voice broke the silence, shaking him to his core.

"Turn around very slowly."

Simon was a control freak, and as he swivelled his head over his right shoulder his normally razor-sharp mind was disoriented and scrambled to process how a stranger had managed to smuggle himself into the back seat of his car without his knowledge. As soon as the intruder locked eyes with Simon, his right hand sprung up like an automated lever, releasing a jet spray from an aerosol, inches from his victim's head. The liquid coating Simon's face was pure cyanide, and as the tiny particles penetrated his skin, the cells inside his brain began to die, cutting off the oxygen supply and causing an excruciatingly painful but swift death.

The murderer continued to move quickly, manoeuvring out of the back passenger seat to open the driver's door, where he carefully dragged Simon's lifeless body out of the car and slid it across the grey concrete floor towards the rear doors of the Escalade parked next to it. It took less than fifteen seconds for him to secure the corpse inside the back of the SUV and, a minute later, the Escalade departed the car park, weaved its way through the early morning commuter traffic in Manhattan and headed west. Waiting in a New Jersey crematorium was a cheap empty coffin ready to receive Simon's corpse.

The thirty-mile journey took just over an hour, and when the SUV came to a stop at the rear entrance of the Jersey State Funeral Home, the double-width white electric doors opened skywards, allowing the vehicle to drive inside, where two men, smartly dressed in black suits, were waiting, standing either side of an open pine casket. Once the coffin had been placed in the cremation chamber, six burners fired up inside the furnace, creating a scorching temperature of fourteen hundred degrees. Ninety minutes later, all that remained of Simon White was a pile of red-hot ashes.

Back inside the laboratory in Neuquén, Franklin noted the confirmation WhatsApp message from the New York hitman. One down, one to go.

Chapter 52

Sydney, Australia

At the age of twenty-eight, Daniel Anderson was the third eldest of the five Franklin siblings and following the brutal killing of Simon was John's final target. In many ways he was the brightest and most successful of the clan because in just five years, from a standing start, he'd created and built a video game company currently valued at over two hundred and fifty million dollars. Daniel had recently floated Wolf Productions on the ASX, the Australian stock exchange, where its public launch exceeded all expectations. None of his competitors or admirers had any idea he'd chosen the company name as an everlasting tribute to his grandfather. The Führer's Christian name, Adolf, was a compound of two old German words – Adal, meaning noble, and Wulf, meaning wolf, and Hitler had chosen the latter as his nickname.

Like the rest of his siblings, Daniel had benefitted from an undisclosed fifty-million-dollar inheritance, courtesy of his late father's Swiss bankers, and that illicit money had funded his start-up. However, the worldwide success of one of his games was the real driver for the business now, spawning a feature film franchise along with countless other merchandising spin-offs. Daniel had single-handedly invented and developed the role-playing game *Secret Tombs* featuring a fictional American archaeologist Jack Pitt, who spent most of his life uncovering hitherto unknown burial sites containing the embalmed bodies of obscure pharaohs buried in the vast sands of the Valleys of the Kings and Queens on the west bank of the Nile.

Pitt was an obvious clone of Indiana Jones, but Daniel was smart enough to provide him with some unique characteristics to escape any claims of plagiarism. The most notable being his mastery of bokator, an extremely rare ancient battlefield martial art that was created by the Cambodian Army and involved close-quarter hand-to-hand combat. It proved to be one of the most popular gameplay fighting features, which fans worshipped as its USP. Daniel practised what he preached and was also a master of the art, having achieved black belt status alongside his fantasy character.

Ironically, in the initial manifestation of the game, Pitt fought against a group of ex-Nazis who were particularly interested in locating the tomb of Nefertiti, one of the most powerful queens in history who ruled Egypt with her husband, Akhenaten, during the eighteenth dynasty. It greatly amused Daniel that his lone adventurer was able to see off a large group of Nazis and, as the publisher, he could take credit for portraying good winning out over evil. However, Daniel's real-life games were being played out under the leadership of his older half-brother, John Franklin, and they involved a direct attack on the Jewish race based in Israel.

As a single man Daniel normally socialised after work with colleagues and friends, and that often involved a visit to one of Sydney's most popular hangouts, the Zephyr Sky

Bar, which offered panoramic views over Darling Harbour as well as their infamous vermouth-inspired cocktails. Daniel was parked at one of the premier tables sited along the north perimeter of the roofline that looked directly out at the Pacific. He was accompanied by two women and another man, all of whom formed part of his key management team. They were celebrating the recent release of a new title that had just stormed to the top of the gaming charts.

Daniel nodded towards Richard Green, the only member of his team who'd been with him from the very start of the journey. They'd met as freshers at Melbourne University where they'd studied software engineering and business. Richard became Daniel's first employee when he formed Wolf Productions in 2017 and was in every sense of the word his right-hand man. Despite sitting outside on an open terrace, the background techno music provided by the in-house DJ was almost deafening, forcing Daniel to shout across to his friend.

"Rich, can you sort out another round and order a few plates of seafood while I make a couple of quick calls."

"Sure, mate. Your best bet is actually inside the dunnies, where you might just be able to hear something."

Daniel smiled as he stood up and crossed the small dance floor, heading towards the men's toilets close to the entrance of the roof terrace. The place was heaving with revellers, and he was oblivious to the middle-aged, blond-haired man who'd been nursing a pint of Foster's for over an hour, his eyes never leaving Daniel's table, as he rose to his feet and headed in the same direction.

The washroom interior was floor-to-ceiling black marble broken up by a line of mirrors above a run of four sinks, opposite six cubicles. Daniel walked to the furthest stall to escape the blaring music that was bleeding through from the bar. He retrieved his phone and dialled one of his many girlfriends, who he planned to meet with later in the evening. His back was half turned from the entrance, and he had a finger in his left ear to help eliminate the noise while he held the phone close to his right ear. The call went straight to voicemail, and he began to leave a message, but was interrupted mid-flow by the jolt of a Glock 17 barrel jamming into the pit of his back. The pistol was hidden from sight by the assassin's leather bomber jacket, draped over his right arm.

The gunman spoke in a whisper. "Just come with me and all will be fine. We're going for a little drive and a talk. So long as you cooperate, you'll be okay. You lead the way out of this dump. My car is parked in an alley a couple of blocks north from here. Just don't try anything stupid."

Daniel processed the initial shock of the confrontation and began walking towards the exit, his brain trying to formulate an escape plan. He'd no idea who the gunman was or what he wanted, but he had no intention of joining him in his car for a mystery drive to find out. As they reached the solo lift in the hallway, he began to fake a physical tremble that soon developed into a full-blown case of the shakes.

"Please don't hurt me. I'll give you all the money you ask for but please don't kill me. I can arrange a bank transfer from my phone and—"

"Shut up, Daniel. Just do what you're told, and you'll be just fine."

Daniel could tell the man was lying, so persevered with his act. "I'm scared, just tell me what you want – I'll give you anything."

"I told you to shut up, you pathetic piece of shit. No more talk."

The two men rode the lift down to the ground floor in silence and departed the hotel through a rear exit, emerging onto a quiet side street where they turned immediately left.

"Just keep walking and take the next right."

Daniel led the way, his head bowed, his body continuing with the fake shaking. A few minutes later they took a final turn into a darkened alley, only illuminated by a glint of moonlight. Parked halfway along, on the right, was a red Toyota Hilux.

"Hold it there and turn around."

The man sounded almost bored as he calmly issued his orders. He could see the frightened, shivering figure in front of him posed no threat and wished he could end it right there in the alley, but that wasn't the job. His victim needed to disappear without trace and that entailed a short drive along the coast and a rendezvous with a colleague who was waiting in a small fishing boat. Then, a couple of miles out to sea, Daniel's body would be weighted down with rocks and heaved over the side as a tasty midnight snack for the sharks. The hitman fiddled inside his jean pocket for his car keys, which he flung towards Daniel, who deliberately fumbled the catch and allowed them to fall onto the cobbled street.

"Pick them up, you imbecile, and get your ass in the driver's seat. I'll join you in the front and tell you where to go. Get on with it."

Daniel carried on playing the fool, groping around on his knees in the dark, searching for the keys, shaking with terror. Finally, he grabbed them and slowly rose to his feet before turning to face the pickup. He could sense the gunman was no more than a foot behind him and the man had momentarily lowered his right arm, so the gun barrel was now pointing at the ground. It would only take a second for the hitman to have Daniel back in his sights, but Hitler's grandson didn't need that much time.

He launched his right elbow backwards and skywards, smashing into the jawbone of the unsuspecting killer, who reeled sideways and fell to the ground like a pile of bricks being emptied from a wheelbarrow. A second later, Daniel's right foot crashed into the fallen man's ribcage with such tremendous force the unmistakable crunching sound of broken ribs echoed around the alley, blending in with howling screams of pain. Rather than hang around to deliver a killer blow, Daniel sprinted forward and leapt into the driver's seat of the Hilux to fire up the engine. A quick glance in the rear-view mirror showed his opponent rolling on the ground in desperation, clutching his ribcage with both arms.

Daniel rammed the gear lever into reverse and floored the throttle, propelling the Toyota backwards at speed, smashing into the stricken man, who disappeared underneath it. Then he braked hard, bringing the truck to an emergency stop. Peering through the gloom he could just make out what appeared to be the shape of a motionless body, lying on the cobbles. But Daniel wasn't in the mood to take any chances. He downed the clutch, changed up into first and sped forwards, aiming the huge front wheels directly at the body, which they flattened like a pancake.

This time he didn't bother to stop to check the damage but slipped into second and drove off down the alley, which he knew led back onto the main street circling Darling Harbour. Daniel's body was pumped full of adrenaline, yet his mind was calmly and clinically working out his options. He pulled the Hilux to a stop about a mile up the road, directly outside a branch of the National Australia Bank which housed four cash machines in the wall to the side of the front entrance.

He was pretty sure who lay behind his attempted murder and, if his suspicions were correct, it meant his half-brother was also in imminent danger. He grabbed his phone and punched in Simon's number, which produced a high-pitched monotone, indicating the phone had been disconnected. Any doubts he might have had instantly melted away. Now he had to think fast.

Christ, he'd written enough escape scenarios for his action hero who always survived, whatever the odds. What the hell would Jack Pitt do in this situation?

For the next five minutes he repeatedly entered his credit and debit cards into the cash machines, emptying out as much cash as they would allow him, before they inevitably stopped working due to excessive use. He knew he had to ditch anything that might help track him down or identify him and that meant the credit cards had to go, along with his phone. He was about to smash it into the wall when he hesitated, thought for a moment, and decided to send off one last WhatsApp message. As soon as he saw two blue ticks appear in the bottom right corner of the screen, he began repeatedly smashing the phone against the brushed steel rim of the cash machine until it was completely wrecked. He pocketed the cash and returned to the Toyota. His plan was to drive non-stop for as long as he could, heading towards the Northern Territory, where he could hopefully disappear somewhere inside the cavernous spaces of the open terrain.

Franklin received the second WhatsApp message he'd been

waiting for, but when he saw the identity of the sender and read the chilling message his blood ran cold.

You made a huge mistake moving against me. As a brother and ally I would have done anything for you. As an enemy, I'll search you out and bring you down.

Chapter 53

Neuquén, Argentina

The Dassault Falcon 8X was a state-of-the-art wide-bodied business jet capable of flying seven thousand miles without the need to refuel. That had been its main attraction when Franklin chartered it for the long-haul journey to transport the sterilisation drugs from Argentina to Afghanistan. As part of the hire, he requested fourteen of the sixteen passenger seats be removed, allowing plenty of room for his precious cargo while the remaining two seats would be filled by Paz and Al Kathib.

The pair were standing inside one of the vast hangars on-site at Presidente Perón International Airport in Neuquén, keeping a watchful eye on the merchandise as the one-metre-square pallets containing the drugs were flipped onto their sides, enabling them to easily fit through the main aircraft door. They were carefully carried aboard by local airport baggage handlers who'd no idea what substance lay inside the small glass bottles, but they didn't really care, because all six of them were being paid four times their hourly rate in cash.

Paz and Al Kathib's focus was interrupted by the sight of

Franklin storming into the hangar through one of the small side doors, his arms gesticulating towards the two men in a frantic motion, summoning them to join him as he headed towards a small glass-walled office in one of the far corners of the hangar. Once inside, he sat down on the only available chair, positioned behind a cheap formica-topped desk, while Paz and Al Kathib took standing positions the other side of it, facing him. The tension in the air was palpable and, as usual, Franklin didn't bother with small talk.

"We've had a massive screw-up in Australia. Daniel somehow avoided his hitman and is on the run. He has the potential to seriously jeopardise this entire operation – and he's a distraction we haven't got time for."

Paz had never seen the man he regarded as the ultimate control freak so on edge.

"What about Simon?"

"He was taken care of, but right now we need to track down his brother."

Al Kathib glided around the desk and perched over Franklin's shoulder. "John, we've an hour before our flight leaves. Let's sort this problem out together, right now. Just give me a moment."

The obsequious Syrian dashed out of the office back into the hangar where he headed for the small pile of cases and rucksacks belonging to him and Paz that hadn't yet been loaded. He unzipped one of the rucksacks and grabbed a black MacBook Air, then hastily returned to the office where he proceeded to bring it to life on the table, the screen angled towards Franklin. It only took him a matter of seconds to log on to the notorious Tor Browser, which provided unlimited access to the Dark Web.

"I'll need a good headshot of Daniel and an instant transfer of funds from you to boost my Bitcoin account on here. We're going to nail that ungrateful bastard by placing a huge bounty on his head."

Having spent the previous ten years behind bars, Paz was out of his depth, and he watched in awe while the Syrian's elegant fingers flew across the keyboard, loading the required information. While Al Kathib meticulously cut and pasted recent photos of Daniel from Google and positioned them within the page, Franklin was on his cell arranging a transfer of five million dollars from one of his numerous Swiss accounts.

They both checked the copy through one final time with Franklin reading it over Al Kathib's shoulder before approving it. The Syrian hit the upload icon.

"The kill order is now live on the Dark Web and with a reward that size, wherever Daniel surfaces – anywhere in the world, someone will be waiting for him. It's simply a matter of time."

Franklin's self-confidence made a remarkable comeback. He eased into his chair and allowed himself the rare luxury of an unguarded smile. "Good work. Now, haven't you guys got a plane to catch?"

For some reason, Al Kathib chose that precise moment to raise a related topic which had always intrigued him about the former presidential candidate, but soon realised that in doing so, he'd made a huge mistake. He hadn't factored in the fact Franklin had no emotional intelligence and didn't function like a normal human being.

"John, you never talk about your son Bill. I assume unlike your siblings you've had no contact since your 'supposed suicide'. It must be tough, and I guess ..."

Franklin cut the Syrian off at the pass with a brutal interruption. His face was slightly distorted with a look of thunder.

"My stupid bitch of a wife has spent the last decade poisoning his mind and has relentlessly campaigned to taint my memory and the incredible legacy of his great grandfather. Of course, for now, like the rest of the world he believes I am dead, but that will soon change. Last year he turned twenty-one; the age my father and I were both told about *Operation Gesamtkunstwerk* and the duties we had to fulfil as the Führer's progeny. As soon as we complete this mission I intend to reappear in his life and educate him on the responsibilities and destiny that come with having the Führer's blood pumping inside his veins. But right now, let's just concentrate on the present and make sure we take care of Daniel."

* * *

The location for the encrypted Zoom call was an internal meeting room on the forty-second floor of the impressive Kirya Tower, one of Tel Aviv's landmark skyscrapers, which accommodated some established government departments, as well as providing a covert office for Mossad's director, Doron Bekher.

The spy chief, who was accompanied by Katz and Vargas, brought the fifteen-minute call to an end thanking Berrettini for the illuminating update documenting the unexplained disappearance of the two Franklin siblings. They were all stunned by the news and Bekher turned to Vargas, curious to get his take on the latest turn of events that seemed to be unravelling at breakneck speed.

Vargas didn't hold back. "All roads lead directly to Franklin. For Christ's sake, the man's a raving lunatic – he's purging his entire family. Every day we get closer to this event, whatever it is, he's taking care of any loose ends. This is the same MO we witnessed with the doctor in El Bolsón who simply vanished because he knew something that threatened Franklin's plan. Doron, I'm afraid to say, we're now just a few days away from what I suspect will be an unprecedented attack on the Israeli people. I think it's time for your prime minister to announce code red status and declare a state of emergency."

Bekher snapped back with a verbal volley of his own. "Based on what, Nic? What do you expect me to tell my prime minister? Hitler's disgraced grandson, who almost became president of the United States, is about to attack us with a stolen batch of antimalarial drugs? We need to know what the impending threat is and where it's coming from. We need evidence, Nic, and we need it fast. I suggest you get your ass back to Berrettini and Hembury asap and try to crack this. I'm sure the answer lies somewhere in Argentina." The Mossad chief switched his eyeline to Katz. "Meanwhile, we'll keep working the case at our end. Leah, I'm keeping you here for now. You'll work out of my office with senior members of our intelligence team as we gear up for whatever's coming our way."

Weirdly, Vargas felt a tinge of sadness about flying back to Buenos Aires on his own. A feeling he doubted Leah shared.

"Understood, Doron. Hopefully Troy and I will be back in the next few days to help bring Franklin's attack dogs down. Bearing in mind he's an LA cop and I'm an Argentine detective, how's our status going to work over here. Can we operate alongside Mossad? Can we be armed?"

"Nic, if you and Troy come through with the answer as to what the hell we need to defend ourselves against, I'll give you both your own battalions."

* * *

The endless long-haul flight from Neuquén to Kandahar took just over nineteen hours, including a brief thirty-minute stop in Ghana to refuel. As soon as they landed, Paz and Al Kathib were whisked away from the airport in an armoured jeep and transported to Taliban HQ, based inside the palace formerly owned by the governor of the city. The pair had visited the dilapidated mansion a few weeks earlier when they'd met up with two senior Taliban leaders, Foreign Minister Abdul-Azim Habibullah and Military Commander Firooz Mohammedzai who, once again, were waiting to greet them. Only this time, the senior members of the Taliban high command were joined by a third man who stood to one side of them in the governor's office.

Akhtar Khairkhwa was a notorious killer on an industrial scale who carried a five-million-dollar price tag on his head, courtesy of the US military. Even though the bounty had been live for over twelve years, no one inside the region had ever uttered a word regarding his whereabouts – the Afghans were either too fearful or too in awe of his reputation to consider giving him up. Even within the Taliban hierarchy, Khairkhwa was regarded as an unchallengeable figure and held legendary status within the country.

He was wanted for questioning by the US regarding an attack on a hotel in Kabul in 2009 that killed eighteen people, including nine Americans. He was also suspected of coordinating and participating in numerous cross-border attacks against the United States and coalition forces inside Afghanistan. His tall, wiry frame was clothed in loose-fitting traditional tribal robes that helped disguise the true level of physical strength beneath them. As Paz couldn't understand a word of Pashto, Al Kathib once again played the role of translator.

The foreign minister formally introduced Khairkhwa, who greeted the two visitors with a solemn pledge.

"God willing, I plan to join you on this crusade to the Jewish state, where we'll unveil chaos and carnage on their bitches as we inflict them with the curse of infertility. We've already cleansed the Jews from our own land and now we'll strike a decisive blow by launching a plague inside the land they stole from the Arab people."

Khairkhwa was technically correct – only six months earlier, following the resurrection of the Taliban regime, the last remaining Jew in the country, Tova Moradi, an eighty-three-year-old woman, fearing for her safety, left the country and fled to Albania.

Abdul-Azim Habibullah, the foreign minister, gestured towards a large table displaying a selection of hot and cold vegetable dishes and a variety of naan breads. "Come and eat with us as this will be your last meal before you set off on your journey to the Holy Land. Tonight, our men will carefully repackage the drugs into hundreds of halal processed-meat packages that will be stored inside refrigerated crates before being placed inside the transport trucks. I understand the drug is stored in 50 ml bottles. How many are there?"

Al Kathib swiftly made the calculations. "We have twelve pallets, each containing three hundred bottles, so three thousand six hundred in total. We've seven targets to hit inside

Israel and we'll deploy varying quantities of the drug at each location, directly into the water supply."

Firooz Mohammedzai, the military commander, a bear of a man, dipped a huge piece of naan into a brown ceramic dish containing a yellow concoction consisting of lentils, olive oil, garlic, and tomato paste – a local dish, known as dal afghani.

"Enough of the maths. Tonight, we eat as friends, and then in the morning we hit the road as brothers."

Chapter 54

Kandahar, Afghanistan

As the morning sun cracked through the pearl-blue cloudless sky, Paz checked his watch. It was 5.10 am and the trucks were scheduled to depart the governor's palace in twenty minutes. He was fully attired in standard Afghan dress: a white tunic shirt and loose-fitting black pants, while his head was protected from the blistering rays by a traditional Peshawari turban. He watched a small group of Taliban fighters secure the back of one truck, his thoughts wandering to what would happen once the operation inside Israel was complete.

Now that Franklin's siblings had been all but neutralised, Paz had no intention of sticking around playing the role of a subservient hitman, constantly at Franklin's beck and call. If he didn't get the opportunity to kill him, he figured he needed to disappear far away from South America to escape his clutches. He'd nurtured a secret yearning to live in the Emilia-Romagna region of northern Italy, ever since he'd visited a second cousin who lived in Bologna, and he knew he had enough money squirrelled away in overseas European accounts to ensure a luxurious retirement in the "red city", where he could indulge his passions for exquisite food and fine wine, along with an unlimited supply of underage Italian rent boys.

His train of thought was brutally interrupted by Al Kathib who energetically grabbed his shoulders from behind and swung him around on the spot.

"Paz, the combination of your olive skin, dark eyes and Arab garb does the trick. So long as you don't open your mouth when we travel through the border checkpoints, all will be well."

Before he could come up with a suitable reply, the menacing figure of Akhtar Khairkhwa joined them, seeming to appear from nowhere, as if he were a ghost. He pointed the barrel of his M4 carbine fully automatic rifle towards the two Volvo trucks that were parked up next to a black Toyota Land Cruiser.

"The small convoy is ready to depart. I'll ride in the cabin of the first truck alongside one of my trusted fighters, Abdul. The commander will follow in the second one accompanied by his driver, Baahir. You two will be behind us in the SUV. We'll head north-west on the Asian Highway towards western Herat, which will take us directly to Islam Qala, the official border crossing with Iran."

It was apparent to Paz the Taliban legend was swiftly taking control of the entire operation and he sensed a power struggle with Al Kathib, who seemed slightly intimidated by his unexpected presence. The Syrian tried to regain some authority by firing off a series of questions, the last of which received a telling response.

"How long should the journey take? Do you anticipate any problems at the border? My friend, of course I'm deeply honoured you've chosen to join us, but your face is familiar to many people across this region, as well as inside the Jewish state ... Could your presence on this trip be a risk?"

Al Kathib regretted his words the moment Khairkhwa stepped forward and locked eyes with him.

"My friend, the journey to the Iran border should take us about ten hours. I've made that crossing many times, so we'll face no issues there. As far as my presence is concerned, it's non-negotiable. It's an insurance policy requested by our supreme leader, who's no fool. He's fully aware of the dangers and potential fallout associated with this attack and needs to know we can trust you and the disgraced American, Franklin, not to betray us."

A small bead of sweat appeared on Al Kathib's forehead as the Taliban fighter paused a moment before ending his reply with a threatening rhetorical question of his own.

"Let's hope, for your sake, you are both trustworthy, shall we?"

* * *

Vargas was back in Buenos Aires and his body clock was all over the place, so his restless sleep wasn't disturbed by an incoming call on his phone. For a moment, he thought it was his alarm kicking in. However, as he picked up the cell and recognised the identity of the caller, his brain immediately clicked into gear.

"Detective Ojeda, really good to hear from you. How are things?"

"Things might just be about to get interesting, chief inspector. A few minutes ago, Doctor Julieta Eduardo woke from her coma and briefly communicated with one of my female officers. She wants to speak with the person in charge of her husband's kidnapping investigation – she believes she may have an idea of what lies behind it. Bearing in mind the bigger picture, I thought you might want to be present when I interview her."

Vargas had already left his bed and was heading for the bathroom. "I'll be on the next flight."

He brought Berrettini and Hembury up to speed in a brief call from the cab taking him to the airport, where he caught a short-hop internal flight heading south-west on the nine-hundred-mile journey to Bariloche. Ojeda sent a car to collect him from the terminal, a twenty-minute ride from the hospital. The officer who picked him up led him directly through the busy reception area to the small corridor where Ojeda was waiting, seated on a black plastic chair outside Julieta Eduardo's private room.

The two men greeted each other with a warm handshake before Ojeda paused for a moment, his hand on the door handle.

"I understand Julieta is quite weak and still under heavy medication, which means she drifts in and out of consciousness. The good news is, when she's awake, she's incredibly lucid."

Vargas could hardly contain himself – he was desperate to go inside.

Ojeda could sense the chief inspector's eagerness and fired off a precautionary note. "Nic, just go easy on her. I know she's a doctor, but the woman almost died. It's more than likely her husband has been murdered, even though we haven't yet found his body, and according to her physician she's still not out of the woods."

Vargas nodded and followed Ojeda into the room where

the first thing that struck him was the natural beauty and vulnerability of the young lady lying in the hospital bed. Her petite frame was wired up to numerous IV tubes, pumping life-saving fluids directly into her veins. Julieta's eyes were closed, but as soon as she heard the soft tone of Ojeda's voice they slowly opened and her lips curled into a small smile of recognition as she saw the detective whom she considered a family friend. Her smile morphed into a quizzical look as she spotted Vargas standing next to him. Ojeda, seeing her response, looked to put her at ease.

"Julieta, it's wonderful to see you awake and looking so well."

The doctor grinned at Ojeda and raised her eyebrows, amused by his obvious untruth.

Ojeda smiled and continued, nodding towards Vargas. "This is Chief Inspector Vargas from the Buenos Aires Police Department who's helping me with the case, as Tomás's disappearance appears to be connected to another investigation."

Julieta settled her dark brown eyes on Vargas, who stepped forward towards the side of the bed.

"Have you found Tomás – or do you know where he is, why he was taken?"

"Doctor Eduardo, I'm afraid we haven't. We're concerned for his welfare and are doing everything we can to find him."

Vargas was lying. He had no doubt Paz's hitman, Rojas, had killed Tomás shortly after the kidnapping.

"Doctor, I understand you might have a theory as to why Tomás was targeted?"

Julieta felt a wave of nausea flood through her as she fought to rationalise her thoughts. Her voice was weak and dropped to a whisper.

"It's something and yet, maybe ... it's nothing ... it may not be connected at all."

Vargas moved closer to her bedside, pulling a plastic visitor's chair with him, and once seated leaned forward. "Trust me, doctor, anything you have to say might be vital in helping us find Tomás." Vargas cursed himself inwardly for betraying her with another necessary lie.

She closed her eyes for a brief respite, summoning up her inner strength to enable her to continue. "A few weeks ago, Tomás told me of a concern he had regarding some patients who were trying to conceive. As an obstetrician he is used to coping with anxious women desperate to have a child ... struggling to fall pregnant ... this was, somehow, different." Julieta paused again, sensing her mind drifting into darkness.

Vargas tried to keep the conversation alive. "How so?"

"Well, it seemed odd to Tomás that such a high number of young women of childbearing age were all failing to conceive, so he carried out some preliminary checks – ultrasound, blood tests, X-rays. He showed me a few of them, and in all cases it appeared, at first sight, as if the women's fallopian tubes were ... blocked ... furred up."

Vargas was hanging on her every word, desperately trying to process the implications of what the doctor was trying to tell him. He sensed she was fighting to stay conscious and so made the decision to push her. "Julieta, did Tomás inform anyone of his findings."

"A few days before he was taken ... he sent an email, a short report, outlining his concerns, along with the X-ray and ultrasound images, to the Ministry of Health in Buenos Aires. He doesn't really know anyone there ... so he also sent a duplicate copy to a senator he'd met a while ago when she spent a day campaigning in El Bolsón … and briefly visited our surgery."

"Do you remember the name of the senator?"

Vargas held his breath and waited for what seemed like an age before Julieta spoke.

"Castillo … Senator Eva Castillo."

Chapter 55

Taybad, Iran

It was the incongruous sight of a black Land Cruiser parked alongside two Volvo transport trucks a few hundred yards off the side of the highway that initially piqued the curiosity of Farzad Nazari, the deputy leader of Jaish ul-Adl, a militant organisation operating in the south-east of Iran. They were a small, fanatical group, fighting the government regime, attempting to gain independence for Sunni Muslims living in the Baluchistan province, currently under Iranian rule.

Nazari remained perfectly still, lying prostrate on the ground, viewing the activity around the parked convoy through the set of PVS-14 night-vision goggles he'd removed from the body of a mutilated US soldier he'd killed by hand during one of his many raids across the border into Afghanistan. As he viewed the four Arabs moving around the campfire, preparing food, he couldn't help but wonder what was really inside the trucks that according to the branding on the outside contained fresh halal meat from Kandahar. Why would such an innocuous cargo require the support and protection of two men who were currently sitting in the front of the Toyota, deep in conversation? What prized cargo were they really carrying?

It didn't take Nazari long to conclude the answer had to be heroin. Afghanistan's annual harvest produced ninety per cent of the world's supply, so it wasn't an unreasonable conclusion, and his brain whirred as he calculated that hidden inside the refrigerated meat containers lay somewhere in the region of twenty million dollars' worth of illicit drugs, there for the taking. The sale of the heroin would provide a much-needed financial boost for his jihadist cause.

It was just a question of time before he sanctioned an attack, but he would allow the drivers to enjoy a last meal before launching a surprise assault with three of his fellow tribesmen.

Paz and Al Kathib exited the front of the Land Cruiser and joined Khairkhwa and the other men by the campfire. The enticing smells emanating from the large clay pot containing a traditional spicy lamb stew confirmed the food was almost ready to be served.

The Taliban leader had been right when he'd predicted a smooth journey across Afghanistan and a trouble-free, swift crossing at the border with Iran. The convoy had travelled non-stop for just over fourteen hours and had set up camp for the night about eighty miles west of the border with Afghanistan. Everything was going according to plan and the men were ready for a hearty meal and a good night's sleep before leaving at sunrise for the next leg of the journey.

Paz helped himself to a plateful of steaming hot stew and sat, cross-legged, on the rough terrain alongside Al Kathib, who seemed happy to make do with a large piece of naan. Khairkhwa was sitting about ten feet away, deep in conversation with a couple of his men and was well out of earshot. To be safe, Paz still spoke in a whisper.

"I'm not sure Señor Franklin will welcome the news our team is being led by one of the most wanted terrorists in the world, whose face is well known to the Israelis."

Al Kathib took his time, digesting a large mouthful of bread before whispering his reply. "I completely agree but we are where we are and I suspect, if you take him out, the rest of the men would turn on us. It seems the supreme leader is smarter than we thought. It's another obstacle – one we have to live with, and if things play out—"

The Syrian never completed his sentence; the conversation was interrupted by the sound of galloping hooves and sporadic gunfire that broke the serenity of the Great Salt Desert, as three white-robed Sunni jihadists, led by Nazari, dressed head to toe in black, approached the campfire on horseback at breakneck speed. The dapple-grey Kurdish stallions were built for pace, and within a matter of seconds they appeared out of the darkness, less than thirty yards from their prey, their riders firing off multiple rounds from their Heckler & Koch G36 assault rifles.

As bullets rained down on the camp, the startled men reacted swiftly, desperately reaching for their weapons, but none of them, Paz included, was as quick or resourceful as Khairkhwa, who rolled backwards down a shallow incline, immediately escaping the glow of the firelight, and disappeared into the coal-black night. As the natural momentum he'd created came to a stop, the Afghan retrieved his M4 carbine, steadied himself and took careful aim at the four figures who'd almost reached the campfire and were now illuminated by the flames.

The automatic assault rifle fired off four rounds, each striking their desired targets. Three were kill shots, bursting open the heads of the jihadist attackers, creating a gruesome visual effect resembling a steel hammer squashing a giant tomato. The fourth shot was just as accurate, deliberately hitting Nazari high up on his chest, tossing him sideways into the air like a rag doll before he plummeted to the ground. The bottom half of his body crashed directly onto the open fire, sending the clay pot spinning off into the sand.

Khairkhwa had correctly identified Nazari as the leader of the tribal invaders – his black attire singling him out, and within seconds was kneeling over the broken body with his peshkabz pressed firmly against the man's throat. His specialist knife had originally been used to penetrate chain mail and other armour, so could easily slice through flesh and bone.

"Why did you come for us? Who are you working for? Tell me the truth and I'll allow you the honour of a swift martyr's death. Lie to me and I'll slice your body into tiny pieces and leave them in the burning sun to be enjoyed by the jackals."

Whatever answer he gave, Nazari knew he was about to die, so he opted for the truth. He nodded towards the Volvo trucks parked about twenty yards away. "I wanted the heroin. It would have provided huge funds to help our cause."

Khairkhwa relaxed the intense pressure he'd been applying to Nazari's throat with his knife, allowing a rare smile as comprehension dawned. He understood why the radicalised Sunni tribesman had mistaken him and his men for drug traffickers. Applying the delicate skill of a surgeon's hand, he slit the warrior's throat in one elegant movement and, within seconds, Nazari bled out. If nothing else, Khairkhwa was a man of his word.

Paz, who'd somehow managed to survive the attack in one piece, watched on from the sidelines, slightly in awe at the solo performance he'd just witnessed. He himself had a history of inflicting great pain and often lingering deaths on victims and recognised Khairkhwa operated on a superior level. The Afghan legend was a fearless, honourable killing machine; an adversary not to be underestimated.

The campfire was almost out, most of it smothered by Nazari's bleeding corpse, but its dying embers still provided a faint, almost sinister-like orange glow, allowing Paz to take in the carnage caused by the assault. The enormous hulk of a body belonging to the Taliban commander Firooz Mohammedzai was slumped on the ground in a twisted heap, entangled with his driver Baahir. Abdul was leaning over the bodies desperately checking, in vain, for any sign of life. Paz noticed he had blood pouring out of an open wound halfway up his right arm that didn't look good, but at least wasn't life-threatening.

The Black Scorpion's thoughts were still scrambled, but somehow he dug deep and snapped back into the moment. As his head cleared, his gut tightened when he realised there was no sign of Al Kathib. He began to scout the area, wondering if the Syrian had escaped the hail of bullets by reaching the cover of one of the nearby trucks. He set off at pace in the dark in search of his colleague, but only manged a few steps before tripping over a prone object that sent him tumbling to the ground. Paz cursed aloud at his clumsiness and looked back for the cause of his fall. Peering through the gloom, he identified the blood-soaked body of the Syrian, whose corpse was lying on the ground, his bulging eyes forming part of a horrific death mask.

The random attack had taken out half their number, leaving just three of them to continue the mission – one of whom was injured. Paz knew he had no choice but to inform Franklin of the disastrous turn of events and reached for his cell. As he keyed the number, Khairkhwa appeared through the darkness and stood in front of him, his face inches away. When he spoke, it was as if he'd read Paz's mind.

"We dump the Land Cruiser here and you ride up front in one of the trucks with me. We'll patch up Abdul and he will drive the other one for now. Once we reach Israel, I'll have him picked up and taken to a safe house on the West Bank where his injury can be treated properly. Then I'll contact two sleepers who I know to be courageous fighters to replace him and Baahir."

Paz was astonished to discover the Afghan legend understood and spoke English. Yet again, he'd underestimated him. Khairkhwa enjoyed the moment and then spotted the phone.

"If you're about to call the American, inform him the operation will still go ahead."

With that, the Afghan turned and disappeared into the blackness. Paz took a few moments to clear his mind before making the difficult call to bring his boss up to speed. Franklin remained silent as he took in the grave implications of the Black Scorpion's report. He felt no remorse about Al Kathib's brutal death, just annoyance; it wasn't an eventuality he had planned for.

Events were spiralling out of control – Franklin couldn't allow that to happen. Despite his better judgement, he resolved to travel to the Middle East where he planned to meet up with the trucks at the Israeli border. From there he would wrest back control from the Taliban mujahid. *Operation Gesamtkunstwerk* had been almost eighty years in the making and there was no way he would allow it to fall at the last hurdle. He owed that much to his grandfather.

Chapter 56

Buenos Aires, Argentina

Within a few hours of departing Julieta Eduardo's bedside, Vargas was back inside the Marriott in Buenos Aires. Hembury and Berrettini listened carefully as he brought them up to speed.

"Julieta was incredible. She was only semi-conscious but gave us some real gold."

Hembury nodded in agreement. "Her husband was so concerned about an abnormal number of his patients suffering from an undiagnosed condition, he sent off a report to the Ministry of Health. But the real game changer was sending a copy to Castillo. She obviously passed it straight through to Franklin who read it and issued a death order. That's where Rojas came in ... but why? What was he trying to—"

Vargas interrupted his colleague, unloading his stream of consciousness. "All the women had the same problem – their fallopian tubes were furred up, making it impossible for them to conceive. Maybe they were all taking part in a drug trial that created disastrous side effects – the blocking of their tubes? Tomás's computer was destroyed in the fire, so we need to contact the Ministry of Health in Buenos Aires and track down the email containing the X-rays and images as soon as possible. They may help provide the answer."

The FBI deputy chief was preoccupied reading an email on his laptop that had just landed. "So far, our guys have found nothing helpful in the doctor's files, unfortunately, but this sounds promising. It could be the breakthrough we've been waiting for. Actually, for the first time since we started working on this case, things are beginning to make sense. Some of our researchers have been looking into the history of Quentiline, the antimalarial drug Paz's men stole from the chemical plant in Córdoba. Listen to this." Berrettini quickly scrolled back to the top of the email before reading aloud. "Back in 1965, a distinguished Brazilian, Carlos Lorenzo, invented a controversial, non-surgical but permanent method of sterilisation that involved injecting the drug Quentiline directly into the uterine cavity, resulting in the formation of fibrous adhesions inside the fallopian tubes. The procedure was irreversible."

For a few seconds, no one spoke, and then Vargas broke the silence.

"Christ, if we're talking mass sterilisation, how the hell is that going to work? Franklin's goons can hardly move across Israel injecting millions of women one at a time."

Hembury was already one step ahead. "Don't forget, the Franklin family ran one of the world's largest pharmaceutical companies for over sixty years. Who knows what kind of wonder drug they might have secretly cooked up? If we're on the right lines, the immediate question facing us, is what sort of delivery system are they planning to use?"

The FBI deputy director cut in. "Troy, you're right. If they've created a drug that can cause sterility in women of childbearing age, how the hell will it be distributed? Will it be airborne or ingested through liquid or food? Unless we can find out in the next few days, we have no way of preventing it."

Vargas leapt out of his chair like a whirlwind and dashed out of the suite without saying a word to his bemused colleagues. As soon as he hit the hotel corridor, he called his sister-in-law Nadia, desperate to warn her she needed to leave the country until the crisis was over. He knew he would sound like a crazy man, but had no choice. He cursed as her home number clicked through to voicemail, especially as the voice he heard belonged to Nadia's husband, Meir, so he couldn't understand a word. He was just about to hang up and try her cell when Meir's message ended, giving way to a familiar, female Spanish voice.

"Hi, friends, Meir and I have decided to take a two-week break. After months of nagging from me, he's finally agreed to show me the beauty of Israel, so we're off on a new adventure. We're leaving our phones behind so we can be free from the joyful distraction of email and Instagram. You won't hear from us until we return when I'll tell you all about it. I'm so excited and can't wait to discover more about my newly adopted country."

As he listened to her recorded message, a giant knot tightened inside Vargas's gut. The pain was almost unbearable.

Chapter 57

Haji Omeran, Iraq

The trucks rumbled their way uneventfully across the Iranian desert and entered Iraq at the border crossing located in the small town of Haji Omeran in the Erbil province. From there, they headed due west, aiming for the Al Karamah border crossing, connecting the Iraqi town of Trebil to Ruwaished in Jordan. Other than stopping for fuel, food and meagre bouts of sleep, the small convoy ate up the distance, and once they entered Jordan, they were only three hundred miles away from the entry point into Israel.

Abdul, whose arm wound was beginning to fester, was driving the lead truck and Khairkhwa was following close behind, accompanied by Paz, sitting next to him in the cabin. For only the second time since they'd met, the Afghan legend decided to converse in English.

"Despite the questionable motives of your American boss, our supreme leader believes this a holy mission we are carrying out in the name of Muhammad, so I'm honoured to die a martyr if that's what it takes. My loathing for the Americans is only surpassed by my hatred for the Zionists who have occupied our land for far too long. But tell me, from what I know of your personal history, you're a South American gangster. What's your interest in this game?"

Paz was momentarily taken off guard by the bluntness of the question, but strangely, having travelled hundreds of miles alongside Khairkhwa, he felt far more comfortable in the Afghan's company than he would ever have expected. He knew, better than most, the incredible sacrifice required to follow a life as a killer and believed that when it came down to the wire, they weren't really that different from one another. He surprised himself by the unguarded honesty of his reply.

"I owe a debt to Franklin that I need to honour, but once we complete the operation, I'll be a free man and I plan to disappear. He's a fanatical psychopath obsessed with his Nazi lineage." Paz paused for dramatic effect. "I'd happily take him out given the opportunity."

* * *

The headquarters of the Buenos Aires Police Department was located at 1650 Moreno Street, in the heart of the city. Deep inside its bowels Vargas sat alone at a small metal table in the vast basement area that held the records department. The chief inspector was about to relive a nightmare from ten years earlier when he'd first set eyes on the contents of a safe-deposit box that had been stolen in a daring bank raid, sparking a national manhunt for the three perpetrators.

The notorious case surrounding Box 1321 had come to define Vargas's career when, back in 2012, his initial investigation into a high-profile robbery in Buenos Aires had spiralled out of control, as it uncovered a historical and political conspiracy that had created global headlines. Vargas had been a key player in a small team that had revealed the secret identity of Senator John Franklin, the Republican presidential candidate. Franklin had come within touching distance of the White House and before he was exposed, he'd been the firm favourite to win the upcoming election.

The explosive contents of the safe-deposit box revealed irrefutable evidence that Adolf Hitler and his wife, Eva Braun, had not committed suicide at the end of the war but had escaped from the infamous bunker in Berlin back in 1945 and created a new life in Patagonia using the alias "Franklin". Now, the man who'd supposedly taken his own life and was known around the world as "The Counterfeit Candidate", Hitler's grandson, had reappeared and was about to launch an outrageous attack on Israel. A nagging distant memory buried deep in the recesses of his brain had forced Vargas to revisit the archived documents from Box 1321.

Spread across the surface of the table were dozens of A4 sheets. Most of the original documentation was typewritten in German and individual pages were protected by wafer-thin transparent polythene covers to help protect them from damage. However, every document inside the box had been translated into Spanish and it was those versions Vargas was meticulously working his way through.

At the time of the initial investigation, his entire focus had been centred around two main concerns: firstly, the need to secure evidence proving John Franklin was Hitler's grandson, and secondly, a financial paper trail confirming Franklin Pharmaceuticals had been created using illicit Nazi funds secretly transferred to Argentina from German-based banks.

Today, a decade later, he was on the hunt for something

completely different. Vargas was convinced that buried in the paperwork somewhere was a vital clue that might explain the nature of the impending attack planned by the Führer's unhinged grandson. He was slightly wrong in his assumption as, hidden in plain sight, was not one but two separate documents relating to the impending biological attack on the female population living inside the Jewish state.

It took well over an hour before Vargas came across the first one. A single piece of paper chronicling an extract from one of the Führer's speeches, dated 30 January 1939, given at the Reichstag. The short paragraph in which Hitler talked about the "complete annihilation of the Jewish race" had a three-word heading that read *"The Führer's Prophecy"*. Vargas felt his heart race as his mind rewound to the covert meeting of the Franklin clan in Bariloche and the presence of a whiteboard in their hotel suite that had the word "prophecy" scrawled at the top.

However, it was the information on a second sheet of paper – that in the original German documents had been stapled to the Reichstag speech, that proved to be the most significant. It was a copy of a telex, dated 26 November 1943, sent from a Doctor Horst Schumann, who was based at Auschwitz to Hitler's deputy, Heinrich Himmler, in Berlin. The Spanish translation was headed *"Operation – Total Work of Art"* that Vargas knew was a literal translation of *Operation Gesamtkunstwerk*.

The report catalogued the grim details of an intense programme of sterilisation that had taken place inside Block 10 of the death camp during the previous six months. It named hundreds of female Jewish inmates who'd been operated on successfully during that period and had been rendered infertile. In some cases, the letter D, contained in a set of brackets appeared at the end of the name, which, he deduced, indicated their failure to survive the medical procedure. The telex went on to confirm the programme would be rapidly accelerated and requested further medical and financial resources to facilitate essential research to help achieve the ultimate ambition of mass sterilisation. Schumann signed off with a chilling message that made Vargas's blood run cold.

Please pass on my personal regards to the Führer and inform him we are doing everything we can to speed up Operation Total Artwork as I know how close the project is to his heart.

Vargas sat motionless in his chair, staring at the report, stunned by the reality that the imminent threat facing Israel could be traced back almost eighty years to the most infamous death camp in history. He had two immediate calls to make and headed for the staircase that would take him above ground where he could obtain a decent signal. He exited the front reception of the building and walked onto the busy street, guzzling down some fresh air before reaching for his phone.

The first call was to Doron Bekher who, much to Vargas's surprise, came on the line within seconds via one of Mossad's complex encrypted phone systems. He knew the director could be speaking from any one of his many secret bases – or indeed from anywhere in the world, although he strongly suspected he was probably in Tel Aviv near the heart of the government, as they were now only a few days away from May 4, the date earmarked by Franklin for the attack.

Bekher was adept at absorbing information quickly but was nonetheless stunned by Vargas's revelations. "Nic, I have to admit I didn't see this one coming, and in many ways it's far worse than anything we could have predicted. If this threat were to go public, the fallout would be nuclear. Can you imagine the scenario? Women would be scared to leave their homes in case the drug was airborne and wouldn't eat or drink anything for fear it had been tampered with. Now we know what the actual threat is, we need to pool our resources to find out exactly how they're proposing to pull it off."

"Agreed. I'm about to fill in Berrettini and Hembury and suggest we schedule a call for later today to formulate a defence plan."

"Amazing work, Nic. Consider yourself an honorary Israeli. I'll fill Leah in at my end and report back to the prime minister, who I know will be incredibly grateful to you for uncovering this obscene plot."

Vargas wasn't quite ready to end the call – there was something else playing on his mind. "Doron, I need to ask a personal favour that involves my sister-in-law who lives in Netanya."

The chief inspector explained his dilemma regarding Nadia's unknown whereabouts and asked if her ID could be issued to police throughout Israel in an urgent attempt to locate her. Doron was more than happy to facilitate the request and was about to hang up when Vargas cut back in.

"Thanks, Doron, I really appreciate that. One last thing, I need your assistance on another matter."

As soon as Vargas finished his call with the Mossad director, his cell alerted him its battery was down to less than five per cent, so rather than phone Hembury and Berrettini, he opted to hop in a cab and head back to the Marriott to brief them in person. Both his colleagues were captivated by the images of the documents he'd photographed with his phone, outlining the origins of *Operation Gesamtkunstwerk*. Once they'd fully digested them, the FBI deputy director brought Vargas up to speed.

"Nic, less than an hour ago I personally briefed the president who, in turn, shared our intelligence with his counterpart in Israel. He also spoke with the British prime minister, who's put the full resource of GCHQ at our disposal. They're now searching the internet for any sign of chatter that might help us track down the whereabouts of Franklin, Al Kathib and Paz. I suspect, wherever they are, they won't be far from the action."

Vargas nodded his agreement. "Okay, Mike, that all makes sense. What's our next move?"

"You guys are heading out to Tel Aviv on the red-eye. Bekher wants you on the ground, ready to help in any way you can. Try and grab some sleep on the flight. I doubt you'll get any once you arrive. You'll be part of a special military task force that will have unlimited access to anyone and anything inside the state of Israel, and, yes, Nic, before you ask, you'll be armed."

Hembury picked up his laptop and headed for the door. He paused and turned to face Berrettini. "Mike, you're right about the sleep, so I hope you booked us business."

Chapter 58

Wadi Araba, Jordan

The Wadi Araba Crossing marks the international border between Jordan and Israel and is one of the busiest in the Middle East, with thousands of workers and tourists passing through it each day. Every morning, eighty per cent of the traffic moves west from the Jordanian port of Aqaba into the seaside resort of Eilat, and in the evening that pattern is reversed.

For the Afghan legend Akhtar Khairkhwa, the ancient crossing point represented the final obstacle on a two-and-a half-thousand-mile journey that had begun three days earlier in Kandahar. As he sat at the wheel of the Volvo truck, slowly edging his way forward in the congested line of traffic, he praised his god, Muhammad, for bringing him safely towards the target. His short blessing was interrupted by the sound of a WhatsApp alert pinging on Paz's phone.

The Black Scorpion was silent as he grabbed his cell and scanned the incoming message. He read it through twice, unprepared for its content. Khairkhwa could sense the mood change inside the cab and demanded to know what was going down.

"Tell me the news you've just received."

Once again, after reflecting for a moment, Paz saw no point in lying to the Afghan. "It's Franklin. He's in Israel, waiting for us in Eilat. He wants to meet at a small café adjoining a large Sonol petrol station, a mile across the border. We're to park up the trucks a few hundred yards before we reach it. Abdul can stay and guard them. He only wants to meet with us."

Khairkhwa wasn't happy receiving orders from anyone. "It was never the plan for the American to be part of this."

Paz snapped back with a mighty conversation stopper. "Well, it was never the plan for Al Kathib to get shot to pieces. Shit happens and plans change."

It took just over an hour to cross the border, and a few minutes later Paz spotted the rendezvous location. The trucks pulled over and parked up by the side of the highway. The exterior of the rundown café was grim – a mix of grey concrete and corrugated metal that looked as if it should have been torn down long ago. The sparse interior wasn't much better, with three beaten-up circular metal tables, each surrounded by a few low stools. It was deserted except for the owner, a rotund old man who looked ready to be condemned alongside his business. His obese frame was resting on a glass-fronted dark wooden cabinet containing a selection of sweet and savoury items, all of which were clearly well past their sell-by date.

Paz and Khairkhwa parked themselves at one of the tables and stared across at the shopkeeper who was occupied working out a word puzzle printed on the back page of his daily paper. Without bothering to look up, he greeted his guests in English, which took them both by surprise.

"I can recommend our tea and coffee or canned drinks but wouldn't trust any of our snacks. If you're looking for food, I suggest you try the gas station next door."

Paz cringed as two Turkestan cockroaches appeared, on cue, from beneath the wooden cabinet, scuttled across the floor and headed for the freedom of the front door. "We're waiting to meet someone, so we'll just hold off until they arrive."

The Afghan had clearly dined in far worse places and immediately contradicted him. "I'll have a strong black coffee and some bread."

The old man cursed under his breath – now he had no choice but to desert his puzzle. He dropped the pencil, folded up the newspaper and resentfully set about his task.

Khairkhwa looked away from the shopkeeper and turned towards Paz. "Where's the American?"

"I've no idea. I'm sure he'll be here any minute."

The two men sat in silence for the following hour. Paz grimaced as he watched the Afghan devour a stale piece of challah bread that had started to turn green around the edges.

Eventually Khairkhwa stood up and walked towards the door. "I've run out of patience. Let's get back to the trucks."

As they exited the café, he spotted the petrol station shop and headed towards it at speed, even though it was in the wrong direction. Paz ran up alongside him as he marched past the fuel pumps.

"Paz, I'll let you into a secret. I loathe the Americans, but I love their chocolate. Abdul and I share a weakness for Hershey bars, so here's a rare opportunity to stock up."

Inside the shop Khairkhwa selected a dozen assorted chocolate bars as well as two packets of freshly made jam doughnuts.

As they walked back towards the trucks, Paz couldn't resist a quick jibe. "For a cold-hearted killer, you sure have a sweet tooth."

The Afghan smiled, unwrapped a bar and took a huge bite.

Abdul was waiting for them, standing by the side of one of the trucks, but he wasn't alone. Alongside him, sporting his trademark baseball cap, stood John Franklin. On seeing his boss, Paz produced the best false smile he could conjure up at short notice while Khairkhwa remained stony-faced.

"I see you enjoy playing mind games, Mr Franklin."

"Your English is very good for—"

"For an Arab terrorist with a price on his head?"

Franklin didn't reply but flashed a quick glance towards Paz, acknowledging the WhatsApp message he'd received earlier from him, warning the Afghan was not a man to be underestimated. He checked his watch and saw it was almost midday. "Look, we've plenty of time to kill before we hit our first target in the early hours. I've booked a hotel a bit more upmarket than the café, where we can run through the schedule for tonight and the next few days." He looked at Khairkhwa before issuing his next instruction. "Have your sleepers meet us in the hotel car park no later than eleven. We have an unmarked Transporter van into which we'll transfer the precise quantity of drugs we require for our first hit."

They drove to the outskirts of the city and checked in to the Star of David, a drab four-star hotel where Franklin had booked a junior suite using one of his many aliases. Abdul, whose wound had turned septic, remained in the cab of one of the trucks in the outdoor parking area, waiting to be collected by two other terrorists who were on their way from the West Bank. The other three men took full advantage of the room service menu before starting work. Franklin laid a large marked-up colour map of Israel out on the surface of a low plastic coffee table.

"The blue dots indicate the locations of the largest and most significant desalination plants in the country. These giant facilities pump seawater directly from the Med into a filtration process that removes the larger unwanted particles. Then the filtered seawater is forced, under pressure, through special membranes that reverse the osmosis process that normally occurs in nature. Only then is the water safe to drink. And that's the point in the process where we add our own man-made secret ingredient that definitely does not appear in nature."

Franklin paused, briefly, as if waiting for a round of applause.

"Between them, these desalination plants provide over six hundred million cubic metres of water a year, supplying the population with well over two thirds of its drinking water. They represent our key targets. In addition, we'll be hitting the major pump station that brings fresh water in from the Sea of Galilee. It's Israel's largest freshwater lake and supplies the entire north of the country."

This was the first time Paz had been privileged enough to hear the full breakdown of the plan as Al Kathib had always played his cards close to his chest and specific details of the operation had only been revealed to him on a need-to-know basis.

"Señor Franklin, how long do you expect this to take?"

"Based on our schedule, the entire operation should be complete in seven days. We work our way north along the Mediterranean coast and then travel east to the Golan Heights, where the Galilee pump station is based. The first operation will begin just after midnight tonight, as the Jews begin celebrating their independence. We start by hitting one of the smaller plants here in Eilat, and tomorrow we travel two hundred miles north to one of the biggest in the country, at Ashkelon. Then we move on to hit four other major plants in Ashdod, Soreq, Palmachim and Hadera. And then finally the pump station in Galilee."

Franklin paused and produced a small white Jiffy bag from the inside pocket of his jacket, which he passed to Paz. "Here's a copy of the schedule Al Kathib and I created for the operation tonight. It details everything we'll need – the interior plant layout showing precisely where the drug needs to be added, along with the exact quantities required. In addition, there's the names of the two guards who are on our payroll. They'll facilitate our discreet entry into the plant. The rear entrance will be left unlocked and unguarded for a one-hour window, allowing us unfettered access. You've also got the cell numbers for the guards, just in case anything goes wrong."

The Afghan was dubious. "How do you know we can trust the Jewish guards not to betray us?"

"My friend, you'd be surprised by what level of betrayal a cash bonus of two years' salary can buy." Franklin paused and smiled at his two associates. "If all goes according to plan, by the time we've finished, ninety-three per cent of the drinking water inside the Jewish state will have been transformed into one enormous sterilisation drug."

Chapter 59

Tel Aviv, Israel

Mossad had booked rooms for Vargas and Hembury at the Orchid Hotel in the heart of Tel Aviv's fashionable beachfront. It made sense as Katz was already based there – her own apartment in Haifa being too far away from Mossad's control centre. As soon as they checked in, she joined them in Vargas's fourth-floor room for a catch-up.

The director had already brought her up to speed, so she was fully aware of the significant progress Vargas had made on the case – which meant that for the first time they all understood the true meaning of *Operation Gesamtkunstwerk* and the imminent threat they were up against. What they still didn't have a handle on was how and where the sterilisation drug was going to be delivered inside Israel, and as they were less than twenty-four hours away from Independence Day, they knew they were rapidly running out of time.

All three of them were pleased and relieved to see one another again. Katz hugged them both warmly, before diving in with some questions. "Nic, the wife of the obstetrician seems a very special woman. Do you think she'll have more to give us when she comes round again?"

"I do, but I'm not sure what. It's possible, of course, that her husband speculated on how his patients ingested the drug that caused the blockage in their fallopian tubes."

Katz seemed anxious to pursue that avenue. "That could be the final piece of the jigsaw, Nic. We need someone at the hospital twenty-four hours a day, ready to question her the moment she wakes up."

"Don't worry, Ojeda is all over that. He has an officer outside her room who'll contact him the moment she regains consciousness."

"Excellent, meanwhile we have half the world's secret agencies searching for any sign of—"

Katz never got the chance to finish her sentence. Hembury cut across her, his voice full of excitement. "Christ, guys. Check this email."

Seconds later they were all peering at Hembury's laptop, scrutinising three grainy black-and-white CCTV images Berrettini had forwarded from Buenos Aires. They featured two males in full Arab garb inside what appeared to be a shop. One image showed the men side by side, while the other two featured solo shots. The FBI deputy director had joined them on speaker via Vargas's phone and explained their relevance.

"These images came in less than twenty minutes ago from our friends at GCHQ in England. After learning about the live threat and vile nature of the impending attack, the Israeli government gave them total access to all cloud-based CCTV cameras inside the country. As their computers run the very latest facial recognition software systems, bingo – they just hit the jackpot."

Vargas was the first to react as no one in the room could make out the faces of the two men. "Mike, where was it taken? Who are they?"

"Here's what we know so far. The images were recorded ten hours ago in a petrol station located in Eilat, just a few miles from the Jordanian border."

Hembury almost yelled at the phone on the table. "Mike, for Christ's sake, who the hell are they?"

"Here's the thing – the software locked on to the guy standing on the right-hand side of the two-shot, even though we weren't looking for him. He's a high-ranking Taliban terrorist named Akhtar Khairkhwa who currently holds the distinction of being numero uno on the US government's most wanted list. He's believed to be responsible for the deaths of dozens of Americans and we've been searching for him for years without any joy. The guy's a cold-blooded killer with a five-million-dollar bounty on his head."

Katz shook her head and, when she spoke, she sounded exasperated. "Mike, how on earth does this help us? Where does he fit in?"

"Calm down, Leah. I'm just getting to the good bit. Flick through to the third picture – the single shot of the other guy."

Hembury clicked on the mouse pad and brought up the image full screen. The features of the Arab in the photo were partially hidden as he was wearing a traditional turban along with a white scarf wrapped high across his neck.

"Here's the beauty of facial recognition, guys. Thanks to GCHQ's software, I can tell you we're all staring at an image of our old friend the Black Scorpion ... Matias Paz."

Vargas banged the table with his fists in jubilation. "Yes! Those killer eyes – I should have recognised him myself. What the hell? What's Paz doing with a Taliban terrorist? This collaboration has got to be down to Al Kathib. Any sign of him or Franklin?"

"Nada. But we must assume they're both close by and, yes, Nic, I'm sure you're right about the Syrian being the middleman."

"What about their vehicle – what were they driving? They were at a garage ... They must have been filling up."

For the first time during the call Berrettini sounded subdued. "Weirdly, there were no vehicles parked outside by the pumps, but what we did learn is that our friend Khairkhwa is a chocolate addict. He bought twelve Hershey bars and a few doughnuts but no fuel. The CCTV cameras covering the forecourt saw them leave the shop and walk past the pumps before disappearing out of view."

Hembury came back in. "Shit. We need to know what they're driving if we're going to track them down quickly. Let's get our asses down to Eilat." He switched his eyeline to Katz. "Leah, how far is it?"

For a moment before she replied, the Mossad agent seemed preoccupied. "It's a decent four-hour drive south or just under an hour if we fly."

Having briefed them all, Berrettini was in the process of signing off when Katz interrupted him.

"Mike, have you updated Bekher on this development?"

"No, I thought I'd leave you guys to do that as you're on the spot. I'm knee-deep in Zooms with the president's office and the agents in the UK at GCHQ. Let's talk again in a few hours when you're in Eilat. As soon as I get any more news, I'll be straight on. Good luck and safe travels."

Hembury leaned down to close his laptop as Vargas switched

off his phone. In doing so neither of them noticed the slight body movement from Katz as she pulled her Beretta 70 from the inside pocket of her cream leather bomber jacket. When they both looked up, the barrel of her gun was pointing in their direction.

Chapter 60

Tel Aviv, Israel

"Is that the same gun you used to blow an enormous hole in Rojas's head, and while we're at it, where's the knife you used to slit Williamson's throat?"

Katz's green eyes had a wildness about them Vargas had never seen before. They flicked between him and Hembury before locking back on to him. "How long have you known?"

"About twenty-four hours, although I've had my suspicions for a while – ever since we raided Franklin's superyacht and the cupboard was bare. It was safe to assume he'd been tipped off, but there was something about your demeanour that was off... as if you were expecting it. When I thought back to the slaying of Rojas at the hospital in El Bolsón, it seemed incredible Franklin could arrange an assassin to get there so fast – but then you and I were staying in a hotel just a few minutes away. The same goes for the killing of David Williamson – once again, you were there with us when he was taken out."

Hembury was desperately trying to process what the hell was playing out in front of him. His astonishment at Katz's apparent betrayal was matched by his anger towards Vargas who'd clearly made the decision not to share his suspicions. He felt deceived by both of them, however, his immediate concern was the dawning reality the Mossad agent had no intention of allowing him or Vargas to leave the room, let alone head to Eilat.

Katz, intoxicated by Vargas's accusations, was intent on finding out more. "How can you be totally sure any of this is true? As far as I can see, it's just speculation."

It was time for Vargas to play his ace card. "Because late last night I discovered the truth about your father."

The Mossad agent seemed startled, and for a moment held her breath as if she knew, at that precise moment, her life was over. Both Vargas and Hembury saw her index finger slightly twitch as it tightened its grip around the trigger of the Beretta. She nodded to Vargas, indicating she wanted him to continue.

"Yesterday I asked Doron to email me your personal file. He was furious and initially refused my request. But he owed me a favour, so I called it in. A few hours earlier I'd been reading through a batch of old documents relating to Hitler and the Franklin family, trying to source a clue that might help us with the investigation, and that process set me thinking about John's father, Richard. The man was a twisted sociopath who, long before he killed himself, arranged for four of his children to be brought up by Nazi sympathisers around the world. These men all worked for the pharmaceutical giant created by his own father, Adolf Hitler, with the aid of Martin Bormann, soon after the end of the war. Many senior executives within Franklin Pharmaceuticals were also direct descendants of other notorious Nazis who'd supported the Third Reich, and who, just like Hitler, changed their names to create fake identities. Then I remembered part of our conversation over dinner –

when we were down south investigating the disappearance of the doctor. You passionately regaled me with the tale of how your family immigrated to Israel from Holland when you were only five because of your father's work. I started delving into his background and discovered he was working for Pfizer as a biological engineer at the time he moved you and your family to Israel. It struck me as a weird coincidence that he worked for one of the big pharma companies – albeit a rival to Franklin's, and it bothered me. So, I kept on digging until I finally hit pay dirt. That's when I knew for sure you had to be the traitor."

Vargas paused, expecting Katz to respond, but she remained silent, fixed to the spot in shock. He took that as a cue to continue.

"Leah, before your father, Hendrik Katz, joined Pfizer, he'd served as a senior board member of the European division of Franklin Pharmaceuticals, reporting directly to Richard Franklin, who, I'm sure, concocted the genius long-term plan to create a sleeper family based in Israel. At the point you joined Mossad in February 2010, nobody had any suspicions about the true provenance of the Franklin Corporation, as the bank robbery exposing the truth didn't occur until two years later, in 2012. So, of course, when Mossad checked out your family's background, no red flags would have shown up. According to your file, your mother was Jewish, although I'm pretty sure that's fake news as well. As the daughter of a respected biological engineer who immigrated to Israel when you were just a child, your backstory was a perfect piece of fiction. Unlike Franklin's children, you weren't adopted, but I suspect you were indoctrinated from a very early age by your Nazi parents to loathe the Jewish race and everything it stood for. No wonder your father brought you up as a tomboy who loved playing with toy guns rather than Barbies. I can well imagine Richard Franklin's warped brain salivating over the idea that one day a fanatical Nazi sympathiser could be placed at the very heart of the Israeli intelligence community."

Finally, Katz broke her silence, her words laden with sarcasm. "Nic, if I could only put this gun down, I'd give you a round of applause."

Vargas hadn't quite finished. "I assume your father's father was a Hitler collaborator?"

Suddenly Katz seemed happy to converse, which Hembury took as a bad sign – it confirmed she didn't expect him or Vargas to survive the confrontation.

"Of course. But my grandfather was a bureaucrat not a soldier. His name was Ernst Abicht. He was a legislation councillor in the Nazi foreign ministry where he worked alongside Adolf Eichmann, helping the SS in their essential work. He was personally responsible for the deportation of thousands of Jews transported across Europe by train to death camps in Austria and Poland. As a little girl my father told me bedtime stories about his work ethic and bravery in trying to solve the Jewish problem. Although I never met him, he was my hero."

Vargas shook his head in disgust.

"You both realise I can't allow either of you to travel to Eilat – not when we're this close to fulfilling a long-held dream."

Hembury couldn't fathom why Vargas seemed so assured when it was apparent their lives were on the line, but then his colleague turned the tables.

"Leah, it's over. Before we flew in today, I briefed Doron on my findings. He's in the next room with four agents monitoring this entire conversation. Rather than arrest you straight away, he wanted to hear it from your own mouth and see what information you might give up when I confronted you. That's why he rigged this room with cameras. Leah, you're a top operative, take a good look around. It shouldn't take long for you to scout them."

Katz wasn't sure if Vargas was bluffing – a thought Hembury shared. Her penetrating green eyes frantically searched the room for any signs of hidden cameras, without success, but then her heart missed a beat when she saw one neatly positioned on the top of a large wardrobe in the corner of the room. A moment later she spotted a second, partially hidden at the side of the headboard of the queen-sized bed.

She rationalised her options as she heard multiple footsteps in the hotel corridor heading her way. Her survival instincts kicked into gear, and she charged across the room, heading towards the open glass doors that led onto a small sun terrace. Just as the bedroom door flew open behind her, she hurdled the five-foot-high balcony rail with an outrageous display of athleticism.

Vargas and Hembury darted after her, closely followed by Bekher and four other Mossad agents. Just before any of them reached the edge of the balcony, the sound of an almighty splash rang out, accompanied by a chorus of hysterical screams from petrified holidaymakers who, moments earlier, had been enjoying themselves in the hotel's swimming pool. Miraculously, as Katz crashed into the water, she avoided direct contact with any of them, and their initial assumption was they'd just witnessed a botched suicide attempt. That idea quickly changed when Leah surfaced with her right arm almost vertical in the air, still tightly gripping her Beretta. The sight of the gun provoked a second round of screams and panic as people desperately tried to escape from the pool.

Four floors up, one of the Mossad agents drew his gun and took aim but swiftly concluded the risk of hitting innocent civilians was far too high to justify letting off a round. "Shit! Let's get down there."

The agents ran off while Vargas and Hembury watched from above as Katz made her way to the side of the pool and heaved herself out. She sprinted away through the landscaped grounds, heading for the main exit. As she disappeared out of view, Hembury turned to confront Vargas head-on.

"Nic, I'm so pissed you didn't trust me enough to tell me about the plan you hatched with Bekher. Not knowing what the play was, I couldn't see a way out for us."

Vargas grabbed his close friend and gave him a warm hug. "Honestly, Troy, I'd trust you with my life and would have told you, but Bekher swore me to secrecy until I could prove my suspicions. He insisted on keeping it on a need-to-know basis so Katz couldn't find out and escape – which she has done anyway, but I should have ignored him. I can see I was wrong. I should have let you in on it."

Down below, mayhem was breaking out as Katz cut a bizarre figure, soaked from head to toe, gun in hand, sprinting wildly through throngs of holidaymakers who were spilling around the grounds in the opposite direction, desperately trying to get away from her. As she approached the grand gated entrance at speed, a uniformed hotel security officer, who'd been observing the chaos, drew his gun, stepped forward and shouted towards her. "Hold it right there or I'll shoot."

Katz didn't even break stride. She fired a single round that almost decapitated him – her trademark kill shot blowing away the top half of his head. She exited the hotel and turned right on to HaYarkon Street, pocketed the gun, slowed down and disappeared into the herd of unsuspecting tourists who were heading for a day on the beach.

Fifteen minutes later, Bekher was back inside the hotel room with Vargas and Hembury, reeling from the fallout of Katz's escape and planning their next steps. "We've a helicopter on standby to run us down to Eilat, where we keep a small safe house we can use as a temporary base. The problem is, we don't know if Paz and Khairkhwa used the Jordanian border with Eilat as a convenient entry point into the country or if they've identified a specific target inside the city. I've a huge team of tech guys running through images of all vehicles that crossed the border in the last twenty-four hours, hoping we might catch sight of them. It's a long shot – thousands of people pass through it every day, so we're searching for a needle in a haystack."

Vargas reached for his overnight bag, which lay on the floor by the side of the bed. "Doron, I think the answer lies somewhere in Eilat. Katz seemed determined to stop us heading down there, and I don't think that would be the case if Franklin's team were on the move."

The Mossad director's face broke into a rueful smile. "I hope you're right, Nic. Tomorrow is Independence Day, so if we're going to prevent this attack, it's now or never."

Chapter 61

Eilat, Israel

Franklin was sitting at an oval marble table in his hotel suite, working through the interior layout plans of the desalination plant in Eilat with the Afghan and the Black Scorpion when he received an unexpected WhatsApp message from Katz. He immediately stood and disappeared into the privacy of the separate bedroom before reading it.

My cover's been blown, so I've gone off-grid. Vargas and Hembury have images of Paz and Khairkhwa at a petrol station near the Eilat border. They're heading down there, probably with Bekher and some Mossad agents, but they've no idea about the proposed targets or the schedule or the meat trucks. No reason why you can't proceed.

Losing his insider was bad news. Katz had obviously been careless and if Mossad didn't reach her first, at some point in the future she'd need to be punished. Franklin sensed his enemies were closing in on him, but while they remained ignorant of the specific delivery plans for the drug, there was no way they could scupper his operation, and by the time they did it would be too late for millions of Jewish women. He strolled back into the lounge area with his self-confidence slightly tarnished but still intact.

"Right, gentlemen, let's run through tonight's plan one more time."

* * *

In 1997, when the Sabha desalination plant in Eilat announced its unique operating system, it made global headlines as the first facility in the world to remove salt from seawater using reverse-osmosis technology. The plant fulfilled all the city's fresh water requirements, pumping fifty-five thousand cubic metres of water a day to meet the needs of over a hundred thousand residents. The high-quality drinking water contributed to the rapid expansion of the city, which boomed, and its reliable arid climate attracted visitors from all over the world – many of whom would suffer collateral damage as a result of Franklin's plans.

Ariel Peretz was a twenty-six-year-old law student who supplemented his meagre government grant by working occasional night shifts as a security guard at the plant, which was located about thirty miles north of the city centre. He was newly married with a three-month-old daughter and the family lived in a small studio flat in a crowded suburb near the industrial port, a run-down district way off the tourist trail.

Ariel was sitting at their tiny dining table revising for upcoming exams, but the baby's incessant crying made it an impossible task. The small flat offered no respite and, despite his wife's best efforts, the baby wouldn't quieten. Finally, he snapped.

"Maya, I can't do this tonight. The exams are in three days

and I need to know this stuff to have any chance of making my grades." He stood up and began to pack his law books into an old brown leather satchel hooked over the back of his chair. "I'm going to the plant, where at least I know it will be deathly quiet. There's only Shimon and Moshe on duty tonight and I'm sure they'll let me use a quiet corner somewhere."

Maya was bouncing their daughter on her knee, trying to entice her with a fresh bottle of warm milk without much success. "Ariel, it's not a library. Are you sure you won't get into trouble if the manager finds out? We really need that money."

The law student walked over to his wife and bent down to kiss her affectionately on the cheek. "Darling, it's fine. No one will ever know I was there."

* * *

The Panther helicopter Bekher had seconded from the military took precisely seventy-six minutes to fly from Tel Aviv to Eilat, where it landed in the private section of Ramon Airport, normally reserved for VIP tourists. A blacked-out Range Rover was waiting on the tarmac close by and the three men were whisked to a Mossad safe house located in the North Beach area, adjacent to the five-star Dan hotel.

The SUV pulled to a stop in the internal garage and Bekher led the way inside. Two minutes later Vargas and Hembury joined him in a surprisingly large high-tech operations room located in the basement. Four Mossad agents were sitting at desks facing computer terminals, scouring hundreds of images of vehicles that had recently passed through the Wadi Araba border crossing.

"Sadly, our facial recognition software isn't as sophisticated as

GCHQ's, but we know how Paz and Khairkhwa were dressed, so hopefully we'll get a break doing it the old-fashioned way. We desperately need to know what vehicle they used to enter the country. Eilat Police have been sent an APB containing their CCTV images – if we're lucky, someone might call this in at any moment."

Vargas walked across to the area where Bekher's agents were scrutinising the colour images provided by the border cameras. "Guys, we have to assume the sterilisation drug has been transported into the country during the last twenty-four hours and, although we have no idea of its size, weight or indeed it's packaging, I suggest you focus on vans or small trucks as opposed to regular cars."

The man sitting closest to Vargas glanced up and nodded to the chief inspector. "That's a good call. Thanks."

Bekher took a seat at the long glass table positioned in the centre of the ops room. It had a large-scale map of the city centre spread out on it. He concentrated hard, hoping it might throw up an answer or a clue as to where the terrorists were hiding out or the location of the target they were planning to hit. "Now then, where the hell are you two bastards hanging out?"

Chapter 62

Eilat, Israel

"Okay, it's officially Independence Day. It's finally time to unleash *Operation Gesamtkunstwerk*. Let's get moving."

Franklin's digital watch displayed 00:01 and, as he glanced down to confirm the time, he missed the arching of Paz's eyebrows, who loathed the anal control freak currently calling the shots. An hour earlier he'd stood in the deserted hotel car park watching with disdain as Franklin supervised Khairkhwa's two sleeper Arab tribesman carefully transfer two-hundred-and-eighty 50 ml bottles containing the drug CDF830 from a wooden pallet on board one of the trucks into a large transparent plastic container which was then loaded inside the back of the Transporter van. After that job was completed to his satisfaction, Franklin insisted everybody remain inside the hotel suite until he was ready to action the attack. Now that time had come, he was like a rampant dog, barking out orders.

"Paz, you drive the van and I'll ride up front with you. Khairkhwa, you travel in the back with your two men, along with the drugs. Remember, there are only two security guards on duty and both will make themselves scarce during the agreed one-hour window. The rear gate will be unguarded and unlocked, and the same goes for the main doors inside the facility. The entrance is wide enough for the van to pass through, and once inside we keep to the right of six huge steel water storage tanks. A hard left and then we drive for about one hundred yards to a red metal door that takes us into the heart of the plant. After that, we'll use the interior layout map to guide us to the exact spot to deposit the drug. We have exactly an hour on-site to carry out the operation. After that, the guards will lock everything back up and it'll appear as though we were never there."

Ten minutes later the Afghan and his men squeezed into the rear of the van alongside the large plastic container and sat cross-legged on the metal floor. Paz fired up the engine and Franklin, in the passenger seat, couldn't resist issuing one final patronising order before the ten-minute journey.

"Drive carefully. The last thing we want is to be stopped by the local police or a random military vehicle."

But a few minutes later, even Paz was forced to suspend some of his initial scepticism as the van passed through the unlocked gates of the facility unchallenged and Franklin's precise instructions took them directly to the main body of the plant. Once he'd parked up, he exited the van and tapped on the rear doors, signalling they'd arrived. As soon as their passengers emerged, Franklin led the way through the unlocked red door followed by Paz, Khairkhwa and the two Taliban fighters, who shared the task of carrying the large plastic container, which was jammed full of small glass bottles.

The unimposing exterior of the main building was misleading, and the five intruders were taken aback by the scale of the plant when they entered. The enormous space was filled with a giant maze of super duplex stainless-steel pipes of varying diameters, manufactured especially for desalination plants. Their unique alloy enabled them to withstand the natural corrosion created by seawater and brackish water, as well as the chemicals used in the reverse-osmosis process. The labyrinth of pipes connected to vast storage tanks, where the water underwent multiple processes of filtration. The only sound inside the plant was the constant eerie drone of water passing through steel, which was occasionally interrupted by the odd high-pitched creak.

Franklin stealthily followed the route marked out on his drawing of the interior, carrying it in his left hand while his right held a Nightsearcher torch that illuminated the way. A couple of times he stopped in his tracks to double-check he was heading the right direction, but it took him less than two minutes to bring the human convoy to a halt at his chosen destination.

The five men found themselves standing in a large open space – a gap between two giant storage tanks, about forty feet apart. Running horizontally between them lay a huge pipe, five feet in diameter, joining the tanks. Positioned about halfway along it was a large steel wheel connected to a panel indented into the curvature of the pipe.

Franklin was light-headed with excitement. He felt truly elated and wallowed in his emotions before issuing the next round of orders. He savoured every second – this was the moment he'd dreamed of for more than thirty years, and now it was within touching distance of becoming a reality. "Paz, turn the wheel anticlockwise for three revolutions. That should release the mechanism and the panel below will free up.

Khairkhwa, instruct your men to bring the container over here and begin the process of emptying the bottles' contents into the linking pipe."

During the next few minutes Franklin was mesmerised, watching the two Arabs slowly unscrew the tops of the 50 ml glass bottles and carefully pour the contents into the opening at the top of the giant pipe. Paz and Khairkhwa, standing next to him, also found the monotonous process of the men repeating the same task countless times strangely hypnotic.

About fifty yards away, discreetly hidden on an upper level, Ariel Peretz had been revising his exam notes on international law when he first heard footsteps followed by the murmur of voices. His initial reaction was a mix of intrigue and fear. He knew the only two security guards on-site were both working the perimeter outside, which begged the question – who was creating the noise down below?

He was sitting at a small metal desk in the open-plan area that the guards used as a restroom where they could grab a break and some food between shifts. The space contained three desks, six lockers, a small fridge and a toilet, and formed the perfect hideaway for Ariel when he needed some peace and quiet to study.

Although he wasn't in uniform, his professional instincts kicked in and his first thought was to phone one of the two guards outside. Then he remembered how poor the signal was inside the plant and quickly abandoned the idea. He had no idea what was going on below him on the floor of the plant, but he knew something was off.

Ariel reached inside his jacket pocket for his key ring that held a small key for the single drawer below the desktop. He slowly turned the mechanism and cautiously slid the drawer open, then reached for his work gun.

He knew it was loaded but checked nonetheless before moving across the open-plan area to the spiral metal staircase leading down to the plant floor. Fortunately, Ariel was wearing trainers and was able to make the descent in silence. Despite the murky gloom, as he approached the giant storage tanks, he could clearly distinguish the shape of five figures, two of whom appeared to be pouring liquid into the central linking pipe.

None of the intruders had noticed Ariel's giant shadow looming over them until it was too late. Although he was nervous, he tried hard to instil a sense of confidence and authority in his voice as he moved to within ten feet of them, his Glock raised in a firing pose. "Stop right now and raise your arms to the sky. Would one of you care to tell me what the hell is going on here?"

The Taliban fighters carefully lowered the small glass bottles they'd been pouring the drug from to the floor before raising their arms in the air, along with the three other men. Franklin struggled to process the moment as his perfectionist, control-freak brain knew full well there were only two guards on duty, both paid handsomely to stay away. So, the question assaulting his mind was, who on earth was the guy wearing denims and a T-shirt pointing a gun in his direction?

"Who are you and how much money do you want to walk away from here and forget you ever saw us?"

As ever when he was in trouble Franklin defaulted to money as a currency for survival. But Ariel wasn't interested in his proposition.

"Okay, you're going to keep your arms high in the air and

329

we're all going to take a slow walk outside. Don't think about trying—"

The security guard was cut short by a voice echoing from the shadows behind him.

"Bend down and lay your weapon slowly on the floor. One wrong move and I'll kill you."

Ariel's heart thumped hard as though it was about to jump out of his chest. He suddenly felt foolish and isolated and did exactly as he was instructed by the cold female voice. Moments later, Leah Katz emerged from the darkness. Within seconds she was standing alongside him, the barrel of her gun pressed firmly against the side of his head.

Franklin almost purred with satisfaction as once again he held the upper hand. "Now, young man. Tell me exactly who you are and what you're doing here?"

Peretz was frozen in terror and struggled to speak. "My name... is Ariel Peretz. I'm a law student and part-time security guard. I take on shifts here... to earn extra money, but tonight I came to study for my exams... I needed some peace and quiet."

Franklin's sinister laugh dripped with venom. "I'm afraid, young man, because of what you've seen, you're about to experience a great deal of that – more than you ever dreamed of. There's no way you can unsee what you saw unfortunately and it's vital no one knows we were here or what we were doing."

Katz pulled her gun away and stepped to the side, looking questioningly at Franklin. "Are you sure we need to go that far?"

Franklin ignored her and nodded towards Paz, who didn't hesitate. He retrieved his Smith & Wesson and shot the terrified student in the heart without a trace of emotion or delay. Ariel's body crumpled to the ground in a heap and, content the crisis was over, Franklin turned to Katz who had lowered her own gun and placed it back in her belt.

"Wonderful timing as ever, Leah. I'm so thrilled to finally meet you in the flesh after all the years of Zoom calls and texts. I know your parents and my late father would be so proud of everything you've achieved on behalf of our great cause."

He moved forwards to embrace her, and she reciprocated, wrapping her arms firmly around his back. They held each other for a few seconds before breaking off the hug. As they moved apart, Franklin's right hand slipped into his trouser pocket from where he withdrew his grandfather's beloved Walther PPK. He fired two rounds into her chest. Katz gazed into Franklin's eyes with a bewildered look of shock and betrayal. He glared back at her as a large red stain spread across her chest and blood sprayed onto the side of his face. Her body fell backwards and by the time her head crashed against the concrete floor she was dead.

Franklin used the back of his hand to wipe her warm blood away from his mouth and stepped forward, peering down at her emerald, green eyes that stared into space. He half turned to face Paz and Khairkhwa who'd watched the scene play out without uttering a word.

"I told you, I hate loose ends."

Chapter 63

F ranklin brandished the gun high in the air as if he were a preacher holding a rare prayer book.

"This Walther PPK belonged to the Führer. It's a treasured, historical icon that belongs to my family. It was an honour to fire it for the first time in my life."

He expected a response from Paz or Khairkhwa, but none was forthcoming. He broke the silence instead. "Katz knew far too much about me and this entire operation. Her very existence posed a threat."

Franklin locked eyes with the Afghan. "Now, because of that unfortunate distraction, we've lost valuable time. Your men still have work to do. Once they've finished emptying the bottles, they need to clear up any sign of blood in here and remove the bodies to the van."

By the time Paz drove the Transporter out of the plant, the five intruders had been on-site for fifty-six minutes, meaning they exited with just four minutes in hand. When they made it back to the sanctuary of the hotel suite, Franklin glared at

Khairkhwa and his two tribesman and issued a fresh set of orders.

"Ask them if there's forest land nearby where they can bury the bodies."

The Afghan and his Taliban fighters had a swift conversation in Pashto. The men walked across to the hotel room door, picking up the van keys from the table on the way.

"There's some woodland about ten miles away in an area called Holland Park. They'll find a suitable spot there to dispose of the bodies."

"Excellent. This evening we'll depart at sunset to head for our next target. We've a two-hundred-mile drive north to Ashkelon. The plant there is four times the size of the one in Eilat, which means the operation will be far more precarious. They have eight guards on-site and we only have two on the payroll. But the pay-off is well worth the risk – we'll be dispensing almost five times the quantity of drugs into the water system, which'll require the contents of three pallets, so you and Paz will need to help carry them in. Once again, we'll hit the plant late at night and our men on the inside will ensure the rear entrance will be open for an hour between midnight and one."

Franklin stood up and walked over to the bedroom, closing the door behind him. As soon as he was on his own, he flopped on the bed and pulled himself into a foetal position. Despite his bravado, he realised the events earlier in the night had been a total fiasco and almost a complete disaster. Even though he'd planned everything down to the finest detail, he hadn't factored in the vagaries of human behaviour. How could he possibly have guessed a freelance security guard would be revising for exams inside the plant on his night off? Had Katz not surfaced when she did, the whole plan could have gone up in smoke – and worse still, he would have fallen into the hands of the Israelis. He thought again of Katz and the role she'd played as his insider in the enemy camp. He had no doubt Vargas and Hembury were already in Eilat, even though he couldn't confirm it. He could sense them breathing down his neck and he knew the noose was tightening.

It had never been part of his plan to be operational, but the unexpected death of Al Kathib had left him with no choice. However, his self-preservation instincts kicked in – he wasn't prepared to flirt with danger a second time. He knew he needed to retreat into the shadows and allow his soldiers to work the frontline, even if it went against his controlling character. Having made that crucial decision he calmed down, and after inhaling a few deep breaths his mind clicked smoothly back into gear. He collected a long white envelope from the bedside table and strolled back into the lounge area where Paz and Khairkhwa were eating chocolate bars they'd appropriated from the minibar. He handed the envelope across to Paz who placed it on the coffee table in front of him.

"These are the full instructions for the Ashkelon hit, along with the internal design layout of the main plant. Something's come up that requires my urgent attention, so I won't be with you on this one." Franklin noticed the suspicious expression on Paz's face but continued to build the lie. "I'm not sure how long I'll be away, but before I leave in the morning I'll prepare similar packages for Ashdod, Soreq, Palmachim and Hadera, just in case I'm held up."

"Where do you need to go?"

"That's outside your pay grade, Paz, but I assure you I'll be back very soon, probably tomorrow night."

He didn't wait for a reply but rose to return to his bedroom. As he made his way towards the door, he could sense Paz's eyes burning into his back and the sensation felt like a multitude of daggers.

Chapter 64

Maya Peretz was in despair. It was midday and she hadn't heard a word from her husband since he'd left home the previous evening. She'd expected Ariel to return from the desalination plant in the early hours, as he normally did when he went there to revise. He'd never been away this long before without making contact and his cell was switched off, which told her something was wrong. In desperation, she called one of the night guards at the plant – a friend of Ariel's, who confirmed her husband had left the plant about two in the morning, which raised further alarm bells because that meant he'd been missing for over nine hours.

There was something odd about the phone call with the guard that further heightened Maya's suspicions. She'd only met Moshe once before, albeit briefly, when he popped into their apartment to drop off a birthday card and small present for Ariel. He seemed a warm, easy-going man with a nice sense of humour, demonstrated by the comic card he hand-delivered that featured a soundalike of Israel's disgraced former president, Benjamin Netanyahu, wishing Ariel a happy birthday. But the man she'd just spoken with on the phone sounded ill at ease and defensive. He couldn't wait to get her off the line – it was as if he was hiding something. Maya was no detective, but she knew when she was being lied to.

Her anxiety level was running off the chart and she decided she'd no option but to call the police. In her panicked state, she'd forgotten it was Independence Day and most of the officers at her local station had taken it as holiday, so her call was answered by voicemail. Instead of leaving a message she screamed hysterically at her phone as though it had betrayed her, before cutting the call.

Maya felt as though she were losing her mind, but knew she had to pull herself together quickly and act rationally if she were to have any chance of finding out what the hell had happened to her husband. She gathered a few essential bits together for the baby and booked an Uber to take them to the police station, about two miles away. On her way there she sat in the back of the taxi, cuddling her daughter, praying she wouldn't sound like a mad woman when she told her story to the police.

The lone duty sergeant at the reception desk was Lavi Kaplon, who was serving out the final few months of his career after a forty-year stint. He was a childless widower and so had volunteered to do a twelve-hour shift on Independence Day. With no family lunch to attend, he was more than happy to pick up the double-time rate for working on a national holiday. He'd had a quiet morning but all that changed the moment Maya Peretz rushed through the door of his station, and he sensed the afternoon would be the opposite.

He listened sympathetically to her story and initially suspected her husband had either done a runner or had another woman in his life. Either way, it wasn't really a police matter, so he was about to send her home when Maya explained her phone call with the guard and her suspicions. Her intuition that the guard was lying touched a nerve, and for the first time since she'd begun to tell her story, Kaplon wondered if foul play was involved.

Then he recalled the confidential email his station commander had received the previous night from Mossad's central office in Tel Aviv, warning of an imminent terrorist threat to the city posed by an infamous Taliban tribesman believed to be in Eilat who, along with a small team, was preparing an attack on an unknown destination. He speculated the desalination water plant might be a potential target and, given the story he'd just heard, he decided, en balance, it was a good idea to call the emergency cell number on the bottom of the email. Kaplon figured he would either sound like an idiot or end up becoming a hero, and with three months before he drew his pension, why not roll the dice?

Forty-five minutes later Maya found herself sitting in a small interview room inside the station, retelling her story word for word to a junior Mossad agent who'd taken the police sergeant's call. Noah Weizman was young, extremely bright, and highly ambitious. His overall appearance was rugged rather than good-looking in the conventional sense. His muscular six-foot frame combined with his dark features and long black hair meant he stood out in a crowd. Not always a good thing for an intelligence officer.

Weizman concluded the unexplained disappearance of Ariel Peretz at the local desalination plant merited further investigation. He knew his boss was desperate to locate the whereabouts of the infamous Taliban terrorist, Akhtar

Khairkhwa, but wasn't senior enough to have access to the highly confidential information regarding the specific threat he posed to the female population inside Israel. Bekher had kept that secret very close to his chest and only a handful of his most trusted agents knew about the potential horrific consequences posed by the sterilisation drug.

The young agent decided to follow his hunch and pay a visit to the plant. He wanted to look around and see what he could find, and despite his protests Maya insisted on going with him, along with her baby daughter, who'd slept soundly through the entire interview. They sat calmly in the back of his red Jeep Wrangler as he drove the short five-mile journey. There were two fresh guards on duty who allowed him entry as soon as he flashed his Mossad ID at the front barrier. One of them jumped into the passenger seat to guide him to the red metal door that gave direct access to the main plant. As they drove through the front parking area, Maya's piercing scream had Weizman flooring the brakes, bringing the jeep to an emergency stop, almost sending the guard through the front windscreen.

"Over there – look over there, by the blue car. That's Ariel's moped. I told you the guard was lying ... Ariel never left here."

Chapter 65

Eilat, Israel

Vargas and Hembury were in the ops room of the safe house, helping four Mossad agents sift through thousands of stills and CCTV footage taken at the Jordanian border in the previous twenty-four hours, searching for images of the Afghan and the Black Scorpion. The fact that the two terrorists had been spotted less than three miles away from the Wadi Araba Crossing at a petrol station suggested they must have entered Israel via that route.

Vargas was using a computer tool to manually zoom in to the faces of two Arabs sitting in the front of a black pickup when his concentration was interrupted by an incoming call on his cell.

"Nic, what on earth is going on? Why the hell have we been arrested?"

Vargas was massively relieved to hear the familiar voice of his sister-in-law, even though she sounded like she would happily kill him.

"Nadia, where are you?"

"Meir and I are up in the north-east of the country, in the

Golan Heights. It's the start of our two-week trip taking us south along the spine of the country and ending up in Aqaba for a few days' snorkelling and beach time ... except our dream vacation turned into a nightmare thirty minutes ago when we had our asses arrested by two Israeli cops. They flagged us down on the highway and took us into custody at the police station in Katzrin. Not a word of explanation as to why until we reached the station, and I was given a phone and a cell number to ring that I instantly recognised as yours. Nic, you'd better have a great explanation or you're one dead brother-in-law."

Vargas was happy to soak up the abuse while he thanked God she'd been tracked down in time. "Nadia, how far are you from the northern border crossing with Jordan?"

He heard her asking Meir for the answer before she replied. "We're about a two-hour drive away. Why?"

"Nadia, I need you and Meir to trust me – at least for the next forty-eight hours. I'm working closely with the director of Mossad, trying to prevent an imminent terrorist attack inside Israel. I can't go into any hard detail, but you need to promise me, as soon as we end this call, you guys will drive into Jordan and find a hotel to hang out in until I tell you it's safe to return. This is so important, Nadia. You must do as I say. If Sophia were still alive and knew what the threat was, I promise you she'd also beg you to go."

Nic's last comment felt like a massive kick to Nadia's stomach. She could hear the concern in his voice, which told her all she needed to know about the gravity of the situation. Her aggressiveness softened. "Okay, we'll go ... we'll go right now. When will this be over – can you at least give me that?"

"I'm not sure, but hopefully very soon."

Nadia was about to hang up when Vargas asked her to agree

to one more request. "Nadia, promise me you won't eat or drink anything until you are safely inside Jordan. And I mean anything."

* * *

The Bell 429 twin-engine light-utility helicopter made an elegant landing on the private helipad belonging to the exclusive Scots Hotel and Spa, which perched gracefully on the Tiberias coastline and offered stunning views over the Sea of Galilee from every suite. The seven-seater aircraft contained only one VIP guest, who stepped out of the chopper and walked across the immaculate lawn to take in the spectacle of Israel's largest freshwater lake.

The two-hour non-stop flight from Eilat had given Franklin the opportunity to recharge his mental batteries after his narrow escape at the desalination plant. As he stared across the vast expanse of water, he knew he was standing less than five miles away from the newly built state-of-the-art pump station which transported almost a million cubic metres of fresh water to the north of Israel every single day. If all went according to plan over the next few days, Paz and his team would hit Israel's five biggest desalination plants dotted along the Mediterranean coast before heading north-east to Galilee, where Franklin planned on joining them to take part in the final assault at the pump station in Tiberias.

Then, having hit all the prescribed targets, *Operation Gesamtkunstwerk* would be complete. After that, Franklin planned to disappear and bide his time until the Israeli people began to appreciate the shocking implications of the attack. He'd wait for the outrage and condemnation to begin. He'd already identified a replacement superyacht, currently moored in the Croatian port of Split, that would eventually become his new floating home, but it wasn't available for three months, so he needed to source another bolthole in the meantime.

As he soaked in the surroundings and contemplated the future, he failed to notice the immaculately dressed bellboy who'd brought his luggage from the helicopter and was now standing in front of him.

"Mr Johnson, welcome to Scots Hotel. Please follow me to your suite. As requested, your full body massage is confirmed for four o'clock and the masseuse will come to your room."

Franklin smiled at the young man and reached inside his trouser pocket for a fifty-dollar bill. Life was good and once again he felt invincible – A Master of the Universe.

Chapter 66

Eilat, Israel

D oron Bekher stormed into the ops room, having just finished a game-changing phone call with a young Mossad agent named Noah Weizman.

"We've had a major break. One of our local agents called in from the desalination plant on the coastal road at the edge of the city, where something very strange has gone down. Grab your jackets and let's go. I'll fill you in on the way."

An hour earlier, Maya had identified Ariel's moped in the car park and Weizman had smelled blood. He'd sensed an opportunity to make a name for himself assisting the director of Mossad with the highly confidential investigation that had, miraculously, fallen into his lap. Despite it being Independence Day, within fifteen minutes he'd tracked down Moshe Stern, the night guard who'd lied to Maya, and, despite his protestations, coerced him into returning to his workplace for an interview he didn't want anything to do with. Faced with an ultimatum from Mossad, however, the guard knew he had little choice.

By the time Vargas, Hembury and Bekher arrived at the plant, Weizman had created a temporary interview room in the manager's office, along the lines suggested to him on the phone by his boss. Stern was already in a state of distress, sitting alone in an upright chair in front of a small table wondering why he was facing three empty chairs. Out of uniform he lacked the presence of a security guard, with his middle-aged paunch covered by a discoloured white T-shirt hanging over the top of his cheap denims, while his double chin wobbled beneath his chubby face. Regardless of the huge chunk of fresh money sitting in his wife's deposit account, Stern was regretting his part in the break-in.

He didn't have to wait long to find out who was going to fill the empty chairs. After a brief handover with Weizman in the main corridor outside, Vargas and Hembury followed Bekher into the small, unimposing office, where they took their seats behind the desk, either side of the Mossad director. The guard instantly recognised Doron Bekher – probably the second most famous man in Israel and certainly the most respected and feared. As he locked eyes with the Mossad icon, he recognised the sheer enormity of the trouble he was in, and his mind turned to pulp. He expected Bekher to introduce his two sidekicks, but that didn't happen. Instead, the director went straight for the jugular.

"Moshe, I'm going to conduct this interview in English, and you're going to tell me everything I want to know because if you don't, I'll personally place your fat ass on a plane with a one-way ticket to Guantánamo, where my American friends will introduce you to the joys of waterboarding."

Stern felt his bowels give way as he soiled himself. Both Vargas and Hembury recoiled at the disgusting smell pervading the air. Bekher had clearly experienced that reaction before and carried on undeterred. His tactics were brutal.

345

"No lawyers, no phone calls. You'll simply disappear and live the rest of your life in a ten-foot square windowless box, only being let out for regular bouts of torture. Moshe, I have no time to play games – the safety of millions of Israelis may well depend on your answers. So, are you ready to talk?"

Stern nodded his head and began reciting his sorry tale. It took the petrified security guard less than five minutes to tell Bekher everything he knew.

"Shimon and I were both paid fifty-thousand dollars to disappear for an hour between twelve-fifteen and one-fifteen in the morning. We had to unlock the rear gates and the main entry door to the plant and turn off all the CCTV recorders. The truth is, no one ever checks them, and at the end of each month the drives are wiped clean, so we thought no one would ever know."

Bekher's voice resembled a drone. "How were you first approached and what was the objective?"

"Everything happened online – the initial contact followed quickly by a fifty per cent down payment. But I swear to you on the lives of my three children, I have no idea who entered the plant during that hour or what they got up to. Shimon and I stayed in the canteen the whole time and saw nothing."

"What about Peretz?"

Stern wiped giant beads of sweat from his forehead with his club-like hand. "Ariel came to the plant from time to time on his nights off to work on his law degree. He found it impossible to study at home because of the baby. When he showed up last night, I was furious, but there was nothing I could do to prevent it. I just hoped he'd stay out of harm's way. I promise you, I've no idea what happened to him."

Vargas turned to Bekher and spoke for the first time,

ignoring the guard. "This operation has Franklin's fingerprints all over it. Excessive payments to buy access is his calling card. We've seen it time and time again throughout this entire case, stretching all the way back to the warden at Valledupar who facilitated Paz's breakout. I suspect Paz and Khairkhwa were here in the early hours and, if that's true, we finally know the delivery mechanism for the sterilisation drug. They're unloading it directly into the country's water supply."

Hembury's mind had already raced one step ahead and he glanced at his watch before speaking. "Jesus, if they added the drug during that one-hour window, it's been live in the drinking water serving Eilat for the last sixteen hours."

Chapter 67

Eilat, Israel

P az checked his watch for the third time in fifteen minutes. It was just after five and sunset was still over two hours away. He understood the importance of moving the huge trucks under the cover of darkness because, with Franklin out of the equation, there was no way of knowing if Mossad was aware of their presence inside their country. He suspected the true reason his boss had opted out of the next hit was because he feared the Israelis were closing in – no doubt working closely with Vargas and Hembury, but there was no way of knowing for sure, so he just had to be careful and play the odds.

The Transporter van in the hotel car park was already loaded with two large plastic storage containers jammed full of tiny 50 ml glass bottles that the two Taliban fighters had carefully transferred from the pallets on board one of the trucks. Paz stared across at the Afghan, who was sitting cross-legged on the floor, studiously analysing the interior plans of the Ashkelon plant laid out in front of him.

Khairkhwa sensed Paz's gaze and glanced up to meet the stare of the Black Scorpion.

"This plant is, as the Americans would say, a whole different ball game. It's the size of four football pitches, and height wise it's constructed over three levels. The pipe we need to hit – the main pipe, is located on the top tier, which means we'll have to carry the drug containers up three flights of stairs."

Paz smelled a possible window of opportunity that might allow him to exit the operation as Franklin was no longer present to call the shots.

"Now Franklin has left us to our own devices, it could be time for a rethink. I believe he's running scared. We were fortunate to escape the plant in Eilat and yet we still have five more to hit, plus the pump station in Galilee. The odds are not so good, my friend. Maybe we should think about our own survival and disappear before—"

The Afghan, who'd been sedate on the floor, flew into action. He leapt up, whipped out his peshkabz from inside his tunic and pressed the razor-sharp blade of the knife hard against Paz's throat. The lightning speed of his movement defied human logic and caught the Black Scorpion off guard.

"I'm here to carry out the commands of the supreme leader, who is only answerable to the Prophet Muhammad. If, God willing, I'm successful in culling millions of Jews, I'll be remembered and revered for all time as the warrior who carried out one of the greatest crimes against humanity in the name of Islam."

Paz just about managed to choke out a reply. "And if you fail?"

"Then I'll die a true martyr and enter paradise."

* * *

The Mossad director spent the entire drive back from the plant to the safe house on the phone to the prime minister. Vargas and Hembury travelled back in a separate car and the three of them met up in the ops room, where Bekher briefed them.

"The prime minister knows he's caught between a rock and a hard place but doesn't want to spook the entire nation, especially on the most important day of the year. Before he takes any action, he needs confirmation from our team of biochemists that the water has definitely been polluted with this evil drug. They'll be on-site within the hour to begin testing."

Vargas asked the obvious nagging questions. "How long before we know for sure, and, meantime, what do you tell the people of Eilat?"

"It's going to be at least three or four hours. Right now, he's briefing the mayor on what we suspect has happened, but the last thing any of us want is mass panic across the country, starting in Eilat. The prime minister and mayor are close friends, and the PM is asking the mayor to go live on local media to declare there's been an accident at the plant involving a small chemical spillage, so just to be safe no one should drink any tap water until further notice."

"What about those women who've already been drinking it. Surely we need to call them in for tests?"

"For now, we have to pray this drug is cumulative in its effect and one or two doses isn't enough to cause infertility. But, then again, it could be too late for some women depending on the efficacy of the drug. I pray that's not the case. Nic, you've got to appreciate, the country is celebrating at street parties, mass concerts or in their own homes. It couldn't be a worse day to declare a national crisis."

"That's no doubt the reason Franklin chose it to begin the attacks."

Hembury raised his white polystyrene cup of black coffee into the air, signalling a toast. "Happy Independence Day, Doron. It appears it's down to us to ensure it remains a day of celebration and not a national disaster. At least we—"

The police lieutenant was abruptly interrupted mid-flow by a loud shout from one of the agents at the other side of the ops room. All eyes locked on the blond-haired young man pointing at the large screen on his desk. "We've found them. We've bloody well got them."

Chapter 68

Eilat, Israel

Bekher sprinted across the room, closely followed by the two detectives.

"Adam, what have you got?"

The frozen colour image framed on the forty-inch screen gave the Mossad director the answer. Although it was obviously zoomed in and a bit grainy, staring back at Bekher were the unmistakable faces of the two most wanted men in Israel, sitting side by side in the cab of a Volvo truck. Paz and Khairkhwa were dressed in the same Arab robes they were wearing in the CCTV images taken from the petrol station.

"Zoom out. Let's see what they're driving."

The young Mossad agent's fingers flicked furiously over his keyboard and when the image changed Bekher was staring at the front and side of a medium-sized transport truck. Branding displayed the Kandahar Meat Company logo under which, in a smaller font, were written the words "Fresh Halal Meat". Bekher banged the desk in triumph and turned to look at Vargas and Hembury who were both eyeballing the same image.

"Incredible. They've driven all the way from Afghanistan. Bloody brilliant way of transporting the drug into the country. Most border guards would be respectful of the cargo and not ask too many questions."

Vargas leaned forward, brushing shoulders with Bekher to take a closer look at the screen. "Adam, can you zoom out any further?"

"Sure, no problem."

Moments later they were staring at a second truck parked immediately behind the first, with identical branding. As usual, Hembury was first in, echoing the thoughts of his two colleagues.

"Christ, those trucks are huge. Just how much of this drug are they smuggling in?"

The Mossad director shook his head, acknowledging Hembury's question. He turned to the young agent who had made the breakthrough they'd so desperately needed. "Adam, it's over twenty-four hours since those trucks crossed the border so, in theory, they could be anywhere in the country by now. We must locate them fast – like in the next two hours. I know what day it is, but we need to throw every resource we have at this – and some. We need an emergency code red APB alert sent out to every police officer and soldier currently on duty. I want every highway service station, hotel, independent car park put on high alert, looking for any sign of those bloody meat trucks. If we can find them, we just might be in with a fighting chance of working out their next target."

"Yes, sir. I'm on it."

Bekher smiled at his young agent and patted him on his shoulder. "Failure's not an option on this one, Adam." He then beckoned Vargas and Hembury to accompany him across the room to a black free-standing divider screen displaying a giant colour map of Israel. He grabbed a red marker from a nearby desk and began circling several small cities dotted along the Mediterranean coastline.

"The desalination plant they hit in Eilat was the smallest in the country. Maybe they hit it first as a trial run, who knows? The ones I'm marking up are monsters in comparison and supply drinking water to millions of Israelis every day. For all we know, they could be planning to hit any of them or, based on the quantity of drugs they've brought into the country, maybe all of them. There are too many plants for us to protect on a day when most of our police and military are out with their families, partying. We have about forty agents on standby, but they're spread all over the country and we've no idea where to send them. The prime minister has spoken with the commander-in-chief of the Defence Forces. He'll send in whatever troops are available depending on where the next strike happens. We just have to hope ..." Bekher paused mid-sentence to study the configuration of red circles on the map he'd just drawn. Then, when he continued, it was as though he were talking to himself. "We're too far away down here – we need to get closer to the danger zone. Look at the map. If we fly back to Tel Aviv, we'll be within forty miles of all five major desalination plants. It might just give us an edge and a fighting chance."

Bekher had already started walking before he finished the sentence, heading for the door.

* * *

It was almost ten at night when the two trucks and the Transporter van pulled up outside the entrance to the Leonardo Hotel in Ashkelon, six miles north of the plant. It had taken the small convoy just over four hours to complete the two-hundred-mile drive from Eilat. Paz and the Afghan had driven the van, while the two trucks had been driven by the Taliban fighters.

Once they parked up, Khairkhwa instructed his men to stay in the car park with the van containing the drug containers, while he and Paz took a room inside the hotel. It was vital they arrived at the plant at precisely midnight, when they knew the rear entrance would be open, so they had just under two hours to kill and didn't waste a minute of it. They meticulously worked through the complex plans, design layouts and timings until they knew them like clockwork, testing each other all the time. Although they had the names of the two guards on the payroll, unlike Eilat there were six others on duty who weren't. Any screw-up, however small, would mean certain exposure.

The Afghan kept to his usual routine, emptying the minibar of all its chocolate, while the Black Scorpion steeled himself with a couple of whisky shots. At eleven forty-five they departed the hotel and returned to the van, where Khairkhwa's two men were waiting in the back, guarding the drugs. Paz jumped into the driver's seat and gunned the engine, while the Afghan took his place alongside him. The attack on Israel's third biggest desalination plant was underway.

Chapter 69

Tel Aviv, Israel

I t was pitch-black when the Panther helicopter approached Ben Gurion Airport in Tel Aviv, and although the main airfield was closed the helipad lights were on full beam, awaiting the arrival of the Mossad director. Two minutes before they landed, Bekher opened a large black metal case that had been strapped into the seat next to him throughout the flight. He triggered a four number combination lock and withdrew two Beretta 70s that he passed to Hembury and Vargas, one row behind. They were all wearing helmets with built-in radios and boom mics.

"These are already loaded with ten round clips and there are spares inside the box. As of now, you're officially deputised Mossad agents licensed to work in the field."

As soon as they landed, Bekher led the three of them into a small hangar, about fifty yards away, that he'd requisitioned from the airport authorities soon after they took off from Eilat. It was empty except for a few pieces of cheap furniture, namely three plastic chairs and a metal table, that had been hastily laid out by two of the hangar cleaners five minutes before they'd arrived. Bekher placed his computer case on the table and fired up his iPad to check for any updates, but nothing had come in. It was almost midnight, well over two hours since the code red APB had gone out, but there'd been no response.

Vargas was studying a photo of the Israeli map on his phone, which he'd taken in the ops room just before they'd left. It highlighted the five desalination plants on the Mediterranean coast that Bekher had circled earlier with a red marker. He held the phone up in the air and angled the screen towards the Mossad director.

"Doron, we can't just sit and wait. Sometimes you need to play the odds. Pick one of these five and let's go. Trust your instincts."

Bekher wasn't a gambler by nature. He was the most highly ranked intelligence chief in the world, who always applied logic to any major decisions but, right now, he knew Vargas was right. He glanced down at his watch. He was running out of time.

"Nic, I don't need to look at the list. I know it by heart. Let's go for Soreq. It's the largest plant in the country. More than a million people get their water from it – over six hundred thousand cubic metres of fresh water a day. That's got to be their next target."

Within three minutes they were airborne in the Panther heading towards the giant desalination plant located less than fifteen miles south-east of Tel Aviv. The Mossad director felt strangely energised having made the decision to leave the airport and head for Soreq but then, in a flash, everything changed. His cell rang and he didn't speak for the entire thirty-second call. The voice doing all the talking belonged to Adam Dayan, the young agent based in the ops room in Eilat. When the call ended, Bekher's voice boomed over the radio headsets.

"Maybe I shouldn't have trusted my gut – it was wrong. The trucks have just been spotted in a hotel car park three miles north of the plant in Ashkelon. We're about twenty miles away. We'll be there in less than fifteen minutes."

* * *

The black Transporter van went unchallenged as it drove through Gate 6, sited on the north-east boundary of the desalination plant. Once inside, it headed south towards the massive three-tiered structure housing the water storage tanks and filtration systems. It was two minutes past midnight and, as arranged, the gate had been unlocked and unguarded. Paz carefully followed the directions on his map, marvelling at the ease of entry. He was aware there were six unfriendly guards patrolling the perimeter grounds but, as far as he could tell, he was driving through a ghost town, and when he reverse parked next to the giant steel doors that led to the main filtration system, everything seemed a little too easy.

Once again, the doors were unlocked and the four raiders broke into teams of two, each pair carrying a large plastic box containing the drugs. Paz and Khairkhwa led the way inside the building, both men gripping a side handle of the container with one hand and an LED torch with the other. They cautiously crept inside, where they were confronted by a giant warren of pipes and storage tanks built over three levels, dwarfing the plant they had penetrated in Eilat.

The heavy boxes were awkward to carry, slowing their

progress, and when they eventually reached the giant metal staircase that ran all the way up to the third level, their hearts sank. It resembled the kind of open steel fire escape you'd expect to encounter at the rear of a major hotel. Each level contained two sets of fifteen steps broken up by a landing. Paz had already done the maths back in the hotel room and knew they had a ninety-tread climb ahead of them.

Khairkhwa sensed the unease of his two men, who, unlike Paz, had not been warned about the mini-Everest they needed to conquer. They'd set their plastic container on the ground at the foot of the steps and were staring upwards at the massive task facing them.

"Brothers, we are about to strike at the very heart of the Jewish race. Prophet Muhammad will grant us the strength and determination to complete this epic task that will be a hammer blow to the Israeli state."

The Afghan's inspirational words hit home, and the Taliban fighters grabbed a handle each and began carrying the deadly container up the first level of metal stairs. Paz was reminded once again, Khairkhwa was not a man to be underestimated.

* * *

The Panther approached the plant from the east and landed on open scrubland about a quarter of a mile away from the front entrance of the complex so as not to alert anyone inside of their arrival. Bekher's right ear had been locked to the side of his cell since he'd learned the location of Franklin's next target. He'd spoken twice on conference calls with the prime minister and the commander-in-chief of the armed forces and separately to Udi Allon, the head of Sayeret Matkal, Israel's elite counterterrorism unit – the equivalent of the United Kingdom's revered SAS.

As the rotors slowed to a halt, the Mossad director dropped from the chopper with Vargas and Hembury and cleared the footprint of the Panther before stopping to peer through the darkness at the massive desalination plant up ahead. It looked as though it had been lifted from a sci-fi movie set. The two detectives noticed Bekher had swapped the phone in his right hand for his Beretta 70. They quickly armed themselves and awaited instructions.

"Okay, here's how it's going to play out. In about ten minutes' time, a Sikorsky cargo helicopter is leaving Tel Aviv, carrying fifteen elite marines from our Sayeret Matkal unit. It's now 00:20 and the flying time is fourteen minutes, which means they should hit the ground at 00:44. CCTV at the hotel where the trucks were found shows Paz, Khairkhwa and two unidentified men leaving the car park in a Transporter van at 23:47, which means right now they are probably inside the plant contaminating the water supply. The prime minister made it clear we can't stand around waiting for special forces to arrive – we need to take action."

Vargas glanced at Hembury, who nodded his agreement. Both men were aware of what was at stake.

"Doron, bearing in mind we have the advantage of surprise on our side, three of us against four of them seems pretty good odds."

"Nic, they're way better than that. We know there are eight armed security guards on-site and my deputy spoke with the one who operates the front gate. Right now, he's rounding up the others to give us backup. It's more than likely one or two of them are on Franklin's payroll but they'll be too scared to show their hand once they see my face. Believe me, they won't want to take on Mossad."

* * *

It took almost ten minutes to carry the drug containers to the third tier and having completed that arduous task the four men formed a human chain and began carefully passing the small glass bottles down the line. When they reached Paz, he laboriously removed the plastic tops and poured the evil liquid into the concave opening he'd located at the top of the main filtration pipe that linked directly to a giant storage tank. The meticulous process continued smoothly for the next twenty minutes and ninety per cent of the bottles were empty when all four men stopped in their tracks, becoming human statues as they heard the distinctive creak of a metal door opening followed by the distant sound of footsteps.

The Afghan kept his feet rooted to the spot but was the first to react to the intrusion, silently easing his rifle out from its hiding place inside his baggy robes. The two Taliban fighters followed his lead. Paz responded by elegantly swapping an empty glass bottle in his right hand for his Smith & Wesson pistol. Khairkhwa then moulded his body shape downwards onto the metal floor where he eased forward to the edge of the landing like a writhing snake, silently hunting an unsuspecting prey. He manoeuvred his semi-automatic rifle along the floor and slightly arched the top half of his frame into an improvised firing pose. Once he was happy, he maintained his reconnaissance position and waited.

Chapter 70

Yehuda Alon, the plant's senior guard, cautiously led the way inside the vast metal maze alongside the Mossad director, closely followed by Vargas, Hembury and seven security guards who instinctively fanned out into a V formation. All of them had their weapons drawn. Alon worked the night shift in the main gatehouse, signing visitors in and out, and had limited knowledge of the intricate workings of the filtration system, which meant neither he nor any of the other guards had any idea where the intruders might be. The gloomy interior of the plant only added to the jeopardy. Bekher's eyes constantly scanned the semi-darkness looking for clues, while the soundtrack of pumping water flowing through wafer-thin porous membranes inside giant steel pipes created a sinister backdrop for the inevitable confrontation.

The Afghan was well versed in leading night attacks on American military outposts, and over many years of combat his eyes had developed an inbuilt night-vision setting. Even though the light levels were minimal, as he peered through the darkness, he spotted the enemy approaching from over thirty yards away. As he focused in on the two lead figures, his mindset instantly changed from fight to flight. He was genuinely startled when a thin glint of light exposed Doron Bekher's face. The presence of the esteemed intelligence chief told him an elite team of Mossad assassins wouldn't be far away. His thoughts flashed back to Franklin, and he suddenly felt betrayed, and at that precise moment he decided he wasn't prepared to die a martyr, if that meant being a fall guy for the American.

Other than Bekher and two plain-clothed men, the assault group consisted of plant security guards, who Khairkhwa knew would pose little or no threat to a killer of his talents. Although he held the higher ground, if he were going to escape, he knew he had no option but to work his way down the stairs and fight his way out before reinforcements arrived. He whispered brief commands in Pashto to his men, ignoring Paz who had no idea what was happening or who was creating the disturbance below.

The Afghan was in his element. Without warning, he moved into a low crouch and charged down the staircase at speed, followed by his two fellow warriors. Paz held his position on the upper tier, at a loss by the sudden turn of events. As Khairkhwa flew down the stairs, he unleashed his unique brand of hell on the advancing group who were caught off guard by the speed and arrogance of the head-on attack.

The Afghan weaved across the concrete floor in a manic zigzag pattern, moving forward all the time, firing off a hail of rounds towards his assailants. While Bekher, Vargas and Hembury instinctively dived for cover, the guards froze on the spot in terror and disbelief, unable to process the sight of the frenzied demon charging towards them. The 9 mm rounds leaving the Afghan's rifle, sliced through human flesh as though it were rice paper and bodies collapsed like a cheap set of deckchairs. Four security guards were slain in a matter of seconds and the Afghan athletically hurdled over their fallen corpses where a gap in the human line had been created. As he pounded forwards, Bekher, who had rolled about ten feet to his left to dodge the attack, caught sight of America's most wanted terrorist and for a split second their eyes met.

The two Taliban fighters who'd held back for a moment during their leader's charge, sprinted forward in a second wave, shooting randomly at the remaining guards who, remarkably, were still upright, rooted to the spot. Even though Hembury had dived behind a large steel pipe running horizontally across the floor and was partially shielded, a random round tore into the top of his right shoulder, causing a reflex action in his hand that released its grip on the Beretta, sending the gun clattering into a mesh of pipework before sliding into the shadows.

Bekher, only a few feet away from the police lieutenant, regained his composure and took careful aim, attempting to take out one of the Taliban fighters. The round hit its target, creating a small black crater in the middle of his forehead and the impact sent the tribesman flying backwards, his limp body smashing into the bottom of the metal staircase. At the same time, as the crossfire continued, the second fighter took out another guard before his heart was pulverised by two swift rounds fired by Vargas, who'd managed to conceal himself behind a pile of dead bodies. As the shooting abruptly stopped, Bekher leapt up and darted down the corridor like a man possessed in pursuit of Khairkhwa.

The Afghan had a decent head start on the Mossad director and sprinted out through the same steel door he'd entered almost an hour before, making straight for the Transporter parked up only ten feet from the entrance to the main plant building. His hearing was just as hypersensitive as his eyesight and once outside his acute senses tuned in to the distinctive hum of a rotor. He figured he had maybe three minutes before the approaching helicopter reached the plant.

Paz had left the keys in the ignition and as soon as the engine flared into life Khairkhwa jammed the gear lever into drive and slammed the throttle pedal to the floor. The van screeched away just as Bekher emerged from the door with his Beretta firmly gripped in his right hand. He knew he was just a few seconds too late, and although he unloaded an entire clip of rounds in the direction of the departing van, they all fell short. The Transporter sped away through Gate 6 and disappeared, with Bekher watching on in despair. He fell to his knees before letting out an anguished cry of fury and frustration.

The Afghan headed north on the coastal highway with the intention of putting as much distance as possible between himself and the plant. His immediate thoughts focused on two objectives: firstly, he needed somewhere to hide out for a while before he could begin the arduous task of working his way back to Kabul. But his passionate desire to return to his homeland was dwarfed by the vow he made to himself, one that inspired him to survive. His second objective was to seek out and punish the arrogant, lying American who'd hung him out to dry and caused the deaths of his beloved brothers.

Chapter 71

Back inside the plant, Vargas was taking a close look at Hembury's shoulder injury. The Los Angeles police lieutenant was slumped on the floor, his back propped against a vertical pipe, while Vargas leaned over him, examining the lesion. He'd already helped to remove his white blood-soaked shirt and was using a strip of it to bandage the immediate area where the bullet had struck.

"From what I can tell the round went straight through. There's a nasty exit wound high up on the back of your arm that needs medical attention as soon as we get out of here, but it's nothing to worry about."

Hembury grimaced with pain every time Vargas touched the wound but knew he was fortunate the bullet hadn't landed a few inches to the right or it would have been a different story.

Three levels above, Paz was furtively peering down at the human carnage and weighing up his options. He was leaning against a large steel water tank, and as he edged slightly forward to take a better look below, the barrel of his gun grazed the side of it, generating a high-pitched screech that echoed around the plant. Vargas instinctively glanced upwards and caught a glimpse of Paz's unmistakable profile before he retreated into the shadows. He turned to Hembury and pointed upwards towards the top level of the staircase.

"The Black Scorpion is up there and right now we're pretty much sitting targets. Troy, are you okay to move yourself around to the other side of the pipe?"

"Yep, no problem, but let's wait for backup before taking him on."

"No way. There might be another escape route somewhere up there and I'm not letting him get away from us again."

Hembury hobbled gingerly around the side of the pipe, his left hand clutched hard against the top of his right arm, trying to stem the flow of blood. Vargas moved in the opposite direction, heading for the bottom of the staircase, his gun drawn. He crept slowly upwards, his eyes focused dead ahead, searching through the greyness for the slightest sign of movement.

Paz had found a fresh hideaway up on the third level. His tall, powerful frame was wedged into a tiny opening between two vertical pipes, drenched in darkness, providing him with a cloak of invisibility. Although he couldn't hear Vargas approaching, his sixth sense told him the chief inspector was on his way up and all he needed to do was bide his time and wait for the right opportunity to strike.

Vargas progressed stealthily up the three levels of metal stairs until he reached the platform on the top tier where he assumed Paz would be lying in wait for him. Two shafts of light cut through the pure darkness, but there was no sign of the Black Scorpion as he carefully scanned the area. He knew, though, that the multitude of pipes and water tanks offered numerous hiding positions he needed to be wary of.

Edging forward slowly, he constantly glanced left and right into the various side openings that were saturated in blackness. All the time his index finger was pressed hard against the trigger of his Beretta, ready to fire at will. The platform ran straight for about thirty feet, and as he approached the halfway point he could distinguish, in the distance, two large plastic containers on the floor positioned alongside a large horizontal pipe that appeared to have an opening at the top. He assumed he was staring at where the sterilisation drug had been added to the water, and the dozens of empty glass bottles on the floor told him the process had already occurred before he arrived. The drug was now in the water supply and the public needed to be warned as soon as possible.

"Place the gun on the floor, chief inspector. Then raise your arms high in the air. Clasp your hands together and slowly turn around."

Vargas had only been distracted by the discovery of the drugs for a few seconds, but that gave Paz enough time to emerge from his shadowy hideout and sneak across to the steel handrail on the opposite side of the platform without alerting his enemy. The chief inspector cursed under his breath at his mistake as he followed Paz's instructions to the letter. A few moments later he was face to face with the Black Scorpion who, incredibly, didn't look a day older than the last time they'd met. Vargas could taste the hatred in the air and knew Paz was about to take his life. Knowing there was absolutely nothing he could do to prevent it was a weird feeling. He wasn't ready to die.

"Vargas, you are personally responsible for taking away ten years of my life – ten of my very best. When I was living, or should I say existing, in that hellhole in Colombia,

I never imagined in my wildest dreams I'd one day be given the opportunity for retribution. But fate has a strange way of balancing up the odds and here we are."

Paz lifted his right arm vertical to his shoulder and took aim with his gun.

"If it's any consolation, your death will be instant, and you won't have to endure ten years of pain and torment as I did but—"

"Paz, it's over. Listen to that sound."

Troy Hembury emerged from the gloom at the top of the staircase and onto the third-floor platform. He moved towards Paz and Vargas, shirtless, still clutching his shoulder wound and unarmed. All three could make out the sound of a helicopter circling above.

Hembury continued to talk as he walked along the platform. "That's the sound of a helicopter about to land at the plant. It contains fifteen elite Israeli soldiers who'll lock this place down. As I said, it's over. Place your gun on the floor."

Paz's mind flashed back to his years of incarceration at Valledupar and knew there was no way he was ever going back. "I'll take my chances and at least I'll have the satisfaction of knowing I took care of you two."

Hembury was less than ten feet away from the Black Scorpion. He realised there was no way he could reach him without getting shot but, equally, he and Vargas were dead men anyway. Plus, there was the small matter of the terminal brain tumour that was going to kill him before too long, so without breaking stride he charged forward and propelled himself through the air like a heat-seeking missile hurtling towards its target. Paz responded by firing two rounds that ripped open Hembury's stomach. The shots didn't have any immediate effect, though, and a moment later the police lieutenant slammed into the upper body of the Black Scorpion. The momentum of the collision carried both men over the top of the metal handrail and Vargas watched in disbelief and horror as the two men, locked together as one, fell forty feet down.

The men plummeted through the air, hurtling towards the ground. Hembury could feel he was on the verge of losing consciousness, but his survival instincts kicked in and he drained every ounce of his remaining strength to cling onto Paz's head with the tenacity of a leech. The horrendous crash as they smashed onto one of the giant pipes below was nothing short of brutal. Even from three floors above, Vargas heard the sickening crunching sound created by Paz's vertebrae cracking into dozens of small pieces as his back took the full force of the fall, while the impact snapped his neck in three places.

Chapter 72

Ashkelon, Israel

Hembury's eyes struggled to focus. His forehead was centimetres away from Paz's and his arms were still firmly wrapped around his foe. The shock of the fall had produced a surplus of adrenaline that had temporarily masked the pain caused by the gunshots, but as it wore off, he felt as though his stomach was on fire. He somehow found the inner strength to lift his head a few inches into the air, allowing a small degree of space for his vision to regain focus. As it did, the first thing he registered were the dead eyes of the Black Scorpion.

Vargas was already racing down the stairs and once he reached the bottom, he turned back on himself to run under the staircase towards the massive steel pipe currently supporting the entwined bodies of Paz and Hembury. As he approached, he feared the worst – there was no sign of movement from either man. Hardly surprising, given the height of the fall. It was obvious when he reached them that Paz's disfigured body had taken the brunt of the impact. He gently rested his arm on Hembury's back and moved next to his friend, bringing his face close to his own. There seemed to be no hope but then he caught a flicker of life in his eyes. It was nothing short of a miracle that he was still alive.

Vargas's body trembled with relief and his eyes welled up. "Troy, thank God. You're a total madman for taking that on."

Vargas suddenly spotted a thick line of blood oozing down the pipe, obviously coming from Hembury's stomach wounds. He knew the importance of keeping his friend conscious for as long as possible and continued to talk. "That's got to be the best gridiron tackle I've ever seen. The soldiers will be here any minute and they'll take you in the chopper to the nearest hospital. Once you're fixed up, we'll find the best casino in Israel and pull an all-nighter, or if you like—"

Hembury interrupted, his shaky voice a mere whisper. "Nic ... I don't think ... I'm going to make it."

"Troy, you're the fittest sixty-year-old I know – of course you'll make it."

But Hembury's eyes had closed and he didn't hear Vargas's reply.

* * *

Less than five minutes later, four elite soldiers, one of who was a paramedic, transported Hembury out of the plant on a wheeled stretcher and onto the helicopter. It took off immediately and headed for the Sourasky Medical Centre in Tel Aviv where a team of surgeons was prepping the operating theatre, awaiting Troy's imminent arrival.

Vargas and Becker were back inside the plant, standing together by the foot of the metal staircase, surveying the bloody wreckage around them. Soldiers were carefully placing the bodies of the security guards into thick black plastic body bags. The area resembled a war zone. The Mossad chief shook his head, trying to take in the full implications of the horror scene that surrounded them.

"Right now, it's hard to process all this. I've just spoken with the prime minister and as soon as we hit sunrise, he's making a national address. He's not going anywhere near the sterilisation angle because he fears the public reaction would be catastrophic. He feels the pure evil behind the attack and the plan to sterilise all childbearing females needs to be buried forever. He'll reference a failed terrorist attack on our water supply, specifically at the desalination plants in Eilat and Ashkelon, and explain how both have been successfully neutralised. He'll inform the public that a very small amount of water may have been contaminated due to the failed attack but not to be too concerned because both plants have already switched to emergency supplies."

Vargas nodded but hadn't really taken in much of what had been said. His thoughts were with his airborne friend fighting for his life.

"Doron, I need to get to the hospital in Tel Aviv. Can I catch a ride on the Panther?"

"Sure, I'll drop you off on my way back. I think the hospital has—"

The Mossad director was interrupted by the ringtone of a distant phone that was coming from the other side of the staircase. He glanced across at Vargas – they both had the same thought regarding the caller's identity. The men darted around the staircase and headed towards the area where Paz's body lay prone on the ground. The closer they got to it, the louder the ringtone became.

Vargas arrived first, and as he leapt down to frisk the corpse the ringing stopped. It only took a few seconds to locate the phone, which he removed from the inside pocket of Paz's jacket, and as he stood up Bekher joined him. He peered at the screen and saw the red number signalling a missed call. Without thinking he pressed it with his thumb. It took a moment to connect but then the dialling tone kicked in, and after just two rings a familiar voice came on the line.

"What's the news? How did it go?"

Vargas felt a shiver run through his body. It was John Franklin. "Here's the news, Franklin. It's over. Your hideous attack has failed. We have the trucks containing the drug in our possession."

There was no response. Despite the silence, Franklin was still on the line, as though he were waiting to glean more information. The chief inspector was more than happy to oblige, delivering the coup de grâce.

"In case you haven't recognised my voice, this is Chief Inspector Vargas of the Buenos Aires Police Department. I'm currently standing on the floor of the Ashkelon plant which is now under the control of Mossad."

Franklin remained silent but continued to listen, struggling to process what was happening.

"One last thing, Franklin. The Black Scorpion is dead and so is *Operation Gesamtkunstwerk*."

The only response Vargas got was the beep in his ear telling him Franklin had hung up.

Chapter 73

Kabul

Eight weeks later

Three black Toyota Land Cruisers pulled up in a neat line outside a large stone-built mansion located in the countryside, forty miles north of Kabul. The rear passenger door of the lead vehicle was the first to open and the distinctive figure who emerged was the world's most wanted man. Following the notorious episode in Israel, the bounty on Akhtar Khairkhwa's head had risen from five to twenty million dollars. The reward was jointly funded by the American and Israeli governments.

Despite the ultimate failure of his mission, the Afghan had received a hero's reception from the Taliban high command and, today, a month after his return, he was attending a special dinner in his honour. It was hosted by the regime's foreign minister, Abdul-Azim Habibullah, who'd recruited him to take part in the operation, and twelve of the government's other senior ministers were present to pay tribute to his extraordinary bravery. As he strode through the enormous hallway entrance, framed by a stunning hand-carved vaulted ceiling, he was flanked by eight bodyguards who'd arrived with him as part of the convoy. When he entered the main dining area and headed towards the top table, he was enthusiastically cheered and applauded by the wives and children of the VIP guests who formed the upper echelons of the Taliban regime.

Two and a half thousand miles away in a subterranean steel-lined ops room hidden deep in the bowels of one of Mossad's secret bases in Tel Aviv, Israeli Prime Minister Reuben Oren sat alongside Doron Bekher, four of his senior cabinet members and the commander-in-chief of the military. The seven men sat in silence as they viewed the live feed from one of their surveillance drones, currently operating at a height of ten thousand feet directly above the countryside mansion in Kabul.

Oren left his chair and walked across to the giant video screen where he stood in front of the black-and-white live image focusing on the whole footprint of the small estate surrounding the main residence. Without turning around, he spoke to Bekher.

"Doron, are we totally sure he's in there?"

"Absolutely. We tracked him all the way from the house in Kabul where we knew he was staying, and our intelligence confirms he is the guest of honour of Foreign Minister Abdul-Azim Habibullah. He was the man who led the Taliban side of the operation and cut a deal with Franklin."

The prime minister remained fixated on the image as he threw out a question to the entire room. "Has anyone got an objection?"

Nobody answered and after a few seconds Oren lifted

his right arm and pointed towards the mansion. "Go ahead. Activate code green."

Doron glanced down at the speakerphone in the middle of the oblong table. He leaned across and pressed a button that opened an encrypted live line to an elite pilot in the cockpit of a F-35 fighter jet. He issued the attack order and five seconds later an Aim-9X Sidewinder missile hurtled through the sky and slammed into the centre of the mansion's roof. The image on the video screen disappeared in a large plume of grey smoke, and while six men inside the room applauded, the prime minister reached for his cell. He typed in a short text and sent it to his good friend, the president of the United States.

You can remove the Afghan from your most wanted list.

* * *

Vargas stood by the side of a small bench on the lawn at the rehabilitation department based in the California Hospital Medical Centre, taking in the scene around him. A small number of inpatients, many in wheelchairs or on crutches, were scattered across the gardens, mostly accompanied by nurses or visitors. For a moment, his eyes fixed on a wheelchair-bound young soldier missing an arm and a leg, obviously recovering from bomb wounds, being comforted by his parents. His heart melted at the tragic scene but then in a flash his spirits lifted as a familiar voice yelled out his name.

"Nic, over here, you bastard."

He spun on the spot and caught sight of Hembury being wheeled towards him at great speed by a young male nurse. Vargas dashed towards him, overwhelmed with joy as he watched his closest friend signal to his nurse to stop pushing, allowing him to stand from the wheelchair and shuffle forwards so the two friends could properly embrace. They hugged for a while before Vargas helped the lieutenant back into his chair. Both men teared up and neither of them said anything meaningful for the first couple of minutes. Then Hembury pointed to a wooden hut at the far corner of the grounds.

"There's a great ice cream parlour over there. Fancy giving an old man a push?"

Vargas roared with laughter as the tension of their reunion drifted away, and he gently wheeled his friend across the grass where he purchased a couple of chocolate chip cones.

"You're looking good, Troy. How's the rehab going?"

"Amazingly, although I've probably run my last marathon. The doctors say it's going to be a long haul, but I should make a decent recovery."

"You know something, that first night you were in a coma in Tel Aviv, wired up to the hilt, I stood at the end of your bed with your surgeon who gave your life chances two out of ten at best. I told him his odds were way off and explained you were the fittest man I knew. Then he told me something remarkable. He said the oxygen levels in your blood were the highest he'd ever come across, so much so that he checked the tests three times to make sure they were correct. He said if anything would save your life it would be that and, look, here we are."

Hembury smiled but was keen to change the subject. "So, guess what? Berrettini's offered me a job when I eventually get out of here."

"Go on."

"It's a consultancy position for security inside the White House. It's helping to look after the big fella. It means moving to Washington but it's a six-figure salary, so what the hell?"

"Troy, I love the sound of that. I hope you said yes."

Hembury winked. "Let's say I'm giving it some serious thought."

"Meanwhile, what's the latest with our friend up there?" Vargas pointed at Hembury's forehead.

"Nic, I've been desperate for you to ask. Despite the trauma my body's gone through in the last couple of months it hasn't grown. Seems the steroids are doing their job."

Vargas punched the air in sheer delight. "Yep, I knew it, I bloody well knew it. I bet it keeps shrinking as well."

Hembury smiled and smoothly changed the subject. "What's the latest news from Doron? How many women consumed the drug in Eilat and Ashkelon before the warnings went out, and how badly were they affected?"

"From what they can tell, it could be as many as twenty thousand including tourists, although so far only fifteen hundred have come forward for tests. Remember, the official line is the water had a chemical poison in it, so the government is inviting everybody: men, women, and children of all ages to come in for check-ups if they used any tap water during those few specified hours. That means they're not raising suspicion."

Hembury was deep in thought. "Presumably younger females could be affected too – you know, before they reach puberty? That really would devastate the future of the Israeli state."

Vargas nodded and then finished off the last of his ice cream cone before speaking. "Do you remember those X-rays taken by the doctor in El Bolsón, which Franklin tried to destroy? They found them at the Ministry of Health in Buenos Aires and they're proving to be extremely helpful to expert physicians in Israel. They hope the drug needs to be regularly imbibed through numerous doses to cause permanent damage to the fallopian tubes, but the truth is no one really knows, so it's going to take months before anyone can be sure. It's tragic if even one woman is sterilised but, God knows, we helped prevent a national disaster."

"Speaking of the Israelis, I see Doron's already executed his revenge on the Afghan. That was some show – wiping out nearly half the Taliban regime. You have to hand it to them; they don't do things by halves."

Hembury was now on a roll and hit his friend with yet another question. "What about Leah, have they tracked her down?"

Vargas grimaced slightly before nodding.

"Doron thinks she's dead – probably at the hands of Paz or Franklin. When his team did a sweep of the plant in Eilat, they found tiny blood stains on the floor, close to the site where the drugs were deposited into a major pipe. DNA checks confirmed the blood came from two sources: the security guard and Katz. We think they were both executed on the plant floor but clearly their bodies were removed, so we can never be totally sure."

"But that still leaves one giant loose end that begs the question—"

Vargas finished the sentence, "Where the hell is Franklin hiding out?"

* * *

The tall, blond-haired bearded man wearing a red baseball cap trailed at the back of the small group of tourists who were being guided around the museum. He wasn't paying any attention to the information being given out because he knew more about the location than anyone alive. After all, the property they were being shown around had once belonged to his paternal grandmother, Eva Braun. Following her death ten years earlier, the house, known as El Negus, was taken over by the Argentine government, who decided to turn it into a macabre museum. It was to act as a lasting reminder of the despicable crimes carried out against humanity by Adolf Hitler who'd lived in a property on the same site, named El Blondi.

While Franklin waited to take possession of his new superyacht, he needed somewhere safe to hide and calculated that the small city of El Calafate in southern Patagonia would be the very last place on earth any of his enemies would expect him to be. He'd rented a farmhouse a few miles out of town, where he kept a low profile and drew great comfort from being so close to where his infamous grandparents had once lived. As the tour finished, he followed the guide through the gardens, heading for the way out. For once in his life, he felt safe, hidden in plain sight.

Across the street, facing the museum exit, a young, unshaven Australian sat alone at a small street café nursing a cold lager. Inside his black leather bomber jacket, a SIG Sauer P226 pistol created a small, discreet bulge. Daniel Anderson had a price on his head, courtesy of Franklin, but rather than lie low he'd vowed to avenge the murders of his siblings and had travelled halfway across the world to do just that. He took another sip of beer and waited patiently for his older half-brother to emerge from the museum.

Author's Note

For me, the decision to write a sequel to *The Counterfeit Candidate* relied on finding another historically based 'big idea' that could hopefully hook the interest of the reader, in the same way the first book did. Now you've read the story, I hope to some extent I managed to achieve that result and *The Führer's Prophecy* kept you guessing, right up to the final page. I loved revisiting many of the characters and hope the enjoyment I experienced during that process will inspire me to complete the trilogy with a final instalment.

The contemporary aspects of *The Führer's Prophecy* may be pure fiction but the legitimacy of the malovelence which lurks behind the idea belongs to the minds of Hitler and Mengele, both of whom sought the destruction of the Jewish people in their pursuit of creating a perfect, Aryan race. As I mention in the story, the phrase 'The Führer's Prophecy', relates to a speech Hitler made at the Reichstag on 30 Jan 1939 where he referred directly to "the annihilation of the Jewish race in Europe". I believe had he still been alive in May 1948, he would have used that same evil phrase when alluding to the newly formed State of Israel, and that disturbing thought helped inspire the plot for the book.

The appalling medical testing on Jewish human guinea pigs that took place inside Block10 at Auschwitz was horrifyingly real and reading about it inspired the fictional idea of Operation Gesamtkunstwerk. In terms of my story, I could well imagine Hitler employing the resources of his massive Pharmaceutical Corporation to research and develop a drug that one day would have the potential to cause the mass sterilisation of Jewish women and the more research I carried out, the darker the plot became. I tried to imagine Hitler's reaction to the creation of Israel and how it might spark him into action.

Mengele did live in secrecy inside Argentina for thirty years between 1949 and 1979, under different aliases, including Wolfgang Gerhard. I believe it more than likely that had Hitler also been hiding in South America, Mengele would have jumped at the opportunity of continuing his human medical research under the leadership of his beloved Führer.

As the idea began to form, recent events in Afghanistan, especially the decision by the US Military to leave behind billions of dollars' worth of military equipment, due to the speed of their withdrawal, plus the Taliban's declared hatred of Israel, inspired me to find a way for Hitler's grandson to join forces with them to strike at the very heart of the Jewish race.

I really hope you enjoyed the return of Vargas and Hembury and although Matias Paz was a malicious psychopath, in many ways I was sad to say goodbye to the Black Scorpion but in the end, I felt he'd enjoyed his "nine lives", so it was time for him to go.

At the time of writing, *The Counterfeit Candidate* is being developed by a film production company as a six-part television series, which is incredibly exciting and prompted me into knuckling down to write a sequel, just in case a second season is needed!

Now you've finished the sequel you'll realise the story isn't quite over. There is one final book to come, which will resolve all loose ends and the series will be known as "The Reich Trilogy."

Here's a taster from the opening chapter of the finale:

John Franklin was just a few seconds away from meeting his maker. As the former presidential candidate crossed the busy street in the centre of El Calafate, heading for his black SUV, he'd no idea he was the moving target of a lone gunman, sitting at a small table at a run-down, street café, just thirty yards away. At that critical moment, it was his hidden wireless earpiece that saved his skin. It broke into life emitting a brief crackling sound and then a second later, the unmistakeable voice of his driver boomed a warning into his left ear.

"Sir, there's a hostile directly west. He's been watching your exit from the museum and has a weapon trained on you. Shall I take him out?"

Franklin slightly stiffened for a moment and then surreptitiously glanced to his left before speeding up the pace of his walk which almost immediately broke into a fast jog. The momentary look told him all he needed to know. The man with the gun aimed in his direction had every reason to want him dead, even though he was a blood relative.

"Intercept immediately ... but don't take him out ... just disable him."

Two seconds later a 50-calibre bullet fired from a Barrett

M107, high powered semi-automatic rifle, ripped into the right shoulder of the would-be assassin and the sheer force of the impact, propelled his body backwards. The gunman was tossed out of the rusted, metal chair he'd been sitting in, while the small handgun he'd been holding, slipped from his grasp and clattered onto the pavement. His head slammed down onto the concrete and although he didn't lose consciousness, he was far too dazed to offer any resistance to what was about to follow. The Lincoln Aviator sped forward from its stationary position and pulled up directly outside the café, where the driver, a massive hulk of a man, leapt out and grabbed the fallen body and heaved it off the pavement, before literally throwing it onto the rear seat of the SUV. Moments later, the front passenger door was yanked open, and John Franklin leapt inside, barking orders to his driver as he slammed the door shut.

"Get moving Hugo ... head straight for the farmhouse."

The whole incident lasted less than twenty seconds and as the Lincoln pulled away at speed, Franklin half-turned over his right shoulder and stared down at the dishevelled figure, whose bloodied body was splayed across the back seat. The man was barely conscious, but his eyes glared back at his attacker, exuding pure hatred. Franklin's lips parted to reveal a malevolent, Joker type grin.

"Don't worry Daniel. Everything is going to be just fine."

A moment later a fist smashed into Daniel Anderson's temple, and everything went black. At least that meant he didn't feel the prick of the hypodermic needle which followed shortly after.

Acknowledgements

Producing a book is by its very nature, a collaborative process and this one was no different. My wife, Charmaine, was instrumental in finding and developing the core idea for *The Fuhrer's Prophecy*, without which there would be no sequel, and she also did several great edit passes on all the drafts, which was an enormous help. Her analytical and creative mind was just what was needed on such a complex plot. Once again, I am also indebted to Victoria Woodside, who did a meticulous job proof reading and fact checking the penultimate draft.

For me, the original artwork design for the sleeve of a book is a key factor in its success and once again I turned to the remarkable Patrick Knowles for inspiration. He designed the cover for *The Counterfeit Candidate* which I thought was powerful and inspirational and I believe he's succeeded again with his sleeve creation for the sequel, *The Fuhrer's Prophesy*.

I'd also like to thank Rob Callow, Hemen Schafeie and Jo Harris at Spirit Entertainment, who make the whole publishing bit appear so easy.

About the Author

Brian Klein is an award-winning Television Director, with over thirty years' experience in the industry. His work regularly appears on Netflix, Amazon Prime, BBC and Sky. Amongst his directing credits are twenty-eight seasons of the iconic car show, "TOP GEAR" and seven seasons of "A LEAGUE OF THEIR OWN ROADTRIP", Sky One's highest rating entertainment show. He has also directed two feature-length films for BBC Worldwide and five entertainment specials for Netflix.

THE FÜHRER'S PROPECY is his second publication – a sequel to his debut novel, "The Counterfeit Candidate."